Haft yelled a battle cry of his own and in three steps was on the startled lancer to his right, inside the swing of the lance. His knife flashed twice and the enemy soldier crumpled at his feet. He dove beyond the bleeding corpse and came up with his own axe. He charged the nearest Jokapcul and chopped deeply into the man's side. He looked around as the giant cut down the sixth Jokapcul soldier. That left only the officer.

Spinner quickly limped over to the startled officer and knocked him to the ground, then dove beyond him to retrieve his quarterstaff.

The officer scrambled to his feet with his sword raised *en garde*. He looked puzzled, as though wondering what Spinner expected to do with the stick in his hands; he didn't seem to recognize the quarterstaff as a weapon. He found out about it almost instantly . . .

By David Sherman

Fiction
The Night Fighters
KNIVES IN THE NIGHT
MAIN FORCE ASSAULT
OUT OF THE FIRE
A ROCK AND A HARD PLACE
A NGHU NIGHT FALLS
CHARLIE DON'T LIVE HERE ANYMORE

THERE I WAS: THE WAR OF CORPORAL
   HENRY J. MORRIS, USMC
THE SQUAD

Books published by The Ballantine Publishing Group are available at quantity discounts on bulk purchases for premium, educational, fund-raising, and special sales use. For details, please call 1-800-733-3000.

ONSLAUGHT

Book One of
DEMONTECH

David Sherman

A Del Rey® Book
BALLANTINE BOOKS • NEW YORK

To Carrie and the AllieCat

A Del Rey® Book
Published by The Ballantine Publishing Group
Copyright © 2002 by David Sherman

www.delreydigital.com

ISBN 0-345-44374-8

Manufactured in the United States of America

First Edition: February 2002

10 9 8 7 6 5 4 3 2 1

PROLOGUE

"You have until the midnight bell's toll, Lord Lackland." The voice of the Grand Vizier of the archipelago nation of Jokapcul cracked like a whip in sharp contrast to the deep wrinkles in his face and the withered skin of his hands.

The Dark Prince looked down the length of his royal nose at the bent old man who dared call him by that hated sobriquet. "I do not need till the bell's toll, old man."

"We shall see." The ancient vizier's voice again cracked like a whip, but on the first words; on the last, it cracked like an old man's. He eased about slowly, maintaining fragile balance so as not to threaten equally fragile bones with a fall, and shuffled out of the sacred circle to where magicians and kamazai stood in solemn watch. He sat in the lone chair. The High Shoton's headsman stood behind the vizier's left shoulder and turned the head of his axe just enough to reflect torchlight onto the Dark Prince's face.

Ignoring the light that sparked in his eyes, the Dark Prince lifted his face to the dome of the evening sky and slowly raised his hands until his arms were parallel to the ground. He began to chant in a deep voice; slow, guttural sounds in a language so ancient and arcane few of the assembled magicians and kamazai had ever heard it.

Away from the sacred circle and its attendant magicians and kamazai, tiny creatures watched from the protection of bushes. Curious, they listened to the words he intoned. One, who understood the words no better than did the humans surrounding

1

the chanter, rested his chin on the shoulder of one who did understand them. *"Wazzim zayyim?"*

The one who understood shrugged his free shoulder. *"Zhimm's wanttin,"* he said briefly, not wanting to miss a word of the chant.

"Wazzim wanttin?"

"Kinollitch."

"Kinollitch whatch?"

"Woour." The one who understood the chanter's words shrugged his shoulder to dislodge the other's chin. The questions were becoming distracting enough for him to miss something.

The one who asked settled back on his haunches and considered for a long moment. Why did the man in the black robe want knowledge of war? What did he propose to do with it? Well, the creature knew a way to find out. Abruptly, he rose on bandy legs and leaned forward to knuckle the ground. He scampered off to where a dozing jinnlette softly ruffled fallen leaves.

In a moment the jinnlette was awake and spinning rapidly enough to scatter the leaves. It swept up the curious knuckle-walker and sped away with him. Midnight was nigh by the time they returned.

In the circle, the Dark Prince still stood chanting, his quivering arms still parallel to the ground. His voice no longer intoned, it croaked through his sore throat. The effort of holding his arms up brought deep lines to his face and tightened the cords of his neck so they stood out in sharp relief. Around the circle, the magicians and kamazai tiredly shifted stiff muscles and joints, anxious for the midnight bell's toll to bring an end to the farce. The vizier dozed in his chair. The headsman once more tested the sharpness of his axe with his thumb.

The jinnlette summoned others of its kind. They whistled to his side through the trees and bushes. The knuckle-walker told them what he wanted. The jinnlettes whistled agreement to the grand joke and began spinning in unison. They spun until they raised a cloud of dirt and leaves and dust the width of the sacred circle and three times the height of a human. They advanced.

The magicians and kamazai stirred and looked in the direction of the approaching whirlwind. The Grand Vizier started awake and looked. The headsman turned his head toward the sound. Everyone looked up, but the sky was cloudless and no wind rustled through the trees around the circle. Only from the one direction was there the sound of wind, and that sound was moving their way. Such a wind could only be magical. The magicians and kamazai on the wind's side of the circle sidled out of its way; none ran, none showed the fear all felt. Only the Dark Prince seemed not to notice.

The spinning cloud moved into the flickering torchlight, its progress slow and stately, without veering from a path that took it directly across the sacred circle. When it passed, the Dark Prince lay crumpled on the ground, his voice stilled. Before him rose a neat stack of tomes.

The Grand Vizier stood on wobbly legs. Immediately, a magician supported him on his right and a kamazai on his left as he tottered into the circle. They stopped within reach of the stack of tomes.

The Grand Vizier commanded with a hand signal, and a magician ran to check the Dark Prince. In response to another sign, the magician supporting him bent and lifted one of the tomes for the vizier to examine.

The tome's cover was the white of milk just beginning to go bad. It was flexible, like parchment, but it wasn't the texture of kidskin. It was adorned with indecipherable script, and an eagle bearing a shield was spread inside a circle. The vizier waved a hand and the magician opened the book at random. Another random opening, and another. The assisting magician lifted each tome in turn and showed its cover and contents to the vizier. All were filled with the same indecipherable script as the covers. But the pictures! Never had the vizier seen pictures of such clarity. The Dark Prince was stirring under the ministrations of the magician.

"Dark Prince," the Grand Vizier said, using the preferred title. "It appears we have not been using the demons in the right way."

He examined the covers of the tomes again. Much of the script was different on each one, but all had three things in common. Each bore the circled spread eagle. Each had writing in the upper left quadrant that began with the strange symbols FM. At the bottom, each bore the legend: FIELD MANUAL, UNITED STATES ARMY.

Whatever that symbolized.

That same night, a third of a world away in the archipelago nation of Frangeria, priests of a half-dozen religions filed into an alabaster temple to observe an experiment to be conducted by a renowned philosopher—or to watch him destroy his reputation and career, which was what most of them expected. The interior of the temple shone with lamplight that reflected from its polished walls. Rows of marble benches circled the room. Brilliantly painted statues of gods and heroes stood in niches mounted higher on the walls than the head of a standing man.

The white-robed philosopher stood calmly in front of the altar and watched the priests. His bland expression gave no indication that he saw the skepticism and disbelief that adorned most of their faces, or that he heard the disparaging words they whispered to each other. They were fools, he knew, to believe as they did. None of their gods had ever manifested themselves, not unless one gave credence to ancient legends and myths. Ancient legends and myths had value, to be sure, but they shouldn't be considered as history. What he was going to demonstrate to them this night was real; he'd seen it himself on his journeys to the western edge of the world.

The last priest filed in and took his place. The High Priest of Tomarnol, the ranking personage in the assembly, sat in the place of honor, directly facing the altar. There was a muffled swishing and bumping as the rest of the priests sat. The High Priest signaled attendants, who moved to extinguish four out of the five lamps.

"Hold!" the philosopher said, speaking for the first time. "There is no trickery here, no legerdemain. What I am going to demonstrate can be seen in clear light. Nothing need be hidden."

The attendants looked to the High Priest of Tomarnol, who in turn examined the philosopher speculatively for a moment before signaling them to return to their stations and leave the lamps lit.

The philosopher bowed thanks to the High Priest, then slowly rotated as he looked at all of the priests. He seemed to look each in the eye, and many squirmed under his gaze.

"You are holy men," the philosopher began. "You hold with your various gods and seek their assistance. You believe not in demons save as foes of gods and man. *Know you that demons are real!* They are not foes of god nor man, and they can be made to do man's bidding."

Tittering broke out in the temple, and cruder expressions of disbelief. The philosopher cocked his head and looked around with the slightest trace of sadness on his face.

The High Priest angrily flipped a hand in the air, and the exclamations ceased. Again the philosopher bowed his thanks.

"I have seen demons do man's bidding," the philosopher continued. "I have learned how to call and command them. Observe and you shall know."

He lifted his face to the dome of the temple, raised his hands till his arms were parallel to the floor, and began chanting in a language few of the assembled priests had ever heard and none knew well. Those who did know a bit of the language were so impressed at the ease with which the philosopher chanted that they never guessed the philosopher knew the language hardly better than they did.

Curiously watching and listening to the proceedings, two smallish creatures scrunched behind the feet of a statue in one of the niches.

"Wazzim zayyim? " one of the creatures asked.

"Nasurre. Zhims nunchiation nawgud," the other replied.

They listened intently for a few more minutes, trying to work their way through the philosopher's mangled vowels and garbled consonants.

"Zhim whanns leadumzhib," one of the creatures said uncertainly.

"Thinzo," the other said slightly less uncertainly. *"Trainem mebbe? "*

"Mebbe."

"Givvim? "

"Whyynaw."

They hopped up from their scrunch and skittered through a carefully concealed crack in the wall behind the statue. By the time they returned, the philosopher's voice was a mere croak and his elbows were resting against his sides, though his hands were still parallel to the floor. Worry about what had gone wrong furrowed his face. The two creatures scrunched back behind their statue and sniggered behind their hands. This was going to be fun.

A thor bearing something in its arms sped into the temple faster than glazed eyes could see. The thor set his burden upright on the altar, then drew his hammer and slammed it against the floor. Thunder crashed and lightning flashed. The priests jumped and shouted, nearly panicked by the deafening noise and blinding light. Swaying with exhaustion and much nearer the hammer strike, the philosopher was knocked from his feet. The priests didn't see the thor as it raced away.

When their vision cleared, the priests and the philosopher were stunned by the vision in command of the altar.

It was a man in a fighting crouch. He spun to face first one way then another until he saw no one advancing to attack him. Then he stood so erect he might have had a spear for a spine.

He was a man such as none of them had ever seen. It wasn't only his near impossibly erect posture or his obvious musculature. It was his resplendent garb—a tunic the blue of the deepest sea and trousers the blue of the purest lake. A bloodred stripe ran down the outside of his trouser legs. Each of his upper arms was adorned with three inverted V's over two saucer-curves with crossed, crossed . . . *somethings* in between. Those adornments were in cloth-of-gold mounted on scarlet. His lower left arm bore four diagonal cloth-of-gold stripes on a scarlet backing. A panoply of rainbow-colored ribbons supporting dangling medallions adorned his left breast, and other strips of rainbow hue were on his right. Golden emblems glittered on the tunic's high collar. Gloves the white of new fallen snow covered his hands. A stiff billed hat sat squarely on his head, its crown as white as his gloves, its flat top slanted back from a peak, and the whole top stood out round like a halo. A gold emblem sparkled so brilliantly on the front of the hat, none could make out any details. The bill of the hat and his shoes were leather that shone so brightly they might have been polished obsidian. An ornately guarded saber hung in a polished black, gold-toed scabbard at his side; no one thought to wonder why he hadn't drawn it when he first thought he might be attacked.

Slowly, the man curled his upper lip with disdain. He looked about at the stunned priests. When he finally spoke, his voice was so loud it knocked down the philosopher who was struggling back to his feet, staggered the nearest priests, and woke sleepers in nearby houses. No one in the temple understood his words. They were in a language even further removed from the temple than the language in which the philosopher had chanted. But the meaning was clear when he bellowed:

"Who's in charge of this circle jerk?"

Trembling with terror, the High Priest of Tomarnol rose to his feet, advanced partway to the altar and prostrated himself.

"Lord," the High Priest's voice broke, "I am the High Priest."

It was several years before the magicians of Jokapcul understood enough of the Dark Prince's tomes to put their knowledge to practical use. It took about the same length of time for the man who came to be known as Lord Gunny to turn the Frangerian sea soldiers into what he called "Marines."

I
INVASION

CHAPTER
ONE

It was harvest time in the Duchy of Bostia, in the nation-less jungle to its north and west, and in the Kingdom of Skragland to its northeast. Harvest time, when the great merchantmen of the fleets of far Arpalonia's many countries filled the freeport of New Bally so that it was said a man could walk the length and breadth of Bostia Bay by simply stepping from ship to ship. The streets and inns, the taverns and brothels of the freeport were flooded with boisterous gaiety and unrestrained laughter. Seamen of scores of nations from the two continents assailed the eyes with the riot of colors of their national costumes, and assaulted the ears with the babble of their tongues. The shopkeepers and innkeepers, the serving maids and whores, the brothel mistresses and gamblers as well, ignored the assaults on their senses and reveled in the money they made from men too long at sea. Even the City Guard stood back and let their visitors party hard, intervening only when life was threatened or property wantonly destroyed.

The silos and granaries and dockside sheds of New Bally were filled to overflowing at harvest time. Mountains of burlap sacks swollen with grain, vegetables, and fruit loomed near the docks, where farmers who reached the port too late to store their crops elsewhere hoped to sell them before the rains came and brought rot. Foreign traders climbed those mountains, prowled the peripheries of the silos and granaries, poked and probed the sacks and piles of grain and produce under the sheds, squeezed the fruit, rapped on the melons and gourds, seeking the best of the foodstuffs. Traders' magicians oversaw the loading of the foodstuffs into the ships' warded holds, where they would be protected from further ripening and the resultant rot during the sea voyage to their destinations.

At harvest time the craftsmen and artisans of the Kondive Islands, across the Turquoise Sea from the great trading port, brought their wares to New Bally to trade. They had jewelry of gold, silver, brass, and gemstones aplenty. Tapestries and rugs were rolled or hung or stacked high for leafing through.

Local merchants stalked up and down the docks, inspecting the goods bought by the merchantmen. Sandal- and zebra- and other exotic woods from the farthest reaches of Arpalonia were there for sculptors and cabinet makers. Myrrh and frankincense came from even farther reaches for lovers and the pious. Iron farm implements from far northern Ewsarcan for the farmers. Weapons of hunting and warfare from near every nation that hunted or fought—which meant from near everywhere—for warriors and hunters. Some few shipmasters offered slaves privately to selected buyers; privately, for slavery was taboo in most nations, and the slave traders could find themselves turned upon by their seamen if the seamen knew the nature of the cargo these captains had borne in hidden holds accessible only through their cabins. Breeding bulls and hogs and horses were presented for sale to ranchers and herdsmen who wished to improve their stock. Lions and tigers and bears were sold for hunting or other, less speakable, sport. Camels and impala and elephants and serpents were offered to zoos or to private collectors, for more exotic purposes than the sellers cared to inquire about.

The annual orgy of trading among the merchants, tradesmen, artisans, farmers, and herders lasted one week, during which most seamen enjoyed a different kind of orgy in the inns and shops and taverns and brothels of the freeport. During that week, those who bought—and their employees and the seamen as well as local stevedores—spent several arduous days loading and shifting and moving and lading until the ships' holds were filled, the stores stocked, the animals herded away, and—perhaps most important—the money counted. More than half of the magicians recently released from apprenticeship could expect to sign aboard a ship. Others found employment in New Bally, the Kondives, or elsewhere in the nearby kingdoms, duchies, and principalities.

When all the cargo was aboard, some shipmasters wanted to weigh anchor and sail on the first outgoing tide for their next port of call, but most gave their crews a last night of shore leave before heading out to sea; it might be a long time before the crews had another chance for drink and women, and too long a time without drink and women can breed sedition or mutiny. More of the masters wanted to stay another night than wanted to deport immediately, so the admiral commanding the dozen or so men-o'-war shielding the harbor from raiders did his best to persuade the impatient ones to wait for the morrow, so the merchantmen could sail altogether in convoy, protected by the warships and the offshore flotilla. He succeeded with most but close to fifty fat merchantmen sailed on the evening tide. Some of them made their destinations.

During the witching hours, that time of the late night when nearly all men, even those who set out to feast and drink and whore the night away, were dead asleep, a fleet of small coast-huggers crept around the headland and into the harbor. With muffled oars they glided to the ungainly ships that wallowed together, spars and tackle and gear creaking and groaning, waiting for their crews and the morning tide. Leaving the dozen shielding men-o'-war at peace for the moment, the first wave of coast-huggers reached the outermost of the anchored merchantmen, and small groups of small men, clad only in loincloths, armed only with long daggers, swung aboard.

Each merchantman had left a mate and two or three seamen aboard overnight as fire watch. It was those the small

bands of small men slew swiftly and silently. The small bands
went the width and breadth of the harbor, stepping from ship
to ship. When they had secured all the fat merchantmen, a
mage among them dispatched an imbaluris to the warlock attending the kamazai who was the General Commanding of
the invasion force. The warlock reported to the general that
the merchantmen were secured. On the kamazai's order,
larger groups of small men, uniformed and armed, crept
aboard the outermost merchantmen and walked the length
of the harbor across the ships. When four thousand of the
ten thousand in the invasion force had reached the docks,
their magician again dispatched an imbaluris to the kamazai's
warlock.

The General Commanding gave another command. Hordes
of small men then swarmed onto the men-o'-war and slew all
aboard. Lost in the creaks and groans of the wallowing ships,
the clashes of battle and screams of the wounded and dying
went unheard on shore.

At the same time, four thousand small, uniformed soldiers
left their landing beach on the headland and marched inland
to encircle the two regiments of Bostian troops guarding the
city's landward approaches. On another command, the four
thousand on the docks moved rapidly into the city, where they
captured the Guard and the city officials, slaying all those
who offered the slightest resistance. They took prisoner all
foreign seamen and soldiers, slew all who failed to surrender
quickly enough. On yet another command from the kamazai,
two thousand of the troops who took the city departed it to re-
inforce those surrounding the Bostian forces. Soon afterward, white flags fluttered above the Bostian encampments.

The conquest was so well designed that not one of the
magical weapons carried by magicians and specially trained
soldiers had to be used.

By dawn it was over. When the General Commanding
came ashore, he was accompanied by the Dark Prince, the

half bastard fourth son of Good King Honritu, liege lord of the mountain realm of Matilda.

"You will have your kingdom, my Lord Lackland," the kamazai said to his companion. During the long years in which the sages and magicians had worked on deciphering the tomes the Dark Prince's magic had wrought, the hated nickname had returned.

The Dark Prince's lips twisted into a smile. Oh, how he hated that name, and he hated no less those who used it. "No small thanks to you, Kamazai," he said. Then his smile straightened and his eyes glowed as he envisioned the arrogant Jokapcul warlord impaled at his command—impaled along with the other kamazai, and that unspeakable High Shoton. He looked forward to the day he would give that command.

The freeport of New Bally was secure in the hands of the Jokapcul invaders, as were the merchantmen and men-o'-war in her harbor. The bivouac of each thousand-man Bostian regiment sat under a white flag. The entire invasion had cost twenty-seven Jokapcul casualties: all wounded, none dead, few likely to die of their wounds.

The General Commanding issued an edict to the Bostian troops, the New Bally Guard, and the captured seamen and sea soldiers of a score or more nations: join us or die.

Without giving their captives a chance to make the decision, his soldiers then grabbed a hundred prisoners and hanged them in full sight of the others. The rest of the prisoners immediately declared allegiance. The Jokapcul executed one in ten of those, singling out the sea soldiers of a score of nations, especially Frangerian Marines, when they could find them. The remainder they held as slaves.

CHAPTER
TWO

The women woke them before dawn.

"You must go," one hissed as she pushed one of the men.

"Hurry, hurry," whispered the other as she tugged at her man.

They acted with such urgency that the half-awake men automatically groped for their weapons before remembering they'd left them on the ship—all they brought with them on shore liberty were the knives on their belts. They grasped their knives and held them ready.

"Why? What's happening?" Haft asked in a low voice. His eyes probed the shadows of the small, dark room.

Spinner listened closely to the indistinct sounds that reached them from the street. He scabbarded his knife when he realized the trouble wasn't in the room with them.

"Go," the one woman urged, and bundled Haft's clothes into his arms.

"Rush," the other hissed as she helped Spinner pull on his jerkin. Both women did all they could to speed the men on their way, made certain they had all their belongings, ensured they left nothing incriminating behind.

"You must be gone," whispered one.

"They will kill *us* if they find you here," said the other.

"Who?" Haft demanded. His eyes probed more deeply into the shadows, his knife held ready to slash or jab or parry if necessary.

"Jokapcul?" Spinner said. The woman nodded.

The women didn't particularly want to save the two men

16

they were quietly expelling from their garret room. The men, of the Frangerian Sea soldiers called Marines, only meant pay for a night's dalliance to them. But the invaders were coming, and the men created mortal danger by their mere presence.

"Let's go." Spinner put a hand on Haft's arm and guided him from the room. "Thank you," he said back into the darkness of the room. The door closed on them.

"What?" Haft demanded. "It's not dawn yet. We paid for the entire night, and the morrow's breakfast as well." If they weren't being attacked, he felt he was being cheated.

"Quiet," Spinner snapped softly. He pulled on the rest of his clothes.

Haft didn't know what the urgency was, but his friend's voice held an edge that made him obey the command. His clothes barely rustled as he pulled them on.

Without consulting, both men pulled their cloaks close around them, green side out so they could slip through shadows with lesser likelihood of being seen.

Dressed, they stood on the small landing outside the garret chamber for a moment and listened. The faint street noises that came to them through the walls of the inn were unexpected at that hour of the night. They crept down the narrow stairs, willing the treads not to creak.

The public room of the inn loomed huge in its darkened emptiness, appeared far larger than it had when filled with boisterous men. It seemed to have hidden recesses where an enemy could lurk until ready to spring an ambush. Spinner ignored the skin-crawling sensation of eeriness that the darkened common room caused. Haft held his belt knife as though it were his axe, prepared to fight off any ambush.

Faint starlight barely filtered through the glazed, unshuttered windows, but it was enough for them to make their way to the door without knocking anything over. They stood at the door and listened to the street outside. The unexpected noises were clearer, but none sounded on the street outside the inn.

Haft released the catches that held the door bar secure, and Spinner lifted the bar from its brackets and set it aside. They eased the door open and slipped out, leaving the door ajar behind them. It didn't bother them that anyone could walk right in to the now unsecured inn; the noises they heard, unmuffled now by walls, told them that barred inn doors would be battered down. Better the innkeeper didn't have to replace his door because it resisted the people coming his way.

Cries rang out in the night; some triumphant, some fearful, some death rattles. Here steel clashed against steel, there a ram battered down a barred door. The noises were coming closer. Haft clenched his hand so tightly on his knife that his knuckles almost glowed white in the night; he wished they had proper weapons, so they could better defend themselves if they had to fight. Spinner was glad they had *only* their belt knives—better armed, they'd be more likely to get into a fight, and he didn't want to fight without knowing more about what they were up against.

"What are the Jokapcul doing? Why are they here?" Haft whispered.

"Two ways to find out," Spinner replied.

Haft nodded; he knew the two ways. The first way, to walk openly toward the street noises, was too risky. They took the second way. They ran toward the corner closest to the approaching noises and peered cautiously around it.

Forty yards away was one of the many squares that dotted New Bally. It was ringed by fifty or more torches held by soldiers. They wore the dun-colored summer uniforms of the Jokapcul light infantry. Another fifty of the dun-clad soldiers formed a second ring inside the ring of torches; the soldiers in that ring brandished swords and spears at the mass of men they encircled, and barked commands at them in the harsh, unintelligible language of the Jokapcul Islands. Some of the men who were prisoners wore the scarlet uniforms and plumed helms of the New Bally Guard. Most of them wore the tatter-rags of the sailors of a score of nations. While

Spinner and Haft watched, more guardsmen and sailors were roughly brought and shoved into the square.

Spinner nudged Haft and pointed. One of the prisoners wore the same green-side-out cloak they did. "Rammer," he said.

Haft nodded. Rammer was their commander, the sergeant of the Frangerian Marine contingent aboard the *Sea Horse*, their merchantman.

Before either could give voice to the question each held—how to rescue Rammer—he looked directly at them and his mouth shaped the single word "Go."

The two looked at each other and saw nothing but deepest shadow, and wondered how Rammer, even with his legendary sharp vision, could have seen them. Without further thought, they obeyed their commander's order and quietly sped to the nearest alley leading away from the square, its guards and their prisoners. They knew they had to get back to the *Sea Horse* and join up with any crew members who might still be aboard and free. They wanted to free Rammer and the other prisoners in the square, but they were essentially unarmed. Before they could do anything, they needed weapons and manpower. They headed toward the docks.

Slowly, cautiously, they made their way through the alleys of New Bally, always careful to avoid stumbling through the middens or stepping into piles of slops. When the street noises and their route threatened to converge, they changed direction to avoid meeting the noise-makers. They went this way and that and sometimes the other, but always they wended toward the docks. The straight-line distance from the inn to the docks was less than half a mile; what with their innings and outings and roundaboutings, it took them more than an hour to travel the distance.

By the time they reached the mouth of an alley that opened onto the docks, dawn was drawing a line of light over the hills of the eastern headland. But they didn't need to see the color of the uniforms, or the narrow-billed, peaked caps of the soldiers standing guard on the ships, to know they were Jokapcul.

Even if they hadn't been able to see at all, the guttural, dog-like barking of the sergeants would have identified the soldiers as Jokapcul. The sight of the enemy soldiers on the ships' decks told them they wouldn't find any of their shipmates alive or free on board the *Sea Horse*. They edged back into the deepest shadows of the alley.

"We've got to get to the ship," Haft whispered hoarsely. "We need our weapons."

Spinner nodded. After a brief moment he whispered, "This way," and headed back and around until they came out again near the end of the docks, where there were no guards. An ancient shed nearly blocked the entrance of the alley they were in, so that from the dockside it might be possible to look at the shed and not realize there was a passageway behind it.

By then dawn was a glow that covered the lower quadrant of the sky. Stars faded away as the glow spread higher.

They slipped unseen into the shed, then Spinner dropped his cloak and started stripping off his uniform. "What are you doing?" Haft demanded.

"Getting us to the ship. Strip." When he was down to his pants, the legs of which reached barely below his knees, he redonned his belt with its single cross-body shoulder strap— his knife was scabbarded on the belt.

Haft looked curiously at Spinner, then realized what he had in mind and likewise stripped down. They bundled their clothes and hid them behind a crate in a corner of the shed.

"Watch your step," Spinner whispered as he pointed ahead.

Haft looked, and barely made out a darker place on the floor where there were no boards, just a narrow hole. He heard the gentle lapping of water.

Back outside, hidden by the night that still lay over the docks, they lowered themselves into the water between the last two ships along the dock.

Ships don't go straight down to the water; their hulls curve down and in. Even when nuzzled together, bumper to bumper at deck level, there is a wide space below their decks at the waterline. In the predawn, the darkness between the ships was stygian. The two paddled blindly through the dark, hands groping for anchor chains, mooring lines, low hanging bumpers, and the flotsam that always accumulates around ships in port. They made noise; they couldn't help it. But the washing of the harbor's water against the hulls masked their sounds from the guards on the ships above.

They didn't try to swim centered between the ships, but swam along them so they could keep track of where they were and where they had to go. They counted the bows and sterns they swam by; the *Sea Horse* was berthed the fourth row out, on the flank of the massed ships. When they were past four ships, they turned right and swam to the very end of the line, to where they were no longer under and between the ships. The sky was by then bright enough that they could make out the curve of the bay's western shore as it bent away from them.

Haft silently cursed the light. Spinner didn't waste thought on it. He held himself steady in the water by grasping the bow anchor chain and looked up to see the best way of boarding the ship. The most obvious was to climb the chain, then use the hawsehole as a step to climb over the rail, but that would leave them briefly silhouetted. Then he saw, a few feet aft of the hawsehole, a darker spot on the hull—someone had left a porthole open below the forecastle, in the hold that was the crews' quarters. He poked Haft to get his attention and pointed at the open porthole.

Haft looked, nodded, and immediately clambered up the chain. At the top he grabbed the edge of the hawsehole and swung himself to the porthole. In a trice he pulled himself through it. A few seconds later his head poked back out. Spinner was nearly at the top of the anchor chain, so Haft reached out to help him through the opening.

"Trouble," Haft whispered. "Smell."

Spinner sniffed. The crews' cabin held the odor of death.

It was too dark in the cabin for them to see, and they didn't dare light a lamp, but in seconds their hands found the source of the smell. Three corpses were dumped in a corner of the cabin. One had multiple knife wounds, as though he died fighting. The others had their throats neatly cut. Their clothing had the feel of sailors' tatters rather than Marines' uniforms.

"The sailors left on fire watch."

"Poor squids."

A moment's blind searching revealed no weapons—not that they expected to find any in the crew quarters. The Marines kept their weapons on their persons or secured in their quarters. Weapons that might be issued to the sailors in an emergency were kept in a locked chest in the bosun's cabin amidships. The sailors each had a utilitarian knife that was of less use as a weapon than the belt knives carried by the Marines. To get weapons, they had to go aft, to their own quarters, hard by the captain's cabin. The main passageway was nearly a hundred feet long, with who knew what in between.

Spinner listened at the hatch. When he heard nothing, he undogged it and eased it open. Three dim watch lights spaced evenly along the passageway that ran from the crews' quarters to the captain's cabin gave a feeble illumination, just enough so two men approaching from opposite directions wouldn't bump into each other. He opened the hatch far enough to step through and signaled Haft to follow. Haft closed the hatch behind himself but didn't dog it—they might have to come back that way in a hurry.

They ran silently on the balls of their feet toward their own cabin, and pulled up short while still a few yards from it. Directly ahead, at the end of the passageway, was the captain's cabin. Just out from it was another hatch on each side of the passageway. Those hatches led to the Marines' quarters, small, inboard cabins, each of which was shared by six men. The hatch on the right—their cabin—was open, and a low glow came from it. Scuffling noises came from inside the cabin. Someone was there. But who?

They slipped closer to the hatch. When they were just outside it, they heard chinking, as of coins being dropped into a pile, and a low, guttural humming. Whoever was in the cabin almost had to be a Jokapcul soldier. But was there only one or were there more? They drew their knives.

Haft stepped away from the bulkhead. Splash light showed him to Spinner. He tapped his own chest and made a gesture. He pointed at Spinner and made another gesture. Spinner nodded. They made ready, then Haft bolted through the hatch and twisted to one side; Spinner followed on his heels and spun the other way.

"Gwah?" A Jokapcul soldier who hunkered over one of the cabin's hammocks stood up at the noise of their entry and looked around. His slitted eyes popped wide, he dropped the coins he was tumbling from hand to hand, reached for the knife at his belt, and opened his mouth to cry out. Neither his hand nor his voice made it before the two were on him.

One hand clapped over the soldier's mouth while a knife point sliced up through his diaphragm to pierce his heart. Another blade slashed though his larynx, and an arm around his chest prevented him from falling to the deck. The two men held the body up until its legs quit kicking, then they dumped it onto an empty hammock.

"He was robbing us!" Haft said indignantly.

"He didn't think we'd be needing our money, I guess," Spinner said dispassionately. The individual chests of the Marines were all broken open and their contents strewn about. Coins and other valuables were dumped on one hammock, personal weapons were piled on another. Other usable items were stacked on a third. The remaining three hammocks were empty. "Let's move fast, his friends might come looking for him."

Frangerian Marines were issued sabers. Haft found his and hefted it, thought for a moment, then put the saber aside. Like many of the Marines, he used the saber mostly for parade and ceremonial duty; he had another weapon he preferred for fighting. "Ah, here it is." On the hammock filled with weapons, he found the axe that gave him his name. The axe's two-and-a-half-foot-long haft was made of ironwood. A half-moon blade projected a foot beyond the end of the haft and an equal distance down its length. A thick spike opposite the blade tapered to a sharp point. A rampant eagle adorned the face of the blade. Haft swung it in a short arc.

"Watch that!" Spinner jumped out of the way of the swing.

"Sorry." Haft didn't sound sorry, but he lowered the axe. He slipped his hand through its wrist strap and let it hang free. He picked up a crossbow. "This one always was better than mine," he said. He slung it over his shoulder and opened a belt box of quarrels; it wasn't quite full, so he opened another and jammed as many of its quarrels into the first as would fit.

Spinner found a full box of quarrels to put on his belt. His crossbow also went onto his shoulder. He opened his chest and withdrew an oilcloth-wrapped bundle. He opened it enough to make sure what it held, then sealed it closed again and tied it to his belt.

"*Lord Gunny Says*?" Haft asked, referring to the manual Spinner had.

Spinner nodded. "Never know when you'll need it." Then he looked at the hammock filled with coins and valuables. "Do you remember how much money you left in your chest?" he asked. Haft shook his head. "Neither do I." Spinner considered a moment, then said, "I have a feeling our shipmates won't be needing any money." He pushed his hands, back to back, into the pile of coins and valuables and shoved them apart. "That pile's yours," he said. He grabbed the coins from the other pile and poured them into a soft leather pouch that he plucked from the pile on the hammock filled with usable items.

Haft considered the remaining pile for a moment. The coins in it were from a score of nations; some from the nations the *Sea Horse* visited in its trading, some from the home nations of the Marines. He wondered if the casual way

Spinner divided the coins made a fair split. He decided they could settle it later if it wasn't, and likewise filled a leather pouch.

Spinner pondered the remaining valuables for a moment. The talismans and decorations, like the coins, were from a score of nations. Some of the coins were Frangerian, but none of the rings or medallions were. Frangerian Marines were all foreigners, since native Frangerians were not allowed to serve their country that way—they were supposed to be traders, merchants, or craftsmen. Some men joined the Frangerian Marines because they sought adventure, some because they had a past they wanted to leave behind. It was the custom for them to adopt fierce, warlike names and never use their own while serving. That custom helped keep the past from catching up with those who wanted only a present or only a future. It also helped them seem more menacing to those they might have to fight.

Finally, Spinner selected three rings that fit and hung two gold medallions on gold chains around his neck. He shook his head sharply. "Why do I feel like a thief?"

"I don't know. *I* don't." Haft started draping chains around his neck, filling his fingers with rings, circling his wrists with bracelets.

"I always thought you were a bit greedy, Haft."

"Come on, Spinner. If we don't take it, the Jokapcul will. Our shipmates would rather have us take their valuables than leave them for the Jokapcul."

Spinner looked calmly at his friend. "You know, we have to swim back to shore. Do you really think you can swim with all that weight?"

Haft looked down at himself for a moment, considering. "Maybe not," he finally said, and removed the smallest medallion, which hung from what looked to be the lightest chain. He looked up. "I'm ready anytime you are."

Spinner looked at all the jewelry his friend wore and shook

his head. "Why do I have the feeling this bay will soon have some very rich fish?"

Haft just looked at him.

Spinner never moved to pick up his saber. Like Haft, he had another weapon he preferred. Tied upright in a corner near the hatch stood a seven-foot-long staff nearly two inches in diameter. Spinner undid the thongs that held it in place and took it. "Let's go."

Again they ran quietly down the passageway. Halfway along, Spinner abruptly stopped and tried the hatch to the bosun's cabin. The hatch was always secured; it wasn't now. The Jokapcul who took the ship had broken it open. It scraped against its frame as it opened.

"In here," Spinner murmured. Haft followed him into the cabin they had always been forbidden to enter.

The bosun was responsible for many things on board the ship. One of his responsibilities was to be keeper of the fire. An orange glow from a brazier fashioned of iron straps gave them a dim light to see by. The cabin was thoroughly ransacked.

"Bosun will have a fit when he sees this," Haft murmured. Spinner grunted. "Oh, right," Haft added. "He probably won't be coming back." He kicked at a small, broken chest leaning precariously against the bulkhead where someone had tossed it. The chest dropped to its side with a clatter.

"Stop that," Spinner said, sharply but quietly. "Keep quiet."

Haft grunted. But after a few seconds it was clear the noise hadn't attracted the attention of anyone on deck.

Spinner breathed deeply and commenced a search. First he peered into the dark recesses of the shattered chest the bosun's mattress normally lay across; the thin mattress was now flung into a corner. Unable to see anything, he probed into it with a sweeping hand. The chest, usually abrim with the weapons that were to be issued to the crew in emergencies, was empty. He picked up the mattress and stuffed it into the chest. The small, broken chest that Haft kicked went on top of the mat-

tress. A middle-size chest that had held the bosun's uniforms
and other garb was also broken open and its contents strewn
about. Spinner haphazardly tossed articles of clothing into it
to clear the floor.

"This isn't the time to clean the bosun's cabin," Haft said
with urgency. He was growing anxious to leave the ship;
every minute they stayed aboard increased their chances of
being discovered.

"I'm not cleaning, I'm searching."

"Searching for what?"

Spinner shook his head. He wasn't looking for anything in
particular, but surely the bosun's cabin held something of
value to them. He picked up the bosun's dress sea-blue cloak
to toss out of his way and a small object fell out of a fold. He
picked the object up, looked closely at it, and said, "Good."
He tucked it into the pouch with his money.

Haft had just enough time to see that it was metal, little
more than the length of a man's knuckle and not as high. In
color, it was a dull silver, with scarlet and yellow flames
painted on it. He recognized the magic house.

"That's a salamander!" he exclaimed. "They're dangerous!" The salamander's house was constructed so that when
its door was open a properly fed salamander could only come
out partway and light a fire. Salamanders were always angry
at their imprisonment.

Spinner shook his head. "There's no magic to using salamanders, all you have to do is keep them fed." He continued
his search until he found a sealed canister, which he sniffed.
"Good," he said, "salamander food." He found nothing else
usable. Even the magician's cabinet built into the bulkhead
opposite the bosun's chest-bed had been stripped, all its arcane contents either taken or broken. "That's all," Spinner
said after his eyes swept the cabin one last time. "Let's go."

The hatch to the crews' quarters now stood ajar and a dim
light shone through it. Spinner was the first through the hatch

and fell over a soldier who was bent over, breaking open a locked chest. Another soldier spun at the noise, drawing his sword. He saw Spinner sprawling across the deck and swung a vicious overhand blow at him.

"Spinner," Haft cried out as he flipped his axe into his hand.

Spinner twisted his body, and momentum changed his sliding sprawl into a roll. The heavy blade of the Jokapcul sword thunked into the deck, just missing him.

Haft swung his weapon at the swordsman, but his blow was deflected by the blade of the man Spinner had tripped over, now on his feet with his sword in his hand. Haft spun out of the way of the soldier's thrust.

In one fluid motion Spinner was on his feet, staff held in both hands, and sidestepped the next slash from the man who'd already swung at him. He started to swing his staff, but had to parry a thrust before his blow struck home.

Haft had problems with his man. The cabin could house twenty sailors, but it was barely bigger than the cramped cabin he normally shared with only five other Marines; there wasn't enough room for him to use his axe effectively. He could parry and jab, but couldn't swing very far. The Jokapcul soldier rushed in with a quick flurry of blows that kept Haft too busy parrying to jab. Then Haft ducked under his foe's swing and tucked himself inside his arm. He gave a short chop to the man's side below his ribs. The Jokapcul gave a sharp, anguished cry and stepped back, his hand clasped against the entrails boiling out of his body. Haft swung his axe in a tight upward circle and brought its blade down on his opponent's neck. The enemy soldier crumpled to the deck, twitched a few times, and died.

Haft turned in time to see Spinner finish off his man. Spinner held the staff in front of him, spinning it like a baton, barely clearing the cabin's deck and overhead, deflecting each blow his opponent directed at him. Suddenly his hands shifted on the staff and one end of it shot out, slamming against the soldier's head with a crunch that left no doubt his skull was smashed. Spinner looked at the crumpled man in front of him for a second as though making sure he wasn't faking.

"Let's go," Haft snapped. They heard a loud voice call out from the deck above.

Spinner reached the open porthole, climbed through, and dropped before Haft reached it. When Haft was halfway through the porthole himself, he heard the splash of Spinner hitting the water fifteen feet below. He scooted through head first and went straight into the water.

The decks of several nearby ships rang with cries of query, but the two in the water paid them no attention. They swam through the darkness under and between the ships. The sun was up now. Quickly, they swam inward in the mass of ships, putting as much distance as they could between themselves and the *Sea Horse*. More voices were upraised on the ships. They heard the stomp of shod feet running along the decks.

Spinner pulled steadily ahead of Haft and turned at the second ship in when Haft was still only halfway past that ship. Spinner sprinted toward the dock. Haft splashed and struggled, weighted down by his weapons and the gold he'd taken. He gasped and foundered, and grimaced as he remembered what Spinner had said about rich fish. He bobbed in the water as he swam, his head below the surface more often than above it.

At last, after once spending almost more time under than he could hold his breath, he grabbed a dangling bumper line and paused to get his breath back. Spinner was right! Cursing silently, Haft jerked chains off his neck and bracelets from his wrists and let gold worth several years' pay fall to the bottom of the bay. Then, unencumbered but for his weapons, pouches, one bracelet, and the rings on his fingers, he was able to continue through the water.

Spinner gave Haft's bare neck a knowing look when the latter joined him at the base of the dock, but didn't comment. Instead, he cocked his head and pointed upward.

Feet tramped hollowly on the wooden deck above their

heads. Jokapcul soldiers were marching directly above them. And with the sun having risen, they could see each other clearly in the shadows between the ships and the dock.

CHAPTER
THREE

A sharp command was barked on the dock, and the tramp of feet slammed one-two to a halt. One pair of feet accompanied by the jangling of gear quick-marched a few paces: by the sound, an officer or a sergeant. Then the man barked a question. A sergeant, officers didn't bark that harshly, not even Jokapcul officers. A distressed halloo answered him from the direction of the *Sea Horse*. The sergeant barked another question, received another distressed response, barked an order at his men. Several pair of feet quick-marched to the edge of the dock. Thuds sounded on the deck of the ship Spinner and Haft were next to as several soldiers jumped onto it from the dock. The disorderly thumps and clinks of men crossing an unfamiliar obstacle marked their passage across that ship to the next one out; they were hurrying from ship to ship to the *Sea Horse*. The sergeant barked another order, and a soldier broke from the line and ran back in the direction from which the formation had come. Then the sergeant growled something low at his remaining men.

Even though they didn't understand the sergeant's words, the growl sounded to Spinner and Haft like he told his men they would now wait in good order for something else to happen, or for the messenger he sent to come back with new orders from an officer. Sergeants of all armies sounded alike, no matter what language they spoke, so it didn't take much imagination for the two Marines to follow the meaning of the sergeant's barked orders and growled commands.

31

Spinner and Haft looked at each other: What do we do now? A formation of soldiers, probably a squad or two, was on the dock directly above them, between them and the shed where they'd hid their clothes. Soon the entire dock area would be alerted and a search organized. It probably wouldn't be long before their clothes were found, then not much longer before they were found themselves. They were armed, but the odds against them were too great; they wouldn't be able to fight their way to freedom, not through an entire army.

Spinner motioned Haft to follow and, careful to avoid making noise, half paddled and half pulled himself from piling to piling deeper under the dock.

Haft at first wondered if Spinner thought they could hide under the dock until nightfall, no matter how many swimmers the Jokapcul sent to search the water. Then he remembered the hole in the floor of the shed. The search for them would probably start on the ships near the *Sea Horse* and in the water around the ships and under the dock. It would be some time before the invaders launched a search on the docks themselves, and even longer before they started searching in the city proper. By then the two of them would have found a place to hide, a place to plan their next step. Somehow they had to free the prisoners. Or at least enough of the Frangerian Marines to fight back. If they could find a safe place . . . If they could find Marines, or even sea soldiers of another nation, held by few enough guards for them to overcome . . . If the prisoners weren't locked away where they couldn't get to them . . . If a thousand other things. But Haft didn't worry about the ifs; he never worried about the ifs. Once they were away from the docks, the odds against them would be greatly reduced. Besides, he had full confidence in his and Spinner's fighting ability.

But first they had to find that hole in the dock, and the hole had to be big enough for them to get through. Was it big enough? Haft couldn't remember. But that was an "if " he'd worry about later—if it had to be worried about at all.

In moments, they reached the seawall under the dock and found more problems. The tide was out, so the bottom of the dock was almost six feet above their bobbing heads, which would make the hole in the dock hard to reach. They paddled about for a few moments, looking for handholds on the barnacle and seaweed coated pilings, searching the darkness above for any hint of an opening in the dock, without seeing or feeling anything.

Haft wondered how deep the water was under the dock at low tide, and he felt with his feet—New Bally wasn't known for the depth of its tides. He found the bottom and stood up. He tapped Spinner, who had to look up at his shorter companion.

Spinner gave a quick shake of his head and stood up, annoyed for not thinking of that himself. The water reached only the middle of his chest. It was shoulder deep to Haft.

Wading was less noisy than paddling and made looking up easier. They continued searching for the opening in the dock above them. Then Spinner probed up with his staff, making as little noise as possible.

After several moments, he said, "I found it." Then he staggered as Haft unexpectedly clambered up to stand on his shoulders.

"Hold still," Haft hissed. He crouched to keep from bumping his head while he felt with his hands just above his head. "We're not directly under it, move a little to your left."

Spinner shuffled, staggered, but managed to keep his balance. There were scuffing noises above his head, and Haft grunted once or twice. Then there was a snap and water splashed onto him. A fresh piece of flotsam bumped into his chest. Haft's weight suddenly lifted off him.

Shafts of light provided enough light that Haft immediately spotted the cask they had hidden their clothes behind. He was half dressed by the time he realized Spinner hadn't joined him. He lay down and stuck his head through the hole.

"This was your idea," he whispered. "Are you coming up?"

"It's too high, I can't reach it." Spinner sounded angry.

"Oh. Right." Haft reached his arm down the hole. "Grab hold, I'll pull you up." There was a splash as Spinner jumped up. Haft's hand didn't stretch far enough to reach Spinner. "Wait," he said, and twisted around to grab one of the cloaks. He knelt by the side of the hole, got a solid grip on the sturdy material, and dropped one end through the opening. The cloak went taut when Spinner grabbed it, then Haft felt his companion climbing. A hand suddenly grabbed the side of the hole and Haft let go of the cloak with one hand to grasp Spinner's wrist. In another second they were both inside.

"You left me down there!" Spinner said. "You had to stand on my shoulders to reach the hole, and you expected me to reach it by myself. If we weren't surrounded—"

"I'm sorry," Haft said, abashed. "I didn't think of you needing help. I forgot."

"You'd forget your head if it wasn't nailed on."

"No I wouldn't." Haft spoke sharply, but he looked away. "Anyway, I remembered, and I got you out of the water."

But Spinner was already dressing and arranging weapons on his person. Haft silently finished doing the same.

Dressed and armed, Spinner put his eye to a crack in the door of the shed. "We've got a problem," he said. In his brief look outside, he saw Jokapcul soldiers crawling over the ships and other soldiers using pikes to probe the water along the edge of the dock. They didn't bother him; two soldiers were walking toward the shed. Clearly junior men, they wore no armor. One carried a sword scabbarded on his back, and the other held a pike in his hands. The one with the sword had a round buckler strapped to his left forearm.

"Hide."

Haft ducked down behind the cask, his axe in his hand. Spinner stood against the wall on the hinge side of the door; he held his staff ready. They didn't have to wait long.

The door creaked open and one of the soldiers poked his head in to look around. He said something then turned back to scan the docks for a sergeant watching him. Evidently nobody was watching them. The soldier said something urgent and came in all the way. The second soldier dashed in behind him. The first one pushed the door shut and leaned against it. They weren't looking in Spinner's direction, so they didn't see him even though he was standing an arm's reach away. They laughed and said something that probably meant "We're out of this worthless search now. Let's rest here for a while and let the other men look for the intruders, who must be far gone." Spinner and Haft didn't understand a word the two men used, but under similar circumstances soldiers of all armies say the same things no matter what language they speak.

But Spinner and Haft didn't want to share their hiding place with two enemy soldiers. And they didn't think the two Jokapcul would want to share with them either.

"Now," Spinner said, and rose to spin his staff at the pikeman.

Haft was already on his feet, swinging his blade in a horizontal arc at the neck of the swordsman, who was closer to him.

The two Jokapcul didn't have time to react before one had his head cracked open by Spinner's staff and the other one's head flew off his shoulders.

Haft sidestepped the falling corpse of the man he'd killed and strode to the door to peer out. "No one's looking, let's go." He started to open the door.

"Wait," Spinner said. He knelt by the bodies and stripped off their shirts. The shoulders of the shirt of the man Haft had decapitated were saturated with blood, but the shirt of the man Spinner had killed was clean. Spinner tied a sleeve of the bloody shirt around the end of his staff and stuck it down the hole to swish around in the water. He pulled it back up at an angle so it wouldn't slip off. He wrung the water from the shirt and held it open to see how much blood still showed on it. He couldn't tell in the dim light inside the shed. "It's wet.

Any blood still on it probably won't show until the shirt dries," he said. "Here, put it on." He thrust the shirt at Haft.

But Haft realized what Spinner was doing and had already put on the other shirt. "No," he said. "You got that one wet, you wear it."

Spinner glared at him.

Haft spread his cloak out on the floor of the shed, made a few folds and closed some snaps in it. The Frangerian cloaks were versatile: not only were they double-reversible so they could be worn with any of four colors on the outside, they also had snaps and concealed straps so they could be turned into packs. Finished transforming his cloak into a pack, tan side out, Haft put his own shirt into it along with everything he was carrying that he didn't want to be seen wearing. He put a Jokapcul hat on his head. "I'm ready," he said. "What's keeping you?"

Spinner muttered something under his breath but made up his own pack and was soon dressed as Haft was, though a bit soggier.

They looked at each other. The sleeves of their new shirts were too short, and there was no point in trying to put on the pants of the much shorter Jokapcul soldiers, so they were only partly dressed in enemy uniforms. Still, at a distance, in dim light, and certainly to the townsmen of New Bally, they could pass as Jokapcul soldiers—Spinner more easily because his dusky complexion somewhat resembled the saffron skin of the invaders. But if a Jokapcul saw them close up, or if they had to speak, or if a Jokapcul even noticed the weapons they were carrying, there was no mistaking them for anything but what they were—impostors. "You know," Spinner said, "if they catch us they'll hang us as spies."

Haft shrugged. "If they catch us, we're dead regardless."

Spinner nodded. He would never surrender, would not allow himself to be captured by the Jokapcul, and he knew Haft would also not allow himself to be taken alive. The Jokapcul were notorious for their ill treatment of prisoners.

No, they'd rather die fighting and take as many of the enemy with them as they could.

There was one chore left. Careful not to get any blood on themselves, they lowered the corpses through the hole in the shed floor so that anybody checking the shed wouldn't raise the alarm. A quick glance inside probably wouldn't reveal the fresh gore that spattered it.

Spinner put his eye to an opening between the boards of the shed wall. Most of the soldiers were prowling the ships' decks. The few on the docks were looking down into the water or watching those searching the ships. No one was looking toward them. "Let's go," he said. He opened the door and Haft stepped boldly through it.

Without seeming to hurry, in seconds they had rounded the shed and entered the alleyway behind it. They headed back in roughly the same direction from which they'd come. This time they didn't skulk through the shadows and sprint across the thoroughfares. Instead they marched in step, side by side down the middle of the streets and byways. They didn't test their luck too much, though. When they saw a uniformed soldier, which was far more often than they wanted, they turned and marched in a direction that took them away from him, or into a street or alley where the enemy soldiers couldn't see them. Frequently they moved in a direction that would have led them back to the docks if they continued, but never for long.

"There seems to be more Jokapcul in the city now than there were before dawn," Spinner said after they'd avoided getting close to enough soldiers to form a regiment.

Haft nodded. "They've taken over the city like flies on a corpse."

Once, they stopped where they could see a small square without being seen themselves. It was filled with sailors packed hip to haunch. Chains linked the captives. Makeshift gallows, just posts with top arms, dotted the square. Bodies dangled from the top arms, two or three to each. More of the hanging bodies were Marines and other sea soldiers than were sailors.

Haft hefted his axe but made no move toward the square. The prisoners were ringed by twenty sword- or pike-bearing guards and a half-dozen archers. As much as he seethed at the sight of the mistreated prisoners, it was obvious that a two-man attack on those guards would be suicide. They moved on.

Twice they hid in alleyways while strings of prisoners shuffled by accompanied by guards who didn't hesitate to beat a man for not stepping briskly enough. Once, they passed near a small stone building with two squads of Jokapcul guards around it. Cries and moans came from the building, and through its barred windows they saw it was filled to bursting with prisoners.

They kept moving, in a generally northeast direction, toward the city wall.

Without help there was no possibility of freeing the prisoners. All Spinner and Haft could do was try to escape the city without being captured themselves. Then cross a continent. Then cross the Inner Ocean. And find their way back to Frangeria.

So it was that the only people who saw them up close were the few citizens of New Bally who were about on that day of foreign conquest, most of whom bowed their heads and ducked away at the sight of the conquering uniform. A few, bolder, spat at the two once they were past. Once or twice someone must have looked more closely because they heard muttered words that sounded like "traitors" from the shadows. Fortunately, the only things cast at them were words.

The straight-line distance they traveled to the wall was little more than twice the distance their journey from the inn to the dock had been the night before, but it took four times as long because of how often they had to avoid enemy soldiers. The New Bally city wall was not as tall as the walls of most big cities, only fifteen feet high for most of its length. As a freeport, New Bally was not often subject to raid or conquest.

Its status as a freeport was generally more valuable to would-be conquerors or raiders than its conquest or the fruits of a raid would have been.

The top of the wall had a fighting step behind crenelations, but it lacked platforms for catapults. Neither did it have the archers' towers with interlocking fields of fire that marked city walls meant to keep out determined attackers. A New Bally city ordinance decreed that a lane wide enough for a troop of cavalry and a company of infantry to pass each other while marching be kept clear on the inner side of the wall. But as New Bally rarely needed to be defended, the ordinance had long been ignored. Vendors had set up stalls along the lane, and shanties were frequently stacked against the wall. By using the city wall, the poor who built the shanties only had to come up with enough wood or brick to build three walls to their homes; two walls if they also built against another shanty.

Spinner and Haft examined the wall from a shadowed position in the mouth of an alleyway. Every fifty paces a Jokapcul soldier stood watch on the wall's top. Most of the guards watched the fields and forests beyond the walls, but many others kept watch on the city itself. To one side of the alley mouth a produce vendor sat cross-legged behind piles of fruit; to the other side, a small merchant hawked the virtues of his brassware. Few people moved back and forth on the lane, the normal cacophony of citizens doing their marketing in the military lane absent.

Directly opposite their hiding place a row of a dozen shanties leaned uneasily against the wall.

"You give me a boost there," Haft said, pointing at the end of the row of shanties—a guard watching beyond the wall stood almost directly above it. "I'll get on the wall and cut down that guard before he knows I'm there. Then I'll toss down a rope for you to climb up. We'll be over the wall and on our way before anybody can reach us."

Spinner calmly looked down at Haft. "And what will we land on when we go over the wall?"

Haft looked up at Spinner, perplexed. "The other side, of course. What do you think?"

"And what's on the other side?" Spinner asked patiently.

Haft just looked at him.

"Is there a moat? Is there a palisade of stakes? Is there a passing company of Jokapcul soldiers? Is there a nearby troop of cavalry or line of archers to cut us down before we reach the cover of the forest? For that matter, how far away is the forest?"

"Oh," Haft said, looking away thoughtfully. "I hadn't thought of that." He straightened up. "Well, it's easy enough to find out what's out there. Let's ask this fruit vendor." He started to step out of the alleyway, but Spinner grabbed his shoulder and slammed him back against the wall.

Spinner shoved his face into Haft's and spoke low but sharply. "If a Jokapcul sees you, he'll know you're not one of them and will sound the alarm. Even if a Jokapcul doesn't see you, the vendor will think you're a traitor. Do you think he'll give a traitor true information about the other side of the wall?"

Haft's brow furrowed in thought. "I guess not," he finally murmured.

"Right." Spinner scanned the alleyway, looking for something else they could do. One of the two buildings flanking them was made of stone, the other of wood. Neither had a door or other opening into the alley into which they could step. Higher, though, perhaps twelve feet above the ground, wrought-iron fencing formed a faux balcony outside a small unshuttered window on the side of the stone building. No light came from within the window. Spinner craned his head back to look higher. The stone building was perhaps fifty feet high. If it had a flat roof that they could reach from inside the building, from the top of it they'd be able to see almost everything they'd have to face on the other side of the city wall.

"Stand here." He positioned Haft under a corner of the wrought-iron fencing and, remembering what Haft had done to him when they were under the dock, vaulted without warning to his shoulders. One hand instantly found a finger-hold on the stone face of the building, the other wrapped around a picket of the wrought-iron fence. Under him, Haft collapsed from the unexpected maneuver and the sudden weight on his shoulders, but Spinner was already pulling himself up and finding toeholds on the wall. He yanked on the wrought iron to test that it was held securely enough to the wall to hold his weight. It gave slightly, but he saw that if he stepped softly it would probably hold his weight. He swung over the top of the faux balcony. The fencing was low, little more than a foot high, and the iron lathing was scarcely half a foot wide. The footing was cramped, but Spinner easily enough managed to hold his balance in the tight space.

"Hey!" Haft snapped.

"Shhh," Spinner hushed at him. "You want someone to hear?"

Haft hushed. He looked up and saw what Spinner had in mind. He wondered how he was supposed to get up to the fencing. Then he put his hands on the wall, looked up, and concluded that he could find enough purchase for his finger-tips and toes.

Spinner put his face close to the glazing and peered through. Inside, it was too dim to make anything out, but he saw no movement. His questing fingers found hinges along one side of the window and he swore about the outward-opening windows. He shuffled to the side of the balcony, away from the hinges. There, he stepped one foot over the side, found precarious purchase on the wall, and slid his other foot as close to the end as it would fit. Holding the wall with one hand, he pried at the edge of the window with his free hand. The hinges squealed but the window opened. Its bottom scraped across the top of the wrought-iron fencing. When the window was open far enough, he leaned into the opening and rolled through. As his foot came off the bottom of the balcony, he thought he felt the iron lathing shift, and he heard metal grating against stone.

For a brief moment Spinner froze. At first he heard nothing. Then he spun around, holding his staff at the ready as he heard a slam and a grunt and the squeal of tortured metal behind him.

Haft looked in through the bottom of the window. His arms were over the sill and hanging on tightly—it was obvious his body dangled outside. His face wore a silly grin. "The balcony broke," he said.

Spinner snorted. "I ought to leave you there." But he held his staff one-handed and grabbed Haft's outstretched hand with the other and pulled him in. He cautiously peered outside. No one was looking into the alleyway. The faux balcony dangled from one end, the other end torn completely from the wall. He closed the window and turned back to examine the room.

It appeared to be some sort of office. It held a desk, a chair, and three high-topped clerk's desks. Along the walls were shelves stuffed with ledgers and cabinets filled to bursting with papers. On one wall hung a map of New Bally. Various locations on the map were marked. The marks all seemed to indicate storehouses, merchants' stores, and government buildings. The harbor was clearly drawn, with the docks and piers annotated. But other than indicating the routes of the highways, the map showed nothing of what lay beyond the city wall. There seemed to be nothing in the room that could help them get away.

While Spinner examined the map, Haft put his ear to the door. When he didn't hear anything beyond it, he tried to open it. It was locked. Spinner joined him at the door.

"This is the only way out," Haft said. He hefted his axe. "I'll break it down."

"Stop!" Spinner put his hand on Haft's arm before he could swing at the door. "If the door is locked, it might be warded by a banshee."

"The window wasn't," Haft answered, and again prepared to swing his axe.

"That doesn't mean the door isn't."

Haft stepped back and looked at the walls all around the door. "No red-eye, no banshee," he said.

Spinner quickly looked around the room again, this time for the telltale red-eye. "You're right," he reluctantly acknowledged.

Haft looked smug. It wasn't often he spotted something important before Spinner did.

With almost no backswing, Haft slammed his blade into the door frame next to the lock. A shattered chunk of the frame fell out. He calmly grasped the handle and pulled. The door opened easily. The locking mechanism clunked to the floor. No banshee wailed its alarm. With a flourish, he bowed Spinner through the open door.

Spinner held his staff at the ready. He stepped halfway through the doorway and looked both ways. The door opened into a corridor that appeared to run the length of the building from front to back. No one was in evidence. He stood in the middle of the corridor and listened. He heard nothing from inside the building.

"Let's find a way to the roof," he said.

CHAPTER FOUR

They glided silently through the building and up its stairs to the roof. The place felt eerily like it had been unpeopled for longer than human memory, though the lack of dust on the floor, except where it was caked thick in the corners, indicated it was occupied regularly and had been used recently. In the top floor of the building, ladder rungs built into the wall of a storage closet led them to a trapdoor in the ceiling.

Spinner climbed up and unlatched the trap. He eased the door up, looked out, and found the flat roof he'd hoped for. He climbed through and motioned Haft to follow. Together, they lay flat and breathed a sigh of relief at the clear, unoppressive air of the roof. But they only rested for a few seconds.

They looked about. A low wall stood above the front and two sides of the roof; the back had no barrier guarding against a sheer drop. To the back, toward the middle of the city, they could see roofs as high as or higher than the one they were on. Many of the roofs were flat. No guards stood watch on any of them. They saw only sky to the front and sides; nothing in those directions seemed to be higher than the building they were on. Staying below the level of the wall, they crept to the front and peered over. In the distance were close-packed trees that appeared to climb rising ground, but the restraining wall was too wide for them to see anything nearby.

"This is no good," Haft muttered and stood up. "That's better," he said.

Spinner sat leaning against the wall and cringed at thought of the guards on the city wall seeing Haft.

Haft stood casually, as though he belonged there and had every right to be on that roof. He knew that someone who looks like he belongs is almost never challenged. Quick glances to the sides told him theirs was indeed the highest building along that stretch of the city wall. Looked up at from the street, he'd be silhouetted against the bright sky, and the observer would see his uniform shirt and probably not be able to make out his fair complexion and red hair.

"We might have a problem," he said when he looked beyond the city wall.

"What?"

"Well, I don't see a moat or palisades or any soldiers outside the wall, but the forest is almost a mile away. We wouldn't be able to reach it before horsemen could run us down."

"See, I told you we needed to find out what was on the other side of the wall before we went over it."

Haft ignored that and continued observing the area. He saw how cluttered the military lane was, with shanties against the city wall and vendors' stalls on its inner side. In some places the shanties and stalls almost completely blocked the lane, so no more than two people could pass at one time. The guards on the outer wall were at fifty-pace intervals for as far as he could see. A gate a quarter mile distant was guarded by at least a squad of Jokapcul soldiers who seemed to be carefully inspecting the slow procession of people, carts, and animals passing out. They allowed no one to enter the city. He was looking for a way over the wall when he heard a jangling of metal and a guttural halloo from the lane below.

Spinner, still below the restraining wall, realized a sergeant or officer saw Haft and was demanding to know what he was doing there. Spinner started looking for a fast way off the roof.

Haft managed not to flinch at the unexpected call. He pretended not to hear it and continued to look around.

The guttural halloo came again, with a sharpness of anger to it this time.

Haft continued casually looking around until his moving eyes seemed to naturally look down. He hoped he was right about the bright sky disguising his complexion and hair. He feigned surprise at finding someone standing below, calling to him. He could see the man was a sergeant from his uniform. Rectangular metal plates linked with iron hoops armored his shirt, and metal-studded gauntlets protected his hands and wrists almost up to the elbows. In place of the peaked cloth cap worn by more junior men, he wore a peaked helmet, slightly flattened front to back. Haft assumed the three black cloth stripes slashed across his chest were rank insignia. He wore a short sword on his belt.

The sergeant barked and growled and made gestures in the manner of all sergeants of all armies. It sounded and looked like he was asking what Haft was doing on top of that building and demanding that he come down. Evidently, this building was in his unit's area and he knew he hadn't stationed a guard on it.

Haft pointed to his ears and shrugged elaborately.

The sergeant bellowed something that had to be, "What do you mean, you can't hear me?" He knew his voice was loud enough to be heard all the way from one end of a parade ground to the other.

Haft pantomimed being clouted on the ears and shrugged apologetically.

The sergeant snarled in disgust. He took a deep breath to calm himself then used a series of elaborate gestures that concluded with his finger sharply pointed to the ground at his feet.

Haft held out his hands and shook his head emphatically. He splayed three fingers on his left chest, mimicking the insignia the sergeant wore on his own—and fervently hoped he was right about it being rank insignia—then pointed to himself and, just as emphatically as the sergeant had pointed to the ground in front of him, pointed his finger at his own feet.

My sergeant ordered me to stay here and not leave for any reason, his gestures said.

The sergeant huffed and puffed and went red in the face. Then he roared something. He gave Haft a last glare and stomped away down the military lane, the rings on his shirt jangling against the metal plates.

Haft watched him for a moment, then dropped down behind the wall. "I don't think it's a good idea for us to stay here any longer," he said weakly. He was almost hyperventilating.

"You're right for a change."

Spinner led them scuttling back to the trapdoor. Inside, Spinner ducked into an empty room and opened his pack. He stripped off the stolen shirt and put his own back on.

"Change," he ordered.

"Why?"

"If you'd been wearing your own uniform, you wouldn't have been dumb enough to stand up where that sergeant could see you."

"But if I hadn't stood up I wouldn't have been able to see what was out there."

Spinner didn't answer; he knew Haft was right about that. Still, he thought they'd be more cautious and therefore safer if they were dressed in their own uniforms.

Haft didn't say so, but he agreed that caution was the better course of action—especially now that they knew what was on the other side of the wall—and also got out of the enemy shirt.

This time they explored their surroundings from the top floor of the building. A window on the side they'd come in from showed no one in the alleyway below. There were no windows on the other side of the building; the adjoining building shared that wall. A window to the rear was mere feet above a roof that abutted the rear of the building they were in. They saw less from the front than Haft had seen from the roof. Except . . .

Where they weren't smack against each other, the shanties

against the wall had middens between them. Some of the middens were more than half as high as a man was tall, and some were piled as mounds standing almost free of the city wall rather than sloped screelike against it. It might be possible for a man to hide behind them and not be seen from the lane.

"We could hide there until dark and then go over the wall," Haft said, pointing at a midden that had space between it and the wall.

Spinner looked at it and grunted. "Unless a guard on the wall looked down. He'd be sure to see us."

"We could pull the top of the midden down on us, to hide us from view."

Spinner simply looked at him. He was repulsed by the idea of being covered with other peoples' rubble, rubbish, and garbage. He said, "We'd make a lot of noise covering up now and getting uncovered again after dark. Someone would hear it and we'd be discovered."

"Do you have a better idea?"

Spinner didn't.

"Then let's do it." Haft led the way back down to the second floor office through which they'd gained entry to the building. Spinner followed, protesting Haft's idea all the way but unable to come up with a better one of his own.

The alley looked as empty as before, and they only heard the sounds of a few passersby on the lane beyond it. The faux balcony hanging by one end blocked their view of whatever might be directly below it, but that blind spot was barely large enough to hide one man—it certainly couldn't conceal a Jokapcul squad waiting to capture them.

Haft eased himself over the sill and slid down until he hung by his fingertips, then let go. He dropped only a few feet and, even though he stumbled when he landed, managed to stay upright. He heard a grunt and a gasp so close together they were almost simultaneous. The grunt was from Spinner when he landed next to him. Haft pulled his axe and spun toward the hidden space below the hanging balcony, which was where the gasp came from.

"No, my lord," said a thin, old man's voice. "Don't hurt me, I mean no harm. I'm merely an old man with weak water." The old man looked as thin as his voice, and his body was bent and sagged with its many years. His garments were so old and patched they seemed to be more rags than clothes. He hurriedly closed the front of his pants. A small puddle glistened next to the wall near his feet. Then he saw how the two men who had so suddenly dropped in on him were dressed and drew himself erect. He rendered an old man's clumsy salute.

"My lords, you are not *them*!" he said in a stronger voice—and they could hear the emphasis when he said "them." "You have come to drive *them* away? I will help you. I will do anything I can to help you expel the invaders." His body resumed its old man's slump.

Spinner stepped back and peered deeper into the shadows of the alleyway, looking for others. He didn't see anyone. "Who is with you?" he demanded.

"No one, my lord," the old man answered. "As I said, I'm just an old man with weak water. I came in here alone to release the pressure so I wouldn't embarrass myself in front of other people. But"—he now spoke in a firmer voice—"I know many people who want to fight *them*, to drive them from our fair city, which hasn't known war in more years than the oldest person in the city can remember." He cleared his throat. "Certainly not for as long as I can remember, and I may well be the oldest living citizen of New Bally. One of the oldest, at any rate." Now that he was over his initial shock, the old man was becoming gregarious. "I don't think anyone in the city wants *them* here. Unless they come as traders. Certainly no one wants them here as conquerors. New Bally is prosperous as a freeport, but if we are a vassal city, we will be poor, and no one wants that."

Haft had to stop the old man's rambling. "You say you will fight?" he asked haughtily.

The old man straightened again and looked at Haft levelly. "I may no longer be able to wield a sword in the manner of young, strong men such as yourself, my lord. I cannot lead a charge into the massed ranks of the enemy, nor will I be a member of our own massed ranks repelling and assaulting. Nonetheless, there are yet things even a bent old man such as myself can do to aid in a battle."

Spinner thought of what the old man had said. He said he could help them. Maybe he could. He said to the old man, "Are there many in the resistance?"

"My lord, all of New Bally will arise when you make your attack. We citizens of this fair freeport ask only guidance to coordinate our fight with yours."

"Good. We are a reconnaissance. We have seen much of value to our army's attack. Now we must return and give our report to our general, but we don't see a safe way out of the city. Can you help us?" He almost hated himself for giving the old man false hope, but if they got out of the city, they might actually run into a counterattacking army that would need what they knew about the Jokapcul in New Bally. He put a hand on Haft's arm to keep him from giving away his ploy.

"Uh, that's right," Haft said. He hadn't needed the warning to realize what Spinner was doing. "We're a special reconnaissance force for the whole army."

The old man's eyes glowed and he grinned broadly, exposing snaggled teeth with gaps between them. "You can't get out during the day," he said. "You have to wait for night. But I can hide you until then and show you a hidden way to the forest."

"Good. Where do we go?"

"Follow me." The old man scuttled, bent over, deeper into the alley, his head swiveling furtively from side to side as he went. At first Spinner shook his head at the sight of the old man moving in a manner such as an old man might imagine

soldiers move when they were on a secret patrol. Then he
realized the old man looked as though at one time he might
actually have known how to move unobserved. He wondered
about that.

Haft was wondering the same thing. He said, "Do you
think he's leading us into a trap?"

Spinner shrugged. "It could be. But we can't stay here. If
he's telling the truth, he's our best hope of getting out."

Still, they hesitated to follow him. Until they heard the
tramp of marching feet approaching on the military lane.

"That sounds like your sergeant coming back with a squad
to relieve you," Spinner said.

"Yes it does," Haft agreed.

They quickly followed the old man into the depths of the
alley. They walked erect and swung their weapons casually,
but were ready for action, just in case the old man was collab-
orating with the enemy—or in case the approaching soldiers
entered the alley before they were out of sight. Just as they
reached the end and ducked into a barely shoulder-wide passage the old man had disappeared into, they heard the squad
come to a halt. A sergeant barked commands, and the sounds
of running feet told Spinner he'd ordered them to secure the
building.

They had to duck and weave and sidle as the old man led
them through a warren of alleys that were often little more than
narrow spaces between buildings and garden walls. They darted
across streets and thoroughfares when no one was looking
their way. As he clambered and hopped over obstructions in
his path, the old man proved far more agile than his wizened
appearance suggested. The deeper they went into the maze,
the more certain Spinner and Haft were that the old man was
exactly what he said—someone hoping to be rescued from
the Jokapcul invaders—and they relaxed their vigilance. It
wasn't long, though they had become hopelessly lost, before
the old man disappeared into a doorway they couldn't see.
They groped blindly for a few seconds, found the opening

and ducked through it themselves. A door thunked shut behind them and light suddenly flared up.

The old man, his body still bent, his grin still wide, rubbed his hands in glee.

He cackled. "They'll never find you here," he said. "The only way to know this place exists is to come the way I led you, and no one can do that unless he knows the way, and there are few who do. No one will show them the way. You'll be safe here until night, and then I'll show you a way out of the city." In the light of the room, he was able to see Haft's axe clearly for the first time. He stared at it for a long moment, then drew himself fully erect, into a surprisingly proper military posture of attention. His grin disappeared and his hands stopped washing themselves.

"My lord," the old man said in a firm voice, "I have not seen the rampant eagle in many years. I did not know anyone still wielded such a weapon. I know if the rampant eagle is nigh, the invaders will soon be driven from this fair city." He gave Haft a courtly bow.

Haft looked at him, puzzled. He glanced at the eagle on the face of his axe, then looked at Spinner. Spinner was looking back, just as puzzled.

Haft cleared his throat. "Yes. It will happen soon. Perhaps sooner than the enemy thinks." He didn't think he sounded very convincing.

The old man looked deeply into his eyes, a touch of uncertainty in his own, but didn't comment on Haft's tone. Instead he asked, "Have you had food?"

Haft's stomach growled—they hadn't eaten since the previous night's dinner.

"You wait here, I'll bring food." The old man opened the door a crack and flitted through, shutting it securely behind him.

"What was that about your axe?" Spinner asked. "The old man thinks the engraving on it means something special."

Haft held it out and looked carefully at the eagle on the blade. He shook his head. "I don't know. It hung over the mantel in my home my entire life. My father said his father carried it when he went off to war as a young man. That was all he ever said about it. I played with it when I was young and playing at soldier. When I ran away, I took it without asking my father."

"Was your grandfather a hero in a war?"

Haft shook his head again. "My grandfather died in a hunting accident when I was an infant, so I never heard anything from him. My father never talked about the war his father was in. I don't even know what war it was, or in what army he fought."

"Maybe the old man will tell us more about it when he comes back."

Haft made a face. "The way the old man reacted to it, I don't think it would be a good idea to let him know we don't know what the eagle means." He stared at the rampant eagle on the blade of the axe and wondered what significance it held that he didn't know about. He remembered the odd looks the axe occasionally got from other Marines, but none of them had ever said anything about it to him.

Spinner nodded and didn't say anything more about the axe.

They looked at their surroundings. They were in a small room—Haft could almost touch both walls with his outstretched arms, and it wasn't much deeper front to back. The light came from an oil lamp in a wall sconce. A rag-covered pile of pine boughs against the back wall served as a bed. A small table against a side wall held an ewer and bowl. A metal plate and cup hung from pegs on the wall above the table. A small chest tucked under the table looked like it was meant to be pulled out for use as a stool. The bare dirt floor was swept clean.

Haft pulled the chest out and flipped up its lid. It was filled with small belongings. There was a set of clothes, a bit newer and less often repaired than what the old man had been wearing. A hairbrush, a small box of antique jewelry—"Put it back," Spinner said—a pocked and ragged-edge stone of un-known origin, a religious medallion, a calfskin-covered book, and a few other objects. The last two objects were of more interest than the rest. One was a miniature painting of a young man and woman lovingly looking at each other.

Spinner indicated the miniature and said, "If that's him and his bride, he's come down a long way." Portraits, especially those as exquisitely executed as the miniature, were costly.

Haft nodded agreement. He was glad Spinner made him put back the jewelry. "How will he buy food for us?" he wondered.

"We'll pay him," Spinner said, and tapped the purse at his belt.

They stared at the other item for a long moment. It was a blue, gold, and red ribbon with a clasp in back, designed to be worn hanging around the neck. A medallion in the form of a five-pointed star with a goddess's head embossed in its center dangled from a padded knot in the ribbon's front. It was the Order of Honor—the highest Frangerian military decoration.

"He was a Marine?" Haft asked.

Spinner shook his head. "He would have been before Lord Gunny came. We were called 'Frangerian Sea Soldiers' then, not 'Marines.' " He looked again at the medal. "If he was, he was a hero."

Reverently, they repacked the chest. Spinner regretted the lie he'd told the old man about them being a reconnaissance, but knew no way to back away from it.

Spinner sat on the chest, and Haft settled a haunch onto the table. They held their weapons in their hands—just in case—and waited.

In moments the door opened again and the old man scurried in with a steaming tray. A wide-eyed urchin of about ten or eleven inched in behind him carrying a brimming pitcher. Her bare feet were filthy and her hair was matted, but she was otherwise as clean as a girl fresh from the bath, and her dress was of fine material and not anywhere threadbare or patched.

Haft moved out of the way so the old man could put the

tray on the table. "My great-granddaughter," the old man said as the girl put the pitcher next to the tray. Then he noticed the chest was pulled out and pain flickered across his face.

"It's all there," Spinner reassured him. "We disturbed nothing." He stood and bowed. "You honor us with your aid."

"My lord," the old man said, returning the bow.

"What were you called?"

The old man looked at him for a long moment before replying in a soft voice, "They called me Tiger."

"Tiger, they call me Spinner and him Haft."

The old man snuffled and brushed the back of a hand across his eyes. Then he removed the cover from the tray.

Haft and Spinner salivated at the aroma of the stew that was exposed in two bowls. The loaf of bread between the bowls smelled freshly baked. The old man pulled a pair of spoons from somewhere within his garments and handed them over. The girl retrieved two cups from somewhere and carefully filled them from the pitcher. In a short while the food was gone to the last drop of sauce and last crumb of bread, and the pitcher was down to the dregs. Haft leaned back and belched contentedly.

"Thank you, Tiger. We needed that," Spinner said politely.

The old man's great-granddaughter looked at them more wide-eyed than before.

The old man bobbed his head several times. "I am glad to do whatever I can to help you rid my city of *them*. Now you can rest until nightfall."

"What are they doing out there now?" Haft asked.

"There is a citywide manhunt," the old man said, glee lighting his face. "Early this morning a large raiding party struck at several of the ships they occupy in the harbor and killed twenty of *them*, including a general or an admiral."

"Really?" Haft asked innocently.

The old man bobbed his head vigorously. "That's what people on the street are saying." He looked at them conspiratorially and dropped his voice. "Personally, I think that's an exaggeration. Had there been such a raid, surely we would have heard the sounds of the battle. Certainly there would have been spontaneous attacks on *them* as a result of the raid."

Spinner nodded gravely. "I agree that such a raid would have caused more interest when it happened. And if a general or an admiral was killed, the Jokapcul would be murdering people wholesale on the streets."

"So it was you who went aboard a ship and killed a couple of *them*?" The old man's eyes twinkled.

Haft opened his mouth to admit it, but Spinner spoke first.

"I told you before, we are a reconnaissance. Reconnaissance teams avoid fighting if possible so no one knows they are there."

The old man nodded knowingly. "Yes, you said that. It is said they have hanged twenty of their prisoners in reprisal. They are not soldiers, they are beasts. Soldiers do not murder prisoners."

Shooing the girl ahead of him, he went to the door. "You rest now, I will return later to lead you out of here." Then they were gone and Spinner and Haft were alone.

"He took off before I could give him money for the food," Spinner said, looking around the barren room again. "I'm sure he couldn't afford to buy it." He fished a gold coin out of his purse and put it on the table.

Haft thought of the young girl, how her clothes contrasted with her feet and hair, and agreed. He added a gold piece to Spinner's.

"We're going to be traveling at night at first," Spinner said. "So we should get some sleep today. I'll take first watch. I'll wake you in a couple of hours." He got off the chest long enough to open it and take out the book, then settled down to read away the time until Haft's watch.

Haft looked at the book and wondered what he was going to do to keep from getting bored during his watch—he read well enough, but it wasn't something he enjoyed. Then he lay

on the pallet of rags-over-pine-boughs and, in the manner of
soldiers of all armies, was asleep in minutes.

It was dark by the time the old man returned. He gave them
a sack that contained cheese, bread, and a sausage. "You have
not eaten in many hours and you have far to go tonight. You
will need this," he said. "Now follow me." He said nothing
about the coins on the table.

In the narrow spaces that framed their route, they couldn't
see enough of the night sky to tell whether there was a moon
out. Still, all three managed to move as silently as spirits
through the night. Nearly blind as they were, not knowing
where they were going, or even where they were, Spinner and
Haft couldn't tell how long the journey took. It felt like a long
time before the old man finally stopped next to a drop.

"Here is a tunnel," he whispered. "It leads to a canal on the
other side of the wall. A long time ago, when I was a boy, the
canal brought fresh water from a forest stream into the city.
Now we have sufficient wells inside the walls, so the canal is
no longer needed and is dry. The grating is gone from both
ends of the tunnel. You can get out here and follow the canal
all the way to the forest. When you reach the forest, you will
be in the Duchy of Bostia. From there you can find your own
way back to your army." Fumbling in the darkness, the old
man found each of their hands and squeezed them. "Go in
safety," he said. "The people of New Bally will rise up and
fight alongside you when you come back with your army."

"We thank you, old friend," Spinner replied, and squeezed
the old man's hand as hard as he dared. "Remain in safety."

Haft hugged him. "We'll be back. We'll drive them out. We
will see you again then, and you will dine richly on our treat."

The two Marines went down into the tunnel, and moments
later were beyond the city walls. In another twenty minutes
they were inside the forest and heading rapidly away from New
Bally on the first leg of their journey back to Frangeria. They
didn't know how they were going to get there or what they

would pass through in between, but they were safer than they had been. Haft wondered why he had promised the old man they'd return.

The Jokapcul invaders didn't pause following their conquest of New Bally. A state of war existed with the Duchy of Bostia as soon as they had captured the regiments guarding the landward approaches to the freeport. Before dusk of the first day, a large element of the Jokapcul force pressed inland. The kamazai who was the General Commanding of the Jokapcul forces left a lesser kamazai, one more adept at civil administration than at command of warriors, in charge in New Bally and went with his forces deep into the duchy.

Lord Lackland, half bastard fourth son of Good King Honritu of Matilda, Defender of the Northern Marches and Guardian of the Western Coast, went with the invading forces, eager to see the booty that would put an end to the hated nickname "Lackland" and leave him once again the "Dark Prince."

THE DARK PRINCE

The Early History of Lord Lackland:
A Speculation

by Scholar Munch Mu'sk

Professor of Far Western Studies

University of the Great Rift

(excerpted from *The Proceedings of the Association of
Anthropological Scholars of Obscure Cultures*,
Vol. 57, No. 6)

It was the custom in the Kingdom of Matilda for a king to
have three sons. The first son became king in his turn. The
second son was bequeathed the title Prince of Easterwood,
and upon the death or abdication of his special uncle, the
second son of his father's father, was given the Easterwood
lands and the title Earl of Easterwood, Defender of the North
and the East. Easterwood was the northern and easternmost
portion of Matilda, and guarded the mountainous kingdom
from raids and wars with the giants of the High Steppes, and
from the strange denizens of the Land of the Night Forest.
The third son was trained from infancy in the art of arms, and
became commander of the armies of Matilda upon the death
or retirement of his special uncle, the third son of his father's
father.

No king of Matilda ever sired a fourth son. That was against
custom, for there was nothing of princely value left to be-
queath to a fourth son: no crown, no border marches, no army.
A fourth son, custom averred, could only lead to civil war, or
some other serious disorder.

It was also the custom in Matilda that while the queen was
the king's only wife, she was not his only woman. Matilda
wasn't the only land in the two continents where a king or a

regent-prince or a duke had more than one woman. But that form of polygamy was conducted openly in Matilda, whereas in the other kingdoms, principalities, and duchies, the concubines of the ruler were strictly back-bedroom affairs, never openly acknowledged. In Matilda, if the queen was barren or if she could not give birth to the requisite three sons, the king still needed three sons from his own loins. While one suspects there were other reasons why a King of Matilda might consort with a woman not his wife, they needn't concern us here. But, if a son had to come from another woman's womb, in Matilda it was thought best that the other woman should also be the king's woman. Even if that son was not born from the womb of the queen, that son by another woman would be presented to the kingdom as the queen's own. Any other children the king's other women might have, well, they weren't the queen's, and thus had no standing in matters of succession, and were never acknowledged to be born to the king. Except . . .

The queen of Good King Honritu, Defender of the Northern Marches and Guardian of the Western Coast, died not long after birthing her third son. The king, naturally, some said, took solace during his time of mourning in the arms of his favorite among his concubines. Some said he celebrated the death of his queen in those arms—but nothing was done to those who so impugned the character of their king, so long as they did it quietly. That was one of the reasons King Honritu was given the sobriquet "Good": he allowed his people the freedom to openly speak their minds—provided they did so discreetly. Two or three nobles who were heard to grumble about the king's dalliance during his time of mourning were beheaded, which quelled further aristocratic grumbling. At the same time, two or three commoners who impugned the king's character too loudly were hanged. Many Matildans regretted the loss of the commoners but none blamed their king; those who were hanged should have known better than to speak their displeasure so loudly.

Good King Honritu waited a decent interval before having

his favorite concubine appear at his side in public: at first only occasionally, then more frequently, and at last constantly. Then he waited until the hints—and they were only hints—of muttering among the nobles ended; the nobles remembered too well the beheadings and none wished to add themselves to that number. He waited a bit longer, until the commoners cheered his favorite when they saw her. Only then did Good King Honritu proclaim the royal nuptials.

By that time his seed had germinated within his new queen, sprouted, and the sprout spawned. This wasn't a problem in and of itself, certainly not if the spawn was a daughter. Even if the spawn was a son, that could be dealt with in any number of ways—most of which had nothing to do with burying the get to avoid admitting to the birth. Truth to tell, down the generations, one or another King of Matilda had in fact sired a fourth son upon his queen, occasionally even more. When that happened, the superfluous sons were simply given over to the motherhood of one of the king's concubines, who raised them as her own. So there had never been any problem of a fourth *prince* in any generation of Matilda's royal house. Until . . .

Unfortunately for Good King Honritu, his new queen wanted to keep her firstborn, and Good King Honritu, Defender of the Northern Marches and Guardian of the Western Coast, was too smitten with his second queen to deny her anything. So, what was to be done with this child? The queen certainly could not have a son who was not acknowledged as the king's.

Overruling his councilors, Honritu reasoned that this fourth son was a "half bastard" and therefore out of the line of succession. The councilors begged to know what a half bastard was, as they'd never heard of any such thing. The king explained that since the fourth son was conceived and born out of wedlock, he was a bastard. However, since the king was his father and was married to the boy's mother, he was only half a bastard, with no more right of succession than a complete bastard. The councilors grumbled that one was either a complete bastard or not a bastard at all, and at any rate, that reasoning begged the question. The king, as kings are wont to do, prevailed.

But no one had given a thought to what it would be like to be the fourth son of the King of Matilda. No one gave a care to how it would feel to grow up being universally known as a half bastard. Anyone should have known that a boy raised as a prince but with nothing to succeed to would risk growing bent. But no one paid it mind. Needless to say, nearly all were surprised when the half bastard fourth son became the Dark Prince, so called for his black moods and his red temper.

The half bastard found the "Dark Prince" an acceptable name, even a grand one. But what he was called by his childhood playmates, his siblings, the nobles, and—worst of all— by his own father, was Lackland. "Lackland" was not an acceptable name to the Dark Prince.

Lackland rankled. Lackland seethed. Lackland envied. Lackland hated. Lackland desired vengeance.

The Dark Prince swore that the mocking use of the scurrilous name would not go unpunished.

There was no royal crown for the Dark Prince to inherit. No Earl of Easterwood for him to become. No armies for the Dark Prince to command. The Dark Prince must remain Lackland for so long as he lived. Or at least for so long as he lived in Matilda.

The Dark Prince planned, but not in hopeless scheming. He knew of the raids the Jokapcul were conducting against the mainland. He understood why those raids were little enough successful that they were considered no more than nuisances, and minor nuisances at that, even with the demons the Jokapcul commanded.

He took to studying seacraft and sea craft, magicians and the control of demons. He did not undertake the study of seacraft and sea craft in order to become a shipwright or a sailor, nor did he study magicians and demons for the purpose of practicing the arcane art himself. He studied the former in order to acquire knowledge tradable to those who had only fishing craft. He studied the latter in order to learn how to gain control over the practitioners of magic.

A day came when a Jokapcul knight was captured during another nuisance raid and was held captive in the king's keep. The Dark Prince quietly visited the captive on a number of occasions, conversing with him in order to ascertain that his understanding of why the Jokapcul raids were merely nuisances was correct and that his understanding of how to make them more serious was equally accurate. Then, one night, he slew the soldier standing guard outside the captive's cell and freed him. Together, they slipped out of the palace, out of the city, all the way to the harbor. There they boarded a small ship that carried them across the sea to the Jokapcul Islands, where the knight got word to the High Shoton of Jokapcul that a parley was requested. This High Shoton was the first shoton in all of Jokapcul history to rule all of the clans and all of the islands of the nation. He agreed to the meeting, at which he listened intently to all the Dark Prince had to say. Then he smiled slyly and agreed to the Dark Prince's plan.

The High Shoton called the Dark Prince "Lackland." So did his councilors, his kamazai, and his generals.

The Dark Prince smiled tightly, but objected not a whit to what he was being called. One day, he swore, the barbarians would regret ever using that name. And when that day came, the Dark Prince, Lackland no more, king—nay, *emperor!*— of the largest and mightiest realm ever known, would gloat over the corpse of the High Shoton.

NOTE: The preceding paper has been based, in part, on studies conducted over the past thirty years on the culture and history and royal family of the Kingdom of Matilda; in part, on official dispatches the author has had access to; and in part, the author must admit, on travelers' tales. It is as its popular tone suggests and as its subtitle clearly states, speculation, and should not be assumed to be fully accurate. By no means should anyone take any action based on the assumption that the preceding paper is a true and accurate portrait in all respects of the events described therein. The author does beg to note, however, that the events describing the natal genesis of Lord Lackland, the self-proclaimed "Dark Prince," and his character as it developed, are matters of public record, well known to scholars of Far Western Studies and to others who have need of knowing what has taken place in the western parts of Nunimar in our lifetime. (MM)

II

ESCAPE

CHAPTER
FIVE

Spinner and Haft walked steadily for nearly two weeks after they slipped out of New Bally in the dark of night. For the first few days they stayed off the roads and skirted the villages they passed, coming close only when hunger and lack of edible game compelled them to risk buying food. Their stealth was prompted by the frequent Jokapcul cavalry patrols they saw during the first days, which they suspected were advance scouting parties for the Jokapcul army. They were soon glad Spinner had brought his copy of *Lord Gunny Says*. They were ship's complement, not field Marines, and had no experience and only limited training on how to live off the land. Lord Gunny had the foresight to have experienced woodsmen write chapters for his manual on field-expedient shelter, edible wild plants, and trapping small game. Each evening, Spinner carefully fed the salamander and used it to light the fire over which they cooked their dinner.

When they hadn't encountered any patrols for a few days, they decided to walk the roads in the interest of greater speed, getting off the road whenever they heard or saw someone approaching. Fortunately, that didn't happen often enough to make road travel slower than off-road, or what Lord Gunny, in the manual Spinner carried with him, called "breaking bush."

For those two days, they still skirted villages. The evening of the eighth day, a day during which they only had to move off the road once to hide from someone approaching, found them nearing a village. That night they stayed in the inn. The main language of the freeport of New Bally was Bostian. Like all Frangerian Marines, Spinner and Haft had picked up enough Bostian to be able to follow a simple conversation in that language. So it was that they heard from other travelers, who more accurately should be called refugees, horrible stories of Jokapcul rapine headed their way. Many of the locals wanted to flee before the invaders arrived. Others in the village weren't talking, they were simply packing to leave.

So it went for the next two days: few stops to hide from someone coming their way, and nights spent in inns listening to rumors to which they didn't contribute. As the rumors became wilder, Spinner and Haft felt a bit more secure. They knew their true nature; the farther away the source, the wilder the rumors. All they had to do to be safe was find their way to the next kingdom, and thence a route to the sea and Frangeria.

And so they got directions to the Kingdom of Skragland, northeast of the Duchy of Bostia. Their rough plan was to cross the lower part of Skragland until they could turn south into the Principality of Zobra and make their way to the port of Zobra City, there to find and sign aboard a ship heading east.

Even though they hadn't seen or heard anyone since entering the forest on their eleventh day, that part of their journey was the most daunting so far. For men as accustomed as they were to the horizon-spanning vistas and unhampered breezes of the ocean, the sluggish air and the closeness of the trees hemming the road in on both sides were oppressive. Tree branches crossed the roadway overhead, blotting out the sky and making the road more a tunnel than a canyon through the forest. They wanted to get out of the forest quickly.

The road was merely an ox cart track, just wide enough for four men to walk abreast if their shoulders touched. If two ox carts approached each other on the road, well . . . Bushes grew between the trees and bulged out over the edges of the road. Save for infrequent deer crossings, there was hardly a space anywhere for even a man to step off the road and into the forest without breaking bush. The grass that grew in the middle of the track between the ruts was evidence that foot, ox cart, or horse traffic along the road was infrequent.

The two talked quietly between themselves in the manner of men who had walked long enough to be bored with walking. But still they were as alert as soldiers in enemy territory. Which, for all they knew, was exactly where they were. One subject they didn't discuss, though, was the men they'd left behind in New Bally. Even though they both knew well that there was nothing they could have done to free the prisoners, they both felt guilt, felt they had abandoned their shipmates.

Haft abruptly cocked his head and listened intently. "Do you hear something?" he asked.

"Other than the birds and insects?" Spinner responded.

"Why else would I ask? Sounds like maybe there are horses on the road behind us."

Spinner shook his head with mock sadness. "You've been at sea too long, my friend. The creaking of tackle and snapping of sails has you losing your hearing. I first heard those horses a good five minutes ago."

Haft glared at Spinner. "Why didn't you say something?"

"They're only trotting, we have a little more time before they come into sight. Besides, I haven't seen anyplace where we can get off the road without leaving sign of it."

Haft turned and walked back a few paces to see what or who was following them, but he could see less than fifty paces to the rear because of the winding of the forest road. The jangle of harnesses sounded closer. A muttered oath drifted to his ears. "Do you think they're looking for us?" he asked.

Spinner shook his head. "Of course not. Not this far away from New Bally. But even if they aren't looking for us, if they're Jokapcul they'd probably be happy to find us. And we probably wouldn't be happy about it if they did."

A space not clogged by a bush appeared ahead. Tracks and

a similar opening in the brush on the other side of the road indicated that this was an animal crossing.

"This is what I've been looking for since I first heard the horses," Spinner said. "Let's see who they are." Haft beat him through the gap.

It was at first too dark to see anything. Just a few feet away from the road the canopy was so dense that almost no sunlight reached the ground. Between the tree trunks, which were larger and not as closely packed as along the road, the forest floor was nearly barren.

Haft turned to the side to go in the opposite direction from which they had been walking and immediately jumped back, swearing and rubbing his thigh.

"Thorn bushes," he muttered. "Be careful."

He probed gingerly with his axe until he found the end of the thorn bushes and went around them. By then his eyes were adjusting to the darkness and he was able to avoid other thorns. He unslung his crossbow from his shoulder and strung it as he went. Spinner also readied his crossbow. If the followers were enemy soldiers, which was likely, and decided to investigate the deer gap, which was possible, they might be discovered. In that case, the two Marines would shoot and quickly reduce the odds against them. If they had to fight, they would probably have enough time to get off two quarrels apiece, perhaps even three, before the enemy closed to side-arm range.

Twenty paces from the game trail, they found a place where they could observe the road without being seen. They also thought they were invisible from the deer crossing through which they'd entered the trees. They were hardly settled in before the riders came into sight.

The horsemen were short, slender men with saffron skin and almond eyes. Their helmets were cone-shaped, slightly flattened from front to back, and bowed out over their ears. A leather sheet hanging from the bottom of the helmets covered the backs of their necks and tops of their shoulders. The helmets had stiff flaps that extended around the front to protect their throats. The bright blue leather was reinforced with small rectangles of shiny metal. They wore blue leather jerkins with shields attached that flared out over their shoulders. Short aprons hung down in the front and back. The jerkins and their flaps and aprons were reinforced with metal rectangles the same way the helmet flaps were. Chain mail covered their arms and thighs. Studded gloves and boots completed their armor. Across their backs, in a scabbard, each man wore a sword more than half as long as he was high, the hilt jutting above his left shoulder. Each held a short lance upright, with the lance's butt anchored in a small cup in the toe of the right stirrup. Jokapcul light cavalry.

The horsemen rode two abreast, and a single man rode alone ten horse lengths ahead of the others. That one held his sword ready in his hand, his lance tucked beneath his thigh. He looked constantly from side to side, examining the woods he passed through. He stopped at the deer crossing, turned his horse to face it, and leaned forward in the saddle to peer into the darkness under the trees.

The officer leading the squad stopped his column and waited for the scout to report. Even if he hadn't given the order to halt, Spinner and Haft would have recognized him as the leader by the scarlet plume that flounced above his helmet and the emerald pennant hanging from his lance. And they knew, if he was a Jokapcul leader, he was an officer, not a sergeant. In the Jokapcul army, sergeants assisted officers, but they never themselves led except in garrison. Unlike the Frangerian Marines, who often had small units led by sergeants or corporals, in the Jokapcul army even the smallest unit had an officer in charge if it was to do anything more than post guards.

The scout barked something at the officer, and the officer advanced. The other men stayed behind. Their horses snorted and pawed the ground. One horse stepped to the side to nibble on a bush almost directly in front of Spinner and Haft. Haft shouldered his crossbow and aimed at the horseman's face. But the horseman didn't look into the bushes, didn't see the death that stared at him; he watched his officer and the scout.

He carried something more than the standard weapons, something that made Spinner and Haft grow weak when they saw it. Slung from a cord around his neck and one shoulder, a tube hung down his side. It was a dull greenish-gray that sharply contrasted with the brilliant colors of his leather armor. Both ends of the tube were flanged. An awkward-looking hand grip protruded from it forward of the midpoint. The two had seen drawings of it; it was called a demon spitter. The weapon was said to be more accurate and longer-ranged than a longbow, and to strike with such violence it could knock a hole in a stone wall.

The two men began to shrink deeper into the shadows. They froze when a small door just behind the hand grip flipped open and a small head popped out. They couldn't see the body the head was attached to, but it looked like nothing so much as that of a flat-faced bat.

"Veedmee!" it said.

When the soldier carrying the tube ignored it, the creature climbed out through the door and onto the soldier's shoulder.

"Veedmee!"

The soldier kept his attention on the scout and officer, who were still examining the animal crossing, and casually waved a hand at the demon, almost as if he was waving at an annoying fly.

"Veedmee!" the demon shrilled angrily.

The soldier snapped something that sounded negative, then turned his head to look at the demon and poked a thumb toward the tube. The demon bit the thumb and the soldier yelped, more in surprise than pain.

The soldier began to slap at the demon, but before his hand reached it, his head snapped toward the officer, who'd barked a question. He shouted back and jabbed a finger toward the demon, careful to keep the finger out of biting range.

The officer said something incomprehensible, but it was clearly a command, and the soldier barked one syllable in reply, then turned his head and growled at the demon. He reached into a pouch on his belt. As soon as the demon saw him going for the pouch, it scuttled back to the tube and crawled inside, then turned around and poked its head back out. It piped joyful noises as the soldier held something the size of a grape before it. The demon snatched the thing from the soldier's fingers and ducked back inside, pulling the door shut so fast it almost snapped shut on the soldier's fingers.

The soldier muttered a few more growls at the demon in the tube, then returned his attention to the scout and the officer. A few of the other soldiers were looking at him, snickering. He glared at them and they looked forward again, some very slowly in what was almost a challenge.

After a few seconds the body of the horsemen started to drift forward, curious to see what had caught the eye of their scout. Soon they were all milling about, crowded together at the crossing. The officer barked a couple of times and growled a few more, but didn't press the issue, and the horsemen briefly danced aside, then ignored his orders.

Haft put his mouth to Spinner's ear and whispered, "We can do it, we can take them. First we get the one with the demon spitter. We can shoot at least half of them before they even realize they're being attacked. Maybe we can get all of them before any of them can close to lance range. Even if they do, their lances are too long to use in the forest. Let's do it." He backed away and aimed his crossbow at the soldier with the demon spitter.

Spinner also thought they could take the nine horsemen without too much danger to themselves, but it felt like a bad idea. It took him a half second to realize what was wrong with Haft's plan. He put his hand on the other's crossbow and forced it down.

"They're probably expected somewhere. When they don't show up, there'll be a search and we'll be found," he whispered.

"We'll drag all the bodies well under the trees. It'll take them a long time to find the bodies. We can be far from here by then," Haft whispered back, and raised his crossbow again.

Spinner pushed it back down. "What about their horses? What if one of them gets away? He'll lead them right back here with a large force to hunt us down. Or what if another picks up the demon spitter and uses it?"

Before Haft could object a second time, the scout dismounted and stepped into the gap. Both readied their crossbows; Haft aimed at the one with the demon spitter, Spinner at the officer.

The scout squinted at the darkness into which he'd stepped. He squinted at the ground near his feet. He barked at his officer, and the officer barked back at him.

The scout growled low to himself and peered blindly about. He took a step to the side, then jumped back with a yelp and smacked a hand against his thigh. Clearly, he'd discovered the thornbushes. The officer growled at him and barked a couple of times. The scout growled to himself, peered around again, barked at his officer. The officer growled back. The scout looked relieved as he turned around and went back out onto the trail. The officer barked at the squad and they got back into formation, with the scout again ten horse lengths ahead. Another bark and they trotted away.

Spinner lowered his crossbow and sighed in relief.

Haft angrily jerked his weapon from his shoulder. "We could have gotten all of them," he complained.

"And a larger force would have come looking for us and we'd really be in trouble then because they'd know we were here and there'd be too many of them to get away from," Spinner said sharply. "And they've got demon weapons."

Haft grumbled and rose to his feet.

"We have to be more alert now," Spinner said. "We know they're ahead of us as well as behind." He didn't unstring his crossbow or remove the quarrel.

"Let's find out where they're going," Haft said.

"I think we have to," Spinner said. The Jokapcul horsemen were going in the same direction they were, and there was no other road for them to take.

They maintained the same miles-eating pace as before, but now they held their crossbows in their hands so they could start fighting at a distance greater than sword length. Their senses were more open to signs besides birds and insects. They talked less. But except for infrequent road apples and nibbled brush, they detected nothing beyond the same oppressive closeness of the forest they had felt before—until late in the afternoon of the next day.

They heard the border crossing before they saw it, and they smelled it before they heard it. Conflicting aromas slowly drifted through the sluggish air toward them.

At first the smells were merely indistinct wafts, hardly enough for them to be consciously aware of. Gradually, the aromas strengthened and steadied and Spinner and Haft realized they were approaching an inhabited area, though they knew it must be either an exceptionally poor village or a temporary encampment that had been in place longer than intended. But they detected the fragrance of well-cooked stew. That told them people were present. Low and unpleasant was the muted stench of a latrine used for too long. Only the very poor, transients, and the overcrowded don't do a better job of disposing of their wastes.

For several hours the forest road had meandered as though it followed an old game trail. About the same time they first heard manmade noises from up ahead, the road bent to the right then appeared to straighten out. They stopped, looking ahead, wondering what lay beyond the bend.

The bushes had been trimmed back there and the lower branches cut from the trees, allowing full sunlight to reach the road; that probably meant it was in sight of someone ahead, and the trimming had been done to improve the field of view—or fire—of whoever was there.

Haft tapped the side of his axe's head against the palm of his left hand as he peered at the bend. Then he half crouched and took a quiet step forward. He intended to approach the bend undetected by whoever might be beyond it and look around it.

Spinner grabbed him before he got beyond an arm's length away.

"Don't worry, they won't see me," Haft objected. "I'm going to get down and look around the base of that tree on the corner."

"That's the obvious place to look from," Spinner said. "If there are guards up ahead and they're any good, that's exactly where they're watching." He thought for a moment longer, then added, "And if they have a magician with them, he's probably got some sort of watch-sprite there."

Haft looked ruefully at the bend in the road, at how well maintained it was, and slowly nodded. "You may be right. Any better ideas?"

Spinner nodded. "There's a deer crossing a few hundred paces back. Let's go into the woods there and get back to a place where we can see what's beyond the bend."

Haft grumbled something indistinct. He didn't like having to backtrack. "All right," he said grudgingly. Just because he didn't like it didn't mean he thought it was a bad idea. The noise of clopping hooves and creaking leather came from around the bend. It might be a horseman approaching from whatever was ahead of them, or it might simply be tethered horses. Neither wanted to wait there to find out, not with Jokapcul light cavalry somewhere ahead of them. Bent over as low as they could without risking their balance, they ran back. At almost every step they expected to hear a cry of discovery from their rear, but none came. When they reached the deer crossing, no one was in sight and they heard no sounds of pursuit. They ducked into the darkness under the trees and paused to let their eyes grow accustomed to the dark.

CHAPTER
SIX

The forest seemed different, though it was no darker or lighter, and the denseness of the trees was the same. There were still thornbushes near the road. But before, they hid under the trees and prepared to fight if they had to. Then, the forest was their friend, giving them cover from the enemy, and they had been within sight of the road. Now they were traveling through the woods, toward something unknown, and out of sight of the road—and that made the forest *feel* different.

Grass and weeds grew between the ruts of the ox cart trail; in the forest, fallen leaves and twigs lay on bare ground under the trees. With no sunlight to evaporate moisture, the soil was wet under their feet. Occasional seedlings sprouted up through the mulch. On the trail, the air moved sluggishly, but it moved; in the bush, it seemed not to move at all but to settle damply on them. Outside, sounds seemed normal, even if somewhat muted by the walls of foliage between which the two men passed. But the thick canopy overhead made sounds hollow, and tree trunks echoed noises, so they couldn't tell how far away a sound was or where it came from. The tree-enclosed road had been mentally oppressive to men accustomed to the vistas of the open sea; it was even eerier under the trees.

Haft grimaced as his eyes adjusted to the relative darkness and he took in their surroundings. "Do we have to go this way?" he asked.

Spinner swallowed. "Can you think of anything better?"

Haft couldn't think of anything better. "We have to go this way," he murmured. He put his words to action and strode into the forest, away from the road, but close enough to make out the wall of foliage that bordered it.

Spinner followed in trace.

Rotting vegetation squished under their feet; fallen branches too soggy to snap collapsed underfoot. Small animals scampered from their path, startling the two men. The two stopped when something that sounded big and particularly dangerous slithered by in front of them, but they couldn't see what made the sound. A flier from the canopy swooped down and squawked its disdain at them. Something high above scattered slops at them and scarcely missed.

They hunched their shoulders, gripped their weapons more tightly, looked fearfully all around through widened eyes—and kept going. Making sure they stayed within sight of the hedge wall that lined the ox cart road, they watched ahead, peered deeper into the forest at their side, and frequently looked to their rear, alert for danger. The journey seemed to take forever, but they kept going. And, after an eternal fifteen minutes, they were rewarded by the sight of yellow-dappled green ahead of them.

Haft started to rush toward the light, but Spinner restrained him.

"We need to check for watch-sprites," Spinner whispered.

"If there are any watch-sprites, we're close enough that they've already spotted us and reported our presence," Haft snapped. "Anyway, I haven't seen any red-eyes."

Spinner didn't think they would see red-eyes there. "Not necessarily. It's gloomy and we've been moving slowly. Not all sprites can see well in low light."

Haft chewed on his lip, watching the light patch of foliage that indicated the bend in the road where they'd stopped. "Maybe you're right," he finally said. "A smart magician wouldn't put a sprite here, he'd use a dryad, they can always see in the forest. So can some elves." He looked at Spinner.

"But why would a magician put a watch-sprite that can't see in the dark in dark woods like this?"

Spinner shrugged; he didn't have a good answer. "Maybe the magician didn't have a dryad or an elf. Maybe he had to use all he had in other places. Maybe he's not concerned about anyone moving through the forest." But he couldn't think of a reason a magician wouldn't concern himself with anyone approaching through the forest. After all, Lord Gunny had drummed into them the absolute need of watching every possible approach route.

As if in answer to Spinner's unspoken question, the cry of a giant cat boomed hollowly in the forest behind them. Suddenly he understood why a magician wouldn't be concerned.

They spun around, ready for battle, but nothing was in sight.

"That sounded like it came from the deer crossing we used," Haft said with an edge of uncertainty.

Spinner agreed. He wasn't sure either, but the deer crossing sounded right.

"What do you think it is?" Haft asked.

"A cat. I don't know what kind." Apianghia, where Spinner came from, was the home of many big cats; given the chance, some of those big cats ate people.

Haft shuddered. It made sense to him that if Jokapcul forces were closing in on the border, someone might want to guard it with big cats. And someone who did that wouldn't need watch-sprites in the forest.

"I don't think there's a watch-sprite here," Haft said.

"Neither do I," Spinner said.

Maybe they did and maybe they didn't think there was a watch-sprite there—or a dryad, or an elf. It no longer mattered—being spotted by a watch-sprite was less dangerous than getting caught by a big cat. They sprinted toward the yellow-dappled green.

As they suspected, the road ran straight once it passed the bend where they had doubled back. At a distance greater than the range of their crossbows there was a gate. It wasn't much of a gate, merely a hinged, counterbalanced bar across the road. The forest seemed to end there.

A uniformed squad of Jokapcul wearing blue leather with metal reinforcing stood in rank facing the gate; probably the same squad that had passed them the day before. The Jokapcul cavalrymen held their swords with the points casually dipped toward the ground, but they looked ready—and willing—to fight.

Immediately beyond the gate a dozen or more men milled about, mostly facing the Jokapcul, scowling and generally looking menacing. They were big men, standing head and shoulders above the Jokapcul they faced. They wore leather jerkins and boots and homespun trousers. Fur capes were draped across their shoulders. The only metal the Marines could make out was the blades of the men's short swords, and banding on their horned helmets and round shields. They were speaking to one another, but Spinner and Haft could not make out any words. From somewhere out of sight came the clang of metal against metal; it sounded more like someone working with kitchen pots than the crossing of swords.

"Must be Skraglanders," Spinner said of the milling, furred men.

"I think so too," Haft said. "We're at the border."

The feline cry sounded again behind them. Closer.

"The Skraglanders might like our help in keeping those Jokapcul out," Haft continued, with a nervous glance to his rear. "We should go and make the offer."

"But the Jokapcul are between them and us," Spinner said. "We'd have to get through them to reach the Skraglanders."

Haft peered down the road. "I don't see a wall." He was right; the gate wasn't set in a wall. All they could see was a small gatehouse. The ground to its side was open; the gate seemed more a symbol of a barrier than a real one.

Spinner looked forward, looked back, judging distances.

The cat cried again, closer still. He flinched. "The cat's tracking us. If we run, we can reach the edge of the woods before the cat reaches us."

"What are we waiting for?" Haft took off through the forest, heading for what he hoped was an open border.

Spinner ran after him, listening for sounds of the cat in pursuit. His staff was long enough and strong enough to blunt the cat's attack if it leaped at him. While the cat was off balance, maybe Haft could get in close enough to injure it with his axe. Maybe. The big cats were fast and agile; even when knocked off balance they landed on their feet. Spinner wanted to get out of the forest before the cat reached them. Maybe it wouldn't follow them into the sunlight. Maybe when they were in the open the Skraglanders would come to their aid against the cat. Maybe when they got out from under the trees they'd have time to aim and use their crossbows. Maybe a huge friendly bird would swoop down and carry them off to Frangeria. Spinner's throat tightened and his breath rasped.

Spinner was concentrating so hard on listening for the cat and considering all the maybes that he didn't see Haft suddenly skid to a stop. He ran into him and the two fell heavily.

Spinner jumped to his feet, both hands firm on his staff. He spun about looking for someone to strike—he thought Haft must have stopped to avoid an attack. His eyes took in everything. Then he saw what made his friend stop so abruptly.

They were at the edge of the forest. Dotted with small clumps of trees as far as the eye could see, farmland lay beyond. A small cluster of cottages nestled under the nearest clump of trees. They heard the sounds of metal being hammered coming from there.

Nearer at hand, twenty-five paces to the right and in front of them, was safety—the dozen milling Skraglanders. The Skraglanders grimaced and grumbled, scowled and shouted at each other, and, less frequently, they turned their scowls at the Jokapcul cavalrymen and shouted at them. The Skraglanders made themselves look as dangerous as they could.

Spinner and Haft could hear their words now, but neither knew Skragish. Still, it was clear that the Skraglanders were discussing the horrid things they'd do to the Jokapcul cavalry should they prove so foolish as to pass through the gate.

At the same distance from Spinner and Haft, but directly to their side, was the Jokapcul cavalry squad. The Jokapcul simply stood in their rank, their swords ready—and in their disciplined steadiness, looked more dangerous than the fierce-acting group they faced. Only one Jokapcul said anything; the plumed officer growled softly, reassuringly, from time to time.

None of them had yet noticed the two strangers.

Of more immediate importance, and the reason Haft had stopped so abruptly, was a simple fence a few paces outside the treeline. It stood as high as an average man was tall. Five strands of wire, evenly spaced from the top to near the bottom, stretched between wooden posts set five paces apart. Thinner wires zigzagged between the main wires. A box was mounted on each post, the kind of box that housed imps.

The border wasn't blocked by a wall; it was secured by an imp-warded fence. Anyone who touched the fence would attract the imps, who would dash out almost faster than sight. These imps were smaller than a woman's little finger, but they were numerous and, in their great numbers, could hold a bull fast to their fence while they ate its living flesh until nothing was left but bones and tatters of hide—they even ate the marrow from the bones. To Spinner and Haft, the safety represented by the Skraglanders was on the wrong side of that fence. The Jokapcul cavalrymen who were on their side of the fence were as dangerous to the two Marines as the big cat that was following them.

"Maybe the imps aren't at home," Haft said, gasping. "Maybe they've been released. Maybe it's a dummy and there never were imps on this fence."

Spinner realized he wasn't the only one who could come up with maybes. He looked along the ground at the bottom of the fence. "I think they're at home," he said, and pointed. A squirrel's tail, something that might once have been a badger, a hare's foot, and several clumps of feathers lay on the ground a foot or so away from the fence.

Somewhere, much closer than before, the cat cried again.

Spinner readied his crossbow. They might have to fight the Jokapcul, or the cat might be on them before they could get to the other side of the fence. In either case, a few bolts from the crossbow would even the odds. Haft noticed and also readied his crossbow.

Sweat beaded Spinner's brow. He looked at the fence. It was too high to jump over without touching the top strand. Spinner looked up at the trees.

"No good," Haft said. "I already looked. None of the branches go over the fence, we can't cross it that way." His eyes searched the trees. "But we can climb one high enough to be out of reach of the cat and wait for it to go away."

"Maybe," Spinner said. "But maybe not. Cats can climb trees too. Only the very biggest can't."

Haft swore. "Maybe this cat is too big to climb trees."

"The biggest ones wait for you to come back down."

The cat cried again. Its voice was clear and they could tell exactly where it was. They turned back to the forest and Spinner paled. It was a kind of cat he knew from Apianghia. "It's a gray tabur," he said. They weren't the biggest of the big cats, but they were probably the toughest. They were forest dwellers who had to deal with thornbushes and other sharp things, so their hides were thicker than those of other big cats. And they could all climb trees. Nearly as big as the two men together, the cat crouched only ten paces away. Iron-hard muscles rippled beneath the black-striped gray coat that rendered it almost invisible in the depths of a forest. It was staring at them. Its jaw worked and its tongue lapped between its teeth, as though it could already taste the men. Bunched shoulders twitched as its forepaws edged forward, bringing it closer to them, close enough for it to pounce.

"A couple of bolts to the chest ought to discourage it," Haft said. "Maybe we'll even kill it." He raised his crossbow to his shoulder.

"No good; skin's too tough. Shooting will just make it mad."

"Right," Haft said. "I forgot that about gray taburs." But the look he darted at Spinner asked: Are you sure of that?

Spinner dropped his crossbow. Haft did the same.

The two concentrated their attention on the cat, tried to think of what to do once it made its move. Only a remote part of their minds noticed a change in the tenor of the voices at the border gate.

The cat continued to inch. Its jaw stretched wide in a yawn, but there was nothing sleepy about it.

"He's about to jump," Spinner said quietly. "As soon as he leaves the ground, we jump to the side. They can't change their direction in midair. When he lands, he's going to have to look at both of us and decide who to go after. That'll give us a little time."

"Right. Time," Haft muttered. "A split second." He had seen big cats in a circus once and knew how fast they could move.

The gray tabur sprang.

Spinner and Haft shoved at each other as they dove apart.

Spinner was right, the cat couldn't change the direction of its leap. But it was very agile; it could and did change its orientation. By the time it reached where they had been, it wasn't pointed straight ahead anymore. It was flying sideways through the air. The cat lashed out with all four claw-extended paws. One hind claw raked across Spinner's lower leg and made a deep, three-inch-long gash in the calf muscle. A forepaw snagged Haft's cloak and got caught up in it. The force of the swipe tore the cloak from Haft's shoulders and sent him tumbling; he slammed against a tree. The cat landed off balance and on its side, hard enough to momentarily knock the wind out of it.

But the respite was brief. The big cat gasped twice and

rolled back onto its feet. It cried again, a deep-throated roar. The gray tabur took only a second to shake its paw free from the binding cloak. Then it swiveled its head, eyes searching for its prey. It saw both of them. Haft, still supine against the tree trunk, was closer, and it bunched to jump at him.

"Climb!" Spinner shouted.

But Haft didn't have time to scramble to his feet and leap for the nearest branches before the cat could get to him—and they both knew it.

Spinner, already on his feet, his bleeding leg ignored, hefted his staff like a javelin and threw it at the cat. The staff hit just as the gray tabur was raising it forepaws off the ground in its leap. The blow staggered it and sent it sprawling to the side. By the time it regained its feet, both men were up in trees. The cat roared out in anger and frustration.

"Go up and get as far out as you can," Spinner shouted. "If we reach branches too slender to hold the cat's weight, it won't follow us." He mentally added, *Maybe.*

Blood from Spinner's calf flowed down his leg onto his foot and he kept slipping as he clambered up the tree. The cat looked from one to the other of the climbing men. The cat went after Spinner. In one bound it was in the branches. The cat slapped at the tree trunk, claws sinking deeply into the wood. A crimson smear was by the cat's nose; it lapped it up and growled low, almost a purr of pleasure at the taste. The cat looked up at the clumsily climbing man and followed slowly, pausing to lick at every splotch of blood. It growled low as it went.

Thirty feet up, Spinner found a branch that allowed him to move toward a branch of an adjacent tree.

The gray tabur stopped licking at the blood. It snarled and moved. In seconds it was on Spinner's branch, crawling faster than Spinner and looking like it could close the gap before Spinner reached the other tree.

Haft had stopped climbing when he saw the cat follow

Spinner. Seeing the gray tabur gaining on Spinner, he yelled at him to hurry.

Acrid sweat flowed from Spinner's armpits, drenched his body, arms, and legs. He pulled himself along faster. The other branch had been level with the one he was on, but now it was four feet above his head because of the combined weight of him and the cat. He pulled himself forward another foot and his branch dipped farther. He glanced back again. The cat had reduced the distance almost by half. Spinner lunged forward and almost lost his balance, but managed to wrap his arms and legs tightly around the branch and hold on. The branch bounced wildly from the sudden movement.

"Hold on, Spinner!" Haft shouted. "That almost threw the cat. He stopped coming after you."

Spinner looked back. The cat wasn't any closer; it was looking down, as though reassessing its situation. Then it looked at him again, growled, and inched forward.

Spinner pulled himself forward again. He was close enough to reach out and grab the other branch, but the vertical gap had increased to five feet. He'd have to stand to reach the branch, and the one he was on was swaying too much for him to think he could do that without falling off.

"There, below you!" Haft shouted. "You can jump onto that one."

Haft was pointing at a branch six feet below and a few feet to the side. Spinner looked. He was sure he could swing down onto it. He glanced back at the cat to see if it was close enough to make the same jump, and almost jumped himself without looking to see where he was going to land—the cat was almost within a paw's reach of his foot. Spinner pulled his feet in close, looked down, and swung off the branch. His momentum carried him the few feet to the branch below, and he let go and fell the short distance. His legs straddled the branch and he fell forward onto it, wincing at the sudden pain in his groin.

Behind him the branch whipped upward from the loss of

his weight. The gray tabur screamed as the sudden movement dislodged its hindquarters. It hung by its forelegs, and the branch creaked in protest.

Spinner scrambled to the trunk of the tree while the cat clawed and pulled, trying to scramble back onto the swaying branch.

"I've got an idea," Haft shouted. "We've got to get him out of the tree. Do something to knock him down."

"Do what?" Spinner gasped back. He could not reach the branch the cat was on, so he couldn't shake it. He saw Haft then, dropping from branch to branch to the ground. Spinner couldn't guess what his companion had in mind.

The gray tabur continued to scream and scrabble. The branch continued to creak ominously.

Haft reached the ground, picked up Spinner's staff, then looked up and yelled, "Do something! Knock the cat out of the tree."

"What can *I* do?" Spinner yelled back. "*I* can't do anything."

"Wouldn't you know it?" Haft muttered. "I always have to do everything myself." He found his crossbow, then stood with his back to the fence. He aimed carefully at the moving cat's shoulder, then pulled the trigger. But the cat and the branch were both moving so much that his quarrel only nicked the skin of the cat's foreleg inches above a paw. The gray tabur screamed again and swatted, as though at an insect that had stung it. But that removed one paw from the branch, and the cat plunged down toward the ground. It swiped and clawed at each branch it passed, but couldn't hold on to any-thing. But each branch it hit slowed its fall enough so that in-stead of crashing to the ground, it landed hard enough only to be stunned.

Haft nocked another quarrel as the cat was falling and shot it again as soon as it hit the ground. He nocked a third and glanced that one off the gray tabur's shoulder before it could lift its head and give it a shake. He was starting to nock a fourth quarrel when the cat sprang to its feet and roared at him. He dropped the quarrel and crossbow, picked up Spinner's quarterstaff and planted one end on the ground next to his foot. The gray tabur charged, and Haft wondered if what he'd had in mind was such a great idea after all. But it was too late to change his mind.

The instant the cat's forefeet left the ground in its final leap, Haft dropped forward to one knee and angled the quarterstaff toward its onrushing chest.

The gray tabur had only an instant to look surprised before it slammed into the end of the quarterstaff. The force of its leap kept it moving forward, but the quarterstaff acted as a lever to lift it over Haft. Still holding the staff, Haft was thrown backward and rolled.

The cat's angry scream when it struck the fence was almost drowned out by the hungry chitter of the imps. The cat screamed and struggled, but the imps held its fur, pinned its head and neck.

Awestruck, Haft got to his knees and watched as the imps killed the cat. Its legs and head and tail thrashed uncontrollably, its body spasmed, its eyes rolling wildly. Blood gushed through holes rent in its skin, bits of fur flew into the air, and white bone began to appear through hide and bloody flesh. The manic chittering of the imps as they gleefully ate the living cat seemed to fill the world until there was no room left for any other sound.

After a few moments the cat moved no more and the imps chittered less as they settled down to feast.

CHAPTER
SEVEN

If Haft hadn't already been on his knees he would have dropped to them in relief. He sagged backward to sit on his heels. He shook so hard he barely managed to keep himself sitting upright. Shivering, wide-eyed and gape-mouthed, he sat for a moment, staring at the remains of the dead cat, moments ago so threatening. Masses of flies were already buzzing around the animal's remains.

Haft was snapped out of his reverie by a weak voice behind him:

"Haft, help me."

Spinner had climbed down to the lowest branches of the tree, but the last drop was higher than he was tall. Crimson still flowed freely from the gash in his calf. Clearly, he was weakened by the loss of blood.

Instantly, Haft leaped to his feet and ran to help Spinner. Gently, he lay him at the foot of the tree and tied a length of creeping vine around Spinner's calf above the gash, to slow the flow of blood so he could examine the wound. But he'd forgotten that other people were nearby.

A gruff voice shouted something, and Haft twisted around. Most of the Skragish border guards were clustered on the other side of the fence. Some of them were looking at what remained of the dead cat. Some, including the one who spoke and seemed to be the leader, were looking at him. Others were glowering to one side.

The Skragish leader—he had to be the leader, Haft thought,

since he was the one addressing him, and he was the only one with a large, purple rosette on his left shoulder—spoke gruffly again. From his bearing, Haft assumed he was a sergeant.

He couldn't understand the man's words, but guessed he was being asked who he and Spinner were. Something was bothering him . . . The Jokapcul! Haft looked sharply to his right, where some of the Skraglanders were gazing. Seven Jokapcul were arrayed in a line there. Three of them had lances leveled at him and Spinner. The other three, alternating with the lancers, held swords at the ready. Their officer stood to their side, his sword at rest, growling orders at them as they advanced. Haft recognized the plumed officer from the day before. He didn't see the demon spitter.

"More trouble, Spinner. Can you stand?" Haft slowly rose to his feet and felt about for his axe. He didn't have it; he must have dropped it when he went for the tree he climbed to get away from the cat. He still had his knife, but it wouldn't do him much good against six men armed with swords and lances.

At his side, Spinner also stood, and drew his knife. Haft gave him a quick glance. Spinner's face was wan and he was unsteady on his feet.

"Anybody over there speak Frangerian?" Haft asked the Skraglanders without looking at them. The only reply was the Skraglander sergeant, who said something that sounded to Haft like: "You're not with them, are you?"

"How about Ewsarcan?" Haft asked in his native tongue. No answer. "What about Apianghian?"

The sergeant said something to one of his men, who turned and ran to the nearby cluster of cottages.

The Jokapcul ignored the Skraglanders. They grinned wickedly as they closed on Spinner and Haft. They didn't stay in a straight line as they advanced; the ends of their short line moved faster than the middle, so that when they reached the two Marines they would form a half circle around them.

Haft didn't want them to get caught with their backs to the

tree. He knew that what little chance they had would vanish if they couldn't maneuver. "Our weapons are nearer the fence," he said softly. "Let's try to go over that way and get them." He thought they could defend themselves if they had their weapons and the fence was to their back. Then, having something at their backs might help.

"I'm with you," Spinner said. His voice was so weak Haft wasn't sure he'd be able to fight.

They stepped away from the tree and sidled toward the crossbow and quarterstaff.

The Jokapcul officer barked, and his men moved sharply in unison to position themselves to block the fence. The six soldiers then began advancing again. Their outermost men were almost level with Spinner and Haft; it looked like they were going to curl around and form a circle around the two.

Everyone stopped when a huge voice boomed out from the fence, "Somebody over there speak Ewsarc?"

Standing on the other side of the fence was the biggest man Haft had ever seen. He towered over the Skraglanders, who themselves were big men. A huge sword dangled lightly from his right hand. He wore a jerkin of white fur. His knee-high boots were fashioned from some tough hide, iron plates lashed over them with rawhide strips. The wrist covers on his gauntlets looked big enough to serve as breastplates for the Jokapcul, and the gauntlets themselves were bigger than most men's helmets. His own helmet was a heavily braced tub; massive horns sprouted from the helmet's top.

As startling and remarkable as his size and accoutrements were, one thing was even more startling and remarkable about the giant. He was leaning down with one elbow on top of a fence post; the wrist of his sword hand rested lightly across the deadly fence's top strand.

Haft had to swallow a couple of times before he could find his voice to speak to this apparition. "I do," he finally croaked. He swallowed again and his voice came out stronger and clearer. "I do. I'm Ewsarcan."

"What are you doing here?"

"We're Frangerian Marines. We managed to escape from New Bally when the Jokapcul took it. We're trying to get home."

"Well there, little brother," the giant boomed, "for people trying to get away from the Jokaps, that's some strange company you're keeping over there. Why, where I come from, those little Jokaps aren't considered good for much but pounding on."

"You're right about that. But they've got us outnumbered and we don't have our weapons. We could use some help."

The giant shook his head. "You'll have to come over here, then. These are border guards. They aren't allowed to cross the fence or go through the gate."

"I already figured that," Haft said. He was looking around for his axe. He saw it, beyond the lancer on the right of the Jokapcul line. "But what about you? Is there any law that says you can't come over?"

"Well, as a matter of fact, the last time I was in Bostia, the duke himself told me never to come back." He looked at the border guards and added, "And I am a guest of these fine gentlemen here. Now, you could say that if I violated the rules they live by, well, I'd be unduly abusing their hospitality."

By then the Jokapcul officer had gotten over his initial startlement at the sight of the giant and realized, even though he couldn't understand Ewsarcan, that the giant was just leaning on the fence and talking. As long as he stayed on the other side of the fence, he was no threat—though the fact that he could lean on the fence without being killed was threatening in itself. He growled an order at his men. They hesitated and looked back at the giant. The officer barked at them. Their heads snapped forward and they resumed their advance.

"On the other hand," the giant said, "I never did much care to do what dukes and such tell me to, and I do like a good fight. Especially against Jokaps. Besides, anyone who doesn't like Jokaps, well, he's got to be a friend of mine." Bellowing a war cry that startled everyone and silenced even the forest noises, the giant bounded over the fence and in a stride was on the Jokapcul. Two of them went down with the first swing of his sword—a lancer decapitated and a swordsman split nearly in two.

Haft yelled a battle cry of his own and in three steps was on the startled lancer to his right, inside the swing of the lance. His knife flashed twice and the enemy soldier crumpled at his feet. He dove beyond the bleeding corpse and came up with his own axe. He charged the nearest Jokapcul and chopped deeply into the man's side. He looked around as the giant cut down the sixth Jokapcul soldier. That left only the officer.

As soon as the giant leaped over the fence, Spinner quickly limped over to the startled officer and knocked him to the ground, then dove beyond him to retrieve his quarterstaff.

The officer scrambled to his feet with his sword raised *en garde*. He looked puzzled, as though wondering what Spinner expected to do with the stick in his hands; he didn't seem to recognize the quarterstaff as a weapon. He found out about it almost instantly.

Favoring his wounded leg, Spinner was almost tentative when he swung one end of the quarterstaff at the officer's head. The Jokapcul easily ducked under the swing then came up lunging with his sword, but had to turn his lunge into a parry when the back end of the circling quarterstaff came at his side. The officer turned his parry into a riposte, and Spinner dodged back, out of the way. Then he had to parry a slash. He tried to thrust inside the officer's guard, but the smaller man was agile and danced aside. The officer came back with a flurry, and Spinner was barely able to fend him off before he managed to start twirling the quarterstaff as he had against the guards on the *Sea Horse*.

The officer laughed at the twirling piece of wood and danced about, keeping his blade away from the spinning quarterstaff and waiting his chance to strike. Suddenly, Spinner stopped twirling the staff and spun an end at the Jokapcul's head. The man pulled his face out of the way and came back with a lunge of his own—a lunge that simultaneously parried Spinner's back-end follow through. Now the officer advanced, slashing and thrusting, and parrying Spinner's blows. He was, obviously, a master swordsman. Spinner concluded the man was just waiting for an opportunity to make his killing strike, and knew he had to do something first.

The officer came at him with another flourish and nearly broke through Spinner's guard. As Spinner backed off, he stumbled. Instantly the officer was inside the arc of Spinner's swing, and Spinner had to fall backward to avoid a sword thrust. The officer's momentum carried him forward, and he tripped and fell over Spinner, who scrambled to his feet first, quarterstaff already swinging as the Jokapcul officer regained his feet. Head and staff met. The officer's helmet flew off and Spinner's backswing caught him full on the temple.

The fight was over. Spinner looked around.

All the Jokapcul were down. The Skraglanders were still on their own side of the fence. The giant was looking at Spinner speculatively. Haft was struggling to free himself from where he was pinioned by one of the giant's arms.

The giant released Haft, who ran to Spinner and threw his arms around his chest, as much to hold him up as to congratulate him on beating the officer.

"I wanted to help you, but he wouldn't let me," Haft said. He glared over his shoulder at the giant.

The giant grinned back and said, "I knew your friend was smart enough to figure out how to beat that Jokap." He winked. "Anyway, if I thought the Jokap was going to win, I would have evened the odds in your friend's favor." He flipped a throwing knife he had concealed in his huge hand, caught it, then slipped it into a recess of his cloak.

"He could have been killed," Haft snapped.

The giant shook his head. "I don't think so. Not a staff-master. Certainly not one traveling with a man who carries the eagle rampant on his axe."

Baffled at what the giant meant by a staffmaster, Haft looked at Spinner. And there was that business about the eagle on his axe again. Spinner didn't seem to notice; he looked like he was about to faint from loss of blood.

"Now we have to get back to the other side of the fence," the giant said. He bounded over the fence.

"Wait," Haft called. "Why don't the imps kill you?"

The giant looked solemnly at the remains of the cat sagging against the fence. "When they've killed something big enough, they take their time feasting on it and don't bother anyone else who wants to cross their fence until they're through. After that they'll kill the next person or animal that touches their fence."

"Then we better go now," Spinner said, and pointed at the tabur. Sated imps were beginning to leave it. Quickly, the giant hopped back to the Bostian side of the fence, gathered their weapons and other belongings, and tossed them over the fence.

Haft climbed over the fence while the giant lifted Spinner over, then bounded back himself. No sooner were they on Skragish soil than the imps that had left the cat rushed toward where the men had crossed the fence.

A shout made them look toward the gate, where two of the Skragish border guards were shouting and pointing down the road. They heard the beat of horses' hooves. The sergeant shouted a command at the two men on the gate, then snapped an order at the rest of his men. Everybody ran to the gate. Haft brought up the rear, with Spinner leaning on him.

In response to the shouted order, the two men at the gate picked up longbows and let loose down the road. One of them gave an excited shout, the other muttered an unhappy oath.

The sergeant shouted a question as he reached the gate. The guard who'd made the excited shout pointed down the road and gave an equally excited reply.

The sergeant rubbed his chin thoughtfully as he looked at where the man pointed.

"What's happening?" Haft called out as he and Spinner approached the gate.

"Two Jokaps stayed at the gate," the giant told him. "When they saw their side was beaten, they mounted their horses and took off. These guards got one. The other one got away."

The two Marines reached the gate and were able to see for themselves. Three-quarters of the way to the bend in the road, a Jokapcul soldier lay on his face in the grass between the ruts, an arrow protruding from his back. Closer to the bend, a horse stood calmly chomping at the grass between the ruts in the road.

The Skragish sergeant talked quietly for a moment, as though to himself, then issued a series of orders. Four of the guards took up positions guarding the gate and stood sharp, like a ceremonial guard. The others relaxed and headed toward the cottages.

"Why don't they go and fetch the body?" Axe asked.

"Sergeant Pilco"—the giant indicated the Skragish sergeant—"considered that. But his orders are still, 'Don't cross the border.' If his men had gotten both of those Jokaps, then I suspect he'd send someone to get them and the horses." He paused and looked around. "If *all* the Jokaps were dead, he could just bury the bodies somewhere and claim they had never been here. Or say they came and went away. But one got away, so the Jokaps are going to know they had men killed here and they'll come for the bodies. If the bodies aren't there, they'll know the guards crossed the border, and there'll be trouble." He paused again and looked someplace only he could see. After a moment his eyes refocused on the dead man laying on the ox cart road. He said quietly, "Probably be trouble anyway."

At that moment, Spinner collapsed.

Haft checked Spinner's wound; the flow had slowed to a trickle, but the flesh of his lower leg was an unhealthy-looking gray and was cold to the touch.

Sergeant Pilco immediately took charge. He called back

the men whom he'd just released from duty, he and the giant quickly prepared a litter, then he directed his men to carry the litter to one of the cottages. He wouldn't let Haft help with the carrying.

"You carry his weapons and pack," the giant translated for Sergeant Pilco.

The cottage Sergeant Pilco led them to was home to a healing witch. She scolded the sergeant for taking so long to fetch the wounded man, then shooed everyone out, including Haft. The giant refused to translate what she said.

"I don't talk that way myself, and I won't repeat it when someone else says it either," the giant explained. "Especially not when a woman says it." He cast a quick look at the healing witch's cottage as though wondering if she really was a woman, and if so, what kind.

Outside, Sergeant Pilco wanted to inspect the site of the fight. Haft and the giant accompanied him, and meanwhile talked. But they didn't talk about the one thing that was bothering Haft: What had the giant meant about the rampant eagle? The old man in New Bally had also made a point of the eagle on his axe. Now that he thought about it, some Marines had looked at the axe oddly, and a few acted deferentially toward him after noticing it, but nobody had ever commented about it except the old man in New Bally. But then, in the Frangerian Marines, no one asked anyone anything about his past—that was a hard and fast rule. And what did the giant mean about Spinner being a staffmaster?

"I'm called Haft. What do they call you?"

"They call me Silent."

"With *your* voice?"

"I'm of the Tangonine people of the Northern Steppes. When one of us goes wandering alone in the world, he takes a vow of silence about the People. You said you are a Frangerian Marine. I know enough about you to know that you are also wanderers in the world, and that you adopt names not your own. You do it, I understand, because it is tradition that Frangerian Marines have no past, no history. For us, it's because names are magic things. If someone knows our true names, he can have power over us. I named myself after my vow."

"For someone who has taken a vow of silence, you're not very quiet."

"The vow doesn't mean I don't talk, merely that there are things I don't talk about."

Haft nodded. Then he said, "Even for a nomad, you're wandering far. Do your people wander much?"

Silent shrugged. "No. But I kept seeing signs of a world beyond the one I knew and got curious about it. Besides, there were people who said the steppes weren't big enough to hold me." He paused and grinned widely, then added, "Or maybe they said the steppes weren't big enough for both of us." He laughed. As big as his voice was, his laugh was oddly pleasing. "If I'd taken all those challenges, I might have found myself the only remaining man of the Tangonine people." He rolled his eyes. "The only man left in a tribe of beautiful women. Hmm. Maybe I should have stayed at home." He laughed again, less loudly.

They reached the fence and stopped talking while they looked at the bodies. The big cat was covered with buzzing flies. Beetles already crawled about on it and burrowed under its skin. Ants scurried back and forth in long columns. The seven Jokapcul were likewise swarming with attendant insects.

"We must do something about the bodies," Haft said after a moment. "Bury them, burn them. Whatever it is the Jokapcul do with their dead."

Silent slowly shook his massive head. "The Skraglanders can't cross the border. Anyway, more Jokaps will be here in three or four days. Maybe sooner. They'll take care of the bodies. Maybe they'll even get here before the bodies start to stink too much."

Haft didn't find that an acceptable response. In Ewsarcan,

where he was from, bodies were never left on the ground—not even the corpses of enemies slain in battle.

Silent and Sergeant Pilco exchanged a few quiet words. The Skraglander seemed disturbed at the sight of the dead men. Silent also looked unhappy. Then Sergeant Pilco's face turned stern and he said a few harsh, strained words. Silent nodded and turned to Haft.

"It's the rules," the giant said. "If the Skraglanders cross the border it will cause a war. Sergeant Pilco doesn't want to leave the bodies there either, but he has his orders. His orders say any man here who crosses the border will be hanged—and their sergeant along with him." He looked away, toward the interior of Skragland. "If the king had his keep here, and had to see and smell these bodies, he'd probably change his mind. But the king never comes to the border, not unless he intends to cross it with an army."

"But . . ." Something on the ground beyond the gate caught Haft's eye. "We've got to get that." He stepped briskly toward the gate.

A shout from Sergeant Pilco stopped him.

He looked back and pointed. "That's a demon spitter! We have to get it."

Sergeant Pilco gave Haft the same kind of look he would give any of his own men he was about to reprimand. He spoke, and his anger was clear.

"He said if you go through the gate," Silent translated when the sergeant was through talking, "or manage to get over the fence without the imps killing you, to get that thing, he will personally hang you. He said there is going to be serious trouble over the deaths of these men, even though his men never set foot into the Duchy of Bostia and had nothing to do with the fighting. He can even blame the dead man on the road on you. But the trouble may be short of war if the bodies are left undisturbed."

Sergeant Pilco spoke again.

"Do you understand?" Silent asked.

Haft nodded. He would do nothing for the dead men. He wondered why none of them had used the demon spitter.

CHAPTER EIGHT

The sleepy border post had been manned for many years by rotations of three guards keeping watch on the gate during the daylight hours and attending to other border post details. It was easy though boring duty. The guards were allowed to bring their families, if they had any, and each was assigned one of the nearby cottages. The king rented the other cottages out to farmers, who could enlarge their farm plots if they did not have houses on their land.

Within the last few weeks, however, because of rumors of an approaching Jokapcul army, the post's garrison had been enlarged to a full squad. The incoming guards displaced the resident farmers, who were sent as refugees toward Oskul, the Skragish capital. Given the compensation offered by the king—farm plots near the capital—the farmers weren't reluctant to leave.

Because a full squad had never before been bivouacked at the border post, it took longer than Sergeant Pilco thought necessary to get his small garrison into proper shape. The shaping-up was further delayed by the arrival of the Jokapcul cavalry squad they had faced over the gate the previous day—and that squad did nothing to establish a proper camp of its own on the Bostian side of the gate, so there was more than the usual amount of stench of human waste about the border post. The border post fairly bustled, and the Skraglander guards who weren't manning the gate worked at preparing defensive positions and rearranging the living quarters to their liking.

The witch tending Spinner knew her healing well. The day after his leg was torn open, Spinner was on his feet, walking around for short periods of time. He limped, but the sewn wound no longer bled and it was obviously mending. On the second day after the fight, he limped less. The healing witch told them through Silent that he'd be able to travel in a few days—so long as he didn't try to walk too far at one time.

Late on that second afternoon, as the border post's evening meal was being prepared, Sergeant Pilco rushed out of one of the smaller buildings. He gathered his men into a group and talked quietly with them for a moment. Silent stood just outside the huddle and listened. When Sergeant Pilco dismissed his men, they resumed washing up or otherwise getting ready for their dinner, but there was a tension in them that hadn't been there before. Silent went to Spinner and Haft.

"A large Jokap patrol will be here before nightfall," Silent told them. "Forty men, maybe fifty. Word is they want this post to hand over the men who killed their soldiers. That's you and me."

Haft looked around the small post. He didn't see anyone he didn't recognize, anyone who might have come as a messenger. "How does he know that?"

"The Jokaps sent an imbaluris with the message, and those demons are fast."

"Then we better get ready to fight," Haft said. "Either that or run away. And I want no part of running away." The way he and Spinner left their shipmates in New Bally still haunted him, and he felt leaving the Skraglander guards to face the Jokapcul would be another abandonment. Still, a part of him knew that Spinner was still too weak for a battle and needed to be taken care of. He turned toward his and Spinner's meager store of possessions, wondering if he should start packing or start preparing his weapons.

"You've got time to eat before you have to go," Silent said.

"We can stay and help fight the Jokapcul," Haft said to him.

Silent shook his head. "Sergeant Pilco said you have to leave. If you stay here, there will be a fight. If you leave, he doesn't think there will be. So you have to go."

Haft looked at him quizzically. "You keep saying 'you.' Don't you mean 'we'?"

Silent shook his head. "You two have to go. Spinner is still too weak to fight properly, and he needs you. I stay here."

"But if we're going so Sergeant Pilco can avoid a fight, you have to go too. You killed more of those Jokapcul than Spinner or I did. They'll see you and demand that you be turned over to them. Then what's Sergeant Pilco going to do? He'll have a choice, hand you over or fight an overwhelming force."

Silent slowly shook his head. "They won't see me, I'll stay out of sight. I've been a guest at this border crossing for too long. If I hadn't gone over the fence to help you, you would have been killed and this patrol wouldn't be coming to find those who killed their men. If the Jokaps cross the border to fight—and we don't know that they will if you're gone—I owe it to these guards to help them. You and Spinner don't owe them anything, except maybe for a few meals." He grinned wryly. "One could even say that because you're the cause of these Jokaps coming, you owe them your absence. I can stay. You have to go."

Haft looked at the giant of the steppes, measured his size. "How can anyone as big as you hide in a small place like this post?"

Silent grinned widely. "When you came to the fence, you didn't see me, did you? Not until I reached the fence and spoke to you."

"We were thinking about the cat following us and didn't see everything. Anyway, if you can find a place to hide here, so can we."

"You are brave and skilled fighters, but your training is for duty at sea and in port, you have no training in how to hide on land. I spent my childhood and youth learning how to fight on the steppes. And I know how to hide in an open area. You have to go."

Sergeant Pilco joined them. His mind was also made up. Everyone was better off if they were gone.

"But the man who escaped, he saw Silent here and must think he's one of your men," Haft said to Sergeant Pilco through the giant. "He must have told his officers that Silent crossed the fence and helped us kill the others." Haft looked at the sergeant while he spoke, even though he was using Silent as a translator and was talking about him. It was the proper way to speak through a translator. Not looking at Silent also made it possible for him to say what he had to say about the giant.

"I'm not sure he could see the fight from where he stood," Silent translated for Sergeant Pilco. "Maybe he didn't know."

"That's not very likely. Not the way Silent gave his war cry."

Sergeant Pilco also did not look at Silent during the conversation. "Silent will stay out of sight. If I tell them you are gone, I won't be lying about the men who killed the Jokapcul being gone. Anyway, that's a chance we will have to take."

There was silence between the two men for a long moment. Even Silent's breathing was almost too soft to hear.

Haft looked at Spinner. His friend was much stronger but he was far from full strength. "Spinner can't walk very far yet."

"There's a better way for you to travel than by foot," Sergeant Pilco said.

Then Silent stopped being merely a translator and became an active participant in the conversation. "Right over there," he said, and pointed.

Haft looked to where the nomad pointed. Beyond the fence four Jokapcul horses still grazed not far from the gatehouse. The horses were hobbled so they couldn't stray while their riders were on foot, and during the two days they'd been unattended, only three had wandered out of sight.

"But we're Marines, not cavalry," Haft said as soon as he realized that Silent and Sergeant Pilco meant they should take two of the horses. "We don't know anything about riding horses."

Silent said something to Sergeant Pilco and the two of them roared with laughter. They thumped each other on the back and shoulders and doubled over with mirth. After a moment they regained enough control to speak, though their faces were red and laughter bubbled through their voices.

"Riding a horse is easier than walking." Silent repeated in Ewsarcan what he'd said in Skragish.

Sergeant Pilco whooped again, then added something of his own.

"He says I say that only because the steppe nomads are born riding horses," Silent told them, "but that's not really true. It's our mothers who are riding when we are born." He laughed again.

Spinner was looking at the horses beyond the fence, his brow furrowed. He tapped Haft on the shoulder. "We should take the horses," he said. "I know how to ride. It's not as easy as Silent says, but it's not hard either."

Uncertain, Haft looked at him.

Spinner started toward the gate and Haft followed, still uncertain. A few steps more and Silent and Sergeant Pilco started to follow.

The guards standing at the gate looked at their sergeant, saw him signal to allow the two Marines through, and let them pass.

Spinner paused to examine the abandoned demon spitter. He was surprised when the door opened when he picked it up. The demon, looking distinctly unhappy, craned its head up at him.

"*Veed ee,*" it croaked piteously.

"Ooh," Spinner said, feeling sorry for the small creature.

"I don't have any food for you." He didn't know whether the spitter demon could eat the salamander's food; anyway, he needed what he had for the fire-maker.

"Veed ee!" the demon croaked again. It sounded more like a demand. It struggled out of the door and stood precariously balanced on the tube.

Spinner shook his head. "But I don't know what you eat."

"Oo no veed ee?"

Spinner shook his head.

Faster than its weakened condition seemed to allow, the demon pounced on Spinner's hand and it chomped on the base of his thumb.

Spinner yelped and dropped the tube. The demon glared up at him, bit his hand again, jumped to the ground then scampered into the trees.

Haft barked out a laugh. "I don't think the demon likes you."

Spinner sucked at the bites and glared at him. Then he returned to the reason they had crossed the border to begin with and cautiously approached the nearest horse. The Jokapcul had left their horses saddled and bridled; after so long without being unsaddled and rubbed down, the horses had to be uncomfortable and irritable. He spoke softly to the horse and held out a hand. The horse tensed and rolled its eyes at him, but allowed Spinner to put his hand on its neck. When Spinner rubbed the horse's neck, first gently, then briskly, the horse relaxed and nuzzled him. Spinner continued talking quietly to the horse. He took the reins in one hand and, rubbing its shoulder and leg as he went, lowered himself to a squat to look at the hobbles. They were broad leather straps around each fetlock, tied with thongs so they were snug enough to stay above the fetlock. A slender but strong chain connected them. Without letting go of the reins, Spinner undid the thongs securing the hobbles. The hobbles off, he stood and placed them across the saddle, then led the horse to Haft.

"Hold him," he said as he handed the reins over.

Haft looked at the reins like they were writhing vipers, but took them anyway. "What do I do if he decides to run away?"

"Don't let him," Spinner answered absently.

Haft looked dubious. How was he supposed to stop an animal so much bigger than he was if it decided it wanted to run away?

Spinner repeated the process with two more horses. Then he led two of them through the gate and had Haft bring the third. Haft was amazed that the horse followed him so easily.

"Three?" Silent said when Spinner stopped next to him. "I'm not going. Really. Besides, these Jokap horses aren't big enough to carry me."

Spinner shook his head. "The third horse isn't for you. We may need to use one as a pack animal. Even if we don't, it's always a good idea to have an extra horse."

"It's even better to have an extra horse for each man."

Spinner looked back, but the last horse had hobbled into the forest and was out of sight. "Three will do for us," he said.

Haft looked relieved. Then he wondered why he should feel relief at only having three horses instead of four when a moment earlier he thought two was two too many.

Silent looked to where the Skragish border guards were gathering at a table under the trees for dinner. "You go and eat now. I'll curry and feed your horses so they'll be ready to go when you have eaten."

While they ate, Silent removed the tackle from the horses and curried them with a stiff comb. When he was through, they looked better and seemed to feel better as well, almost frisky. He gave them each a nose bag of oats then joined the others at the table. Sergeant Pilco sat down with them just as they were finishing their meal. He had a sheet of paper in his hand.

"I drew up a map for you," Silent translated. "Parts of it I copied from my military maps, parts of it I drew from what I know of where you are going." He looked at them solemnly.

"That means this is a more accurate map than anything Guard Command has issued to me here." He put the map on the table and oriented it so the directions he traced on it would be in the same direction they would take.

Spinner and Haft nodded and spoke their thanks.

"Here's where we are." A finger thunked down on the map. "The road you were on coming here continues northeast. Follow it about two miles and you will find a branch heading southeast. Take that southeast branch. It doesn't get much traffic. It goes through farm and ranch land, very lightly populated, so you won't have to worry about running into the wrong kind of people. About two, maybe three days along, I'm not exactly sure—and I don't know the kind of land you will be going through because I've never been there and the person who told me didn't say—you'll reach a main road." His finger traced the winding side road he wanted them to travel to where it butted against another line. "Turn right, onto the main road. That is the main north-south road through the kingdom. Go south. It will take you to Zobra. I haven't heard any rumors of Jokapcul being there, and technically we're at peace with them, so you shouldn't have any trouble at the border crossing. If you do, ask for Sergeant Waffno. He's an old friend of mine. The last I heard, he was stationed at that crossing. Tell him I said he should take good care of you. Then you'll be all right. I don't know enough about Zobra to draw a map that'll do you any good, but once you're there, you shouldn't have any trouble finding Zobra City or some other seaport. Then you should easily be able to find a ship heading your way." He pushed the map to them and sat back, through with his instructions.

Spinner and Haft huddled over the map to examine its details. They had one or two minor questions, but they didn't think they'd have any problems following it. They thanked Sergeant Pilco for his help. He shook their hands and left to see to his men and assign the defensive positions they would take when the Jokapcul patrol headed their way arrived at the border.

The healing witch wanted to spend a few minutes with Spinner before she released him as her patient. While he was with her, Silent showed Haft how to saddle and bridle the horses. Haft wasn't sure he got the lesson down. He wasn't sure he wanted to either. When their saddles were back on, the horses looked proud, almost eager to be ridden. Haft looked at them with some measure of trepidation.

The witch gave Spinner some herbs and vials of ointments to use, and made sure he understood her instructions. Before he left, she glanced at Haft, tapped one of the ointment vials, and softly said something. Spinner glanced at Haft, nodded, and said something back. Though they didn't understand each other's words, they managed well enough to understand each other's meanings. That sufficed.

When they were through saddling the horses, Silent gave Haft brief instructions on horsemanship. "You kick the horse in the flanks when you want him to go," the nomad said with a twinkle in his eyes. "When you want him to stop, you pull back on the reins. Pull the reins to the right when you want him to go right, to the left when you want him to go left. There are better ways to control horses, but those are the easiest commands to learn. Most horses are very obedient, so you don't have anything to worry about. Now mount up."

He showed Haft how to put his foot in the stirrup and swing himself into the saddle. Haft managed on the second try. The horse, a young mare, looked over her shoulder at her rider as though wondering why she got the amateur. Haft mis-understood her look; he thought the horse was thinking, I'm going to get you.

Spinner mounted his horse, a stallion old enough that its randiest days were behind him.

A Skragish guard lashed a sack of food onto the saddle of the third horse, a gelding, and they were ready.

"Travel safely, my friends," Silent said, and gripped each of their wrists. Sergeant Pilco did the same.

"Thank you for saving our lives," Spinner said.

"We will meet again someday," Haft said to Silent. He remembered promising the old man that they'd be back and wondered why he was telling strangers who helped him in strange lands that he'd see them again instead of simply saying good-bye, as he always used to.

They rode east.

Haft wouldn't say he hated horses. He certainly wouldn't say he was afraid of them. If possible, he wouldn't say anything at all about horses. But if he had to say something, he might admit to being somewhat uncomfortable with horses. Why not? He was a Frangerian Marine, and despite the name of the ship he'd sailed on, there weren't many horses at sea. As it was, the horse he rode was a nice enough mare. She was normally a docile animal given to a Jokapcul cavalryman who was new in the cavalry. The Jokapcul army wasn't so concerned with the comfort and well-being of its soldiers that it made a habit of providing neophytes with steeds that would be easy to handle. They'd just as soon give the new man the most unruly horse, on the theory that if he managed to survive, he'd be a tougher, better soldier. Besides, the more experienced cavalrymen had more sense than to try to ride rammy horses into battle—or even on parade. But the small patrol that went to the border with Skragland was showing the flag, and the army didn't want to send a horseman who didn't look like he was an accomplished cavalryman. So that new man had been given an easy horse to ride.

But Haft didn't find the mare so easy to handle; no matter how he kicked at her flanks or pulled on her reins, she wouldn't go at the speed or in the direction he wanted her to. When he kicked, she galloped ahead, and the bouncing almost threw him out of the saddle. When he yanked back on the reins, she skidded to a stop, and the sudden halt almost threw him over her head. When he tried to turn her, she turned in a complete circle no matter what angle he wanted her pointed in. When he didn't do anything, she followed a pace behind the extra horse, which Spinner led with a halter. Haft didn't think he should be bringing up the rear; he thought he should be leading so he would be the first to fight, to defend Spinner if they came upon an ambush.

Spinner managed not to laugh at his friend's discomfort. After a mile or so of watching Haft's frustration, he said, "If we're going to face any danger, it will come from the rear, not the front. So I'm glad you're bringing up the rear."

Haft snarled something, but stopped trying to make his mare lead the short column. At least he wouldn't have to try to turn her as long as she was merely following, he told himself. Besides, playing rear guard was a graceful way out of displaying his inability to control the beast.

The southeast-branching road Sergeant Pilco had directed them to was little more than a footpath; an even lesser road than the one they'd followed through the forest leading through Bostia to Skragland. Slight and unrutted as it was, the Skragish sergeant had to be right about it being little traveled. After an hour or two, they started seeing the farms and ranches he had said were along it.

The road wended its way through a gently rolling landscape spotted with clumps of trees. Some of the tree clumps were naturally growing copses, the remnants of an ancient forest. Others were groves of fruit or nut trees—the first signs of agriculture they saw. Then, here and there among the groves and copses, vegetable plots marked small farms. Many of the plots and some of the groves had farmhouses standing next to them, but not all. The vegetable plots were usually fenced with low-growing thorn hedges to protect them from the small herds of cattle that grazed the uncultivated areas. None of the herds were attended. It appeared that the cattle were fenced by the same kind of low-growing thorn hedge that protected the vegetable plots.

They saw few farmers about, and didn't approach any of the ones they saw. The farmers went about their farmerly chores and seemed to ignore the strangers riding by. At one point Spinner and Haft stopped to examine an unattended vegetable plot that came to the edge of the road. It was recently tilled, planted with winter crops. Weeds sprouted wildly among the planted furrows.

"Nobody's tending these fields," Haft said. Most of the fields were in the same untended condition.

"I get the feeling the people expect war and decided to abandon their fields before the invaders come," Spinner replied. "There won't be enough food to feed the people in the spring." He swept his arm at the grazing areas. "There should be more cattle here too."

As if in echo of his words, a cry called their attention to a small group of farmers driving a small herd of cattle out of a distant field. The farmers took their herd northeast. Haft watched them. How many people, he wondered, would live long enough to worry about spring crops if the invasion came?

Spinner had never done much riding, and he had last sat a horse more than a year and a half earlier, before he ran away to Frangeria and signed up with the Marines. Although he did know how to ride a horse, riding worked certain muscles in ways he wasn't used to after so long, and he was sore by the time they stopped to set camp for the night in a wooded hollow. Still, riding was much easier on his mending leg than walking would have been, and they'd covered more than twice the distance they could have had they walked at his slow pace.

Haft was more sore. He was also chafed from the rubbing of his thighs against the saddle.

"The healing witch thought you might get chafed," Spinner said when the horses were unsaddled and hobbled. "Rub this where it hurts." He handed Haft a fired-clay vial of salve.

Haft removed the vial's lid and sniffed. *"Pffww."* He jerked his head away and held the vial out at arm's length. "I can't put that on my legs. I won't be able to stand anywhere near myself if I stink like that."

"You might not be able to walk in the morning if you don't." Spinner turned away and busied himself brushing down the horses.

Haft wanted to stomp away, but he had too many stiff muscles, so he tried to look dignified while walking with his thighs held gingerly apart. Later, after a furtive glance at Spinner to make sure he wasn't watching, he lowered his breeches and applied the salve to the insides of his thighs.

Spinner made a small campfire, opened the food sack, and found bread, sausage, and cheese. The package also held a packet of aromatic leaves for tea. He got out his tinderbox.

"Why aren't you using the salamander?" Haft said as he joined him.

"I gave it the last of its food a couple of days ago. I don't know how long it's safe to use a salamander without feeding it."

"Oh." Haft edged away. He didn't want to be near if the salamander managed to get out of its house.

They ate quietly. It was late and they'd had a long day. The unaccustomed riding had tired them as if they'd force-marched the same distance. After Spinner layered dirt on the fire to make sure it was out, they went to sleep early. It was unlikely that anyone all that unfriendly would come across them during the night, so they didn't set watches.

"My thighs don't hurt," Haft said in the morning. "The salve worked."

"The stink didn't keep you away from yourself either," Spinner said.

Haft snorted. Then his eyes opened wide when he saw Spinner saddling the horses.

"You don't think we're riding again today, do you?"

"My leg still can't take a day of walking, and we can go far-ther on the horses. We're riding again today."

"Uh, well . . . all right, you ride. I'll walk."

Spinner finished with the gelding's saddle and lashed the food bag over it. He rested his arms on top of the saddle and looked across the horse's back at Haft. "Did you use all of that salve last night?"

"No."

"Good. Then you've got some for tonight if you need it. Let's go." He grinned. "Today we should be better at riding than we were yesterday. So today we go faster. We'll get far-ther by going faster."

"I'm not . . ." Haft backed away from the horses.

"Suit yourself." Spinner mounted the stallion and led the gelding back to the road. In a couple of steps he had the two horses moving at a canter.

Haft grabbed his mare's reins and trotted behind at a pace he thought he could keep up for hours. It wasn't too bad at first; the pace Spinner set was one Haft could maintain for a while. After half an hour, though, his breath was coming in harsh rasps and his legs were burning. Had the pace been just a little slower, he could have kept it up all day. After an hour he was beginning to stumble. Not long after that he stopped, his chest heaving and his legs trembling. The mare placidly stopped with him. When he had enough control over his legs again, he mounted his horse. The mare galloped until she caught up with the other horses, then contentedly cantered along a pace behind the gelding.

The roll of the landscape increased until its steepness allowed for fewer vegetable plots and grazing areas. The patches of old-growth forest were larger and closer. After some hours Spinner's horse-riding muscles were back to proper trim and he was certain his leg wound was fully healed. Haft was beginning to act like he'd spent his entire life on horseback. But the mare still looked over her shoulder at him from time to time and snorted as though she were still thinking, Amateur.

It was late afternoon when they came to an inn, which wasn't marked on Sergeant Pilco's map.

SECOND INTERLUDE
WHENCE THEY CAME

An Outline of the History and Cultural Development of the Peoples of the Jokapcul Islands

by Scholar Munch Mu'sk
Professor of Far Western Studies
University of the Great Rift
(excerpted from *The Proceedings of the Association of
Anthropological Scholars of Obscure Cultures*,
Vol. 57, No. 7)

Until the past few years, Jokapcul was known throughout the two continents, where it was known at all, for two things: the multiplicity of its volcanic islands, and the combative nature of its people. All the peoples of the two continents—at least those who knew of Jokapcul and lived on the western part of Nunimar—were content with the Jokapcul fighting constantly among themselves. That kept them so busy through the ages that they hardly ever bothered to cross the Jokapcul Sea or to sail south to the Turquoise Sea or to invade anyone else. For as long as anyone could remember, they had conducted only minor coastal raids.

According to legend, the Jokapcul Islands were first populated by coastal fishermen who were blown away from western Nunimar in storms. The islands of the chain are craggy and steep, with much barren rock. At first glance the islands seemed to be inhospitable in the extreme. However, during the time it took those first castaways to make their boats seaworthy again, to build new boats, and—perhaps most important— to build up their courage to recross the Jokapcul Sea, they discovered that fishing was much richer in the island waters than in the coastal waters from which they came. Even more remarkable to the fishermen was the ease of hunting land animals. On their western side, the islands were washed by a cold sea current that brought with it frequent fogs and rains, so the islands were much wetter than the continent, and fruit trees and other edibles grew in abundance in the islands' valleys and flatlands. In short, life was much easier in the islands than it had been along the continental coast. So the fishermen resolved to stay. There was only one problem with their resolution: the fishermen had no women among them.

Legend says some of the fishermen made their boats seaworthy, built up their courage, and sailed east to bring their women back to their new homes. But a very serious problem arose: some men had women, some men didn't; men who didn't have women raided those who did for the purpose of stealing away their women. Legends describe the shortage of women as the origin of the warlike spirit of the Jokapcul people.

And those legends are probably true, as stealing women has remained a staple of warfare on the Jokapcul Islands up to the present. There is some doubt, however, about the truth of the legend about the origin of the first Jokapcul settlers. That doubt arises from a simple fact: with their saffron skin and almond eyes, the Jokapcul don't look at all like any of the peoples of Nunimar. On the other hand, their improbable language seems to be derived at least in some small part from the same root language as many of the languages of western Nunimar.

Other legends say some of the earliest fishermen to inhabit the islands were blown there from the Kondive Islands by storms, and that the first wars were fought between Kondive Island fishermen and far-ranging Nunimar coastal fishermen. Those legends too have the ring of truth about them; only in recent times have the Kondivers become purveyors of luxurious trade goods. Before then, the people of the Kondive Islands were known and feared as pirates. Still, the appearance of the Jokapcul people is unlike the appearance of the Kondive Islanders, and there is no common root to their languages. In fact, nobody knows where the original Jokapcul came from.

Even though they constantly warred among themselves, as their population grew wildly and their culture matured the Jokapcul agreed on one thing: foreigners must be kept out. Life in the islands was too rich and too easy—when the islanders weren't warring among themselves—to share with anyone from the mainland or from other archipelagos. The fisher-boats all went out armed, and none hesitated to attack any alien craft, Jokapcul or foreign, that entered their waters.

Thus, over the centuries a culture grew. Each island had its own clan that warred against neighboring islands' clans, and the winners always stole young women from the losers. Sometimes the clans of two or more nearby islands would make truce with each other and combine forces to conquer another, larger and more powerful, island clan, but such alliances almost never lasted longer than it took to achieve the immediate goal. Most often they didn't even last that long. Some islands were too small to support a clan large enough to defend them against their neighbors, so they became dependent fiefdoms, though to whom they were in thrall changed from time to time as the island clans warred with one another. More than one clan grew on a few of the larger islands, so unremitting war took place on them.

At the top of each clan is an individual who calls himself the "shoton," a term that may be fairly accurately translated as "baron," or "count," though most who claim the title would give it a more grandiose translation, such as duke, earl, or prince. A few, usually those who have conquered their neighbors, claim that the proper translation is "king." Some three centuries ago there was even one who, having conquered all the other islands within two days' sail, announced that the proper translation was "emperor."

Directly beneath the shotons are the kamazai. In the military forces of Jokapcul, kamazai hold positions similar to those held by the highest ranking generals in the armies of the two continents, albeit with some significant differences. The kamazai are not men who enter an army and, through diligence, skill, and increasing knowledge of warfare, advance through the officer ranks until they achieve generalship. Instead, they are men who, through force of arms, power of personality, and—most frequently—treachery, are able to assemble an army of their own, which they then offer in service to the local shoton. Kamazai are ranked as higher advisers to the shoton than any other advisers. They are always to be seen at the right shoulder of their shoton, and they are always in deep consultation with their shoton for the purposes of planning wars, invasions, and conquests. No kamazai worthy of the name ever overtly plans a defense; defensive planning is seen as a sign of weakness, to be done only by those who can't attack. Any kamazai who is thought unable to attack is promptly attacked himself.

The Jokapcul word for "knight" is a garble of barks and growls totally impossible for any nonspeaker of the language to pronounce, so knight is the only word ever used to name the third rank of the Jokapcul hierarchy.

The knights correspond, roughly, to the officers of civilized armies. Like the kamazai, however, they do not lead through skill, force of personality, and learning. They lead by the simple expedients of brutality and intimidation. Their subordinates are beneath them in all ways and are treated as less than fully human. Higher ranking knights treat subordinate knights in the same manner. A proper knight is nearly as happy fighting his peers and superiors as he is fighting the army of an opposing clan. After all, once he has won enough battles and acquired a great enough reputation as a fighter, he may have the opportunity and means to raise an army of his own and become a kamazai himself.

Everybody else is below the knights and have as their sole reason for existence the support of the shoton, the kamazai, and the knights. The "people" may be fishermen, herders, farmers, craftsmen, merchants, priests, or anything else. They are subordinate and subject; subject not only to having all their belongings and other worldly goods taken by shoton, kamazai, or knight, but to be called upon to serve in the army as common soldiers.

One might think that an island nation such as the Jokapcul would have a strongly developed naval tradition, but it doesn't. Perhaps this is because their progenitors were coastal, not deep-water, fishermen.

For more centuries than anyone knows, Jokapcul armies fought each other, Jokapcul stole each other's women, Jokapcul developed newer weapons and fighting tactics, and Jokapcul kept foreigners away from their shores. Until twenty or so years ago.

Then a new man became shoton of one of the more obscure island clans. Nobody outside of Jokapcul is quite sure which island he started out on. Even his birth name is unknown to the outside world. The dominant legend of his early rise says that one day he simply walked into the courtyard of the local shoton, dressed in rough leather armor of home-made manufacture and carrying a sword that had long since seen its best days, and unceremoniously slew the shoton's kamazai while that worthy was reviewing the palace guard. This audacious act so shocked the palace guard that before any of them could react, the stranger wrenched the helmet from the dead kamazai and placed it on his own head. He then announced to the palace guard that *he* was the new kamazai, and dared anyone who disagreed to face him in single combat. None did, and he instantly became the shoton's first councilor. Then, before even a season passed, the new kamazai, in full sight of the army and populace during a festive ceremony, drew his sword, lopped off the head of the shoton, and elevated himself to that position.

At that point there could have been a rebellion, for the deposed shoton was, as shotons go, kindly and therefore popular with the army and the people. But the new shoton allowed no time for a rebellion to foment. Within days he led his army in an invasion of a neighboring island. His army won that war. In living memory, it was the first successful invasion conducted by the obscure island clan. That invasion cemented him in the hearts of the knights, and the knights didn't care what the people thought. That invasion was followed by another and another and another until every island within a day's sail was conquered. Each conquest was followed by a brief consolidation, a simple two-step process: (1) the conquered shoton was publicly beheaded; (2) the kamazai were offered a choice of joining the old shoton in death or of joining the new shoton in conquest of the world. Personal loyalty not being a notable strength of the Jokapcul, nearly every kamazai pledged his loyalty to the new shoton.

In order to successfully carry out the conquest of all the islands, the new shoton took a step never taken before by any shoton. He promoted his best kamazai to the new rank of sub-shoton and promised them regency over large sections of the rest of the islands—provided they conquered and held those islands. The newly appointed subshotons set to work with a diligence that would have been admirable had it been applied to a pursuit other than invasion and conquest.

Ten years after the unknown man in homemade armor slew his first kamazai, all the Jokapcul Islands were held under his rule. He styled himself the High Shoton of Jokapcul and established his capital on Kokudo, the largest and richest island of the archipelago. The next several years were spent in consolidating his rule. As one of the steps in the consolidation, he took to wife the most beautiful daughter or sister of each clan chief—except for his victorious kamazai, there were no other shotons. Soon, because the warlike Jokapcul were no longer allowed to war among themselves, it was necessary to find a new way of making war. And so it came about that what had once been occasional raids on the mainland increased both in frequency and ferocity.

But the Jokapcul had no true deep-sea craft or deep-sea

skills, and many of the raiding fisher boats were lost in the rough seas between the islands and the mainland. Moreover, because the Jokapcul had early stripped their islands of forests to clear them for settlements and farmland, they no longer had the resources to construct ships. Further, since the isolated Jokapcul had little more knowledge of the mainland than the mainlanders have of the Jokapcul—and there is a great deal more of the mainland to be ignorant of—the raids were not very successful. And that lack of success bred a measure of discontent.

To further complicate matters for the High Shoton, there are enough islands and clans that he had not even a passing acquaintance with many of his wives. The clan leaders and ka-mazai whose daughters and sisters were taken to wife by the High Shoton had expected some measure of influence with him. Such influence could not come through wives who were unacquainted with their husband. That bred more discontent.

The High Shoton was facing rebellion. He had too many wives to become acquainted with all of them, so he could not forestall rebellion by granting influence through them. The only other distraction he had was raids on the mainland, which weren't very successful, and he had no way of immediately gaining deep-sea capability or knowledge of the geography of the mainland.

That was when, fortuitously for him, Lord Lackland, half bastard fourth son of Good King Honritu of Matilda, self-styled the Dark Prince, requested parlay.

III
THE INN

CHAPTER
NINE

The road topped a ridge and a valley opened before them. Spinner stopped, and Haft, peering into the trees, would have ridden his horse into the back of the gelding if the mare hadn't stopped on her own. The road they were on ran almost straight across the valley. The slopes of the ridges flanking the valley were wooded, and the forest came down the valley from the north as far as the road. From the road south, the valley had been cleared for several hundred paces. Directly ahead of them, alongside the road and a hundred paces beyond the end of the trees, a wooden fence formed a corral next to a stable. Several horses stood quietly in the corral while a stableman saw that the food and water troughs were properly filled. Thirty paces beyond the stable stood the largest building they'd seen since leaving New Bally. Farther away, set back from the road, was another building, bigger than the stable but smaller than the main building. That outbuilding had no windows they could see and its door was strongly barred. It looked more like a fortress than a barn to Spinner, except that he couldn't see any embrasures to fight from in its sides, or crenellations on its top.

Three or four workmen were engaged in chores around the main building. A painted wood sign hung from an iron arm above the door, indicating that it was an inn.

"What are we waiting for?" Haft demanded when he saw the sign, and gave his mare a kick in the ribs.

The inn should have been an inviting sight to Spinner as

well, but it wasn't. He grabbed the mare's bridle as she started to go past and stopped Haft.

"Look at the sign," Spinner said slowly.

"What about it? It's the name of the place."

"What's the name?"

Haft peered at it. It had a painting of a man who looked like he was running: one leg and one arm slightly bent at hip and knee, shoulder and elbow; the other arm and leg were more sharply bent; the head was tucked down. He couldn't tell how the figure was clothed—it was painted a solid black. He couldn't make out the three words written under the figure.

"The Racer?" he guessed. "The Running Man? I don't know. Can you read it from here? Your eyes are sharper than mine. Anyway, what does it matter what the name is? I never heard any warnings about Skragish inns. Let's go. I'm hungry and thirsty and I want a bath with soap." He flicked the reins to start his mare toward the inn.

Spinner didn't let go of the bridle. The mare rolled her eyes as though to say, Make up your minds.

"I can read the sign," Spinner said quietly. "It says, 'The Burnt Man.' "

Haft's brow furrowed. "What an odd name for an inn." He looked at the sign again. Yes, the figure on the sign could have been the corpse of a man who had burned to death. "Well, I've heard the Skragish are an odd people. But this just looks like an inn. The Rose and Thistle back home looks just like it." When he flicked the reins, Spinner let him go. The mare eagerly cantered into the trees, headed for the stable and corral.

Spinner sat on top of the ridge a moment longer. The Burnt Man, he thought, so odd a name. He wondered what significance it had. And the size of the inn bothered him. It was as big as any he'd seen in New Bally. He looked all around the glade, but the only road he could see entering the valley was the one they were on. The road was wider here than it was closer to the border, and looked as if it bore more traffic—

even though they'd seen no one else traveling it—but it was still just a little side road. It didn't seem likely that enough people would pass that way, at least not on the road, to support so large an inn. And he was curious about a low rumble he heard somewhere in the background. Wondering all those things, he tapped the stallion's flanks with his heels and slowly followed Haft.

The stableman was as helpful and friendly as any Spinner had ever met, and once they found a language they could all speak—Frangerian, as it turned out—he was more talkative than most. He assigned stalls to the three horses, unsaddled the mare and the gelding, and had their tackle hung before Spinner finished unsaddling his stallion.

"Now you don't worry about a thing, sirs," the stableman said. "I'll take right good care of your horses. Me and horses, we get along fine." The horses seemed to agree; they closed around him and nuzzled at his face and shoulders. They nickered when he gave them sugar cubes. "And don't you worry none about cost neither," the stableman continued, while briskly rubbing at the horses' necks and ruffling their manes. "The price of a stall for your horse is included in the price of a room for yourself. If you're only stopping for a meal, the price of oats for your horse is included in the price of your dinner." He leaned away from the horses to look at Spinner and Haft. "I know what you're probably thinking when you hear that, and you're wrong. When you go inside and pay for your meal and your room, I think you'll find that the price you pay is about the same as you'd pay for a meal and a room at an inn that charged extra for bedding and feeding your horse." His chest puffed and he looked smug and proud. "The Burnt Man doesn't gouge its customers, no sir. And we're mighty proud of that. And there is entertainment, the finest entertainment to be found within a week's ride. That makes The Burnt Man a very profitable inn. We get lots of happy visitors coming back. Now you go inside and see Master Yoel. He'll take right good care of you." Stepping away from the horses, he shooed the two men toward the inn.

"See? Nothing to worry about," Haft said. "A name is just a name. I think I'm going to enjoy being here tonight." He strutted toward the inn. "I wonder what the entertainment is."

"What's that noise?" Spinner said. The low rumble he'd heard on the ridge top now resolved itself to a drone that came from the far side of the inn. He'd wonder about the entertainment later.

"We'll find out about that noise soon enough," Haft said. He reached the inn door, flung it open and strode through.

Spinner followed, less grandly. He knew that something was wrong. The inn was too big for where it stood; he'd never heard of a stableman in an out-of-the-way inn like this who spoke as many languages as this one seemed to; and there was that name. Well, he'd watch for whatever it was, he decided, and hope he was ready for the trouble when and if he discovered it. He only hoped he wouldn't discover it too late to do anything about it.

Spinner was surprised when he stepped over the threshold. Even though few of the windows were unshuttered and open, the interior of the inn's main room was as bright as the day outside, lit by a light with an odd, bluish tinge to it. Before he could locate the source of the strange light, or even get any more of an impression beyond the fact that there were several customers sitting about, the innkeeper bustled over to them—if a thin man can accurately be said to bustle.

Master Yoel was shorter than Haft, and a stoop made him look even shorter. His eyes were widely spaced and his nose beaked. His scalp was exposed by an almost perfect disk of baldness; a few strands of hair combed across the front of his scalp completed the circle of hair.

"Good young gentlemen, welcome to The Burnt Man," he said in Frangerian. He alternated briskly rubbing his hands with briskly drying them on his snowy white apron. "Come in, come in." He let his hands and apron go and waved his new guests into the room, put a palm on Haft's arm and aimed him at an empty table. "Would you like a flagon of beer? How about a crock of wine? If you can read, the slate over the kitchen door has today's menu. Not that I think such fine-looking young gentlemen as yourselves can't read." He got them seated and made sure their chairs were stable and they were comfortable. Then he started to recite the day's menu.

"Don't bother," Spinner interrupted, somewhat sourly. "We can read the menu for ourselves." The innkeeper talked so fast about so much that Spinner didn't even wonder how it was he knew to talk to them in Frangerian instead of starting with Skragish and then having to work his way through other languages until they found a common tongue.

"Of course you can, of course you can. I meant no harm or insult, I was merely trying to be helpful."

"Well, a flagon of beer would be most helpful," Haft said eagerly.

"Beer, instantly." The innkeeper shot a hand up and snapped his fingers. "Doli," he shouted. A serving maid darted to his side. His voice sounded like the crunching of gravel when he spoke to her in Skragish. The maid curtsied and dashed off. "Will you be wanting a room for the night?" the innkeeper said, returning his attention to his guests and his tongue to Frangerian. "Did the stableman see to your horses? Do you want a bath?" His nose nearly crinkled when he said "bath." "I recommend you be in this common room tonight for our evening's entertainment. Nearly all of our guests find it to be grand. Even the farmers and woodsmen hereabouts find our evening's entertainment to be grand. Soldiers come from garrisons four days ride distant—sometimes even farther—to see our entertainment."

"That sounds great," Haft said. "What is your entertainment?"

Master Yoel lay a finger alongside his nose. "You'll have to wait until tonight to find out. But I guarantee you won't be disappointed."

"We do want a room for the night," Spinner said. "And we will want a bath. First, though, what we want is to sit here and quietly drink a flagon of beer, to rest from our day's journey. In a while we will order dinner." Then, knowing the sometimes suspicious nature of innkeepers, he opened his purse and put a small gold coin on the table. "This should more than cover our stay, should it not?"

The innkeeper snatched up the coin and held it close to his eye to examine. One side held the visage of a fierce-looking, helmeted man, the other had a crossed sword and lance. Words in a strange language were inscribed on it. "Jokapcul?" he asked. When Spinner nodded, the innkeeper bit into the coin, then looked closely at the tooth marks he'd left in it. "Well, I guess this will be legal tender here soon enough. And if it isn't, it's still gold and can be melted down." He peered at them from under lowered brows. "You don't look like Jokapcul. Not that I've ever seen one, of course. All I know about them is what I've heard from travelers who have stopped at my humble inn. I hear they are a gnomish people with orange skin and hair blackened with dripping tar." He looked pointedly at their weapons, then back at them, and asked, "Are you soldiers of some foreign army fighting them? Does your being here mean the Jokapcul are coming this way?"

"We aren't Jokapcul," Spinner said. He ignored the other questions—and the implication that he and Haft might be deserters. "This coin was legal tender where we just came from."

The serving maid addressed as Doli returned with two flagons of beer and put them on the table.

"If I may have your names, good sirs?" Master Yoel pocketed the coin. "I'll keep a tally and give you your change on the morrow."

"They call me Haft. He's known as Spinner." Haft either didn't notice or chose to ignore the glance Spinner gave him.

"Anything you need, Master Spinner, Master Haft, Doli will attend to you."

Haft's look was close to a leer. "Anything?"

"Anything within the powers of this humble inn," the innkeeper assured him.

Doli smiled wanly, curtsied, and hastily retreated.

Master Yoel made an almost perfunctory bow and left them alone. Spinner watched him walk away. Had the innkeeper really looked at his purse as though weighing it, or was that merely his imagination?

Haft tilted his head far back and upended his flagon as he poured half the beer down his throat in one gulp. "Ah," he sighed deeply, and thunked the flagon down. "I needed that."

Spinner drank his beer more slowly, almost as though drinking merely out of politeness. Trying not to be obvious about it, he examined their surroundings.

Eight other men occupied four tables, drinking and eating quietly; one man sat alone, three were at another table, the others were paired. It seemed to Spinner that all eight were making a great show of ignoring everyone other than their own companions—except for the lone man, who seemed almost too obvious about ignoring everybody, while being constantly aware of everyone.

In addition, a man and woman with a half-grown son and daughter, a young boy, and perhaps an older aunt, sat around a large table. This family of six didn't seem as comfortable as the men did, and they sat hunched over their dinner dishes. The women and girl seemed closed in on themselves, the man and the older boy kept darting nervous glances at the other men.

Spinner noticed that all six occupied tables, including the one at which he and Haft sat, were in the same area of the large common room, then he realized that was because several serving maids were engaged in cleaning the rest of the room. Two of the maids diligently cleaned the unoccupied tables, and two more swept and mopped the floor in the larger, unoccupied area. Another industriously cleaned flagons, mugs, bowls, and serving dishes at a counter that also held spigots for beer kegs. She kept glancing toward them, but the others seemed to keep an eye cocked at the other customers. Spinner thought the one watching them was Doli, the serving maid who had brought them their beer. The maids were all dressed alike, in pastel blouses, though each wore a different color, with very short, puffed sleeves and necklines so wide and deep that they couldn't help but expose themselves when they bent over. They all wore floor-length, dark blue skirts that bellowed out because of the many petticoats worn under them, and a small bonnet topped each maid's head. A workman carrying a hammer and a small box of tools rushed in, made a repair on a shelf, and hurried back out.

As for the room itself, swinging double doors into the kitchen were next to the counter with the dishes and spigots. A stairway opposite the entrance probably led upstairs to the rented rooms. Trophies and weapons adorned the walls.

Spinner could tell that most of the weapons were for hunting, though a few were for war. There were bows—long, short, and cross. There were short jabbing spears, javelins, and lances, on up to a halberd and a heavy cavalryman's pike. A variety of knives and swords were arrayed around a two-handed sword that was mounted point down on the wall. The smallest blades were at the top and bottom, the largest in the middle, so the hilts formed an almost perfect circle.

And there were trophies on the walls, most of game animals. A fearsome hog's head with sharp tusks hung over the serving counter. The huge white pelt and head of a bear from the far north was splayed on the wall opposite the swords. A large dais or small stage was against the wall, under the bearskin on a wall. There were skins of cats, large, small, and in between, and the heads of mighty horned ibexes and mountain sheep, as well as common antelope and antlered deer. But the most striking trophy was a battle standard from an army or regiment Spinner didn't recognize. It hung on a stand in a corner. Wires attached to the wall stretched out the banner so it almost seemed to be fluttering in a breeze. Two archaic suits of plate armor of an unknown style flanked it.

What most interested Spinner, though, was the source of the light. More accurately, the sources. Milky-white panels he thought were vellum, more than a pace long and less than half that wide, were set in rows in the ceiling. The panels glowed with an inner light that didn't flicker like the light from candles or oil lamps. The slightly bluish light seemed to diffuse through the room so that it cast no shadows—or at least no shadows with sharp edges; it was dark under the tables.

Spinner nodded sharply and snapped his fingers in understanding. "That's what that noise is," he muttered.

"What noise?" Haft asked.

"The rumbling. I've heard of this but never seen it. I'll wager there's a troll hut out back where we couldn't see it when we came to the inn."

"A what?"

"A troll hut. A troll lives there. That's what makes these lights. This is troll-light."

Haft looked at the ceiling as though noticing the light for the first time. "I've never seen lumination like this before," he said. "Now explain to me, what is troll-light?"

Spinner didn't answer immediately. He was too busy wondering how even a country inn as grand as The Burnt Man could afford the services of a magician who was a trollmaster.

"Yes, sirs?" an unexpected voice said from their side, interrupting Spinner's thoughts of the troll hut and its magician, and distracting Haft from the question. It was Doli responding to Spinner's finger-snap. Spinner noticed she didn't lean forward when she curtsied, so the deep scoop of her pale blue blouse did not compromise her modesty. "Are you ready to order your dinner?" she asked.

Haft quickly drained the rest of his beer and thrust the empty flagon at her. "Refill," he said, smiling. He belched contentedly.

At this mention of food, Spinner realized that, yes, he was

getting hungry. But she had easily spoken to them in Frangerian. Too readily and easily, he thought. How did she know a language that could hardly be spoken by anyone local? "Do you always speak Frangerian?" he asked.

"No sir," Doli replied. "But we get many foreign visitors here, so each of the girls is required to speak at least two languages in addition to Skragish." She looked around and seemed to make a calculation before saying, "The serving maids here now speak eleven foreign languages among us."

"That's a lot of languages." Another puzzle. From where did this place get so many foreign customers that its staff had to speak so many languages? Spinner wondered. The Burnt Man was hardly located in a center of international commerce, like, say, the inns of New Bally—and even the inns there didn't have serving maids who spoke so many languages. "Do you speak Apianghian?" he asked in that language.

"Oh, no sir. But we do have someone who speaks a language that sounds like that one."

"Is she here now?"

"No sir." Doli gave him a crooked smile. "But she will be this evening."

Spinner nodded, wondering about Doli's odd smile.

"How about Ewsarcan?" Haft asked in his native tongue.

Doli seemed to think about that for a moment, to roll the sounds of Haft's words about in her mind, then said, "I think Honni speaks that," and turned to call to one of the other serving maids.

"Never mind," Haft said, switching back to Frangerian. "I was just curious. Maybe later I'll want to talk to Honni."

Spinner looked at the posted menu. "What's the house specialty?" he asked.

"That's Burnt Man pie, sir."

Spinner didn't want to know what Burnt Man pie was. He ordered the venison stew.

"I always like to try new things," Haft said. "I'll have the special."

"Yessir, Burnt Man pie is—"

"Don't tell me, let me be surprised," Haft said, and did his best to look cosmopolitan.

To Spinner, Doli said, "More beer for you, sir?"

Spinner hefted his flagon; it felt half full. "I'm fine," he said.

Doli gave her straight-backed curtsy again, and hurried to the kitchen.

"Burnt Man pie?" Spinner said.

"Sure, why not? I'm in a foreign country. That's one reason I went to Frangeria. I wanted to travel to strange countries. Meet exotic people. Eat new kinds of food."

"That's three reasons."

Haft shrugged.

In a moment Doli was back with another flagon for Haft. He took it from her hand and drank deeply, then settled back to relax. In a few minutes she returned with their dinners. The aromas wafting from the bowls set them both to salivating, and they attacked the food. Burnt Man pie turned out to be a pork pot pie.

"It's a bit salty for my taste," Haft offered. "I don't think I'll get it again."

Later, when they were sated, the innkeeper showed them to their room, and guided them to the bath as soon as they dropped their belongings on the beds.

The bathing room was lit by oil lamps that gave it a warm, cozy glow. They lay back in the tubs for a long time to let the steaming water leach the dirt from their pores and the road-ache from their bones. While soaking and almost half asleep, Spinner wondered briefly why he didn't hear the low rumble from the troll hut. When they got out and dried themselves on fat towels, they were surprised to find that someone had laundered their clothes. He heard the troll's rumbling again.

"The troll here works hard," he said when he saw their clothes were clean and dry, and warm to the touch.

"You'll have to tell me about this troll," Haft said.

Spinner wondered about that again. But he was tired. "Let's sleep on it," he said.

"Great idea! We'll be fresher for the evening's entertainment," Haft said gleefully.

They slept for two hours and awoke refreshed. They dressed quickly. Except for their belt knives, they left their weapons in the room.

CHAPTER
TEN

The common room was filled almost to capacity with men. The only women immediately visible were serving maids, of whom there were a good many more than had been present earlier. It was a lively and raucous bunch. Everyone was drinking, and many were eating as well. The lights were dimmer than they had been earlier. Spinner looked at the ceiling and saw that only every third row of panels was aglow. The stage alone was brightly illuminated. The bearskin had been removed from the wall behind it and replaced by a curtain.

Two brightly clad entertainers, a juggler and a tumbler, were on opposite sides of the small stage. The juggler twirled knives from hand to hand, while the tumbler flipped and rolled between the front of the stage and its back. Every few seconds the juggler threw a knife in the direction of the tumbler; the knife always seemed to just barely miss. They formed so straight a line on the wall behind the tumbler, they might have been positioned there with a carpenter's level. As he threw the knives, the juggler replaced them from a stack on a small table at his side. The customers didn't seem to pay much attention to the entertainers, so Spinner assumed they weren't the entertainment of which Master Yoel had boasted.

The serving maids wound their way through the crowd with trays heavy with flagons, carafes, bowls, and plates. They seldom flinched at or objected to the pinching fingers or groping hands they passed. Most of them seemed not to hear the bawdy remarks cast in their direction, though a few laughed and

143

made remarks back. Like the serving maids on hand in the afternoon, they wore blouses with wide, deeply scooped bodices, but their skirts were shorter and not puffed out with multiple petticoats—the better to make their way through the mass of men and tables.

Spinner didn't see Doli. He wondered how long it would take before they were located by a serving maid who could understand one of the languages he and Haft spoke. Then he realized the lack of a common language would likely not prove any barrier to ordering beer, and wondered again why the inn required serving girls who were adept in a variety of languages.

"Iyii-ee," Haft said when he saw the crowd. "Let's find a table and get some beer."

"Where'd they all come from?" Spinner mused, looking around at the mass of men in the room. He shook his head; he could find out later. He followed Haft.

The common room was crowded, but they found a small, unoccupied table. Almost at once, a serving maid with an empty tray under her arm appeared at their side. She rattled off rapid-fire words in three or four languages, then looked at them expectantly. None of the languages was familiar to either of them. The girl had to bend over to hear and be heard, and Spinner couldn't help but see even in the dim light that there was no undergarment beneath her blouse.

Haft grinned and pointed at the flagons being raised by the men at an adjoining table. The girl nodded and left.

Haft looked almost mortally offended; for all the reaction the girl made, he might as well not have had his hand caressing her haunch when he ordered the beer.

Spinner looked about the room at the other men. More than half of them were dressed roughly and had the dusty look of men fresh off the road. A few were soldiers, most in the Skragish army. But some wore uniforms of other armies, not all of which Spinner recognized. He wondered how men of so many armies came to be gathered in an out-of-the-way inn in a sparsely populated area of rural Skragland. Some of the uniformed men also noted the Marines' uniforms; they nodded and tipped their flagons or mugs. Spinner saluted them back.

A surprising number of the men in the room were merchants or other tradesmen. Judging by the richness of the gold and gems displayed on their fingers, hanging around their necks, or festooning their coats, some were very rich merchants. Spinner thought it odd that such men would crowd themselves into the common room of a country inn, no matter what the promised entertainment.

He decided then that he'd like another look at the stable and corral. They must be fillcd. A short reconnaissance of the forest surrounding the valley glen would have to reveal many trails, perhaps even roads, that made no obvious entry into the large clearing around the inn.

"Your beer, sirs," a voice said in Frangerian. It was Doli. She bent at the knees and hips rather than at the waist to put down their flagons, exposing herself no more than she had at dinnertime. "Master Yoel has instructed me to put this on your account," she added when Spinner pressed a copper coin into her hand. "You don't have to pay now."

"That's not for the beer," Spinner said. "It's for you. I thank you for your service."

"Oh, no sir, we don't accept gratuities from the guests," Doli said, and tried to press the coin back into his hand. "It's against the rules."

"Do the rules say you are supposed to keep the guests happy?"

She gave him a suspicious, almost wary, look. "Yessir."

"It pleases me to give gratuities for service well performed."

"Thank you, sir." Doli stopped trying to return the coin and it disappeared into her clothing. Spinner couldn't be certain in the low light, but he thought she blushed. After making sure their needs had been met, she went off to take care of other customers.

Haft leaned close. "What's the matter with you? She didn't

even bend over and give us a peek. I think if I patted her arse she'd slap my face. She's no fun. What are you giving her money for?"

Spinner held his mouth close to Haft's ear to answer. "There's something strange going on here," he said. "Maybe I can learn something about it from her."

Haft leaned back and looked around. "What's strange? I don't see anything strange. This looks like—" His voice jerked off as Spinner grabbed the back of his neck and yanked him close.

"Quiet," Spinner snapped. "I don't know. A lot of little things don't add up. If there is something wrong here and you go around yelling about it, we could wind up in serious trouble. So keep it down."

Haft reached up and pulled Spinner's hand off his neck. "No need to get so rough about it." He turned pointedly toward the stage.

Spinner stared at him for a moment. When he was sure Haft wasn't going to say anything else he shouldn't, he also looked at the stage.

The juggler and tumbler were finished with their act. They bowed to desultory applause and disappeared behind a curtain that blocked the view of the doorway behind the stage. No sooner had they left than a troop of five midget acrobats cartwheeled onto the stage, accompanied by a round of laughter. The stoutest of the midgets stood on the stage, while two others clambered onto him and stood facing each other on his shoulders. A fourth climbed up and stood on those two. The last one eeled to the top, where he made a handstand on the fourth one's upstretched arms; the hand stander's feet brushed the ceiling.

Haft laughed and clapped and cheered at the acrobats along with a significant number of the other customers. Still, fewer than half of them seemed to be paying attention to the stage. Almost all were drinking, though.

Spinner drank slowly, pondering all the things he found

to wonder about at The Burnt Man. He didn't notice when the acrobats left the stage and the snake charmer came on. He hardly noticed when a sudden change in the tenor of the shouting announced the appearance of a flutist and three dancing girls. So far as he was concerned, the fire eater might as well have not appeared. Nor did he much notice the few times Doli exchanged his empty flagon for a full one; certainly he didn't notice how much more often Doli replaced Haft's empty with full.

It wasn't until the lights went out on the stage and silence fell over the room that the music of finger cymbals and a tambourine drew Spinner's attention.

The darkened stage was bare, and the music came muted from behind the curtain, the quiet in the room an expectant hush. Spinner blinked with recognition at a stringed instrument that softly joined its voice to the finger cymbals and tambourine, an instrument he hadn't heard in a very long time.

There was a rustling of cloth, the curtain opened and someone slipped through. The singing of the tambourine and finger cymbals was no longer muted. The stringed instrument sang in a stronger voice. Spinner's breath caught in his throat. The entire world seemed to have stopped, as though waiting to learn what the music was about. Then the music stopped, the stage lights came back up, and Spinner found himself looking at the most beautiful woman in the world.

She stood, a motionless figure of dynamic gracefulness about to erupt into movement. Her feet were wide apart and pointed sharply away from each other, her hips cocked far to one side, her torso curved in an impossibly sinuous S. Her face was in profile, her arms stretched languidly above her head. She held a tambourine in one hand; the other was poised to beat a tattoo on it. She wore tiny cymbals on the lesser fingers of both hands, but the cymbals were as motionless as she, and as silent as her audience.

A noise like a distant waterfall filled Spinner's ears and

seemed to slowly grow closer. His body felt like it was expanding, while at the same time it shrank to insignificance. All the other people in the room vanished from his ken, as did the trophies and weapons on the walls; the very room itself ceased to exist. The entire universe was reduced to himself and the woman he watched.

She was gold. From the top of her head to the soles of her feet, she was gold. Her hair, her eyebrows, were the color of honey. Her eyes were amber. Her skin was radiant sunshine. The short vest that left her shoulders and arms bare and didn't fully meet between her breasts was cloth of gold, as was the narrow sash girdled low on her hips. Her pantaloons of sheerest fabric were likewise gold, as were the scantiest briefs she wore under them. The diadem that circled her head was of gold chains and gold coins. Gold bands circled her upper arms, gold bangles dangled on her wrists, gold rings adorned her fingers, gold hoops hung from the lobes of her ears. Gold coins depended from the hem of her vest and spanned the girdle of her pantaloons. The only relief from all of her gold was the black of her eyelashes and the scarlet of her lips, fingernails, and toenails. And a strange, silvery anklet.

Spinner had forgotten to breathe and his vision excluded everything but the woman on the stage. He felt faint. He felt that if something didn't happen soon, he might die from expectation. His heart thudded to beat its way out of his chest. And he didn't care. To die with such an angel filling his eyes couldn't hurt, would cause no sorrow.

The golden girl abruptly snapped her lesser fingers together, releasing a tintinnabulation of bells and wind chimes. She tattooed her tambourine with a primitive beat, and Spinner's heart beat in synchrony. She stamped a foot that raised a thin cloud of dust from the stage. The unseen stringed instrument sang out a wild, swirling song.

The Golden Girl danced. She spun and twirled and shimmied and shivered. She wove her arms through the air in impossible patterns. She bent in places no one could bend, and at times seemed to face both front and back at once. Her hands fluttered at the ends of her arms like birds; now songbirds flitting about building their nests, now a gyrfalcon swooping for food to feed her nestlings. She became a cat stalking the forest, then a deer fleeing the cat's pursuit. Through it all, her cymbals clashed, her tambourine tattooed, her feet stamped, her coins jingled and jangled. And always the strings sang their wild, swirling song.

Somewhere, some time, Spinner remembered to breathe. He no longer felt faint, his heart no longer tried to beat its way out of his chest. He was aware of only the Golden Girl dancing on the stage. Dancing, it seemed, only for him.

After what felt like an eternity that took no time at all, the music stopped and the Golden Girl curtsied so low she was almost prone on the stage, her legs folded beneath her and arms spread wide to her sides. The lights over the stage went out.

There was a long moment of silence, then every man in the room applauded and stomped and yelled for more. The din grew, the sound of the applause and yelling a solid wall. The sound grew until it seemed it would shatter the windows of the inn. But the Golden Girl's performance was over and she made no curtain calls.

After long moments of near pandemonium, the noise began to ebb. When it subsided to the point where a man with strong lungs could yell loudly enough to be heard farther than across his own table, Master Yoel bounded onto the stage. Beaming, he held his arms up for quiet. Quiet came, but only after several more moments, and then only relative quiet.

"Thank you, gentlemen, thank you," the innkeeper called out. His voice carried to most of the room and set off another round of cheering, though not as loud as before. Master Yoel, still beaming, waved again for quiet. It slowly came, and the volume dropped until there was little more than a muted buzz throughout the room.

"Thank you again, gentlemen," Master Yoel began. "I know you love the Golden Girl, but her performance is done. If you want to see more of her, you will have to come tomorrow night when, I promise you, she will perform again." The yelling and cheering started up again. Master Yoel preened as though it was for him. After a couple of moments basking in the applause, he waved his arms and patted the air until the cheering subsided.

"It is nearing that time, gentlemen," he said when the room was again quiet enough to make himself heard. "In less than an hour the magician will put the troll to sleep for the night and our only light will come from candles and oil lamps. Those of you who have been here before know that when the troll goes to sleep, so does The Burnt Man. Until then, though, you can continue to drink. The kitchen will remain open for another half hour, so if you're hungry, this is the time to order food. I'm glad you have enjoyed our entertainment this evening, and I hope you all will come back again very soon." Finished with his little speech, Master Yoel jumped off the stage and slowly, as though leading a solemn procession, walked through the room. Here and there, he stopped briefly to speak to someone, and when he did, he looked as though he was bestowing a benediction.

Master Yoel stopped briefly at their table. "Did you enjoy the entertainment?" he asked.

"Very much," Haft answered. He was still breathing heavily from the impact of the Golden Girl's dancing, but Spinner was still too bedazzled by the dance to notice the innkeeper.

Master Yoel cocked an eye at Spinner and laid a finger alongside his nose. "Your friend seems smitten."

"He does," Haft agreed, more than a touch of amusement in his voice.

Master Yoel nodded, then went on without another word.

Haft followed the innkeeper with his eyes. It took the man several moments to reach the kitchen. He paused before going through the door, and turned three small cranks on the wall next to it, two of them more than the other. Abruptly, the room was lit like day—all of the vellum panels on the ceiling glowed with their slightly bluish light. Spinner blinked at the sudden light, but otherwise paid it no attention; his eyes were on the stage.

"What'd he do?" Haft asked Spinner. He had to poke his companion to get his attention and asked his question again.

"Oh." Spinner looked at the cranks Haft pointed out. "He signaled the magician to make the troll work harder."

Haft scowled at him. He wanted to know more about the troll, but Spinner clearly wasn't going to say much of anything until he got over being mesmerized by the Golden Girl, so he looked around for Doli to order another flagon of beer.

In time, Master Yoel came out of the kitchen to announce that it was closing. Haft thought the innkeeper was giving them the once-over, but shrugged the feeling off.

Immediately afterward, as though the innkeeper's voice had snagged his attention, Spinner murmured, "Beautiful," shook his head, and became aware of his surroundings. He blinked again at the light as though seeing it for the first time. He looked around. Fewer than half the tables were occupied, and as he looked, more men got up and left. Those few who remained were still drinking and boisterous, but despite the occasional raucous laugh, were less loud than before the Golden Girl's performance.

Spinner looked at Haft, though Haft had the impression his friend didn't really see him, and said softly, "She's the most beautiful woman I've ever seen."

Haft nodded. "She may well be that. And the way she moves, I'll bet she'd be a lot of fun in—" A sharp look from Spinner cut him off. "Well, a lot of fun."

Spinner nodded slowly, still looking hard at Haft. "Very much fun," he solemnly agreed. Then he noticed his flagon for the first time since the end of the Golden Girl's dance. He lifted it and drank deeply. Doli was there before he could even look around for her. She had full flagons with her.

"You enjoyed the entertainment?" she asked.

Haft laughed loudly. "It was wonderful," he said. "But him! Why, I think Spinner still hasn't come back to earth from it."

Spinner glowered at him and took a drink to hide what he thought was a burning face.

Doli curled her lip in a wan smile. "Yes, Alyline is very . . ." She paused, seemed to think better of what she was saying, and finished, ". . . a very good dancer."

"Alyline?" Spinner asked.

"That's her name, the Golden Girl." The corner of her mouth twitched, and then an expression of fear flickered across her face. "We aren't supposed to say her name. You won't tell Master Yoel I said it, will you?"

"Of course not," Spinner said. Haft echoed him. "But why aren't you supposed to say it? Alyline . . . it's a beautiful name, as beautiful as she is."

Doli shook her head. "I can't tell you." She rushed off before they could ask her anything else.

Spinner shook himself all over like a wet dog, then, with an effort, looked bright and fully aware. "Well, my friend, that was some entertainment!" he said.

"It was," Haft agreed. "I wish we could stay another night and see it again."

Spinner nodded wistfully, recalling in his mind's eye the wonderful dancing of the Golden Girl, Alyline.

More tables were emptying, and serving maids who weren't taking care of customers started cleaning the tabletops. One serving maid facing away from them bent over a table to wipe its far side. Looking down as he was, Spinner saw the hem of her skirt ride far up over her calf. He saw that she was wearing a wide, silvery anklet like the one on the Golden Girl's ankle. He looked around at the others. Every serving maid whose ankles he could see had the same kind of anklet. The anklets were perhaps an inch wide and half that thick. They fit snugly, with no opening, though there was a place where the anklet was thicker than elsewhere. The wide place looked like a join, where one end fit into the other.

Haft signaled Doli for a fresh flagon. When she came, she stood between him and Spinner. Curious, Spinner reached for Doli's skirt and pulled it up a few inches so he could see her ankles. Doli ignored him until he asked, "Why do all the serving maids wear those anklets?"

Doli jerked her skirt out of his hand and spun away, her face suddenly pale. "D-Don't ask about that. You never saw that." She hurried away from them.

"I didn't know you had such an interest in women's jewelry," Haft said.

"I don't, but that's an odd-looking anklet. All the serving maids seem to wear one. So does Alyline."

Haft shrugged. Not that he was unable to appreciate a well-turned ankle, but his area of interest in women's legs lay higher.

"It must mean something," Spinner murmured.

Few of the other tables were still occupied. The porters came out and started moving the empty tables and chairs to one side of the room; one of them wheeled out a large tub filled with steaming, sudsy water; several mop handles stuck out of the tub.

"We should go before they mop us up with the rest of the refuse," Spinner said. He drained the last of his beer and stood. Haft did the same.

The innkeeper came out of the kitchen to announce the common room was closing. There was mild grumbling from the few men still drinking, but they also emptied the last of their beer or wine and stood to leave.

Master Yoel intercepted Spinner and Haft on their way to the stairs. "A moment of your time, young gentlemen?" He led them away from the path of the other men going upstairs.

"You liked our Golden Girl?" he said to Spinner.

Spinner nodded. "Everyone did."

"Ah, but you liked her more than most, or I miss my guess."

"Perhaps."

Master Yoel laid a finger alongside his nose. "Would you have an interest in more than merely seeing her dancing on a stage before the public?"

"What do you mean?" Spinner knew full well what the innkeeper meant. His heart raced and his breath came rapid and shallow. He was sure his face flushed. Yes, he did have an interest in more than seeing her dance on a stage in full public view; he wanted more than just to watch her dance.

"If you are willing to part with another gold coin, you can have the rest of the night with her." The innkeeper's eyes shined bright and moist. "Alone," he added meaningfully.

Spinner's vision again narrowed, but this time it was from anger. "You *sell* her? And how many others have had her tonight before you offered her to me?"

Master Yoel held up placating hands. "None, young sir, I swear. I do not casually allow access to the Golden Girl. It is only when one such as yourself comes around, one who fully appreciates her for everything she is, that I offer her. Her price is dear. She can only be offered to a man who truly desires one such as she, one who can truly appreciate so magnificent a woman."

Spinner's vision narrowed further. He wanted to kill the innkeeper, who despoiled such beauty, such a wonder, as the Golden Girl. The large muscles in his neck, shoulders, back, legs, and arms swelled and grew hard, battle-ready. His fists clenched, ready to strike. The look he gave Master Yoel made the innkeeper blink and swallow.

Haft had had too much to drink to notice Spinner's rising anger, but he broke the tension by slapping him on the arm. "Do it, man," he said. "Do it. I'll never hear the end of it if you don't. I may not hear the end of it if you do, but it'll be easier hearing about how it was than having to listen to what might have been."

Spinner started. He turned to Haft with threat in his face. Then he realized that Haft was right. If he didn't part with a gold coin for the night with Alyline, he would forever yearn for her, and forever hate the innkeeper. Alyline would be a distraction for him for a long time to come, perhaps too great a distraction for the dangers they might be facing on their journey back to Frangeria. But if he gave the innkeeper a coin and had his way with the Golden Girl, that would clear the mists from his mind and he would know she was a woman like any other woman, not the angel he thought he saw on that stage. Abruptly, Spinner relaxed.

"One gold coin for the rest of the night it is," he said. A small part of his mind noted the hungry way the innkeeper glanced at his purse as he withdrew a coin.

"This way, good sir," Master Yoel said softly when the coin was safely in his palm. He led Spinner to the curtain behind the stage and went through it.

Haft looked after them for a moment, then mounted the stairs to their room.

CHAPTER
ELEVEN

A corridor behind the curtain went only a few paces before it turned to the left. The only illumination came from the light filtering through the curtain from the common room on one end, and into the other end from whatever place was around the corner.

Master Yoel walked the short distance to the end of the corridor, felt along the edge of a ceramic half column, then fiddled with the bottom of a frieze a couple of feet beyond on the opposite wall. The innkeeper tugged on a tassel from a hanging tapestry, stepped to the wall facing the tapestry and inserted his fingertip into a recess Spinner didn't see until Master Yoel's fingertip disappeared into it. The innkeeper didn't turn at the corner at the end of the corridor; instead, he placed both hands on the blank wall at the corner and shifted them in a strange pattern. After the innkeeper removed his hands, a section wide as a door slid aside in the wall and exposed a stairway leading down. Flickering orange light came through the hidden doorway. The flickering briefly gave Spinner the terrifying impression the cellar was on fire and Master Yoel was leading him into a conflagration.

Master Yoel looked over his shoulder at Spinner, simpered, then scampered down the stairs. Spinner stood at the head of the stairway for a moment as he realized there was no fire below, and eyed the stairs suspiciously. The source of the orange light was an oil lamp that flickered at the bottom of the stairs, which went down much farther than one would expect for a storage cellar. At the foot of the stairs there was a doorway to the left. Spinner couldn't see what it opened into, and wished he had a weapon like the saber he had left behind on the *Sea Horse*. But wishing wouldn't create a sword. He put a hand on the hilt of his belt knife for reassurance, remembering the hungry way the innkeeper looked at his purse. But, still, he followed the innkeeper down the stairs.

No ambush waited at the doorway below, which revealed another corridor, its walls carelessly whitewashed stone. There was no troll-light, just what was provided by oil lamps sitting on shelves. Curved, polished brass mirrors behind the lamps reflected uneven orange light into the corridor. Set into the walls at intervals of about three paces were stout timber doors inset with tiny windows shuttered from the outside; they looked like the doors of prison cells.

"The women who work in the inn," the innkeeper said over his shoulder, "their quarters are down here. The doors are thick, you won't have to worry about the noises they make tonight disturbing you."

That sounded vaguely threatening to Spinner; it meant that no one behind those doors could hear any noise he made either. He loosened his knife in its sheath and listened carefully for the sound of a door stealthily opening behind him.

But robbery was not the innkeeper's motive for leading Spinner into this cellar corridor. He stopped outside one of the timber doors and rapped on it. Then he opened the door and bowed Spinner through. Spinner noticed that Master Yoel didn't have to unlock the door before he opened it. He went through the doorway ready, he hoped, for anything. He started at the click of a lock being turned in the door as it closed. What he saw then erased all thought of the door or the possibility of ambush.

At first he could not believe he had been magically transported to a heavenly seraglio. Several dozen candles lit the room with a soft glow; some of the candles burned in wall sconces, others sat in candelabra on low tables. Many-hued curtains festooned the walls and draped the ceiling. Woven carpets were piled on the floor to such a thickness that walking on them was like walking on a firm mattress. Large cushions were scattered here and there, perhaps as seats. Cushions were piled behind the curtains against the far wall—or where Spinner surmised the far wall was. The colors of all were pastels punctuated by gold, save for the carpets, which were the yellows, reds, and browns that make up the color of gold.

Four pictures hung, two on each side wall. One was a painting in an archaic style, of horsemen spearing a leaping stag; another, with skewed perspective, showed a walled city from a nearby height. A third was of a palace courtyard, with many women dressed as the Golden Girl had dressed for her dance, walking through it, sitting, or standing about. The fourth painting brought a pang to his heart, for it was of a vase of pangia flowers, flowers he hadn't seen since he left home.

A bronze statuette of a dancer who could only be the Golden Girl graced one of the tables, unclothed save for her sash, jewelry, and coins—and she had no anklet. Spinner was looking at the carved ivory elephant cow and calf on another table when he realized he wasn't alone in the room.

In a corner, seated on a cushion on the floor with her ankles crossed in front of her, was the Golden Girl.

"I almost thought you would never see me," she said in a voice that was half husky, half wind chimes. She stood, and her movement seemed to Spinner even more graceful and effortless than had her dancing earlier.

At the sight of her, his throat constricted and his tongue felt swollen.

The Golden Girl glided softly toward him, and he became aware that she was not wearing the same costume that she wore for her public dancing—now she had on a flowing, diaphanous gown that covered her from neck to floor. Or would have covered her except that he could see through it, and it was all she wore. "He said someone would pay for me tonight," she murmured seductively, and held a languid hand out to him.

Spinner wanted with every atom of his body to reach out to that hand and take the woman. But the sight of her body through the gown stopped him for a moment; he had to simply look at her. Her breasts were more perfectly proportioned and set than he imagined any to be. Her waist dimpled more smoothly than he could have guessed when he saw her on the stage, even though he saw it clearly there. Her belly curved deliciously. Her hips flared so gracefully he thought he could bury himself in their embrace, locked in by her legs, and never come out. The fine hair of her pubes was the same color as the hair on her head.

He looked at her for so long she became impatient. "Come and take what you have paid for," she said at length, and in those words there was an indication that she had not chosen this rendezvous, and the message that he could look and touch and take, but never possess. All that, in the edge to what she said, jarred his mind to awareness, and he finally realized the language she had been speaking. It was unflawed Apianghian, but her words sounded odd, with the musical rhythms her voice held.

He suddenly found his voice. "You speak to me in Apianghian," he said in his native tongue—a language in which no one else in the inn had spoken to him, or heard him speak, except, briefly, Doli.

"Of course. In what other tongue should I address a countryman?"

"But you aren't Apianghian," he said weakly, shocked by her claim of kinship. "Apianghians are like me, dusky and dark haired. You are fair and golden."

A corner of her mouth quirked. "You lowlanders," she snorted. "Hemmed in as you are by seas and mountains, you think you are all there is. None from the lowlands ever visit the mountains—except for the royal tax collectors." She shook her head scornfully. "If Frangerian traders never came to your shores, you'd think you were the only people in the entire world."

"You are from the mountains?" he asked, as though she spoke a riddle, which her words may as well have been from the welter of confusion he felt. Some part of his mind reminded him that he'd learned as a boy that the people of Apianghia's northern mountains were golden of hair and fair of skin.

"From the northern mountains, yes." Her lips curved in an ironic, almost mocking smile. "But if you prefer, I can talk to you," she switched languages, "in Frangerian. You must have had a reason for leaving home if you have become a Frangerian Marine. Perhaps you wish no reminder of your home." A trace of taunt entered her voice. "Maybe you are sorry you came to me? Maybe you want to leave now?"

"How do you know I'm a Frangerian . . ." His voice slowed and stuttered to a stop. He was barely capable of coherent thought.

A corner of her mouth twitched. "Everyone knows the uniform." She pulled the flowing gown close around her, as if not allowing it to flow would make the cloth opaque; one arm half covered her still-seen breasts, the other partly concealed her loins. Suddenly she was just a woman—the most beautiful woman Spinner had ever seen, but just a woman. No longer was she the mystical houri of only a moment before.

Spinner blinked rapidly, swallowed a few times, struggled to control his thoughts. A woman of the Apianghian north— he accepted her claim—a dancer, and . . . and . . . He couldn't make himself form the word, so far from home. And dancing in a Skragish inn? How could such a thing be?

He must have said this last thought out loud, because she told him: "I'm a slave, ninny. What else would I be doing here? Why else would I be dancing for uncouth strangers? Or doing those things you can't bring yourself to name—things you wish me to do with you?" Her voice was sharp, and she glared at him with eyes that hated.

He dropped his eyes. Embarrassed, he dropped to sit on one of the cushions.

"A slave?" he asked weakly.

"A slave," she snorted. "This inn is a staging post for slave trading. Now, you paid for me. Be the man you think you are and take what you paid for." She stepped forward until her feet came into his downcast view. What he could see of her gown flowed again.

He was horrified at the thought of her being a slave; slavery was outlawed in all lands that were recognized as civilized. He'd heard that it still existed in some places, but hadn't been sure he could believe it. Anyway, the tales he'd heard had slaves working as fieldhands, or beasts of burden, living short lives of brutal labor. Never had he heard of them as public entertainers and . . . and . . . He still couldn't say it. Thoughts of what he'd had in mind—what had he had in mind?—tumbled chaotically through his head. He twisted his face to the side so he couldn't see the Golden Girl's feet.

She laughed at him. It was a harsh, mocking laugh.

Spinner cringed. A slave? Slavery in itself was evil. But to enslave a woman as beautiful as this one? To make her, to make her . . . Spinner felt he must be as vile as those who enslaved her.

The Golden Girl abruptly dropped into a flat-footed squat. She grabbed his hair and jerked his head toward her, shoved her face into his so her eyes stared at him from less than a hand's breadth away. "So, you wanted me freely, is that it? You wanted me to come to you out of love, or from passion? You? A man I've never seen? Is that what you thought?" She snorted. "Or did you see me dancing and think I had no more pride or self-respect, no more desire for something better, than a back-tavern whore who will hike her skirts for any man with a copper in his hand? Did you think I was like that?"

Spinner squeezed his eyes shut; his face contorted as though cutting off a flood of tears.

The Golden Girl dug her fingers deeper into his hair and

twisted hard. "Open your eyes when I'm talking to you," she said through clenched teeth. Her knuckles dug painfully into Spinner's scalp.

She kept twisting his hair and digging her knuckles into his scalp until he opened his eyes—opened them to gold. The honey of the skin around her eyes radiated at him the anger of bees whose hive was being raided; her straw-colored eyebrows were lightning bolts striking at him; her black eyelashes were the rims of storm clouds coming to wash him away. Her amber irises seemed to grow and grow until they were ready to engulf him, to cast him inside the large pupils where he would fall forever, screaming until he despaired of crashing on a bottom that wasn't there.

Hair tore from his head as he yanked it out of her grip. "No!" he gasped. "I didn't think you were a—a . . . I didn't think you would come to me from love." His voice was so low she could barely hear him. "I didn't think . . ."

"That's right," she snapped, "you didn't think. You saw me, you got engorged. Men. *Pfagh!*" She pushed roughly at his face and stood, turned and took a step away, folded her arms. She didn't look back at him when she continued, "When lust strikes a man, he never thinks of the woman, of who she is or of what she might want. He only thinks of relieving the pressure in his groin, he only thinks of his own pleasure."

"No!" he wailed. "That's not true!"

She spun on him, bent at the waist, her fists clenched at her sides, her face that of a fury, the transparency of her garment ignored. "No? Then why are you here? If you weren't thinking only of your own gratification, why did you pay the slavemaster a gold coin to own me for a night?"

Anguish rippled across his face.

"Here. You paid. Take." She almost tore her gown, whipping it over her head. She stood unclothed before him, resplendent in her defiance.

He looked away from her, filled with self-loathing. "I didn't know you were a slave." His voice broke when he said it.

Then, so suddenly it surprised even him, he was overtaken by anger, filled with resolve to right the wrong of this enslavement. He was a Frangerian Marine, one of the most capable fighting men in the known world. He stood and looked into her eyes. When he spoke, his voice was strong and firm. "Get dressed. As of now, you are no longer a slave. I am not alone. I will get my companion and my weapons. We will set you free. And woe be to the man who tries to stop us."

She laughed bitterly. Then her body slumped and she was no longer defiant in her nudity, she was just naked and vulnerable. Her arms briefly moved to cover her nakedness before they surrendered the attempt and fell away.

"You can't free me," she said softly, her voice wavering.

"I'm a Frangerian Marine," he said boldly. "And I am here with another. There is nothing we cannot do."

She lifted one foot, indicating the odd, silvery anklet. "There is nothing you can do about this," she said, flat-voiced. She went through the frieze of curtains and collapsed on the pile of cushions Spinner thought must be a bed. She lay curled, her body heaving with silent sobs.

He followed the Golden Girl through the curtains, sat on the cushions next to her and gathered her gently into his arms. He tried to comfort her by putting protective hands on her back and shoulders but was so aware of the soft, warm flesh he touched, her magically silken skin, that without volition his thoughts started wandering from protecting to taking. Desperately he looked around for something to cover her with, any barrier to put between his hands and her skin. The only thing he saw was the thin gown she'd discarded, and it was out of reach. He grabbed one of the curtains hanging from the ceiling and yanked it free. It was as diaphanous as the gown she no longer wore, but he draped it over her anyway. He could still see her through it, could still feel all the warmth of her body, but it was nevertheless a barrier to the touch of her skin on his hands, flimsy as it was. It was enough to allow him to keep his mind on comforting and protecting.

"There there," he said awkwardly. He clumsily patted her shoulder, tried to convey that everything would be all right, suspected he was failing abjectly.

Sobs wracked her. After a few moments they began to subside. A few moments more and they ceased altogether. She pushed away from him and sat up. She smiled wanly and could only glance at him for another moment or so. Then she held her head up, firmed her expression, used a corner of the curtain to wipe tears and running mascara from her face.

"Thank you for wanting to free me," she said, as though it was of no consequence. "I thank you for your consideration. But there is nothing you can do. So," she cast aside the curtain he'd covered her with and lay back on the cushions, arms held open to him, "come and take what you paid for. I grant it less unwillingly now."

For a long moment Spinner was torn between two of the imperatives of a young man: to take the object of his lust; or to right a vile wrong. He decided that lust could wait to be satisfied another time. He covered her again with the curtain, even though he recognized how futile a covering the curtain was.

"Get up. We will go now. You're free." He made to stand up, but before he could rise to his feet, the Golden Girl lifted her foot and sharply kicked his shoulder with her heel.

She threw off the curtain and plunked her ankle onto his shoulder. "Do you know what that is?" she demanded.

He looked at her in confusion.

"On my ankle."

He looked cross-eyed at her ankle. "It's a bracelet for your ankle."

She snorted. "Do you know what kind?"

He shrugged one-shouldered, so as not to dislodge her foot from his shoulder—he liked the physical contact. "No."

"It is a summoner. It calls an azren."

He shook his head. "An azren?"

"A death-demon. There is an azren in the forest beyond the

inn. Every night the anklets summon it to us in our sleep and we dream of it." She shuddered. "The dreams are always of it killing us."

"That's horrible." He wanted to take her in his arms and hold her, protect her, but couldn't without dislodging her ankle from his shoulder.

"*Pfagh!* That's not horrible. What is horrible is what happens if one of us tries to leave." She glared at him, but moisture that glistened in the corner of her eyes gave lie to her anger. "The azren doesn't hurt us when it comes in our dreams. But if we go beyond the inn yard, the anklet summons the azren and it kills whoever has gone forth.

"I saw it happen to a serving maid who'd only been here a day or two. She said she wouldn't be a whore at the slave-master's whim. She said she didn't believe in demons. She ran for the forest. I couldn't see the azren, I only saw the way it cut her to bits. She screamed in agony until it had cut her so much she could no longer scream. It was horrible." She slid her foot from Spinner's shoulder and rolled onto her side into a tight ball. Her voice was muffled as she said, "That is not going to happen to me."

Spinner was shocked at the Golden Girl's tale. He'd never heard of an azren. How could anyone go through this valley? He asked the question as soon as he thought it.

"The azren feeds on our dreams," the Golden Girl said. "And the slavemaster sometimes sends it an 'offering.' If a slave here displeases him, or a new slave is injured or ill, he sends that one out to the azren."

That almost made Spinner disgorge his evening's food and drink. He bent over the Golden Girl's feet to examine the anklet more closely. It was, as he'd noted, thick and wide. What he earlier thought was a larger section of it did seem to be a locking mechanism. In the center was a small opening that could be a keyhole. On the opposite side from the wide place he found what looked like a hinge.

"Where is the key?" he asked.

The Golden Girl shuddered but didn't answer.

Spinner picked up the curtain from where she tossed it when she showed him the anklet, and again draped it over her nakedness. He tucked her in, then lay down with his chest against her back and curled his legs under hers and wrapped his arms around her. She was shivering; he was sure it wasn't from cold—the room was too warm. She gripped the curtain's hem with her fingers and pulled it snug under her chin. He stroked her hair and murmured little nothings into her ear, little nothings that he hoped were soothing.

They must have been because shortly afterward she stopped shivering and twisted around in his arms to snuggle up facing him. He had to straighten his legs to allow her to. Her hands were loosely balled in front of her face. She opened one and caressed his cheek.

"You cannot get the key," she said, half wistfully. "He will not give it up. But it's sweet of you to think of it." She brushed her lips against his and wiggled in closer; somehow the curtain became dislodged and he felt her naked body against him, and his clothing felt more coarse than it ever had before. The Golden Girl must have thought so also. "Your clothes are rough, they scratch me," she said. She slid her hand from his cheek to the bottom of his jerkin and started to pull it up.

He put his hand on hers and pushed it and the jerkin back down. "No," he said, thick-voiced. "We can do that later. When you are no longer a slave, when I come to you because you want me to." Saying that, he realized he wasn't being like Haft. Haft would not say no under the same circumstances; Haft would help her undress him. "I said I would free you and I will. Where does Master Yoel keep the key?"

She pulled her head back to look into his eyes and laughed at him. "Master Yoel? He doesn't have the key. He's not the slavemaster."

"Then who is? I'll take it from him and free you."

She smiled a sad smile. "Master *Gro*uel is the slavemaster. You can't get the key from him."

"I can get it from anyone." He thought about the name she gave. "Grouel? That's a name I haven't heard."

"He's Jokapcul. It is said he's a master swordsman as well as a slavemaster. I think he is. I've seen him spar with men who others have called master swordsmen. He always wins."

Spinner swallowed. A Jokapcul here? As a slavemaster? He remembered that afternoon, when the innkeeper claimed he knew nothing about the Jokapcul, had said he'd never even seen one. And they hadn't seen any Jokapcul since the fight at the border—certainly he hadn't seen any at The Burnt Man. And the slavemaster was a swordmaster, or so Alyline said. Jokapcul swordsmen were supposed to be among the best in the world—and their swordmasters were supposed to be the very best. The only Jokapcul swordsman he ever faced had been the officer at the border, and he had been very good. Perhaps their swordmasters weren't all that much better than their average. If they weren't, he could stand a chance against one of them—if he couldn't find a way to avoid a fight. And he had been weak and wounded when he'd beaten the Jokapcul officer.

"Every swordsman loses sooner or later," he said. "Besides, I don't have to duel him to get the key."

"How else would you get it?"

"I'll find a way."

She looked into his eyes but didn't ask how.

"You said you saw a serving maid killed by the azren?" She nodded. "I saw anklets on all the serving maids. Are they all slaves?"

"Yes. The innkeeper gets to keep all the most beautiful women who come through here—until they are no longer so beautiful."

"Who keeps the keys to the locks on the doors down here?"

She laughed, a harsh cough. "These doors aren't locked, except when a man is with a woman he has paid for. The slavemaster isn't afraid that any of us will run away. How would we escape the demon?"

"Are there any men who are slaves?"

"Everyone who works here is a slave except for the innkeeper, his wife, the stableman, the chief cook, and the traveling entertainers." Her voice was bitter. "I'm the only entertainer who is a slave. The slavemaster has a few men-at-arms who aren't slaves."

"How many men-at-arms does he have?"

She shook her head. "A dozen. Maybe half that many. Maybe more. I don't know."

"Where do the men slaves sleep? Are they down here too?"

"No. I think they are kept in rooms above the stable."

"What about all the men in the common room? Who are they?"

"Some are local herdsmen and farmers. Others are travelers. Most of them are slave traders, or handlers or teamsters for them, or their guards. Why are you asking all these questions?"

"So I'll know what I'm up against."

"Up against? With only two of you?" She pounded a fist on his chest. "Don't be so stupid. There is nothing you can do."

But there was something he could do. He didn't yet know what, but he was sure he could find it. He had to. There was one more thing he wanted to know. "Master Yoel said something when he was leading me here—he said the doors to the rooms are thick, so I didn't have to worry about being disturbed by noise anyone made. What did he mean? Why are the doors so thick?"

The Golden Girl's body shook with fury inside his arms. "The serving maids are slaves—some men think that means they are property, not people. If a man wants to, and pays enough, the slavemaster lets him hurt the girls. Sometimes a serving maid spends the night with a man and is never seen

again. I don't know whether they are killed or merely maimed
and sent on somewhere else."

Trying to contain his anger, Spinner held her tightly. The
wrong being committed there was even worse than slavery.
When he righted the wrong, someone was going to pay
dearly. "This will all end tomorrow, I promise you," he said
softly. "In the meantime, sleep. I will protect you tonight.
When you are free, we can do more than simply me protect
you."

She looked at him oddly, and he chose to interpret it as
gratitude. In reality she was thinking him a fool to turn down
the chance to be with the most skilled lover he would ever
meet, in favor of something intangible he might receive after
accomplishing the impossible.

She turned her back to him, curled up, and went to sleep,
secure in the knowledge that the fool wouldn't ravage or
otherwise harm her during what was left of the night.

CHAPTER
TWELVE

When the Golden Girl woke him, Spinner felt like he'd barely closed his eyes. Faint light came from a few guttering candles.

"It is dawn," she said. "A man waits outside the door to lead you to your room."

"But—"

She crossed his lips with a finger. "No buts. It is the rule." She helped him to stand and to straighten his clothes. She softly took his hand in hers and led him to the door. When she opened the door for him, she stood behind it so the man outside wouldn't see her naked body. She gave Spinner a sad smile. "Thank you," she said softly.

Spinner smiled and nodded at her. He thought she meant to thank him for the rescue he was going to effect. He watched the door close, then turned to follow the man to the stairs. He thought he recognized him as one of the handymen he'd seen the day before.

"What's the matter, didn't you get any sleep last night?" Haft asked when they were seated in the common room waiting for their breakfast. He laughed raucously at his own joke—he knew *he* wouldn't have slept if it had been him spending the night with the Golden Girl. "Or did she kick you out of bed?"

Spinner smiled wanly. "Actually, we did get a little sleep near the end," he said, and tried to look happier and more energetic. He had to look more like someone who'd had a memorable time. "If you'd just spent a night with someone like her and you were leaving, knowing you would never see her again, you'd probably be bawling." He laughed, and hoped the laugh didn't sound as hollow as it felt.

"Right," Haft said dryly. He patted the pile of their belongings and the sack of food they'd bought to eat on their journey that sat on a spare chair at their table. "We have to get on the road." He leaned back and looked wistful. "But it was nice last night. A hot meal, a hot bath, cold beer, a proper mattress . . . though somehow I don't think my mattress was as comfortable as yours." He laughed even more loudly than before.

Spinner's answering grin was weak and he could only manage a chuckle.

Their food came and they were silent as they ate. They had a different serving maid; Doli wasn't in evidence in the common room this morning. Neither of them asked where she was. Spinner could make a few guesses, but wasn't sure. The only guess he didn't dislike was that she had the day off, but he suspected the serving maids weren't given days off. If what he suspected had happened was true, that would be one more man who would regret—no matter how briefly—what he'd done at The Burnt Man.

Other tables were occupied, but not many. Two merchants sat together talking in low voices over their meals. Men in homespun occupied three more tables. None of them seemed in any hurry to eat and move on. Spinner thought the merchants must be slave traders, the other men in their employ. He tried not to show the hatred he felt for them.

Master Yoel appeared at their table just as they finished eating. With a flourish, he presented the bill to Spinner. Spinner quickly looked it over, decided it was more or less accurate; no item seemed unduly high. He held out his hand. The innkeeper hesitated, then dropped three copper coins into his palm.

Spinner smiled at him but didn't say anything. He didn't have to; he knew Haft would.

"You seem reluctant to give change, innkeeper," Haft said calmly. He picked up the bill and made a show of examining it. "Could it be you have overcharged us somewhere?"

"But, good young sir," Master Yoel sputtered, "it's all there. Every tittle. There is naught on that reckoning that doesn't belong. If you think of what you have paid for similar services in other inns, you will see that my prices are quite reasonable."

Haft looked at the bill a moment longer then let it slip from his fingers as though it were a thing of no consequence. "Make change more quickly in the future and you will avoid suspicion," he said solemnly.

Spinner stood. "Has the stableman readied our horses?" he asked.

"I'm sure he has, I sent word for him to do so."

"Then we will be off." Spinner gathered his belongings in such a way that the innkeeper couldn't help noticing how ready to hand were all of his weapons. "Good day, Master Yoel."

He walked to the entrance with long, purposeful strides. Haft followed almost on his heels. When the door was open and he was about to step through, Spinner turned back to the innkeeper, who was about to disappear into the kitchen, and said in a voice loud enough to be heard by everybody in the room, "Treat all of the women who work here well, innkeeper. Especially the Golden Girl. You never know when a family might take offense to the rough treatment of a daughter, or a sister."

Master Yoel gave a start at the words. He turned to look at Spinner. Fear shot quickly across his face, to be replaced by a study of innocent confusion.

Haft had no idea what Spinner was talking about, but he gave the innkeeper a sharp look, as though he did and was firmly with Spinner. After all, come what may, he was firmly with Spinner.

"I always treat all of my workers well, young gentleman,"

the innkeeper said. His hands fluttered about aimlessly. "Especially the entertainers. Most especially the Golden Girl."

"Then see to it that you continue to do so," Spinner said. He stepped outside and strode toward the stable.

In a step or two Haft was alongside him. "What was that about?" he asked.

"Be patient. I'll tell you once we are out of the valley."

"Right. You said you'd tell me about the troll too. I'm still waiting."

"Wait a little longer." He looked ahead. There weren't as many horses in the corral as he might have expected from the crowd he thought had stayed at the inn overnight, nor even enough for the men breaking their fast in the common room. The only carts he saw were two wagons that looked like they were used by farmers to carry produce to market. He saw nothing that appeared to belong to a merchant.

The stableman had their horses ready. The horses looked happy and ready to go.

"They look like they had as good a time last night as we did," Haft said when he saw how the horses pranced.

"Probably better," Spinner said dull-voiced.

Haft looked at him oddly, but didn't ask anything—yet.

"Well, good sirs," the stableman said, "was the bill as honest and level as I told you it would be? Was the entertainment as fine? Do you understand now why people come back and back again? And how soon will you return for more entertainment?"

"It was, it was, I do, and sooner than you may suspect," Spinner answered. He quickly checked the tackle on the horses and found the stableman had done a better job of saddling them than he himself could have. "But right now the sun is up and we have far to go, much to do, and we must be off." He quickly mounted his horse and flipped the stableman a copper coin. "With thanks for your trouble and your good care for our horses," he said.

"No trouble, none at all," the stableman said as he deftly

caught the coin. He looked like he was ready to talk for as long as anyone was there to listen. Spinner didn't want to stand around listening. He had to tell Haft what he'd found out about the inn and make plans for their return.

"Let's go," he said.

Haft hesitated and looked warily at the mare. No matter how confident he'd been on horseback the day before, a night under a roof and in a bed had taken him away from the horses, and now he was no longer so sure of himself.

"There are things you want to know that I'll never tell you if you don't get on that horse right now," Spinner said, and tapped his horse's flanks to get him moving.

Haft sighed and mounted. Spinner was already leading the gelding along the road before Haft was settled in the saddle. He let the mare canter to catch up.

In minutes they were in the trees again, and Spinner kicked the stallion into a canter. He wanted to put distance between them and the inn before he stopped and told Haft what they were going to do—and why.

Haft didn't want to wait. "What's wrong with you this morning, Spinner?" he demanded as soon as he got the mare to trot alongside the stallion instead of trailing the gelding. "You just spent the night with the most beautiful woman either of us has ever seen, but from the way you've been acting, anyone would think you had a miserable night. You looked like you had something on your mind at breakfast, and that something wasn't the great time you had last night. As a matter of fact, you've been looking like you're getting ready for a battle. You gave the innkeeper a hard time over the bill, which looked fine to me, I might add. Then there was that thing you said to him when we were leaving. Anybody would think you were threatening him. You've been short with me every time I asked a question. And you were curt with the stableman when he was only trying to be helpful and friendly. And if that isn't enough . . ."

He looked sharply at Spinner. "You aren't listening to a

word I'm saying! You aren't listening, and you sure aren't doing any of the telling you said you were going to do." He shook his head and glared at the forest that surrounded them. "I could wish we'd run into some robbers, just so I'd have a chance to hit somebody." He glanced at Spinner again. "And maybe, just maybe, some highwaymen would wake you up so you'd get around to telling me what's going on."

"Don't worry," Spinner said grimly. "You'll get your chance to hit somebody. But it won't be highwaymen."

"He lives!" Haft exclaimed with a grand sweep of an arm. "He talks! He listens! At least a little bit. Why, he probably breathes! Maybe he'll even do some of the explaining he promised." He looked at Spinner and dropped his voice to a normal level. "Well, what about it?"

The whole time they were riding through the woods, Spinner was watching the trees along their route. He finally saw a break in the forest edging the road where a slab of exposed bedrock wouldn't take their horses' hoofprints. "In here," he said.

"Hey, where do you think you're going? Don't you remember what happened the last time we went into the forest? I don't think we'll find an imp fence to help us if we run into another cat." Objecting all the way, Haft followed.

The trees on the side of the ridge were different from those in the lowland forest they'd passed through in Bostia; they weren't as tall and their canopy wasn't as dense, though their trunks were thicker. Seedlings and saplings sprouted up through the earth between the trees, but most of them looked stunted. Bushes grew in scattered thickets and much of the ground was open. Sunlight dappled the ground, mostly around the bush thickets. The exposed bedrock only extended a few paces inside the forest before earth covered it. There were a lot of deer tracks, along with myriad tracks of lesser animals. Haft looked closely but found no trace of large predators. Boulders, some small, some the size of a hut, lay scattered about.

When they were far enough into the trees that they couldn't be seen from the road, Spinner stopped, looked about for a route to take, then picked what seemed to Haft to be a random direction, one that led up the ridge at a shallow angle.

Haft nervously kept all of his senses open to any sight, sound, or smell of danger. Insects buzzed about and a cloud of gnats swarmed around them. A few birds cawed in the tree-tops, and an occasional one swooped between the trunks, scooping up flying insects.

But nothing big or that sounded dangerous slithered across their path, and no chittering treetop dwellers scattered slops in their direction. And Haft heard no cries of cat, detected no sign of followers or ambushers. For all he could tell, he and Spinner were the first human beings to enter that stretch of forest.

Spinner kept looking downslope, toward the inn's clearing, seeking a place where they could observe the clearing without being seen. He found a spot where a hut-sized boulder and a large fallen tree trunk were lodged together between two larger trees. From the tree trunk, they had a clear view of the inn, which was almost due west of them, and their horses would be out of sight hobbled behind the boulder. A soft breeze came through this opening in the trees; it wasn't much of a breeze, but it was enough to disperse the cloud of gnats.

"I didn't see any sign of hidden roads coming off the one we just left," Spinner said when they stopped. "Nor any sign of horse or cart traffic under these trees."

"No reason you should," Haft said.

"Yes there is," Spinner said. "Sit down and I'll tell you all about it."

"Do we really have to wait for night before we can go in and kill those fiends?" Haft asked when Spinner finished.

Spinner slowly nodded. "Before we go in to kill those fiends and free the slaves, we have to have a plan. Do you have a plan?"

Haft shook his head.

"Neither do I. Let's watch below and see what goes on. Then we can make a plan. What we observe today will help us make that plan. Also, we don't go in until after the troll is put to sleep. And I'd like to know where the troll's magician lives."

"You keep mentioning the troll like you know something about it. Will you tell me about this troll?"

"See that hut?" Spinner pointed to a small stone out-building near a corner of the inn, where they couldn't see it the previous day. "That's probably the troll hut. I don't know how it does it, but a troll under the proper care of a magician makes light." He remembered how his and Haft's clothes were clean and warm when they finished their baths the day before. "Sometimes the trolls even make heat. Darkness will favor us when we go in tonight, so we need to wait for the troll to go to sleep. There are other things a troll can do besides make light and heat—some of those things can be dangerous to the unwary. We don't know what this troll can do other than make light and warm up clothes, so that's one more reason for us to wait until it goes to sleep before we go back to the inn."

"What if it wakes up while we're there?"

"It won't. I think. What I've heard is that when a troll is locked in a troll hut, it wakes and sleeps at the bidding of the magician who controls it. We don't have to worry about it once it's put to sleep for the night. Not unless we're there long enough for the magician to come back and wake it again."

"You think. I distinctly heard you say 'I think.' That means you don't know."

Spinner nodded. "I've never seen one. All I know is what I've heard."

"And you don't know for certain that what you've heard is right."

Spinner shrugged.

*   *   *

The morning sun lit the grounds of the inn before it warmed the ridge side on which they sat. At first the only people they saw on the grounds of the inn were laborers doing chores; there seemed to be four of them, but neither Haft nor Spinner could be certain, as the laborers they saw were never all out at one time and there was no way of knowing if all of them were outside; there might be more inside. Still, before the sun rested its rays on them, a few of the soldiers they'd seen in the common room during the night's entertainment came out. Some got horses from the stable, others just walked away. Some of the soldiers followed the small road to the northwest, the direction from which Haft and Spinner had come. Others went southeast. Whenever soldiers went southeast, Spinner and Haft worried that they would see where they'd left the road and come looking for them. None ever did.

It wasn't until the mid-morning sun was warming their backs that anything odd appeared in the inn's glade. A merchant, accompanied by a few men in workers' clothing, walked across the glade to the trees on its southern verge, where there didn't appear to be a road or any other entrance to the glade. They didn't walk together, but spread out as they went, entering the forest at wide intervals. A few moments later faint sounds drifted up from within those trees, the neigh of a horse, the jingle of tackle, a creak of leather, a grumble of wheels beginning to turn.

Spinner and Haft looked at each other.

"That's why there weren't enough horses in the corral," Spinner said.

"Or any merchants' carts about," Haft added. He slipped off the log and stood in a crouch that kept him out of sight from the inn. "Let's go take a look at what's there," he said.

Spinner nodded, but didn't leave his seat on the tree trunk. "You're right, we need to look over there. But not yet. Let's wait until we see if any others are going that way any time soon." Where they sat, he could see the tops of the trees in the valley to the south of the inn. The foliage looked solid; there didn't seem to be another clearing. Maybe there was a concealed roadway. If there was, they wouldn't find much when they looked.

Haft jittered a bit. The waiting they'd already done had him anxious to act. But he had to concede that Spinner might be right about waiting a little longer. "All right." He sat again. Even though he tried to be quiet and patient, that wasn't in his character when there was action to be taken; he sat fidgeting. He stopped when another merchant and attendant workmen left the inn by its back entrance and headed to the south side of the glade. He started again when they were gone.

In a short while the sun was almost directly overhead, and Spinner said, "We should eat."

Haft hopped off the tree trunk. "I'll get the food," he said, just as Spinner knew he would. Spinner wasn't hungry; he just wanted to give Haft something to do.

Several more merchants and their helpers left the inn during the early afternoon, all of them spread out as they walked south to the trees. Each time merchants and helpers disappeared into the southern trees, the faint sounds of horses being harnessed and carts driven off drifted up from the valley. None of the merchants or their helpers returned to the inn. Spinner found that very curious. If he hadn't heard the sounds of horses being harnessed, he would have thought the merchants and their men were meeting wagons driving past on an unseen road.

It wasn't until the dinner hour that anyone came out from under the trees: a merchant, three helpers, and five bound people.

One of the helpers ran ahead to the inn. He came back out in a moment with a short, bandy-legged man wearing a drab cloak with a cowl pulled over his head. The bandy-legged man moved with a grace and confidence that was a startling contrast to his common-looking clothing and his short stature; he moved as though he should be wearing regal finery. Instead of walking toward the approaching merchant, he and the helper angled toward the fortresslike outbuilding. The merchant with his other helpers and the five prisoners also went toward the outbuilding.

"New slaves being brought in," Spinner said. He grabbed Haft's arm to keep him from rushing off to rescue the new slaves.

"But we've got to do something about this," Haft grumbled. "We have to free them."

"We will. Tonight. I swear." Spinner had studied the short man as well as he could, but the distance was too great for him to make out anything but his overall shape and the way he carried himself. He was sure he hadn't seen the man in the common room last night; his form and his confident attitude were too distinctive to be missed. Still, he thought there was something familiar about him. It took a couple of moments for him to realize what it was. "He's the slavemaster," he said. "The Golden Girl told me the slavemaster is a Jokapcul swordmaster. That man has the size of a Jokapcul and the movement of a natural swordsman. He has the key to the anklets. We have to find out where his room is."

"How are we going to do that?"

Spinner shook his head; he didn't have any idea. He wondered if the two of them together could stand up to the man, but he didn't look forward to finding out. He also wondered where the men-at-arms the Golden Girl had mentioned were—and how many there might be.

After a few minutes the merchant and his men emerged from the slaveholding building. The helpers rushed ahead, evidently looking forward to the comforts of the inn. The merchant followed more slowly; he was counting money. A few minutes more and the slavemaster came out. He made certain the stout door was firmly barred, then returned to the inn.

Soon, another merchant emerged from the south side of the forest, again with helpers and slaves. The slavemaster went into the outbuilding with them as well. That merchant was also counting money when he left the slave-holding building. The slavemaster stayed inside. A while later and two merchants with seven helpers and nearly two score slaves came from the forest and went into the outbuilding.

"I wonder how many slaves are in there," Spinner said softly.

"We've seen half a hundred or more delivered," Haft replied.

"And we didn't see any leave. There were merchants at the inn last night, they must have brought in slaves yesterday. How many did they bring? They must still be in that building."

Haft looked at the building and frowned. Several hundred people would make that building very crowded. He shuddered to think what it must be like inside. "We've been watching all day. Nobody has taken in food or brought out slops," he said.

"Maybe they don't feed them. Maybe they make the slaves stay in their own waste."

Haft cringed, then grew more resolute. "I look forward to killing these fiends tonight."

Spinner nodded but made no comment. He didn't look forward to the raid, and wouldn't until he knew how they were going to carry it out. And even then he might not look forward to it.

The dinner hour came and went. Spinner and Haft ate another cold meal. The road past the inn began to fill with men on foot and horse, locals and soldiers coming to the inn for the evening's entertainment. Windows lighted up on the inn's upper floors. Through one on the second floor they saw the slavemaster enter a room. Two men were with him and they wore what were obviously uniforms, though neither Haft nor Spinner recognized the army they represented. Not until the last man in closed the door did the slavemaster take off his cowled cloak. Now they could see his face, even though they still couldn't make out details. By the color of his skin he was certainly Jokapcul. His garb was utilitarian, the kind of clothing a man would wear if he knew he was going to be outside, perhaps the kind of clothes a man would wear if he expected bloody action.

"Last night in the common room I saw several men in that uniform," Spinner said. The uniforms were brown and green, indicating that their army moved in forests and probably hunted brigands. The only distinctive part of the uniforms was orange epaulettes. Spinner thought back, seeking details from his memory. "There were three at one table, two at another. I may have missed some, I don't know. At least two of them noted our uniforms and saluted us with their flagons."

The slavemaster appeared to give his men instructions, then the two bowed and left the room. The slavemaster moved to a part of the room that was out of their sight.

"Now we can make a plan," Haft said. "We know where the slavemaster sleeps, we know where to find the key, and we know how to recognize his men-at-arms."

Spinner nodded. "Now let's go and see what there is behind the trees to the south." He looked at the slave-holding outbuilding. "And after that, take a closer look at that place."

CHAPTER
THIRTEEN

South of the clearing they found a wagon park skillfully hidden under the trees. All of the underbrush was cleared from an area almost half the size of the inn's glade. Many of the trees in the park had been felled as well, but they were felled selectively. The trees that were left standing were those whose tops formed the canopy. Anyone looking down on the valley from the ridge sides would see only a continual sea of treetops and never guess at the existence of this park. While the remaining foliage overhead blocked most of the direct sunlight, it was not as dark there as elsewhere under the trees.

Half a dozen wagons stood horseless side by side between the mouths of two roads that emptied into the park from the south. At least two more roads entered the park—one from the east, one from the west. There were no obvious openings into the park—not even a footpath—from its north side, the direction of the inn. Two corrals held thirty or so horses, another corral was empty. Near the corrals there was a wood-frame building far larger than needed by the one hostler they saw tending the horses; smoke rising from the building's chimney flowed into an inverted tub, from which radiated an elaborate arrangement of tubes that led the smoke to far places, where it was diffused through the treetops. No pillar of smoke could rise to show a fire below.

Haft hefted his axe. "We can strike our first blow against the slavers here," he said softly. They squatted behind bushes left standing at the edge of the clearing, and peered through its branches.

"No," Spinner said.

"Why not? One man, he'd be easy to take."

"For several reasons," Spinner said slowly as he continued to examine the hidden park. "First, more slave traders may yet come before nightfall. They'll raise an alarm if they don't find him. They will surely raise an alarm if they find him dead. In either case, if an alarm is sounded too soon, we won't be able to free the slaves. Second, there are probably more hostlers, maybe even guards, in the building. Third, there may be watch-sprites we haven't spotted who would see and report us if we enter the clearing." He paused deep in thought for a moment, and Haft started looking around for any sign of watch-sprites. "And last," Spinner finally said, "do we really know that a man who is merely caring for horses deserves to die for the crimes of those who own the horses?"

Haft stopped looking for watch-sprites and looked at Spinner. "If he knows he's helping slavers, doesn't that make him guilty as well?"

"Possibly," was as much as Spinner would commit himself. Though he thought Haft's argument had merit, he didn't feel like discussing the philosophical differences between slave trading and working for slave traders. And he was more interested in freeing the slaves and getting away safely than in killing the helpers. "Or he might be a slave himself and have no choice in the matter. But regardless of his possible guilt, there are too many risks involved in killing that hostler now. I've seen enough here." He scuttled backward.

A corner of Haft's mouth twitched at Spinner's unwillingness to kill this helper of slavers, but he backed off as well. If the hostler was a slave, he shouldn't be killed.

They had stayed well inside the forest while making their way from where they'd observed the inn, but while they were examining the hidden park the sun dipped below the western ridge leaving the valley in shadow, even though the sky above was still day blue. Going back, they skirted the edge of the clearing, just inside the trees. They stopped once when they saw a man in the robes of a magician's apprentice come out of the woods on the west side of the glade.

The apprentice carried a metal container by a handle on its top. From the way the apprentice tilted to one side as he carried the container, it was obviously heavy. The apprentice went directly to the troll hut, where he put the container down and pulled a large ring of keys from a pocket of his robe. The apprentice unlocked and opened the door, picked up his container, and closed the door behind him when he entered the hut. After a few moments the troll stopped its rumbling and metallic noises came from inside the hut.

Haft poked Spinner. "Remember? When we were in the bath, you said you thought the troll stopped its rumbling for a short while?"

Spinner nodded; yes, he remembered very well.

"Do you think the apprentice is feeding the troll?"

"I don't know, but I can't think of what else he might be doing."

Shortly, the metallic noises stopped, and a moment later the troll's rumble began anew. The apprentice came back out and locked the door. His step was much lighter going back to the woods to the west of the glen than when he came in, and he swung the container lightly at his side.

"Now we know where the magician lives," Spinner said when the apprentice was out of sight.

"What good does it do us to know where the magician lives?"

Spinner merely shook his head. He knew that commanders on military operations always had to know more things than they ever used, simply to make sure there wasn't something they needed to know or do that they didn't. Then he grinned and looked at Haft. "It tells us what way not to go when we leave here."

Haft grunted. That didn't sound to him like enough reason

to bother with. And it didn't tell them how far away the magician lived, which he thought might be a worthwhile thing to know; the farther away, the longer it would take the magician to arrive if he decided to investigate what happened later that night.

No one else was in sight moving about the glade, so Spinner and Haft continued circling close to it. When they reached the spot where the forest came closest to the slave barn, they stopped.

"We may as well see if we can find out how many are in there," Haft said.

Spinner didn't reply. He was thinking about how to free those slaves later on. He said, "While we're doing that, we can check the door and find out how securely it's barred."

Haft crouched over, darted from the trees, and ran straight to the back of the slave barn. Spinner followed close behind.

They hunkered down against the back wall of the barn. Looking up, they made out narrow windows tucked up under the eaves. The stench that filled their nostrils came in the air carried down from those small windows—but it felt as though the fetid aroma oozed through the very walls.

"They do make them live in their slops!" Haft said. "It smells like the slops are never removed." He was very angry, and his voice showed it.

"Maybe there's a slops pit just on the other side of this wall," Spinner said, but he didn't believe it. He understood how Haft felt; he wanted to strike out at someone himself. He thought of the Golden Girl being held there when she was first brought to The Burnt Man.

From inside the building they heard the low keening of someone trying desperately not to cry. Several other voices failed in an attempt not to cry. Someone else moaned, yet another wailed.

Haft raised a fist to pound on the wall to get the attention of the imprisoned people inside; he wanted to tell them they would be free before morning. Spinner saw the motion, grabbed Haft's wrist and held his hand back.

"Don't," he said. "There may be guards inside."

"Then let's go inside now and kill them," Haft whispered harshly.

"We can't do anything here until we've dealt with those inside the inn," Spinner said.

Haft jerked his wrist from Spinner's grip but made no further attempt to strike the wall.

"Now let's examine the front," Spinner said. The sky was almost as dark as night, and the moon was several hours from rising, so the darkness they crept through along the side of the building was almost complete. Ahead of them, glowing windows showed where the inn was. In the lead, Spinner saw someone, probably Master Yoel, peering intently out a window that looked like it was in the kitchen. The innkeeper turned to say something to someone out of sight, then peered out again; he seemed to be searching both the glade and the ridge to the west.

It was fortunate that he paused to look at the innkeeper for a cold light flooded the front of the slave barn then. Spinner instinctively stepped back into Haft before he froze in place. Haft froze as well when the front of the barn lit up—except for his eyes, which darted everywhere looking for danger, and his hand, which adjusted its grip on the axe. But where they were the side of the slave barn remained in darkness, so no one ran at them with weapons raised, no cry of alarm sounded.

"What is that awful light?" Haft asked with a tremor in his voice.

"Wait here," Spinner replied. He lowered himself to his belly and slithered to the corner of the slave barn. He lay his head on its side in the dirt at the corner of the barn and inched far enough forward that he could see the front. Hanging on a wrought-iron arm above the barn door was a globe that hadn't been visible from their hiding place on the ridge. The globe glared with an internal light so bright it illuminated the front of the barn almost like day.

Still, no one ran toward him with weapons raised, no one cried an alarm. Spinner took another moment to observe what he could of the door. It didn't appear to have a lock on it, merely a heavy bar holding it closed. If that was all that secured the door, it would be an easy matter to open it when the time came. He slithered backward until Haft tapped him on the feet.

Spinner described the unexpected troll-light above the door while they made their way back to the observation post, where they'd left the horses.

"Why didn't we see it last night?" Haft demanded. "Did you do or say something this morning to make them suspicious? Do they expect something to happen tonight?"

"Last night I didn't look out any windows in the direction of that barn so I wouldn't have seen the troll-light," Spinner replied. "Did you look out there?"

Haft didn't answer. He didn't remember looking out a window last night either.

The mare seemed glad to have Haft return to her—that's how he chose to interpret the nip she gave him: a love bite. He didn't want to think she bit him because she was angry about being left alone, hobbled, and tethered to a tree; he wasn't comfortable enough with horses to be around one that was mad at him.

"It is many hours yet before we go into the inn," Spinner said, "and we'll have to travel many hours beyond that before we can rest. So we better get some sleep."

Haft grunted. He didn't want to wait many hours before they entered the inn. But he understood why they had to. He said, "I'll take first watch."

Spinner lay down against the tree trunk and was asleep in moments.

Haft sat on the tree trunk and watched the inn. The first

thing he saw was something else he hadn't noticed the night before: twin lamps flanked the sign board above the inn's door. The lamps weren't a flickering orange like every other lamp he'd ever seen illuminating an inn sign at night. These lamps gave out a steady bluish light. Maybe Spinner was right, he thought, and the lamp had been lit over the slave barn door last night and they didn't see it simply because they hadn't looked outside.

He looked at the lighted windows and tried to recall what rooms in the inn they opened onto. Serving maids rushing about with trays, and cooks sweating over caldrons and spits told him which set of windows opened into the kitchen. A corner window showed the counting room; though he didn't see anyone there, he made out a clerk's high desk and a scribe's low one. The windows of the common room were closed and shuttered. Haft had never thought about it before, but he realized now that every inn he'd ever seen that offered entertainment kept its common room windows closed and shuttered during the entertainment, or at least shuttered if not closed. He realized it must be to prevent passersby from standing outside a window and watching and listening to the entertainment without having to pay for food or drink. That was a wise move on the part of innkeepers, he thought.

Only a couple of windows were lit on the third floor, and those glowed with the warm, flickering light of oil lamps. Haft recalled there weren't any troll-lights in the room he and Spinner had rented the night before—a room in which he spent the night alone. He didn't see any movement through the third story windows. There were more bright windows on the second floor. In most of them he could make out men dressing or doing other things that looked like preparations for going out. Most likely they were getting ready to go down to the common room for the entertainment. These were probably men who'd been to the inn before and knew the best was kept for last.

He didn't have to decide which lighted window on the

second floor belonged to the slavemaster's room—only one window glowed with the cold blue of troll-light. He fixed that window's location in his mind and tried to visualize the layout of the second floor. Though he didn't think he'd been in that part of the inn, he assumed the second floor was laid out in a simple manner. After a moment's thought he was sure he could find the room without hesitation. If only he could find out where the men-at-arms spent their nights. He kept watching, but none of the windows gave any hint of that.

A steady trickle of men trooped to the inn door even after the entertainment had begun. Every time one of them arrived and opened the door, a spurt of raucous laughter came to Haft's ears, often accompanied by a few notes of music. Nobody left.

In time, Haft's eyelids began to sag. He woke Spinner to take the watch so he could sleep. Before he lay down he briefed Spinner on what he'd seen, neglecting to mention only that he thought he knew the way to the slavemaster's room.

Spinner whiled away his watch the same way Haft had his. A part of his mind noted the same things about the same windows, and that troll-lights were unseen above the ground floor except in the slavemaster's room. He didn't put much thought into how to quickly find that room once they were inside the inn. He was more concerned with where the slavemaster's men-at-arms would be once the inn had gone to sleep. He also wondered how the slave traders would react if there was enough noise to wake them. He thought it likely that most of the men spending the night in the inn were slavers or in their employ.

He sent his mind back to the night before and how the innkeeper acted oddly in the corridor to the hidden stairs: Master Yoel must have been sending signals of some sort, or deactivating warding spells, to make opening the hidden door safe. The first three would be easy to duplicate, he thought. There must be a lever or a trip of some sort on the column and the frieze and inside the hole in the wall. But which tassel did

he tug, and did it make a difference if a different one was
tugged first? He moved his hands about in the dark, trying to
remember the pattern the innkeeper used on the false wall.

The easiest thing would be to force the innkeeper to open
the door to the hidden entrance to the cellar. He was sure that
any other possible entrances to the cellar were locked or
warded. Unfortunately, trying to get the innkeeper to open the
way might also be the most dangerous thing to do. Was there
another way to gain entrance?

Men started drifting out of the inn, singly and in groups—
the evening's entertainment was over. When the door opened
to let customers out, Spinner saw that the lights were up in the
common room. Revelers went by foot and by horse, in both
directions on the road; some went straight into the forest to
the north. Spinner didn't see any go south across the glade to
the hidden wagon park, nor did any go to the southwest, as
had the magician's apprentice after he put the troll to sleep.
More windows flickered to light in the upper floors of the inn,
and through them he saw men preparing for bed. The windows Spinner was most interested in, though, were those near
the slavemaster's room. The bluish light in that room had
gone out some time earlier.

Lamps were lit in the rooms on both sides of the slavemaster's quarters. Two men entered each of those rooms,
wearing the uniforms of the slavemaster's men-at-arms. One
man in each room undressed for bed, while the other busied
himself with other matters. Then the lamps went out and the
doors opened while the men who hadn't prepared for bed left.

Spinner was certain there were at least five men-at-arms.
The Golden Girl said there might be a dozen or more. Two were
accounted for, asleep in the rooms flanking their master's.
Where were the others? Spinner had a feeling they wouldn't be
hard to find—but he had a very uncomfortable feeling they
might find him and Haft first.

Maybe what they should do first was go to the stable and
free the handymen and laborers, the male slaves who were

quartered there, and arm them. Then it wouldn't only be two Marines against an unknown number of men-at-arms. No, it was likely the handymen wouldn't believe they were truly being freed or that they could take on the slavemaster's men and win. If they helped and the rescue failed, their lives—if they were allowed to live—would be even worse than they were already. Spinner knew that he and Haft would have to deal with the men-at-arms and get the key to the slaves' anklets from the slavemaster. That had to be the first step. Only when they had it and began unlocking the anklets would any of the slaves believe them.

They were going to need a diversion to ensure that the men-at-arms wouldn't organize themselves and attack them. In the confusion caused by the diversion, they could get into the slavemaster's room, somehow bypass warding demons, slay him, and take his key. Then they could freely move through the inn and get into the cellar to free the Golden Girl and the other women slaves.

In his mind, Spinner rehearsed going along that short corridor behind the stage, fingering the trips on the column, the frieze, the hole in the wall, tugging the tassel, moving his hands on the false wall, going down those stairs, opening the door to that candled room with the drapes and cushions. He tried not to think about finding another man with the Golden Girl.

A flicker of movement near the troll hut caught his eye. Enough light from the globe above the slave barn's door reached the troll hut for him to see the apprentice opening the door. Light that seemed to emanate from the apprentice's hand flicked on inside the hut and was visible for a second before the apprentice closed the door, but not long enough for Spinner to see anything inside it. In a moment the troll's rumbling stopped and all the remaining bluish light in and around the inn went out. The apprentice came back out. A cold light he held in his hand blinked out as he stepped through the door.

The glade was dark except for a few oil lamps flickering in some of the upper floor rooms of the inn and lamps in the kitchen, where Spinner could see the serving maids and cooks completing their night's cleaning. A short while after that, the innkeeper inspected the kitchen. Then three men-at-arms appeared to escort the serving maids out. Spinner assumed they were taking them to the cellar. He wondered if a guard was kept in the cellar corridor overnight. He hadn't seen one the night before, but maybe one was posted only after any men who paid for the night with one of the women were locked into the rooms with them; he had gone down while the kitchen was still being cleaned. It might be that other men were led into the cellar afterward. Well, that was a problem he and Haft would have to deal with when and if they encountered it.

The innkeeper sent the cooks out of the kitchen, then went around himself to put out the lamps and candles. He carried the one remaining lighted lamp when he left the kitchen and closed the door behind him.

A moment later the door to the counting room opened and the innkeeper entered it with the lamp in his hand. He went through the room and into the next, where he looked out the window as though searching the glade and ridge side for intruders. Then he pulled the shutters closed and Spinner could see no more. But he knew where to find the innkeeper now—either to kill him or to get his assistance in opening the hidden door to the cellar. At no time did he see the innkeeper or anyone else place a ward on the kitchen door. Maybe, he thought, the reputation of the inn was such that Master Yoel and the slavemaster were confident that no one would enter unbidden during the night.

The time for observation was over. It was time for action. Spinner woke Haft and they briefly discussed what they were going to do. Haft particularly liked the diversion Spinner came up with.

CHAPTER
FOURTEEN

Spinner and Haft assumed there were no watch-sprites hidden about watching the glade. They made that assumption partly because too many people had walked freely about the glade during the day; if guardian watch-sprites were present, how could they tell the difference between those who were allowed freedom of passage in the open valley and those whom they were supposed to report? The sprites would be crying false alarms constantly, unless—and this was something neither man wanted to think about—dryads were on watch, who only watched at night. So they simply gave the slave barn's guards a wide berth while they walked across the dark glade to the back of the inn.

To satisfy their curiosity, they did pass close to the troll hut.

"Pffew," Haft snorted when they were a few feet away. "Why didn't you tell me they stink like that?" He cupped a hand over his mouth and nose to block the acrid, oily smell emanating from the small building.

Spinner coughed softly and covered his own nose and mouth. "Because I didn't know," he whispered.

The air around the troll hut felt like it would be visible if there were light to see by. They hurried past, trying not to breathe.

"They even make the troll live in its own slops!" Haft said. "I wonder why it doesn't break free when the magician's apprentice comes to feed it?"

Spinner shook his head. He knew nothing about trolls' living habits. "Maybe trolls like living in their own slops," he said. "Or maybe it's chained so it can't break free."

The kitchen door was sturdy wood on its lower half, but its upper half was set with a grid of small glass panes. Haft tested the door. It was barred from the inside. Without hesitation he drew his knife and sharply smacked the hilt against a bottom corner glass pane. Large shards fell to the floor inside the door and shattered, making more noise than either of them wanted. They froze for a moment, listening, but heard no sound, not even a halloo from the guards outside the slave barn.

Haft used his knife to pry out the remaining shards of glass and carefully set them down, then he stuck his hand inside and felt around. The bar was too big for him to lift out one-handed without dropping it, and the noise of the bar falling on the floor would surely excite some interest inside. He withdrew his hand and broke the other bottom corner pane. Again they froze and listened for any sign that someone had heard the breaking glass, and detected no sound or movement.

Together, Haft reaching in from one side and Spinner from the other, they lifted the bar and turned it around so it stood on one end, leaning against the wall next to the door. Haft quietly swung the door open. They slipped inside and eased it closed. Then they stood for several moments, again waiting to see if someone would come to investigate the noises and letting their eyes adjust to the greater darkness inside the inn.

No one came, and in a few moments they could make out the vague forms of the stoves, ovens, and counters that filled the kitchen. They didn't bar the door behind them; they didn't want to leave any secured doors between themselves and their exit in case they had to retreat in a hurry. Weapons held ready, they padded softly, cautiously, to the door to the common room. Haft opened it just far enough to squeeze through. He stepped to one side, and Spinner slipped through and closed the door behind him.

The common room was even darker than the kitchen had been, and at first they could make out nothing except a faint sliver of warm light where the stairway to the upper floors was. They held still and listened. All they could hear were the sounds of a sleeping building: somewhere someone coughed; someone else snored loudly; someone cried out during a nightmare. Haft tapped Spinner's arm, and they crept toward the faint light at the stairwell. When they reached the stairway, they climbed along one side of the stairs to reduce the chances of a loose tread squealing underfoot.

The stairway went up several steps, then turned right at a small landing. A few more steps and it made another right turn, so when they reached the second floor, they were facing back, over the common room. At the top of the stairway a corridor went perpendicular to the head of the stairs. At each end and in the middle, another corridor branched off from it, leading toward the front of the inn. A low-lit lamp was at each intersection. The lamps gave just enough light to guide a night-waker who had to find his way to the privy closet. The walls of the corridors were white, and on both sides every few paces along them were the dark rectangles of doors. The two men looked for the glowing red-eyes of watch-sprites but didn't see any.

Spinner no longer wondered what such a large inn was doing in so isolated a place; he now knew that most of those rooms were needed by the slave traders and their employees, or by those who provided goods to them. He didn't think many of the rooms were let out to innocent travelers such as himself and Haft, or to local people who came for an evening's entertainment. So it wouldn't bother him if some of the sleeping men were injured, even killed, by the diversion they had planned.

Haft pointed along the corridor to the right and made a sign. Spinner nodded. First, though, they had to create their diversion. They took the corridor to the left and turned into the adjoining corridor to the far corner of the second floor, where the stairway to the third story began. Above, they saw a light so dim they weren't sure whether it was there or they were seeing an afterimage of the light on the second floor. They didn't notice the small round holes high in the walls at the end of the corridors, holes behind which sprites watched without showing their glowing eyes.

They mounted the stairway to the third floor as cautiously as they had climbed from the common room. The third floor of the inn wasn't as big as the second; its corridors were narrower, its ceiling lower. There was a door at the end of the corridor at the foot of the stairs on the second floor, but on the smaller third floor there was a shuttered window next to the head of the stairway. The corridor the stairs emptied into went straight across the building to another window. As on the second floor, three corridors branched off from it, but they were closer to each other, as were the doors. One small lamp guttered at the ends of the corridors that met at the head of the stairs. The light was dim enough on the third floor that they couldn't see the small holes facing onto each corridor from high on the walls.

Spinner signed to Haft: They were above the end of the common room that held the stage; they would create their diversion at the opposite corner of the third floor.

Haft nodded and set out that way.

As they passed the first two intersections, alert for lurking danger, they looked down them. The middle corridor had no light of its own. They turned at the far corridor and started checking doors near its end, looking for an unoccupied room. They found one right where they hoped to—on the outside, near the corner opposite the common room stage.

After making sure the shutters were tightly closed, Haft used his tinderbox to light the room's oil lamp. By its warm glow they saw that the room was small and sparsely furnished, exactly like the one they had rented the night before. It held two narrow pallets, one against each side wall. Their thin mattresses would suit the Marines' purposes perfectly. Spinner slit one open with his knife, Haft cut open the other. They were filled with feathers, horsehair, and straw. The stuffing was sticky and moist from the sweat of the many men who had slept on the mattresses.

"It feels too wet," Haft whispered. He had his tinderbox ready to strike a spark. "I'm not sure I can light it."

"I've seen wetter things burn when lit by a salamander," Spinner answered confidently.

Haft looked at him. "Is it still alive? I thought you ran out of food for it a couple of days ago."

Spinner nodded. "I did." He drew the salamander's house from the pouch he carried it in. "I don't know if it's still alive. It's worth a try."

"If it's still alive, it might be able to get out of its house."

"I hope it will."

Haft's eyes widened with fear. "Be careful it doesn't bite you," he said, remembering the demon from the demon spitter.

Spinner spared him a glance. "Only if it can get to me." He shook his head. "This one won't bite. If it gets me, I'll go up in flames." Haft started backing away as Spinner studied the tiny house and the bed frames. He'd already thought about how to open the door without the salamander attacking his hand if it got out, and was sure he knew how to do it. Fairly sure. "You wait in the corridor," he said.

Haft half opened one side of the shutters before he backed out of the room. Spinner knelt by the end of the beds and placed the salamander house on its side on the floor, the lever that opened the door against the leg of the bed. He backed into the corridor, lowered his staff to the floor, and slid it toward the salamander house until it touched.

"Back away," he said. He couldn't keep fear of the salamander out of his voice. He gave his staff a sharp shove to jam the house against the bed leg. The lever popped the door open, and the salamander shot through the small door. It was still alive—and much thinner than it had been. The small demon flickered with yellow, orange, and blue fire as it whipped about; its voice crackled and hissed in fury.

With no human hand to punish for its hunger, the demon flailed at the straw and cords and wood; everything it touched burst into flame. In seconds the mattresses were engulfed and flame was eating at the bed. Fire lanced across the floor and began to lick at the walls.

"You did it!" Haft whispered. "I didn't think you could! Let's go." He grabbed Spinner's shoulder and yanked him away from the growing conflagration.

They withdrew to the nearer corner of the corridor and squatted in the deepest shadow they could find to wait for the guards in front of the slave barn to see the fire and sound an alarm.

Tendrils of smoke began to drift out of the open door. After a few moments Haft tensed and looked down the adjacent corridor; he thought he heard another sound above the pops and crackles of the growing fire. All he could see along the corridors' lengths were the small lamps at the far end of each. The other sounds came from the direction of those lamps.

"I think someone's coming," Haft murmured, his eyes searching for the invisible sources of the sounds that were coming closer.

"I hear it too," Spinner said. He looked as well.

They eased to their feet with their weapons held ready and peered intently toward the lamps. Nothing moved, but they were certain they heard the shuffling of feet along both corridors. Did the air along the corridors somehow waver in the night? Or were the flickering, almost invisible shadows the result of overactive imaginations fueled by tension?

Spinner's mouth and throat went dry. He tried to work up some saliva so he could swallow and wondered, if someone was approaching unseen, how he could effectively swing his staff in a corridor that was narrower than the length of the staff. Haft looked uncertain and held his axe ready to strike or to parry a blow.

More smoke flowed into the corridor as the fire grew large enough to light the hallway.

Suddenly, someone cried *"Fire!"* from the outside— apparently the fire had eaten through the shutters and the guards at the slave barn saw the flames. A moment later a loud gong tolled somewhere, followed by the noises of men waking in fear and confusion.

"Now," Haft said.

The next step of the plan was to run along the corridors, pounding on doors, shouting "Fire! Fire!" But before they could take a step a voice boomed from directly in front of them: "What do you mean by this abomination? Who do you think you are to cause this destruction in my home?" Eight men appeared before them, four in each corridor. All eight were armed, swords at the ready. The armed men didn't appear at the far ends of the corridors; they were suddenly *there*, three or four paces away, wearing the green and brown uniforms of the slavemaster's men-at-arms. Even in the darkness of the corridor, Spinner and Haft could make out that each man had a woman sitting on his shoulder, and each woman wore a long, diaphanous robe through which her voluptuous form could be glimpsed. No, not women, they were too small, not much more than a foot high. The miniature women giggled and cried out in tiny voices that tinkled like chimes.

"Lalla Mkouma," they said between giggles. *"Lalla Mkouma!"*

"Wh-What?" Haft stammered.

"Yield!" one of the swordsmen demanded.

Haft faced the quartet coming through the firelight, and Spinner faced the other four. Haft yanked his eyes from the tiny women and answered the command by flying into the four he faced. His axe swung in a diagonal arc that just

missed the walls and ceiling. The nearest man tried to parry
Haft's blow but couldn't get his sword up in time. He screamed
as the axe chopped off his arm at the shoulder, but stopped
when the blade buried itself in his heart. Haft jumped back,
pulling his weapon free as his victim collapsed facedown.

The miniature woman who'd sat on the dead man's shoulder landed on her feet. Tiny fists on her flaring hips, she stared
briefly into the corpse's face, then reared back and spat on it.
Then she scurried along his side until she reached his hand.
She jumped up to stomp on it with all the force she could
muster.

Distracted by her antics, it was a moment before Haft noticed the lunging sword and slapped at it with his axe. Then he
forgot about the impossibly small women and slashed back-
handed at the man who had almost struck home on him. The
spike backing his axe blade sunk into the man's belly and he
fell backward, clutching his middle and screaming. Haft took
a step toward the remaining two men facing him. One nervously licked his lips. The other lunged.

Haft sidestepped and swung his axe in a shallow overhead
arc at the man who, overbalanced, staggered forward. The
man-at-arms gave a surprised grunt and splayed flat on the
floor.

The remaining man gasped, spun, and fled down the corridor. Suddenly he vanished. Haft didn't hesitate. He drew his
arm back and threw his axe in a flat trajectory. Its blade thunked
into thin air. The runner screamed briefly. Insanely, he was
visible again, his hands flung out toward the walls. He
crashed to the floor. The tiny female figure on his shoulder
tumbled when she hit the floor and scampered away.

Spinner was having a harder time of it. The narrowness of
the corridor hampered use of the staff; he could only rotate it
perpendicular to his front, thrust and jab. Still, when Haft
turned from his fight, his companion was dealing with only
two men-at-arms; two others were down. The remaining two

were slowly forcing Spinner back to the wall, where he would be even less able to maneuver his weapon.

Haft whipped out his belt knife and threw it, and one of Spinner's attackers went down, the hilt protruding from his throat.

The sudden loss of his partner distracted the remaining man for an instant, and Spinner cracked him alongside the head. The man staggered into the wall, and Spinner speared him in the throat.

The fight had lasted less than a minute. Eight men-at-arms were down, only one still alive, the one Spinner had jabbed in the belly and groin. A few room doors were open and their occupants were looking out, trying to find out what the excitement was about. Spinner and Haft ignored them.

Without a word, Haft ran past the now rapidly spreading fire to retrieve his axe from where it stood in its last victim's back. He had to run through flames to rejoin Spinner, who was kneeling at the side of the lone survivor, demanding to know how they got so close without being seen.

"The Lalla Mkouma," the man gasped, holding himself low. "The Lalla Mkouma. Invisibility." He moaned softly; it was painful for him to speak. Slowly, he took one hand from his injured parts and moved it to his throat.

"What? How?" Haft asked when he heard the man's explanation. He went to the man he'd downed with his knife, pulled it free, turned to the wounded man and slit his throat. Then he wiped his blade clean on the man's shirt.

"Why did you kill him?" Spinner demanded. "He wasn't able to fight anymore."

"He might be able to again before we are away from here," Haft said without looking at the last dead man. "Hey!" Something small gripped his knee, then a weight hung from it. He looked down. One of the miniature women was climbing his leg. "Whoa, wait a minute!" he said, and shooed at her with one hand.

The tiny woman ignored his hand and quickly gained his

shoulder. She wrapped her small arms around his neck and tinkled into his ear, *"Oo nizzem. Oo kilm baddum. Ee likuu."*

"Spinner?" Haft turned to his companion for help as another of the miniatures clambered to Spinner's shoulder. The tiny figure snuggled against Spinner's neck and spoke into his ear. Then she swung one leg over his shoulder so she straddled it. Her diaphanous robe lengthened and spread out, and she spun it wide enough to engulf Spinner. They vanished.

"Spinner! Where are you?" Haft screamed.

"Where did you go?" Spinner's voice replied from where he vanished.

Haft realized the voluptuous creature on his shoulder was twirling her robe around him. Air was moving around him like a tiny whirlwind.

"I'm right here. Can't you see me?"

"No. I hear you, but I can't see anything where your voice is." Spinner reached out tentatively to where Haft's voice came from and felt a rapidly moving stream of air. He pushed his hand past the resistance and felt Haft's chest.

"By the gods," he swore. "These creatures make us invisible.

"Naw kretue!" the thing on his shoulder tinkled into his ear. *"Lalla Mkouma! M'likmoo! Oo nizzem."*

"How do we make them stop?" There was an edge of panic to Haft's voice.

"Rubbum egg," the Lalla Mkouma on his left shoulder piped into his ear.

"What?" Rubber egg?

"Rubbum egg," she repeated. *"Gimmum han."*

Cautiously, not sure of what the creature meant, Haft shifted the axe to his left hand and raised his right to his shoulder. Tiny hands gripped his finger, pulling with more strength than he would have expected so tiny a creature to possess. When his fingertips reached what must have been the thigh of the Lalla Mkouma, she said, *"Rubbum."*

Despite feeling that there was something distinctly wrong

about caressing the leg of the tiny woman, Haft gently rubbed her thigh. The Lalla Mkouma giggled into his ear and her robe settled out of its spin.

"I can see you!" Spinner exclaimed.

"Rub her thigh! That makes them stop."

Spinner did as Haft said. He reappeared.

More doors were open by that time, and more men looked out. Most of them saw the fire and cried an alarm. The few who saw Spinner and Haft reappear said rapid prayers and followed the panicked exodus of those already in the corridor. "We'll need another one of these little ladies for the Golden Girl," Spinner said.

As though invited, another of the miniature women climbed onto each of them and snuggled against the free side of their necks.

"Now we have a better chance of getting the key," Spinner said grimly, but his eyes rolled uncertainly toward the female forms on his shoulders. "Make us invisible again?" he asked.

The woman on his left shoulder giggled and spun her robe. The two men vanished.

They ran through the growing crowd of men struggling to the stairway in the far corner of the third floor. The only other way down was to jump from the windows. They pushed and shoved and yanked running men out of their way. The crowd panicked more as men were pushed aside by invisible beings. Some of the fleeing men ducked into rooms to get out of the way of the phantoms who were knocking them about. Several fought their way to windows, concluding that the dangers of a drop of more than twenty feet was better than being mauled by phantoms or getting crushed by the panic in the corridor.

None of the men rushing to leave the second floor had seen flames, and none of them had seen a ghostly fight or been shoved by phantoms; their flight was less panicky though equally confused. Spinner and Haft pushed against the flow of men toward the stairs leading down to the common room then ran around the outside of the second floor to reach the slavemaster's quarters.

Behind them, someone was trying to bring order to the chaos and organize a fire brigade to combat the flames.

CHAPTER
FIFTEEN

Four men-at-arms stood outside the open door to the slave-master's quarters. Spinner stopped. He heard Haft continue to move toward them and held out an arm to stop him; the guards weren't looking down the corridors, but at a green, dimly glowing ball that hovered in midair at waist height before them. He also noticed a few shimmers and glints of light in the air at throat and ankle level between them and the guards.

Spinner pulled Haft back far enough around the corner for them to talk without being heard by the guards. In a few words he described the shimmering wires he'd seen. Haft thought the glints were probably from wires stretched across the corridor. Neither had a guess about the glowing ball.

"It might be a counterspell to the power of the Lalla Mkouma," Spinner said. "Remember, right before the soldiers appeared in front of us, the voice that demanded to know who we were? The slavemaster must also be a magician. He knew exactly where we were and told his men. Otherwise they wouldn't have been able to come at us the way they did. He probably knows the Lalla Mkouma are protecting us."

"How could he know where we were?" Haft asked. We didn't see any watch-sprites, no little houses on the walls."

"I don't know how, but he must have known. And he probably knows we have the creatures."

"Naw kretue!" an annoyed voice tinkled into his ear. *"Lalla Mkouma!"*

"Lalla Mkouma," Spinner nervously corrected himself, then hurried on. "His men are ready to make us visible when we attack them. So we have to get close enough to stop them before they can activate the counterspell. It looked to me like there are few enough wires between here and there for us to avoid tripping on them if we're careful."

"And the slavemaster is supposed to be a master swordsman as well," Haft said. He was beginning to think the situation through and was becoming cautious. "As soon as we attack his men, he will join in the fight and we'll lose whatever advantage surprise gives us. So we have to find a way to avoid fighting with him and his men at the same time."

Spinner looked with admiration at where he was sure Haft was. His companion didn't usually think things through so clearly. "Do you have another idea?"

"Maybe. Wait here."

Spinner reached for him but grabbed at air—Haft was already gone. Spinner stayed put. As long as the Lalla Mkouma worked its magic on Haft's shoulder, he knew he had no way of knowing where to search for him. He listened. He couldn't hear Haft's movement, but sounds from farther away indicated that the fire brigade was getting itself better organized.

A moment later Spinner jumped at Haft's voice near his ear.

"There's another door open between here and the slavemaster's room. We can go in there. Maybe his window is still open. If it is, the outside wall is rough enough to give us handholds so we can climb across it to the window. I looked—his shutters are open. We can climb inside and catch him by surprise. By the time his men come in to find out what the noise is about, we should have taken him and the key. We can probably get out without having to fight them."

Spinner stared at the empty air his friend's voice came from. "Haft," he said slowly, "I can't believe you came up with this idea."

"What do you mean? It'll work."

"I know it will. It's brilliant. It's just that you never think like this."

Haft flushed at the praise, but his voice was calm when he replied, "You always do the thinking, I never have to. This time you didn't, so I did."

Spinner grinned. "Maybe I should give you more chances to think. Lead the way."

Haft put an unseen hand on Spinner's arm and said, "This way."

The open door they headed for was the third door before the slavemaster's room. Along the way they ducked under one throat-high shimmering light and stepped over two at ankle level.

They reached the open door without being noticed and then leaned out the window to examine the wall. The stones weren't cut true, and the gaps where they joined weren't filled with mortar.

"That looks easy enough," Haft whispered.

Spinner wasn't as sure.

Above, men were shouting as they worked to put out the fire. Below them on the ground, men were scurrying back and forth, doing what little they could to assist in the fight against the fire. Others clustered in small groups between the inn and the slave barn, watching the fire flaring from the windows on the third floor.

Spinner examined the crowd. "I don't see any of the women who work here," he murmured.

Haft grunted. He didn't see any of the women either. "Maybe they're on the other side of the building."

Spinner didn't reply. He turned his face toward the Lalla Mkouma that had first climbed to his shoulder. "Do you understand what we're going to do?" he asked.

"Yss," she replied. "Ee goam oo." She pressed her miniature bosom into his cheek as she leaned around his head to chatter something at the Lalla Mkouma on his other shoulder.

The other chattered back, then clambered to the floor and

up onto a small table. *"Ee way'um ere,"* she piped. Seconds later she was joined by one of Haft's Lalla Mkouma.

"Haft, are you ready?" Spinner asked.

"On my way," Haft replied. He climbed through the window, probed down with his toes, searching for a hold, and found one quickly. Reaching across with one hand, he found a space between stones where he could get a firm grip. He pulled himself out the rest of the way and let go of the sill. In a few seconds he had shuffled far enough away from the window for Spinner to follow.

In seconds Spinner found himself clinging to the outside wall, high enough up that if he lost his grip and fell he might break a leg when he hit the ground below.

"Stop," Haft said when he reached the closed shutters of the next window. The shutters were well-constructed and tight; as far as he could reach, he couldn't find a fingerhold across them. But the sill protruded from beneath the shutters. "I'm going to try to go below the window," he said, his voice at normal volume. By then the people on the ground were making enough noise to mask any noise he and Spinner made. Haft stretched one leg downward; it was a long stretch before his questing toes found another gap they could slip into and hold his weight. He lowered himself and the protruding sill offered better purchase than the stones had.

"I'm across," he said when he reached the other side. The stretch down wasn't as difficult for Spinner because he was taller, but the traverse wasn't as easy, likewise because he was taller. But he made it to the other side with no more difficulty than Haft had.

The shutters of the next window were open; the sill would give an easy grip and allow them to pass it quickly. But it was one of the rooms the men-at-arms occupied, and a lamp was lit inside, so anyone there might hear them. Haft stopped at the side of the window, shifted his hands and feet, then stuck his head inside the window to look around. There was only one corner of the room he couldn't see into, but the room looked empty and the door was closed. He could lower himself far enough to cross with his hands on the stone below the sill or he could take the chance that nobody was in the corner he couldn't see.

He told Spinner what he saw and what he was doing and took the chance. He was across the window faster than he'd covered any other part of the wall. Now it was only a few more feet to the slavemaster's window.

"Wait here while I look inside," Haft whispered when Spinner caught up with him.

Haft listened carefully at the corner of the window. Even if nobody was talking or moving about, occupied rooms tended to sound occupied. No one was talking in the slavemaster's room or moving about, nor could Haft hear any breathing. But the room sounded like someone was in it; his ears didn't detect the hollow quality of an empty room. He slowly eased himself down the wall to where his fingers could get a purchase on the stone of the wall below the sill, and took another shuffling step to his right so he could look over the sill.

No one lunged at him, no one was even looking in his direction, but what he saw inside the room made him more afraid than he had ever been. Not even the gray tabur or the seven Jokapcul cavalrymen he and a wounded Spinner had faced frightened him as much.

The slavemaster was alone in the room. He wasn't wearing the nondescript cloak he wore when he went to the slave barn. In its place he wore armor of leather and metal plates similar to the armor worn by the cavalrymen, but more ornate. A finely wrought, ornate sword stood ready to hand. It was longer than the Jokapcul cavalry sword. Another sword, shorter than the saber issued to the Frangerian Marines, was next to it. The shorter sword wasn't as ornate as the longer one, but it was more suited to swinging in that room. Haft thought if he was armed and armored thus, the slavemaster must truly be the master swordsman the Golden Girl said he was. What unnerved him, however, was something else. The slavemaster was

hunched over, talking to a hideous winged demon with red,
glowing eyes. The demon was the size of a large owl and had
claws bigger than the claws on the biggest eagle Haft had
ever seen. And they were both talking Jokapcul.

Haft suddenly wished that Spinner hadn't noticed the odd
anklets on the serving maids, that he hadn't asked the Golden
Girl about them, that she hadn't told him, that he himself
didn't care about the evil of slavery, that they had simply continued on their journey. Two young Marines, especially two
very good and self-confident Marines like them, could go up
against a very good swordsman and expect to win. But a sorcerer, or even a high wizard, was entirely too powerful for
them to face, and this slavemaster was certainly that.

He was about to move back, to urge Spinner into the open
window they'd passed moments before so he could tell him
they had to end this quest, to give it up, when an unearthly
scream came from the side. He jerked his head in that direction and saw another apparition, one even more frightening,
hovering a few yards away: a hoard of bees silently buzzed
just beyond Spinner's other side. They were in a formation,
mimicking the shape of a winged demon like the one the
slavemaster was talking to.

Abruptly, the bees began buzzing loudly. They swarmed
past Spinner, around Haft, and into the open window to the
slavemaster and the winged monster. Slavemaster and demon
jerked their heads toward the bees. The buzzing of the swarm
changed in pitch and tone, then the winged demon looked
past it to the window and garbled something. The slavemaster
jumped to his feet, the smaller sword in hand, and raced toward
the window.

Realizing it was too late to retreat, Haft did the only thing
he could: he heaved himself over the windowsill, tumbled
into the room, and rolled in a direction that would take him
past the charging enemy. His hip clipped the slavemaster's
shins as he went by, causing the man to stumble. Haft surged
to his feet and stood rigid, holding his axe ready. Somehow,

the Lalla Mkouma on his shoulder held her grip and kept spinning her robe. The slavemaster regained his balance almost immediately and slowly pirouetted, the sword held ready in both hands, looking intently into all parts of the room, but as quietly as Haft stood, he couldn't be seen or heard.

Two of the guards from the corridor burst through the doorway simultaneously and were briefly jammed together in the door frame. Once through, they stood in place and looked around when they saw what their master was doing; each had his sword at the ready. Haft sidled one step away from them. The slavemaster said something that sounded to Haft like Skragish, and the two men-at-arms stood shoulder to shoulder before the door. The slavemaster backed toward them, slashing his blade from side to side.

Outside, Spinner heard Haft's shout and then a thud and knew Haft had gone into the room. Haft was inside facing the enemy, and Spinner couldn't leave him alone. As quickly as he could, he scuttled the rest of the way, thrust his staff through the window and heaved himself onto the sill before his eyes completely took in the tableau. He froze momentarily, recognizing the danger of the three slashing, advancing blades. One of the two men-at-arms still in the corridor stepped into the doorway, sword at the ready, to block anyone who managed to pass the blades in the room.

Spinner lunged the rest of the way through the window, landed running, hefted his quarterstaff horizontally across his front and began spinning it. The staff became visible.

"Get the man!" he shouted as he crossed the center of the room. Before the startled guards could react to his voice, the ends of his staff slammed into them and knocked them into the doorjamb. Spinner windmilled the staff into the two stunned guards again. One cried out in pain and stumbled to the side, clutching a shattered arm, the other just collapsed. A trickle of blood leaked from his left ear. Spinner twisted the staff then thrust it at the face of the man in the doorway. That guard flew backward into the fourth man, who was just turning to see if he should give up his post in the corridor to join the fight in the room. Spinner followed the third man through the doorway, felled the fourth with one blow, then kicked away the nearby swords so that none of the men-at-arms could get them quickly if they recovered enough to rejoin the fray. Spinner didn't think any of them would; two of them looked to be dead, and it would be a long time before the man with the shattered arm fought again.

Haft moved instantly when he heard Spinner shout then race past him. He stepped forward and swung his axe in an arc that should have caught the slavemaster in his middle. But the tiny woman on his shoulder squealed in terror and stopped spinning her robe around him—he became visible again. With the fastest reactions Haft had ever seen, the slavemaster simultaneously threw up his sword to parry the swing and jumped back out of its way. The Lalla Mkouma squealed again, wrapped her arms tightly around his neck and resumed the furious robe spinning.

As he looked for an opening past the axe, the slavemaster slowly shuffled his feet from side to side and slid forward, his blade held before him, its tip at chest height, shifting from side to side. He growled low in his throat as he came forward; it sounded as though he was saying, "I can't see you, but you can't get away from me in this narrow room."

Haft knew that was right; sooner or later the two would be in contact. Behind him, Spinner was reentering the room after dispatching the last of the guards.

"Where are you?" Spinner asked then, as the slavemaster spun to face this new threat, and Spinner quickly added, "Don't answer. You can see my staff, maneuver on me."

The slavemaster chuckled, growled, feinted a lunge toward Spinner's voice, then made a vicious backhand swing toward the middle of the room where he thought Haft was. He came closer than he knew—Haft barely managed to bow his middle out of the way of the blow of the blade. The slash struck the outside wall of the room and seemed to bury the sword in the plaster and lathe all the way into the outer stone. Haft stepped forward to strike at the unprotected slavemaster, but the blade wasn't stuck. With lightning reflexes, the slavemaster pulled it out of the wall and danced away from Haft's blow. Like Spinner's staff, the axe was visible when Haft swung it. But Haft was fast enough that a corner of his blade slashed across the metal and leather armor on the slavemaster's belly, raising sparks from the metal and slicing through the leather. Red slowly oozed around the cut. Haft moved again. The slave-master responded with a flourish of strokes that met only air. He chuckled again then growled something before moving toward Spinner once more but this time not as a feint, and Spinner had to shield himself with swings and spins of the quarterstaff. Only Spinner's great skill with the staff kept him from being skewered by the sword.

Haft desperately looked for an opening to get the slave-master off Spinner, but the sword's reach, despite its short length, was greater than the reach of his axe—and he had a more than healthy respect for that blade. The slavemaster was swinging his sword in wide arcs that carried almost all the way around to his back. Each time he swung, the tip of the blade sliced into a wall and left clean cuts in it. The swings came so fast that Haft had no time to step inside their arc and land a blow of his own. The slavemaster was slowly backing Spinner up until he was almost at the far wall.

Then Haft saw that the slavemaster's swings were coming in an almost regular rhythm. He edged himself to a position to the swordsman's right rear and, timing himself, brought his axe around and down as fast as he could to intercept the swinging sword. His swing missed the arm he aimed at and buried itself in the planking of the floor—but the axe handle hit the blade and carried it down. The slavemaster spun off balance and only saved himself from falling by letting go of his weapon. He darted past Haft, who was trying to pry his axe from the floor. Spinner raced after him, but the shift from defense to attack allowed the slavemaster to get to the bench, grab the longer sword, and turn to face him. Spinner pulled up short.

The slavemaster gave the room a rueful look. He started to advance again then, and for the first time noticed the emblem on Haft's axe. He stood erect, brought the hilt of his sword to his face, and bowed in salute. When he straightened he said in thickly accented Frangerian, "I didn't know anyone still carried the rampant eagle." He grinned widely. "I always did want to fight the very best." He cocked his head and looked again at the axe, which Haft was still trying to dislodge from the floor. "But you don't know its magic, do you? So you aren't the best. Oh, well." With a shriek, he attacked.

Haft had to let go of his weapon and dive out of the way of the sword blow. He came up with the short sword in his hands.

Spinner struck at the slavemaster with his staff, but the slavemaster spun away, taking only part of the blow. Still, he stumbled, and Haft immediately jumped in and thrust his sword through the slavemaster's chest.

The Jokapcul shuddered and slid off the blade. He clutched the wound in his chest with one hand and grasped the edge of the bench top with the other. He tried to stand, but his attempt was feeble and he tipped over, falling heavily on his side. His eyes misted and he gasped for air. A froth of blood bubbled from his chest and dribbled from the corner of his mouth. He said something, but his voice was weak. His native tongue had an incongruous, plaintive tone. Then his expression went blank.

CHAPTER
SIXTEEN

Spinner and Haft rubbed the thighs of their respective Lalla Mkouma to stop the magic, and they became visible again. They looked at each other, drained by the fight they knew they could just as easily have lost. They looked at the miniature woman on each other's shoulders who at full size would have been beautiful almost beyond belief, and burst into tension-relieving laughter. Startled, the Lalla Mkouma resumed twirling their robes, and the two men again vanished from sight, which only made the Marines laugh harder.

But they laughed only for a moment. There were more men-at-arms to be dealt with, and they had to get into the cellar to free the women before the fire reached them.

Spinner dropped to a knee to search the corpse for the key to unlock the slaves' anklets. Haft looked on the table and through chests. The Lalla Mkouma saw there was no immediate danger and became still.

"Don't bother," Spinner said. "The key is too important for him to leave lying around. He had to keep it on his body or in his clothing." He grunted as he pulled a key ring from inside the armor. "Here it is."

One of the keys was tiny and looked exactly the right size. Spinner picked up the short sword, gave it a few tentative swings, and decided he could use it though it felt and handled differently from the saber he'd trained with. Too many of the spaces in the inn were too narrow for him to properly use his staff.

"Now let's find Master Yoel."

"Wait," Haft said. As soon as Spinner told him to stop looking for the key, he'd noticed the ugly, winged demon the slavemaster had been talking to when he first looked in the window—he'd forgotten the thing in the heat of battle. The swarm of bees was still hovering near it. Spinner now saw it for the first time.

"What are you?" Haft demanded.

The fearsome-looking demon cringed back from him.

Haft grinned at the creature's fear and hefted his axe. "I know you can talk."

"Imbaluris," the demon whimpered from behind its arms. *"Naw hurd'um. Mezzger."*

"You're a messenger?"

"Mezzger!" the demon repeated.

"What are they?" Haft pointed at the bees.

"Zeekums. Tellum whar oo-um."

Haft considered this. "Can they find Master Yoel?"

"Yass'um." The demon gabbled at the bees. They swarmed out of the window.

Haft drew back from the demon and turned his face toward the Lalla Mkouma on his shoulder. "Is it telling the truth?"

"Mebbe," she piped. She made a face at the messenger and said something in a language Haft didn't recognize.

The messenger replied and vigorously nodded behind its arms. The bees returned in a few moments and buzzed at the messenger. When the bees finished, the imbaluris gabbled something Haft couldn't understand.

The Lalla Mkouma on his shoulder listened intently, then piped, *"Ee tellum. I zhow oo."*

"Let's go." Spinner turned toward the door but stopped before he'd taken a full step. "Listen!" he snapped.

They heard the excited sounds of people approaching outside the room.

"Out the window," Haft said. He was over the sill before Spinner reached the window.

The two Lalla Mkouma they'd left behind were waiting, and clambered onto their free shoulders. Climbing down the wall was easier than climbing across it had been, and they were on the ground before anyone in the corridor entered the slavemaster's room.

The sky above the inn shone bright, and sparks flew through the air, threatening to set a grass fire around the building. Men ran about stomping on the embers as soon as they struck the ground. Some of them congregated by the slave barn, but they were unceremoniously turned away by the guards stationed in front of it. A few edged toward the forest, but once they saw how dark it was under the trees, they too turned back. Most of them, though, milled about in front of the inn, looking more like a herd of cattle huddling together for protection from a wolf pack than a mass of men who could cause problems for the two Marines. There were no women in the crowd.

Crying about the valuables they had to retrieve from their rooms before the entire building burned down, a clot of merchants was trying to force its way back into the inn. Others just stood back.

"We can distract them," Spinner said, nodding at the merchants and their men.

"What do you mean?" Haft replied. He twisted his axe in his hands, as though aching to bury it in one of the slave traders.

"By freeing the troll. Let's go." He ran toward the rear of the inn.

"But we don't have time!" Haft shouted, looking up at the flames that now engulfed most of the inn's top level. Spinner neither replied nor stopped, so Haft ran after him.

The shed door was secured by a simple latch. Spinner stared at it for a long moment and slowly lifted his hand to it.

"What are you waiting for?" Haft snapped. "If you're going to open it, open it!"

"I've heard tales . . ." Spinner mumbled. Then fast, so

he couldn't stop himself, he flipped the latch and flung the door open.

Light from the fire splashed dimly into the shed. They could vaguely make out a boxy object along one side of the small room. A cable snaked from one side of the box into a hole in the dirt floor. Another cable runneled from the other side to an odd contraption that looked like a framework with a seat, handles, and footrests. There was no sign of the troll.

Haft clutched at Spinner's sleeve. "Time's wasting, we've got to go."

Then a shadow on the floor beyond the box stirred and rose. It moved toward them and resolved into a gnarly creature shaped roughly like a man. It was the troll, and it stood chest high to them. The troll raised a knuckly hand to Spinner and poked a broken talon at him.

"Veedmee," it rumbled.

Spinner recoiled from the troll so quickly he would have collided with Haft had the other Marine not already stepped back and readied his axe.

"Veedmee!" the troll rumbled louder. It took a menacing step toward Spinner and rolled its lips to expose a mouth full of sharp, serrated teeth.

Spinner was at a loss for words. Not only did he not have any food to offer the monster, he had no idea what it ate. And it looked ready to bite him. He had to suppress the feeling that he should just hold out his hand and get it over with.

Then the Lalla Mkouma on Haft's right shoulder chimed at the troll. The troll, who had raised its taloned hands, stopped and listened intently to her voice. Then it cocked its head toward the hubbub coming from the front of the inn and rumbled something at her. She chimed back, and the troll spread its mouth in a wide grin and shambled toward the crowd noise. Seconds after it vanished around the corner, shrieks were heard above the noise.

Spinner and Haft exhaled loudly in relief.

"What did you tell it?" Haft asked.

"I tellum zhem veed um," she chimed.

Then Spinner said, "The innkeeper's quarters."

They retraced their route to the corner of the building and around it, where merchants were still nerving themselves up to force their way back into the inn for their valuables. Others were standing back just watching.

A lamp was now lit inside the first floor room, where the innkeeper lived. The Marines hurried past it to the window that opened into the room with the clerk's desk, what they thought was the counting room. No lamp was on inside, but the shutters were open, exposing the glazed windows.

Haft pushed up on the lower sash. It didn't budge. He glanced around. Nobody was looking in their direction. He rapped the butt of his axe against one of the panes and looked around again. No one paid any attention to the sound of breaking glass. He reached inside, undid the latch, pushed up the lower sash, and climbed in. Spinner followed.

A slit of light showed beneath the door connecting to the next room. Probing with their feet so as not to knock anything over, they crept softly toward it. They paused at the door and listened. From beyond it they heard Master Yoel's excited voice talking at length in Jokapcul. When he stopped, he was answered by a muffled voice, as though it was speaking from a deep hole.

The hollow voice spoke for a short time; Master Yoel replied with something brief and plaintive. Then they heard a flapping of leathery wings, followed by silence. After a moment there was a low keening from the room. It sounded like the innkeeper was crying.

"Only one way to find out," Haft murmured.

"Wait," Spinner said softly, and addressing the Lalla Mkouma on their shoulders, said: "Make us invisible."

When the Lalla Mkouma had twirled their robes to accomplish the task, Haft tried the door, found it wasn't locked, and pushed it open.

This room was larger than any of the guest rooms they had

been in. Only one lamp was lit, but it gave enough light to see by. A large bed with a massive wooden frame stood in one corner, the rumpled clothes on it showing the haste with which it had been vacated when the alarm was sounded for the fire. A huge wardrobe loomed next to the bed and took up most of that wall. Several plush chairs sat around a richly carved table on a lush rug in the middle of the room. A pitcher and two fine cups were on a tray on the table; evidently, the innkeeper had been entertaining company when the alarm was sounded. A bit of lace that might have been a female night garment showing through the rumpled bedclothes made that seem more likely. Both men wondered which of the serving women the innkeeper had been using before he was interrupted by the fire. A few objects hung on the walls; one that caught Haft's eye was a golden dagger in a golden sheath on a gold-linked belt. In the corner opposite the bed was a simple desk with a small wooden cabinet on it. A plain wooden chair was in front of the desk. Master Yoel was standing in front of the desk, manically pulling things from the cabinet and stuffing them into a leather sack that sat open on the chair. He keened as he grabbed and stuffed, and his thin shoulders shook with his crying. He didn't look up at the sound of the door opening. No one else was visible in the room.

Haft stepped to the crying man and clamped a hand on his shoulder.

The innkeeper jumped and cried out.

Haft dropped his voice a few octaves and ordered, "Take us to the cellar."

Master Yoel looked about, eyes darting, mouth agape. He tried to pull away from the unseen hand that held him, but Haft's grip was too tight. His keening grew higher.

"N-No, Master," he managed to croak. "I did nothing. It is not my fault. If your wizard didn't know a sorcerer was about, how could I know? I beg you, Master, do not harm me!" His eyes focused on a spot somewhere off Haft's shoulder.

"Where are the women you have imprisoned?" Spinner demanded.

The innkeeper's eyes suddenly focused, and shot to where Spinner's voice had come from; but there was nothing for them to see there. He murmured something indistinct.

"Say it again," Spinner snapped.

"In the cellar, just as you ordered, Master," the innkeeper said more clearly.

"As I ordered?"

The innkeeper sank to his knees. "But you did, Master. The imbaluris brought your message just now. 'Let the women turn to ash,' you said. I was but following your command. You know I always obey."

"Take us to the cellar," Spinner ordered.

Haft yanked the terrified man to his feet. "Do it now," he snapped, "or your death will take longer and be more painful than you can imagine." He didn't know who or what Master Yoel thought he was talking to, but realized he could take advantage of the man's fear. The innkeeper shuddered, and Haft gave him a shove that slammed him into the doorjamb. "To the cellar. Now! Move!"

The innkeeper stopped his keening and started whimpering. "I-Instantly, Master," he said, and scuttled through the door, Spinner pushing at his back. As they moved, the golden dagger lifted itself off the wall, hovered in the air for a few seconds, and vanished. Haft smiled. The leather sack Master Yoel had been filling also disappeared.

The innkeeper touched one place and then a second on the wall in the counting room. A section of the wall slid out of the way to reveal a narrow stairway leading down. Dim light showed at the bottom of the stairs. When he didn't start down immediately, Haft gave him a shove. He staggered down several steps, got a grip on the banister and caught his balance. He descended the rest of the way quickly.

A turn at the foot of the stairs opened onto a corridor.

Spinner recognized it as the one along which he went to meet the Golden Girl the night before.

Haft shoved the innkeeper to the first door. "Open it," he snapped.

The innkeeper fumbled with the latch but got the door open. It was pitch-black inside.

"Get a light," Haft ordered.

Master Yoel took a lamp from a wall sconce, then led the way into the room. The lamp showed a room as small as the one where they'd set the fire. Doli and another serving maid were huddled on the narrow beds, blinking against the sudden light and whimpering; they could hear the commotion in the inn above and were afraid. They were wearing short night-shifts, and their anklets glinted evilly.

Spinner said, "Be quiet, Doli. You're safe now. Wait, we'll be back soon." She started violently when she heard a friendly voice, but saw only the innkeeper. Spinner yanked the innkeeper out of that room and closed the door.

"Open the next one," he ordered.

The second door opened onto a room that looked exactly the same. Two serving maids were huddled on their narrow beds. Neither was familiar to Haft or Spinner. One cried out when the innkeeper was shoved into the cell; the other merely hid her eyes from the sudden light.

"Don't be afraid," Spinner said gently. "We're here to help you."

"Give him the key," Haft snapped before Spinner could reach for an anklet.

"Why?"

"For the same reason you didn't try the key on Doli first. The anklets might somehow be warded." Haft's words were punctuated by the crash of a beam collapsing somewhere above them.

Spinner grabbed the innkeeper's hand and put the tiny key he'd taken from the slavemaster's ring into it.

"Now release the women," Haft ordered him.

"Master? I don't understand what you mean, Master." He still didn't realize who he was talking to.

"The key. Unlock the anklets."

Master Yoel dropped to his knees, terror in his eyes. He clasped his hands before his face and looked at where the voices came from. "But Master," he pleaded, "the spell. If the anklets are removed, the azren won't know who it can devour." He swallowed loudly. "If it does not know, it will devour everyone!"

"It will not. I will not allow that!"

The serving maids made no sound except for their quiet whimpering, their eyes fearful as they watched the innkeeper and searched the shadows to see where the bodiless voices came from. Spinner assumed they probably didn't understand Frangerian. He wondered if the innkeeper put any significance on the language they were speaking—or was even aware of it.

"Do it!"

"But Master, you ordered me, on pain of death, never to release any of the slaves for so long as they remain useful."

Spinner thrust the point of his sword an inch from the bridge of the innkeeper's nose, so Yoel could see it. "You said you always obey me. Your death will indeed be painful if you refuse to do this now." He wondered again who the man thought he was.

The innkeeper's eyes crossed as he stared at the unwavering sword point that had suddenly appeared before them. He recognized the blade and crumpled to the floor. Haft kicked him in the ribs, and Yoel crawled to one of the narrow beds. He clutched the serving maid's ankle and inserted the key into the hole.

The anklet popped open and fell off the woman's ankle to lay inert on the narrow bed. The freed slave giggled nervously before she flexed her ankle.

Spinner felt a wave of relief wash over him.

"Now the other one," Haft ordered.

Master Yoel turned around and unlocked the anklet on the

other serving maid. The first was already on her feet, standing in the doorway, bouncing up and down on her toes, a wide grin splitting her face.

Haft grabbed Master Yoel and threw him onto the deserted bed. In an instant he had snatched the key out of the inn-keeper's hand and locked the anklet firmly around his ankle. Master Yoel looked horror-stricken at his bound ankle and opened his mouth. Before he could get a sound out, Haft grabbed the second anklet and locked it around his other ankle.

"Now let's see how you like living with demons," he said.

Only then did Master Yoel manage a wail of agony and de-spair that seemed to come from the deepest depths of whatever it was he used for a soul. He leaped to his feet and raced wildly from the room, shoving aside his invisible tormentors and knocking the serving girl from her feet. He pounded along the corridor, the way they had come, and back up the stairs.

"Do you think he's trying to run away?" Haft asked blandly.

"I don't think he'll get far if he tries," Spinner answered coldly. "Lalla Mkouma, show us so we don't frighten the women." The women gasped as the Lalla Mkouma returned them to visibility.

Master Yoel bolted up the stairs to his chambers. He looked about wildly for something he could use to remove the anklet. There was nothing.

"The laborers," he gabbled to himself. "They have tools. They can free me." He raced from his chambers, through the counting room and kitchen and out the back door. In his panic he didn't notice the open door of the troll shed. Wide-eyed and gasping, he sped toward the stable. Halfway there, the azren leaped from behind a tree to block his way.

The demon was tall and cadaverous. A blue shirt hung

lankly on its body and a strip of filthy cloth was bound around
the crown of its head. Its hands held a hammer and chisel.

"Myne," the azren gargled.

Master Yoel stopped so fast he almost fell. He quailed before the apparition, then gathered himself and stood as tall as
he could. "Not yours!" His voice broke on the shout. "You
are mine. I am master!"

"Oo weare." The azren gestured toward Master Yoel's
ankles with the chisel. *"Myne."*

The azren normally attacked instantly, but it hadn't. Its
hesitation restored Master Yoel's confidence. He stepped
toward it, his face contorted with fury.

"Not yours! I am master. You do my bidding. I bid you go
into the inn, go down to the cellar. You will find two men.
They are yours. You can also have the women, as many as half
of them." That would do it. The azren would kill the invisible
men; he was sure there were two of them, that's how many
voices he had heard. And when the fire was put out he'd still
have half of the women. He'd be ahead of the game with half
the women left. After all, his master had told him to "let the
women turn to ash."

The azren cocked its head as though considering Master
Yoel's orders, or how best to do his bidding. Then it lowered
its eyes and looked at the two anklets the man wore.

"Myne," it gargled again, and slammed the chisel low into
the innkeeper's belly. It swung the hammer and drove the
chisel in so deep only Master Yoel's spine kept it from coming
out of his back.

Master Yoel screamed in agony and clutched at the chisel,
but the azren jerked it out and slammed it into his belly again.
And again. And again, until the screaming stopped and the
innkeeper was dead. Then it fed.

It didn't take long. First they went back to Doli's room and,
in a few words, explained to her what they were doing and the
need for speed. Above them the fire raged ever louder. The

two women they'd already freed were proof of what they promised. Doli translated for them. Then her cellmate and the other two ran down the corridor, opening all the doors but one, telling the rest of the slaves what was happening. Soon the two men were surrounded by serving maids soon to be free. Haft knelt on the floor and unlocked the anklets as quickly as he could grab fresh ankles. Under other circumstances his hands would have lingered on the ankles, but not now. Now he was in a hurry. The fire sounded like it was completely out of control, and they had to get out of the building before it collapsed on them. It was even possible the innkeeper had regained control of himself and was organizing a party of armed men to come down to the cellar after them, or to ambush them when they came out. He had no time to waste. There were slave traders about, he knew that for certain, and even if nobody was preparing to avenge the death of the slavemaster, or doing the innkeeper's bidding, the slave traders would want to stop those who would free the slaves.

"Get dressed," Spinner ordered the women. "As soon as everyone is free, we're leaving here. You can't travel in those night-shifts."

Most of them ran to don blouses and skirts as soon as their ankles were free, but not all wanted to.

"*Ptaugh,* I'd rather go naked into the world than wear the garb of The Burnt Man's slaves," one said.

"I'd love to see naked women running about," Haft said. "But right now it is better to wear something. You can get new clothes once you are away from here."

They might have grumbled as they went, but they went quickly; the smoke that was settling in the corridor lent an urgency to their dressing. Whatever they chose, they all dressed.

But Alyline, the Golden Girl, the one for whose sake Spinner most wanted to free the slaves, wasn't there. Her door was the one that wasn't opened. Spinner took the key from Haft as soon as the last anklet was removed from the last serving maid.

"Guard them," he said, and went alone down the corridor to the one closed door.

No banks of candles lit the room now. Spinner had to carry a lamp from the corridor to see his way. Alyline, the Golden Girl, lay asleep on the pillows behind the hanging frieze of gossamer drapes. She wore the same diaphanous shift she had when he'd entered the room the previous night. When the light from the lamp crossed her eyelids she whimpered and drew herself into a ball. He ached at the thought of the nightmares she must suffer. He knelt at her side and placed the lamp on the floor where it wouldn't shine directly on her eyes. Then, as gently as he could, he unlocked the anklet and removed it. He leaned over her and brushed her lips with his.

"Awake, Golden Girl," he whispered. "Wake to freedom."

Her eyelids fluttered open. As soon as she saw a face so close to hers, her eyes widened fearfully and she jerked back, hard against the wall. Her lip trembled and she said weakly, almost mournfully, "He told me no one paid for me tonight. He promised."

Spinner hid his shock and recovered almost instantly. He leaned back so his face was in brighter light and held up the anklet.

"No one paid, and you are free." He reached out a hand to her, but pulled it back when she flinched from his touch.

He knelt quietly, keeping his face where she could see it in the lamp's light, and holding the anklet where she could see it as well. A long moment passed before her wide, staring eyes focused on him.

"You? Why are you here now? You left."

"This is why I am here." He dangled the anklet on one finger and let it swing back and forth until her gaze shifted to it.

She gasped and felt at her ankle. "Where is it?" She sat up and looked at her ankles, felt them with both hands, pulled up her shift until it bared her entire legs and looked at them in shock. Then she slowly turned her face to him, her eyes even wider with wonder and her mouth agape.

"You did it! You said you'd free me, and you did!"

Spinner could only nod, the lump in his throat too big to allow him to speak.

She bounced up onto her knees, threw her arms around his neck and kissed him. Then she pushed herself away and her face fell.

"The slavemaster won't let you take me away. His men-at-arms will kill you for this."

Spinner shook his head. "The slavemaster is dead, and Haft and I killed his men-at-arms."

Her expression lifted, but fear was still in her eyes. "But Master Yoel, he also has men. They won't let you go."

"Master Yoel has been dealt with. You needn't fear him." Spinner sounded more confident about that than he felt, but the innkeeper's panic when last seen made it unlikely he would be a threat before they were safely away.

"There are slave traders here. They won't let the slaves be freed."

Spinner smiled at that. "I don't think we have anything to worry about from them. They have other things to do." He couldn't stop a grin from spreading across his face. "Haft and I have been very busy this night." He quickly told her about the fire. "Now, I am going out into the corridor. You get dressed and join us. But hurry. We need to be far from here by the time the sun comes up."

He put a hand on her cheek, leaned forward and softly kissed her.

For the first time, Alyline noticed the female forms straddling his shoulders. She made a face and muttered something that ended with ". . . men!"

Spinner blinked, then stood, gave her a loving look, and turned to leave. "Hurry," he said over his shoulder when he reached the door.

"That took you long enough," Haft complained when Spinner rejoined him. "We've got to get out of here." He started herding the women toward the stairway. "Where's the Golden Girl?"

"Getting dressed."

Haft shook his head. "You didn't have time for that," he muttered.

"And I didn't do that." Spinner looked away, his face burning.

All the serving maids milled about talking among themselves in the confines of the corridor; some were laughing nervously. They were getting skittish. They wanted to be out of the cellar and on their way to wherever they were going. Someone giggled in a high pitch that rose toward hysteria. It was cut off by a slap that sounded clearly throughout the length of the corridor, and was followed by muted sobs.

The Golden Girl's door opened and she emerged quietly through the half-open door. She wore the same costume she wore for her performances, down to the tierra and jeweled girdle. The women already waiting stopped talking, and most of them turned their backs on her. When they started talking again it was in lower voices, tinged with disdain. Haft shook his head and grunted. He led the way up the stairs.

"Alyline!" Spinner said, almost in a squeak. He cleared his throat to get his voice under control. "You aren't going to dance now. We're leaving. Go back in and put on proper clothes to travel in."

She snorted. "You have seen all of my clothing. Would you rather I traveled in my bed-shift? You'd be able to see all of me if that was how I dressed—as you well know."

"N-No, no. That's not what I mean. I mean, put on a regular dress. Or a skirt and blouse."

"I don't have a dress, or a skirt and blouse. I have this and the night-shift and that is all." She twisted her lips in a wry smile and said bitterly, "The slavemaster didn't think I'd need anything else. He didn't think I'd be going anywhere."

Spinner's gaze darted about, and seeing how the other women were dressed, remembered they had different length skirts. Probably they all had more than one blouse, though none of them seemed to be carrying a bundle of clothes.

"Borrow clothes from one of the other women," he blurted.

She snorted. "None of them has any clothes for me."

Spinner quickly looked at the women who hadn't yet gotten to the stairway. The backs they displayed were visibly stiff.

"Can one of you—" he began, but Doli cut him off:

"We are wearing all of our clothes. Nobody has anything to let her wear."

Haft had come back to the foot of the stairs to move the women up in an orderly way. He grinned when he realized what was going on. "If that's all the clothes she's got, it's all right with me. Let's get out of here." He looked at the Golden Girl and grinned wider. He was going to enjoy traveling with a woman who dressed like that.

Spinner glared at Haft, looked at the Golden Girl, glared again at Haft. "I'm going upstairs," he said finally, and brushed past the women leaving the cellar.

Haft grinned after Spinner's retreating back, then turned his attention to the other women, to keep them moving. When the last one reached the foot of the stairs, he bent over and looped as many of the anklets around one arm as he could carry.

"Just in case I run into one of the slavers," he murmured to himself. "If I get a chance to make any of them wear one of these, I will."

CHAPTER
SEVENTEEN

At the top of the stairs to the common room, Spinner turned left. At the end of a short corridor there was a dressing room. Spinner had seen dim light from it when the innkeeper led him to the cellar the previous night. A door from the dressing room opened onto the grounds between the main building and the stable. He looked and listened carefully at the outside door. There didn't seem to be anyone outside. Inside the inn he heard the roar of the raging fire and the clamor of many men shouting at each other as they struggled in vain to slow the progress of the blaze. It didn't sound like they were conducting a search.

Spinner didn't think anyone would check the dressing room for fugitives, at least not until they were through fighting the fire. Looking up, he saw that the entire third floor was engulfed, and flames licked through several windows on the second floor. Thick smoke bellowed around the side of the building, and he wondered how many men were dying in the flames. Then, remembering that many of the men were slavers or in the employ of slavers, he felt less concern for their lives.

As they reached the head of the stairs, the women heard the fire, and panic threatened to rise among them. He had wanted to group everyone in the dressing room, but the fire was moving too fast for anyone to remain in the building. So, after everyone had crowded into the dressing room, he said to the women in a hushed voice, "Follow us. We're going to the stable to free the people held there. You must hide *behind* the stable while Haft and I go inside. You'll be safe there."

Haft put down all but three of the anklets and slipped through the door, then Spinner guided the women through it single file. "Quickly, silently," he urged each one as she went past. They followed Haft past the corral to the stable. Spinner saw that there were no horses in the corral and he concluded they must all be stalled inside the stable. Noises from inside confirmed his suspicion. The two men quickly moved the two dozen women behind the stable, where they couldn't be seen from the front of the inn.

"Wait here," Spinner told the women when they were bunched together. "Keep silent. Do nothing that will attract anyone's attention."

Doli translated his words into Skragish for the other women. She seemed to be the calmest of the newly freed slaves, perhaps because she was the only one who spoke Frangerian and knew what the two men were saying without having to wait to be told.

Other than one: Alyline, the Golden Girl, could also understand what Spinner and Haft said, and seemed in good spirits. Spinner looked longingly at her. Someone had to be in charge out there while the two men were inside freeing the laborers, and he wanted to give her the responsibility, but none of the other women had opened her door while he and Haft were freeing them, and most of them had been hostile to her since then. He bit his lip, then through Doli told them, "Doli is in charge until we get back. Wait quietly, be still, and you will be safe." Unless someone comes here for some reason and discovers you, he thought. But he couldn't think of any reason other than flight for anyone from the inn to come that way.

Spinner said to Haft, "Let's go," and they padded quietly around the corner of the stable to a door and stopped outside it. "Do you remember where the stairs to the upper level are?" Spinner asked.

"No. I hoped you did."

Spinner groaned. He asked the Lalla Mkouma to make them invisible again.

The two extra little women clambered down. *"Ee wai' ere,"* they piped up at the men.

Inside, stalls lined a central aisle the length of the stable. They each took a side of the aisle and walked toward the end, feeling their way along the stall gates. If there were a place without a stall, that might be where the stairs were—or at least a ladder to the loft.

The stable smelled strongly of hay, and oats, and of course horses. The animals had awakened during the excitement of the fire, but no excited men had run into the stable, and even though the ruckus around the inn had grown instead of abating, it didn't come nearer, so the horses remained relatively quiet. A few had even gone back to sleep. The stable sounded normal to Spinner; the noises made Haft edgy.

Three-quarters of the way down the aisle, Spinner found a ladderlike stairway. He signaled to Haft, and they carefully started climbing. At the top of the stairs they stepped through a doorway and, by feel, realized they were in a corridor that ran the length of the stable above the inner bank of stalls. The smell of fresh hay and oats was stronger in one direction than in the other, so Spinner concluded that direction led to a hay loft. He led Haft the other way. They had covered nearly half the distance when a spark was struck and a lamp flared.

Standing there, invisible, Spinner and Haft blinked rapidly in the sudden light. Three paces away, the friendly stableman was doing the same. He held the lamp in one hand. Only he didn't seem so friendly now—he wasn't smiling, and he held a sword. The man leaned forward and held the lamp out ahead of him, moving it from side to side so the light reached the entire length of the hallway. He said something in a language Haft and Spinner didn't understand, then hefted his sword threateningly and peered around suspiciously, shining the lamp along the corridor. When he still couldn't find anything amiss, he muttered, lowered his sword, turned, and went back along the corridor.

Spinner and Haft, padding as softly as they could, crept along behind him.

The stableman turned as though to go through an open door, then abruptly spun, slashing across the corridor with his sword. The blade passed harmlessly through the air and hit the wall on the other side. He poked the lamp forward again and peered down the corridor, but again saw nothing. He stood straight and, ignoring the door he'd been about to go through, walked farther down the corridor, again muttering to himself. He settled on a stool. Evidently he had been sitting there, posted to guard the laborers like a prison warder. He left his lamp lit and darted suspicious looks wherever he thought he heard movement.

A voice came through a doorway. It sounded like it asked, "What's the matter out there?"

The stableman answered, and to Spinner and Haft it was something like: "Nothing. Just my imagination. Go back to sleep."

Now they knew where the laborers were kept—or at least one of the handymen.

Haft hugged the wall and advanced along it until he was only two or three paces from the stableman. His foot kicked a pebble he didn't see in the uncertain light. The stableman looked wide-eyed at the stone that seemed to roll of its own accord, then up at the sound of a sudden, sharp step. There wasn't anybody there, and he prayed his fear was merely his overheated imagination. The axe head that suddenly appeared in midair did not seem to be his imagination, but it felt real when its side struck his head, and then he was unconscious.

Haft wasted no time or sympathy in locking an anklet on the stableman. He grabbed the man's sword before straightening up.

Spinner was already in the room the other voice had come from, visible again, talking in Frangerian to the three frightened men kept in it. "The slavemaster is dead," he said. "We have the key that will unlock your anklets and free you."

One of the handymen darted his eyes about. "We? I only see you," he answered.

"That's because you're not looking hard enough," Haft said as he stepped into the room. He held up the key. "As soon as I unlock your anklets, you can join the serving maids we've already freed and take off. Who's first?"

The man who had spoken translated for the others. Not surprisingly, no one volunteered to be the first man freed. "Ah, you don't trust me," Haft said. "You think this may be some trick by the slavemaster. Well, I don't blame you for being suspicious, I'd probably feel exactly the same way in your place. Recognize this?" He held up an anklet. The handymen flinched when he snapped it closed. With a dramatic flourish, Haft held the anklet where the men could see the keyhole, inserted the key and turned it. The anklet fell open. "See? Perfectly safe."

One of the men growled something then stuck out his ankle to be freed. In a moment all three of the handymen were unshackled and leading Spinner and Haft to another room, where three more laborers slept.

Before they descended to the stable, Haft asked if any of the men knew how to use a sword.

The man who spoke Frangerian said, "I served in the Bostian army. That's how I came to know your language." He was of average size, but had muscles like slabs of stone.

"This is yours, then," Haft said as he handed the man the slavemaster's sword. "What's your name?"

"Fletcher."

"Can you use a bow as well as make arrows?"

"Yes."

"Maybe we'll find one for you." Then to the others, "As soon as we can, we'll get swords for anyone else who can use one."

When they realized they were being offered weapons, another man admitted he had served in an army. Haft gave him the stableman's sword. Suddenly everyone claimed to know how to fight.

Several of the women were bunched at the corner of the stable, peering anxiously toward the inn. Doli wasn't completely successful at getting them back out of sight; she had more success keeping them quiet.

"You were gone a long time," Doli said. "They thought you were lost or had left us. They thought if they went back to the inn they could claim they managed to escape through the flames, and nothing would happen to them when they were discovered."

Haft started to object angrily that they hadn't been gone long, but he stopped when Spinner held his hand up.

"That's all right, as long as everyone is still safe," Spinner said.

"Three of those who were too afraid ran away," Doli said. "I told them to wait for us in the trees, but they said they were too frightened to stay nearby. They wished us luck, but they are fleeing."

Spinner looked through the night toward the north. "I wish them luck as well," he said slowly. "I'm sure they'll need it. Now, back around the corner, everyone."

When they were all grouped together again behind the stable, he said, "In a moment you're going to cross the road and hide under the trees. Haft and I have to get weapons for the rest of the men." He indicated the freed laborers. "We also have to give the people in the inn something more to worry about so they won't come looking for us before we get away. Fletcher will be in charge while you wait. Now, go!"

Spinner and Haft raced back to the inn and entered the still deserted dressing room. More men milled about in front of the building than before, and its upper stories were wreathed in flames. They left the outside door open and opened the shutters to let in as much light as possible. As they ran through the room, they each grabbed a cloak.

Haft said, "Weapons!"

"Right—and confusion," Spinner added. Invisible, they headed to the common room, which was deserted. A few men were peering fearfully through the door as though expecting to see the fire dance down the stairs. The snap and crackle of the fire was audible, and embers shot out the stairwell, but no flames had yet licked into the room.

Spinner and Haft ran to the blades on the wall, which were secured with wire. Spinner unsheathed his belt knife and sliced through the wire. One of the men looking through the entrance saw several swords magically lift themselves from the wall then disappear when Spinner pulled them close to his body. The man in the doorway screamed and pointed, but by the time the other men looked, there was nothing to see. Spinner hurried to another part of the wall and added a longbow to his collection of swords but could find no arrows to go with it. He wrapped the weapons in the cloak Haft gave him.

"Now for confusion," Spinner said.

Haft grinned, then charged at the men looking in through the doorway. He threw a shoulder into the chest of one man and slammed his fist into the face of another. Screaming, the two men tumbled backward into those behind them, who leaped backward, cursing.

Spinner followed close behind Haft. When he was near enough to the men outside the door, he swung the bundle of weapons like a big club, slamming it into one man, who was tossed into his companions. They all went down in a heap. Spinner and Haft stepped on the downed men as they ran toward the crowd milling in front of the inn.

Haft thought of the slaves and decided just knocking people down and frightening them wasn't enough; men who dealt in slaves enraged him. He swung his axe at a slaver, and the fat merchant barely saw the descending blade before it hit him at the base of his neck and clove deep into his chest. Haft yanked the axe free of the falling man, spotted another slaver a few feet away, took two steps, and hacked the man almost in two. He killed two more slavers before men in the crowd realized there was someone unseen in their midst sowing bloody murder. Panic radiated around Haft.

Meanwhile, Spinner ran about wielding his bundle of weapons. He couldn't pick his targets as Haft did; his weapon was too unwieldy and he wasn't bent on vengeance. Even so, as he waded through the crowd, men went down pell-mell in front of him. In moments, all the men still on their feet were in full rout, trying to escape the deadly magicians they couldn't see. Many armed men flung down their weapons in their flight.

"Haft!" Spinner shouted when the crowd was scattered.

"Here," Haft cried back.

Spinner looked toward his voice and saw the axe blade dripping gore. "That's enough," he said. "Let's get back to the others."

Haft looked ruefully at the fleeing men. He wanted to kill more slavers, but he knew Spinner had made the wiser decision. In the short time they might have left before someone could start to organize a defense, it would be impossible to chase down enough of the fleeing men. "Let's go," he said, then followed the sound of Spinner's footsteps.

As soon as they were across the road and under the trees, they stroked the thighs of the Lalla Mkouma to return to visibility. Twenty paces inside the forest everybody was waiting for them. They handed out swords to the men.

"I found you a bow, Fletcher," Spinner said. "I don't know if it's any good though. No arrows."

"Thank you," Fletcher said. "I can always make what I need." He bent the bow to test its flex and nodded. He seemed satisfied.

"Now we have to free the people in the barn," Spinner said. "We'll go through the trees to a spot closer to the barn where you'll wait for us again." He paused while Doli and Fletcher translated. "Freeing the people in the barn should only take a few moments." He looked back at the clearing. Small knots of men were beginning to gather, looking back toward the inn, but most of the men had run out of sight. There were a half dozen men-at-arms in front of the slave barn. They looked like they didn't want to be there.

"Let's go!" Spinner and Haft led their group parallel to the road and through the forest until they were near the east side of the glade.

Spinner tried to drape a silken cloak over the Golden Girl's shoulders; she stepped away from his touch and shrugged from under the cloak before he let go of it. He was surprised, but didn't have time to wonder about her actions. He dropped the cloak at her feet.

"Everyone wait here," he told the group, then turned to Fletcher. "I want you to come with us," he said. "Assign one of the other men to take charge until we return." He waited a moment while Fletcher did that, then he, Haft, and Fletcher ran across the road to the barn.

Six torches stuck into the ground illuminated the guards without allowing them to see very far into the night; the only direction they could see anyone approaching from was the inn, where a man would be silhouetted against the flames that raged through the building. Spinner, Haft, and Fletcher stopped in shadows from which they could see the front of the barn.

"Do you know them?" Spinner asked.

Fletcher nodded. "Master Yoel's men. He hires only the worst. Most of them have been cashiered from one army or another. He feeds them well and lets them have the women for free. He never makes them pay any gambling debts they owe him. He has their loyalty."

"Do they know you?"

"Yes."

"Are you friendly with any of them?"

Fletcher spat.

"Then here's what we'll do."

* * *

"Yo, guards!" Fletcher said as he stepped into the circle of torchlight.

The guards started at his words and hefted their swords. They relaxed when they saw who it was, but still held their weapons at the ready. They looked past Fletcher into the shadows.

"What do you do here, laborer?" one of them asked. "Why aren't you putting out the fire?"

"Have you seen Master Yoel?" another asked.

"Is it true, Master Yoel wore a demon anklet and tried to run away?" a third asked.

"I still think we should run while we can," one mumbled.

Fletcher didn't answer their questions. He walked briskly toward the guards, showing his empty hands. The scabbard belt was draped awkwardly over his shoulders, with the scabbard hanging down his back and the hilt of the sword behind his head.

"Stop there!" the first guard snapped, lifting his sword threateningly. "Answer our questions! Why are you here where you don't belong? Where is Master Yoel? What is happening out there?" He took a menacing step toward Fletcher, then a grunt behind him made him spin around. What he saw froze him for an instant.

One of the other guards was on the ground, his head rolling several feet away. An axe hovered in midair above the corpse. A second guard was crumpling from an unseen blow. The axe swung at the third man, but the guard who'd challenged Fletcher never saw it land; as soon as the man's back was turned, Fletcher drew his sword and ran the guard straight through, the point of the sword appearing briefly in the man's chest. The guard collapsed as another man fell to Haft's axe. Spinner's staff took still another, and Fletcher killed the last guard before either of the invisible men could reach him.

Fletcher stood over the man's body, grinning down at the corpse. "I've wanted to do that for a long time," he said.

Haft clapped him on the shoulder. "I understand. Now, let's take their weapons." In a moment they had more swords and scabbards slung over their shoulders and as many more knives in their belts.

When Haft stepped up to the barn door, only his axehead was visible.

"Let them see us," Spinner said. They stroked the thighs of the Lalla Mkouma.

Haft didn't bother examining the barn door to see how it was secured, he simply flailed away at it with his axe. It shattered in three blows. They stepped inside and recoiled from the stench before calling out to the people inside. "Does anyone in here speak Frangerian? Ewsarcan? Apianghian? Skragish?" They ran through the litany of languages they had among them. Some voices answered in those languages, more of those inside simply whimpered.

"Come outside," they said in Frangerian, Ewsarcan, Apianghian, Skragish, and whatever other languages they could manage. "We are taking you to freedom. The slavemaster is dead."

"So are many of the slavers who brought you here," Haft added in each of his languages.

Slowly at first, then with mounting eagerness, the people began to stumble out.

"Keep quiet," Spinner ordered when the prisoners started raising a babel of voices. "Some of the men who brought you here are still about. There aren't enough of us armed to fight them all off."

"Let them come," someone said. "We will kill them with our bare hands."

A low chorus of growls agreed with him.

"Not now," Haft told them. "Maybe later you'll have your chance."

The three of them started moving the former slaves, who numbered nearly a hundred, to the road and across it to where the others waited.

"Fletcher, you're in charge," Spinner said when everyone was together and listening. He and Haft handed over the weapons they'd taken from the guards at the barn. "Decide who should have these and distribute them. A dozen armed men should be able to protect everyone for the moment. Now, follow this road until it reaches a main highway. Take the highway to the north. It will lead you to Oskul, the Skragish capital. You can find safety there, and probably a way home as well. Haft and I have other places to go, other things to do. Good speed and fare thee well." Spinner moved the Lalla Mkouma from his right shoulder to the Golden Girl and pulled her along. He and Haft and the Golden Girl, invisible, raced away, back across the road and into the trees on the glade's east side. They ignored the cries from behind, the voices of people who wanted their saviors to stay with them, or at least stay long enough to be thanked.

The Golden Girl struggled in Spinner's arm. "What do you think you're doing?" she demanded. "Where are you taking me?"

"I'll tell you all shortly," Spinner said. "Trust me for now."

"Why should I trust you?" she replied, but stopped struggling.

In their haste and movement, they didn't hear the footsteps behind them.

THIRD INTERLUDE:

THE NATURE OF DEMONS

A Brief Discourse on the Purported Nature of Magic and Demons

by Scholar Munch Mu'sk
Professor of Far Western Studies
University of the Great Rift
(excerpted from *The Proceedings of the Association of Anthropological Scholars of Obscure Cultures*, Vol. 57, No. 9)

On several counts, magic is a difficult topic on which to discourse. First, not everybody agrees that magic exists, or if it indeed does exist, how efficacious it is. To further complicate the discussion, those who agree that it does exist disagree most vehemently on the proper form in effecting it. Regardless of their stance on other questions, one thing on which the practitioners of and believers in magic agree is that all magic is in the control of demons. Beyond that sole point, the scholar finds naught but disagreement.

Nevertheless, a careful study of the literature and skillful interviewing of practitioners and witnesses have taught this scholar a number of things about the arcane arts.

First: the existence of magic and demons. Over the course of several years, I have undertaken an informal statistical study of belief in magic. There appears to be a distinct correlation between geographic location and belief. For example: Where I live and work, the University of the Rift, belief is so little as to be almost nonexistent; in the Kingdom of Matilda, in the unnamed lands, and in Bostia, belief is high. One might naturally assume that in the environs of the world's premier university, belief in superstition and other nonsensical ideas would be scarce. Further, one might naturally assume that in more intellectually blighted areas such as the west of Nunimar that superstition and other nonsensical ideas would be more common. If discussing trivial matters such as a belief in men with heads in their chests, the hazards of walking under ladders, etcetera, one would be right. However, when one looks further and discovers that belief in magic and demons is only slightly lower in Skragland than in Bostia, slightly lower in the Princedons than in Skragland, lower yet in the Easterlies than in the Princedons; and that such belief is slightly higher in Apianghia than near the University of the Rift, and slightly higher in Ewsarcan than in Apianghia, a pattern begins to emerge. To wit: There is an inverse correlation between distance from the west coast of Nunimar and belief in magic and demons, and that relationship between depth and strength of belief and distance from the west of Nunimar leads this scholar to suspect that demonkind has a homeland, and that its homeland is somewhere off the coast of Nunimar, most likely in an undiscovered archipelago south or southwest of the Jokapcul Islands, if not in the Jokapcul Islands themselves.

(In view of the admission of personal belief in magic and demons implicit in the preceding sentence, this scholar must state here that he personally knows of entirely too many reputable persons, including highly respected scholars and philosophers, who hold such beliefs to be able to discount them as nonsense or superstition. Which is to say, magic and demons very nearly *must* be real. This scholar, having never personally encountered magic or demons, cannot state categorically that they do exist, but the evidence is so strong that allegations of their existence must be taken seriously.)

Second: form of control. Traditionally, which is to say according to legend and myth, magic is accomplished by means of arm waving, gestures, chanting in arcane languages, and commands given in such arcane languages. The literature on magic, both scholarly and popular, is heavy with examples of magical practitioners who effect magic through controlling demons by exactly such means. The literature is also filled with examples of magical practitioners who never use such traditional methods. The conflicting examples, roughly equal in proportion, suggest that either (1) the traditional accouterments are not necessary, or (2) that some demons require the gestures and language, and others will perform for humans without them.

Third: demon types. Careful study demonstrates that demons come in generally two types: intelligent and unintelligent, with many subcategories of each type. There appear to be limited numbers of other demons which are, for the most part, quiescent until called upon and are capable of performing one feat on only one occasion. With few exceptions, each kind of demon can perform one feat of magic—conferring invisibility, starting fires, speeding messages, explosive saliva, etc. Intelligent demons can be enticed to do the bidding of magicians, or indeed, according to numerous accounts, persons who are not even magicians. Intelligent demons have language, of a sort, and can, for the most part, understand human speech, though their own speech is frequently unintelligible to human beings. No one knows why the intelligent demons perform feats of magic for their human masters. Some suspect they do it out of curiosity, others that it is a form of perversion among them, yet others that it gives them an excuse to wreak damage on humans. A fortunately small number of intelligent demons appear to function out of sheer malevolence; payment is negotiated with such demons. Unintelligent demons have no known language, are never enticed, never perform on verbal command, must be imprisoned, and must be coerced to work their magic. Another point on which all sources agree is that demons must be fed. What they are fed appears to depend on the kind of demon, as the literature provides numerous recipes for feeding demons. Intelligent demons that are not fed will simply abandon their human masters; the unintelligent ones will die within their prisons or lose weight until they are able to escape said prison. The unintelligent demons are reputed, sometimes, to cause serious harm to their masters, even death, if they escape their prisons.

Fourth: the efficaciousness of magic. All demons must be treated properly in order for them to perform their magical feats. Many of the intelligent demons appear to form bonds with their human masters, which bonds are not necessarily strong nor positive. An intelligent demon may, on occasion, change allegiances without warning if its bond is negative. If its bond is momentarily negative—for example, if it hasn't been fed recently—it might refuse to perform without actually abandoning its master. Or a demon might decide to perform at a level less than optimal. Malevolent demons may arbitrarily decide that negotiated payments for services rendered are insufficient and break their agreements, to the extent of causing severe harm, even death, to their masters. If inadequately imprisoned, unintelligent demons will escape, frequently doing harm to their masters. Ultimately, the efficaciousness of a demon's magic depends on the appropriateness of its employment.

In conclusion: It appears to be possible, if not probable, that magic does indeed exist, that it is performed by demons under the (partial?) control of human masters, that the demons have a homeland, and that the frequency of their appearance is inversely related to the distance from that homeland. More study is required to come to firm conclusions, and it is fervently hoped that other scholars, perhaps those with closer affiliation to practitioners of magic, will contribute to the study.

IV

FLIGHT

CHAPTER
EIGHTEEN

The horses startled when running people they couldn't see were suddenly among them, and the stallion reared then kicked out, barely missing Haft.

"Be seen!" Spinner shouted as he skidded to a halt. He wrapped an arm around the Golden Girl and jerked her to a stop.

The horses were startled again as three people suddenly appeared among them, but they settled down quickly. The mare gave Haft a love nip when he got in range. Haft tried to avoid receiving any other expressions of affection from the mare as he moved to untether her.

"You ride this one," Spinner said, lifting the Golden Girl onto the gelding; the horses were already saddled.

"What do you think you're doing?" the Golden Girl demanded. "You've sent everybody else off to freedom, and you're keeping me as your own slave?"

"What? No!" Spinner said, shocked and perplexed. It wasn't the reaction he expected for freeing her; she sounded as if she didn't want to be with him at all. "The others will probably be safe in Oskul, but who knows how long it will take them to get home from there, or even if they'll be able to get to Oskul with the Jokapcul invading Skragland? Haft and I are going back to Frangeria. Apianghia is right across the bay from Frangeria. I can get you home from there."

Before either of them could say anything more, Haft softly called out, "Spinner!"

Spinner turned. Haft had his axe raised, looking back the way they'd come. Spinner readied his staff as three figures broke from the trees into the tiny clearing. He was about to swing at the nearest figure when he recognized Doli. Then he saw that one of the others was Fletcher. The third person was also a woman.

"What are you doing here?" Spinner demanded. "Fletcher, you're supposed to be taking everybody to Oskul."

Fletcher shrugged. "The other men can guard them. I have no desire to go the capital of Skragland. Besides, I think it will be safer traveling in a small party than a big one."

"You treated me well at the inn," Doli said. "You never treated me like property. And when you saw we were slaves, you both risked your lives to set us free. I'm going with you."

"This is my wife," Fletcher said, pointing to the other woman. "Master Yoel kept us apart. You have brought us together again." Fletcher put an arm around his wife. "Her name is Zweepee."

"But you can't go with us," Spinner insisted. "We'll be traveling fast, and we only have three horses. You can't keep up with the horses on foot, and they can't go fast carrying six people."

"We must get away from here, *now*," the Golden Girl said. "Let them come with us."

Doli pushed Spinner toward the stallion. "Get on!" she said. "I'll ride with you." Spinner mounted and pulled her up behind him.

Fletcher jumped onto the mare and lifted his wife onto the front of the saddle, where he could cradle her in his arms.

The Golden Girl gave Haft a glare that told him not to even think of doing anything, and reached a hand down to help him onto the gelding's back. She kept her feet in the stirrups and her hands on the reins. "Watch where you put your hands," she snarled as Haft adjusted himself behind her.

Then the three horses were pounding up the ridge side as fast as they could, around trees and dodging low branches. By the time they stopped, sheets of lather dripped off the horses' flanks.

Spinner reined in the stallion. "Everybody off the horses before we kill them." They weren't near the road—or at least he didn't think they were. "Let's make camp and get some sleep. I don't think anybody will come on us very soon." His adrenaline rush was over and he was too tired to worry about how he was going to get rid of the extra people in his party.

But, unexpectedly, he did have another worry. The Lalla Mkouma on his shoulder piped, *"Veedmee!"*

"What?"

"Veedmee!"

The other Lalla Mkouma chimed in with the same demand.

The Golden Girl chuckled as she returned her Lalla Mkouma to Spinner's free shoulder. "They want to be fed," she said.

Perplexed, Spinner looked at her. "What do we feed them?"

She shrugged innocently. "You're the magicians with the demons. Why do you expect me to know how to control them?"

"But—" Spinner and Haft both yelped as the Lalla Mkouma bit their ears.

"Veedmee!" they piped.

"But we don't know what to feed you!"

"Oo naw niz!" one of them said. Then all four clambered to the ground—Spinner's pausing on her way down to bite his hand—and scampered off, but not before delivering surprisingly hard kicks to the Marines' ankles.

The Golden Girl laughed; the others maintained an embarrassed silence.

Moments later they made their sleeping arrangements. Fletcher and Zweepee found a bush to crawl under for privacy. Haft looked from the Golden Girl to Doli. The former stood rigid and threatening, and the other looked longingly at

Spinner. Haft made a disgusted grimace, then cleared a space at the foot of a tree and lay down alone.

Oblivious to her defiant attitude, Spinner stepped up to the Golden Girl and held his cloak open wide. "It's roomy enough for two, Alyline," he said softly, and started to close the cloak around them both.

The Golden Girl's knee went to his groin. It wasn't a kick, she simply put it there with more emphasis than a lover would use. "Aye. And if you wish to keep your manhood, you will give me that cloak to use by myself."

Spinner flinched at the touch of her knee. Again he was surprised by her attitude. Her reaction was so different from her seductive pose the previous night.

"I . . . But—But I didn't . . ." he stammered in a high-pitched voice.

"That's right," she cut him off. "And you won't. The cloak . . ." She held out a hand in an imperious manner and made a motion as though to knee him more sharply.

Spinner hopped back another pace. "But—But—"

"I sleep alone. Give me your cloak so I can cover myself."

He whipped the four-sided reversible cloak from his shoulders and held it out for her to take. She did and disappeared behind a tree.

Mumbling and shaking his head, Spinner took a couple of steps and sat down heavily. He sat muttering and shaking his head for another moment or two before wrapping himself in the silk cloak he'd brought for the Golden Girl and reclining. He didn't even bother to clear the ground of sticks and stones. He rolled onto his side.

A moment later he felt pressure against his back. Doli whispered near his ear, "I will keep you warm."

He tried to shrug off her enveloping arms and drew the cloak closer around himself. "I want to sleep alone," he said. "If someone comes upon us while we sleep, I can rise to meet them more quickly if I am alone."

His words stung. "You didn't act that way with the—with Alyline," Doli accused.

Spinner curled himself into a ball and tugged the cloak closer.

Haft watched from his spot. Even though he couldn't hear what Spinner and Doli were saying, their movements told him as clearly as words what was going on. He shook his head at his friend's dense-headedness. Well, there was no help for it. He stood and picked up the other silk cloak. He padded to where Doli rolled away from Spinner and bent over to touch her on the shoulder.

"Here," he said quietly, "you can use this for your bedding." He draped it over her shoulder and backed off. It was just a friendly gesture, but he thought that if Spinner wasn't interested in her, it didn't mean Doli had to remain alone. He returned to his tree and slept in his cloak. He smiled in his dreams; he dreamt that Doli realized the futility of her desire for Spinner, and that she'd decided that he, Haft, was really quite a sterling chap.

Angry voices snapped Spinner awake. He groped for his quarterstaff as he rolled from under his cloak. He experienced an instant's disorientation, all it took for him to realize that he heard only one angry voice—and another voice protesting innocence. The protesting voice was Haft's. The angry voice was the Golden Girl's.

"It's mine, really," said Haft. "I won it in battle."

"You did not!" the Golden Girl accused. "You stole it from Master Yoel, just as he stole it from me. It's mine and I want it back."

"But—" The sharp report of a slap stopped Haft's protest.

Spinner put down his staff. He sat up and rubbed the sleep from his eyes. The sun was full up. Spinner looked toward the voices. The Golden Girl straddled Haft's middle, leaning over him, grabbing at something he clutched to his chest. The sunlight that reached down through the treetops glinted off her garments. Sunlight also shined off whatever it was Haft held to himself. Pretending she wasn't watching, Doli stood some distance to the side. Fletcher and Zweepee sat where they had slept.

Spinner stood up and groaned. He was sore and stiff; the ground was hard. He arched and twisted his back to loosen it up, then slowly walked to where Alyline straddled Haft. She looked so beautiful that his heart ached at sight of her golden beauty. Even when she was angry, she was the most beautiful woman he had ever seen. As he walked he looked only at her and forgot about the stiffness in his back, his neck, and his shoulders. When he reached them he squatted next to her and placed a protective arm around her shoulders.

The Golden Girl twisted toward him and shoved with both hands, hard. He fell backward.

"Keep your hands off me; I'm not a slave anymore."

Spinner sat back, propping himself up with his elbows. "But I meant no harm. I only meant to—"

"I know what you meant. You men are all alike. You see me dance on the stage, you see my dress, you know the innkeeper sold me, and you think I'm a back-tavern whore. Well, that's over. No man will touch me unless I desire it, and I do not desire you to touch me. At the moment all I desire is that this offal give me back my knife."

Haft tried to slither out from under the Golden Girl, but she twisted around and slapped a powerful hand on his chest, pinning him and driving the air from his lungs.

"You think that hurts? You claim to have been in fearsome battles. Well, I tell you, little man, you have felt no pain, been in no fight so terrible, as what you will experience if you do not give me my dagger right *now*." She grabbed the hair on his chest and yanked.

Haft gasped and looked wide-eyed at the harridan. She seemed ready to kill him. "Well, if it means that much to you, *here*!" he said in an unsuccessful attempt at bravado.

The Golden Girl deftly caught the spinning scabbard belt

with her free hand. She kept Haft pinned with her hand as she moved both feet to the same side of his body. Then, erect, she clasped the belt low on her hips with the scabbard on the left side of the middle of her belly. The scabbard lay diagonally, the hilt ready to hand. She smiled down at Haft. "Thank you," she purred.

Haft rolled away as fast as he could and only raised himself to his feet when he thought he'd gone a safe distance. The Golden Girl slowly turned and smiled that same predatory smile at everyone else. "This dagger is mine," she announced proudly. "It was given to me at birth. It is the sign of Djerwohl, my birth status." She dropped the smile and gave Spinner a cold look. "Do you have any food, or are we to forage like the others you sent off on their own? If you do, we should eat before we move on."

"I have food," Spinner said. He retrieved the bread, cheese, and sausage from his pack. There was little enough and it would not last long. They would definitely be foraging soon.

They sat to eat their meal cold without even a small fire for tea. Throughout the meal, nobody had a chance to ask what "Djerwohl" was.

"You made me leave Mudjwohl behind," the Golden Girl said to Spinner. "I don't think I will forgive you for that."

"Mudjwohl? I left you alone to dress. You could have taken anything you wanted. I didn't tell you not to bring anything."

She looked like she wanted to spit—on him. Instead, she spat at him with words. "You fool. Mudjwohl is the sothar player. He is—" She took a deep breath. "—he was, my musician. He was in the group you sent to Oskul."

He wasn't sure what the problem was, unless she and this Mudjwohl had a relationship more than that of dancer and accompanist. And he didn't want to ask about that. If they did have a deeper relationship, he was glad the musician had been left behind. Nonetheless, he spoke in a conciliatory tone. "How was I to know? You told me you were the only entertainer who was a slave."

This time she did spit, and barely missed his foot. "You lowlanders are as ignorant as you are arrogant. Anytime a Djerwohl dancer says *I* in referring to her dancing, the reference includes her sothar player. She is not a dancer without the sothar."

"But—"

The Golden Girl made to spit again, and Spinner dropped a piece of cheese in scooting away from her. Where *had* the seductress in the woman gone?

"Those three"—she indicated the other freed slaves— "have no money. I don't know how much money you have, but it's probably not enough to see us all the way to Frangeria and me to Apianghia." She fingered a few of the coins that adorned her costume. "I will not spend any of these, I assure you. If you'd had the sense to bring Mudjwohl when you abducted me, I could have danced at inns and castles along the way to make money for our travels. Now I may never dance again." Her look impaled Spinner, made him feel like an insect displayed in a case.

"But—"

Again she cut him off. "But you left Mudjwohl with those going to Oskul." She moved close enough to jab his chest with a sharp fingernail. "Because of your ignorance, I cannot earn money for us by dancing." Each word she spoke was punctuated by a jab. "Do not think that when you run out of money that I will pay our passage by opening my legs." She shot a glance at Doli. "Perhaps another of our number would do that, but I will leave you and travel alone first." She pulled away from him and patted the hilt of her knife.

Doli was outraged by the implication that she would whore to make money for their travels, and shifted as though to leap at the Golden Girl, but swallowed and sat back when the Golden Girl placed her hand on her knife.

"Believe that I can take care of myself when I travel alone!" she finished.

"Then how did you become a slave?" Doli murmured. Nobody heard her.

The Golden Girl then turned to her food and had no more to say, which satisfied Spinner, who hunched over his own food. He didn't understand the woman. Why was she treating him this way? No one else felt like talking after the Golden Girl had vented her anger.

After a bit Spinner stopped pretending to eat and walked away.

As soon as he was able to do so gracefully, Fletcher stood and went in search of trees with branches suitable for making arrows. He had enough to make a dozen shafts by the time Spinner called them all together to move on.

"The horses won't last long if we continue to ride double," Spinner said. He looked at Fletcher and decided the man was fit enough. "The women will ride and the men will run alongside the horses for a way, then we will all walk until the men and horses are ready to run again."

"I can take my turn running," Alyline said.

Spinner was saved from having to argue the point by an approaching sound. It was a chuttering, banging noise that sounded like it was in the treetops, except that it was growing louder too fast to be an animal traveling the treetops.

"Take cover," Fletcher shouted. "Get behind the trunks of trees with the thickest branches and leaves. Don't let it see you!" He fit his own action to his words, dragging his wife and the gelding with him. In a moment all six people and three horses were behind four trees. Haft and Doli were together behind one with the mare; Doli gave Haft a don't-touch-me look, which Haft innocently ignored. The Golden Girl took the stallion and hid behind another tree. The glare she shot Spinner when he tried to join her sent him off to a tree by himself.

The chuttering, banging noise grew until it was like thunder in the trees. When it seemed to be directly overhead, Spinner risked a look upward. Drifting through the air was a huge red cross. At least it appeared huge to Spinner. He wasn't able to judge its size because it was somewhere above the tree-tops. In only a few minutes the cross flew through the sky more rapidly than a horse could run and disappeared to the east, taking its noise with it.

"What was that?" Haft asked in an awed voice.

"A flying carpet," Fletcher answered reverently.

Haft blinked. "It didn't look like a carpet to me," he said.

Fletcher shrugged. "That's what they're called."

"It was so fast," Spinner said softly. "No horse can run that fast."

The Golden Girl snorted. "You think that was fast?" she sneered. "I've seen a flying carpet go so much faster it would make that one look like it was standing still, and it screamed like the damned."

Spinner looked at her uncertainly. He didn't want to believe anything could move that fast. But then, he never believed any of the tales he'd heard about flying carpets. And now he'd seen one with his own eyes. There must be more things possible than he knew.

"Do you think it is looking for us?" Zweepee asked her husband.

Fletcher slowly shook his head. "I don't know."

"Whether it is or isn't, we have to go," the Golden Girl said. She bounded onto the stallion's back. "Ready?"

Haft looked nervously about, gnawing his lower lip and thinking about the flying carpet. It reminded him strongly that the land about held unknown dangers. "We should have flankers," he said. "Lord Gunny says a column on the move needs flankers for security."

Spinner gave him an odd look. "There are only six of us," he said patiently. "How can we manage flankers?"

"We can't. But we should have them anyway."

Spinner snorted.

CHAPTER
NINETEEN

Doli looked to Spinner for assistance getting on the mare, but Spinner wasn't looking at her and she finally gave a grunt and pulled herself into the saddle. Then she grunted in disgust at the way Spinner was ogling the Golden Girl in her skimpy attire. She shot Haft a sharp glance, one that told him not to think of offering assistance. Haft shrugged and made sure he didn't stand too close to her.

Fletcher tenderly helped his wife mount the gelding.

As soon as the other women were mounted, the Golden Girl wheeled the stallion to the east and took the lead. She set the pace at a brisk trot that the running men had trouble keeping up with. In a couple hundred paces the three men were all panting from the effort.

"Slow down, Alyline," Doli snapped.

The Golden Girl ignored her.

Doli heeled the mare in the ribs to make her move up to the side of the stallion but the mare maintained her position behind the gelding. Doli wanted to scream in frustration. Instead she snapped again, "Slow down, you're going too fast for the men to keep up."

The Golden Girl urged the stallion into a gallop, and she was soon lost to sight in the trees ahead of them.

"Zweepee, slow down," Doli snarled in Skraggish. "Let her go on by herself." She reined the mare in to set an easier pace for the running men.

Zweepee brought the gelding to a halt. When Fletcher

reached her side, she put out a hand and stroked his sweating brow. "You set the pace," she said softly. "So we don't wear you out."

After a mile or so the Golden Girl found a small clearing with a fallen tree. She stopped the stallion, dismounted, and sat on the tree trunk to wait for the others. She was determined not be ordered about, now that she was free again. She was sitting regally erect when the others reached her.

Doli leaped off the mare as though she'd spent her entire life as a horsewoman and stalked to the Golden Girl. She stood with legs apart, fists on hips, to confront her.

"What do you mean, setting so fast a pace? Have you no consideration for the men? If there is pursuit from the inn or if someone else attacks us, the men will need to have enough breath and strength to fight."

The Golden Girl stared silently at the forest to the east as though planning a route.

She still had nothing to say when Spinner stepped next to Doli and said, "Don't run ahead of us; we don't know what danger may lie ahead. And wear this." He tried to hand her the silken cloak, but she didn't take it, and he dropped it onto her lap. After a few seconds she looked down at the cloak as though she had placed it there herself while resting. Then she stood next to the stallion and casually tossed the cloak over the horse's withers. Spinner half raised his hand to touch her arm. She turned, still with her back to him, and without speaking led the stallion away before his hand reached her. She didn't put on the cloak.

They all walked for another mile, and then, on Spinner's order, two of the women remounted. The Golden Girl instead insisted that one of the men take a turn riding. Spinner was just as adamant about her riding. Haft took Spinner's side of the argument. He quickly realized he had made a mistake.

"You've been inside for too long," Haft said. "Spinner and I are used to traveling long distances on foot. And Fletcher is used to hard work outside. We men can run better than you."

The Golden Girl spun toward him, her face only inches away from his. "You think dancing isn't physical work?" She stood in a small patch of sunlight that caused her clothing to glint sharply with every movement. She looked Haft up and down and snorted. "I could run farther than you any day. When you are gasping, and staggering to keep your feet, I could run around you in circles." She spun from him and leaped onto the stallion's back. "*Pfagh!* Men, they're all the same!"

Spinner, hurt and confusion in his eyes, stepped to her side. She sidled her horse away from the placating hand he reached out to her and didn't give him a chance to speak. When he dropped his hand, she smiled down at him sweetly and said, "If we have to fight anyone later on, I think I'll use your staff. Since you're too stupid to take a turn riding, you'll be too tired to use it yourself." She sharply heeled the stallion and had him gallop ahead a few hundred paces before she slowed him to a walk and let the others catch up. Then she galloped ahead once more. By the time she stopped for them to catch up again, they had gone far enough to walk the horses once more. She waited for the others to reach her. This time no one said anything to her about racing ahead. They rested quietly and then simply followed when she rose to lead the way. Except for Spinner. He hurried to walk by her side. Just before he reached her, she ducked under the stallion's neck and walked with the horse between them. He tried to talk to her over the horse's back, but she appeared not to hear anything and he soon gave up.

At the end of that mile of walking, the Golden Girl again offered to let one of the men ride. Again they refused. Again she galloped on ahead and waited for them when it was time to walk once more.

And so it went until late in the afternoon when, with the sun's rays casting their shadows far ahead of them, they finally reached the highway that led to the Principality of Zobra.

* * *

The "highway" was no more than a gash in the woods twenty or thirty paces broad. They couldn't tell for sure how wide it was because the river of humanity flooding along it obscured the far side. It was by and large an orderly flow. The people on the nearer side were flooding south. Those on the farther side were pouring north. Some bore packs on their backs. Others carried belongings in baskets bouncing from poles balanced across their shoulders. Some had ox carts with belongings piled higher than was prudent. Others carried children in their arms or ancients on their backs. Their faces bore haunted looks, hunted looks, looks of unfettered fear. For the most part they trudged voiceless, the only sounds the tromping of their feet, the creaking of their carts, the lowing of their oxen, the cries of distressed infants.

The only disorder in the river came from some few swimmers in the highway's tide of humanity, richer and ruder than most, who rode on horses or in horse-drawn carriages, plowing their way through the foot-weary, forcing the ox carts almost into the trees. Shouts and cries, curses and threats, trailed those richer and ruder few, who cursed and threatened back. But whether afoot or in ox cart, whether by horse or by carriage, the people on the highway were all the same—they were refugees.

"I think not all those ahorse will reach where they are going," Fletcher said after an aged woman with a bundle carried over her shoulder was knocked from her feet and nearly trampled by a dusty coxcomb when she didn't scamper from his path quickly enough.

"I think you're right," Haft said, caressing the handle of his axe.

Spinner stood next to them while the dandy ran the woman down. He nodded. Sooner or later one of those with a horse would push the wrong person the wrong way at the wrong time. Then the anger would ripple up and down the river of people and everyone with a horse would be dragged down.

"Where are they going?" Doli asked. She sidled the mare next to Spinner so that her leg pressed against his arm.

Spinner shook his head. "The better question is why are they going anywhere?"

He stepped away from Doli and the mare, into the moving stream of people. Haft and Fletcher, realizing what he was doing, entered it at other points.

"Excuse me, good man," Spinner said to the southbound farmer he fell in step next to. "Where are you going? Why do you go?"

The farmer turned a gaunt visage to him. "Haven't you heard?" he said. "There's been an invasion from the north. An invasion by the dwarves and the denizens of the Night Forest. Oskul has fallen. It is said that the king was sundered limb from limb by the invaders. I have heard that the dwarves and the dwellers of the Night Forest are now rampaging through the countryside. Everyone they find they shackle as prisoner or slave. If they don't kill them first."

Spinner thanked him then stepped out of the human river and back into the trees, where he made his way to the others.

"A townsman told me the Jokapcul invaded from Bostia," Haft said when Spinner was through. "And that the king himself is leading the army against the invaders. But he doesn't think the Skragish army can beat the Jokapcul."

"A deserting soldier told me an army of magicians rained destruction on Oskul," Fletcher said. "That soldier didn't know if the king was dead or alive, but he heard he had been taken prisoner and refused to give his parole." He and Spinner exchanged a look. Each was wondering about the fate of the freed slaves they had sent on their way to the Skragish capital. But neither man spoke of it; it was too late to do anything to help them.

"If Oskul has fallen, why are as many people going north?" the Golden Girl asked.

She dismounted and donned the silk cloak for the first time, wrapping it close around herself. Without a glance at her companions, she waded into the stream. They quickly lost sight of her.

Zweepee spoke and Doli translated. "Wise of her to put on that cloak. Half naked and wearing all that gold, she might not make it more than a few paces through those men."

"I don't know," Spinner said. "The refugees are probably too interested in fleeing to bother her." But his face didn't reflect any confidence in his words.

Doli dismounted and stood close to him, the front of her arm against the back of his, her breast brushing the side of his arm. Spinner looked uncomfortable but didn't move away.

"With that tongue of hers," Haft said, "I don't think anyone would survive bothering her."

The Golden Girl was barely out of sight before Spinner started worrying about her. Doli clasped her hands around his upper arm and held him close when he made a move to follow onto the highway in search of her. Alyline was gone long enough even for Haft to start worrying.

Doli furrowed her brow at the men's concern. She made a move and said, "You don't know her as well as I do. Wait longer." She left unspoken her obvious feelings: small loss if she's gone.

It wasn't much longer before Alyline returned. The dappled gray of her cloak kept her hidden from their sight so that she was almost among them before they saw her approach.

"I talked to several people," she said. "They all said the same thing: Zobra has been invaded from Bostia. These refugees are fleeing into Skragland because they think its armies are closer than their own and can give them protection."

"What about Zobra City?" Spinner asked. "Did anybody say anything about the port?"

She shook her head. "None of them are from that far away. But none of the rumors they told me say the port is threatened."

Lost in thought, Spinner looked south. After a few moments he snapped out of it. "We have to chance going south," he said in a firm voice. "We can't travel on the road, though. We'll have to continue cross-country. Let's go back into the trees." He offered no further explanation, waited for no questions or suggestions, simply led the way back into the forest. Only when the women were mounted again did he notice that Haft wasn't with them.

"Where—" But before he could finish his question, Haft broke through the trees. He was riding one horse and leading two more.

"I think we'll make better speed if we have more horses," Haft said, grinning.

"What? Where?"

Haft shrugged eloquently. "A trio of those rich men pushed the wrong man the wrong way at the wrong time. When I left, people were stripping the valuables off them."

Spinner looked at him speculatively. "Might that man afoot have been a Frangerian Marine?" he asked.

Haft shrugged. "Could have been. I wasn't looking at him when it happened. My eyes were on the horsemen."

Fletcher laughed. "Whoever he was, our thanks to the man afoot. Don't you agree, Spinner?"

Spinner paused, looking hard at Haft for a few seconds before replying. Then he grinned broadly. "Yes, we owe that footman our thanks, no matter who he was."

The women, Doli and Zweepee, at least, cheered Haft.

In seconds Fletcher was on the gelding with his wife behind him, and Spinner was on one of the extra horses Haft had brought. They cantered due south. Haft didn't complain at all about being on a horse.

After an hour's ride, Spinner judged them far enough from the highway that a small fire wouldn't attract the attention of the refugees. Stars were visible in the eastern sky, and they had little time to find firewood before it became too dark to look for more. Fletcher saw to the horses while the others scoured the ground for kindling. It wasn't until they had a small blaze burning that they made any other preparations for their campsite. Spinner parceled out their food, the meager supply of sausage, cheese, and bread. There would be enough left only for the morning meal. Quickly, water was boiling for tea. Their water was also running low.

"It bothers me," Spinner said halfway through dinner, "what that farmer told me about the dwarves and the Night Forest dwellers. Do you know anything about them, Fletcher?"

Fletcher shook his head. "Very little. Both are secretive. The dwarves stay in their mountain valleys northeast of Skragland. I've never heard of them invading another country, though they could. What the farmer said about the denizens of the Night Forest must be wrong, though. The Night Forest doesn't come near Skragland." He lost himself in thought for a long moment, then continued, "They did invade the Easterlies about eight years ago. It took almost five years to force back the invaders." He shuddered. "The strange beings who live in the Night Forest are fiercer than what I have heard and seen of the Jokapcul. And even more brutal. Some say they aren't human."

Spinner felt little reassured. From what he remembered of the maps he'd seen, he agreed that it was unlikely the denizens of the Night Forest had entered the war on the side of the Jokapcul—at least, he was sure, they hadn't invaded Skragland. But he'd heard the dwarves were fearsome fighters who had a long-standing conflict with Skragland. It was possible they were in the war; if not actually on the side of the Jokapcul, at least opposed to some of those who were fighting the western islanders. Well, the direction they were traveling was taking them away from the dwarves.

Once the remnants of dinner were cleaned up, Fletcher took the shafts he'd cut that morning and set to work barking them and planing their surfaces smooth with his belt knife.

"In the morning I'll find feathers," he said. He looked at what little he could see of the ground around them. "Somewhere, I'll find stones I can use to chip heads. Then I can get us fresh meat."

"We can also hunt," Haft said, pointing out his crossbow.

Fletcher nodded. "So long as there have been few hunters about. You have to get close to game to bring it down with a crossbow." He paused in his carving and looked at the crossbow. "I've sometimes wondered, why do Frangerian Marines use crossbows instead of longbows?"

Haft looked at his crossbow intently; that was a question he'd never considered.

Spinner, however, knew the answer. "Because of ship-to-ship fighting. The longbow has the advantage of range and speed in firing, true. But range means little between ships. You see, when a bowman shoots, his ship is bobbing up and down in the water and so is his target. If you're moving when you shoot at a moving target, it's only by chance if your arrow even comes near your target. So you have to be close in order to shoot if you want to strike home. But still, even close, both you and your target are moving—even once the ships are grappled together for boarding. A quarrel doesn't fly as far as an arrow, but it flies faster. That means there is less time between your shot and your hit, so you have a better chance of striking your point. And at its range, the crossbow is more accurate than the longbow. A crossbow throws its bolt with more force than a longbow throws its arrow." He drew a quarrel from its pouch and held it up. "Look at the head of this bolt. It doesn't have flanges like the head of an arrow, it's no more than a pointed cap. This point can punch its way through thicker, harder armor than your arrowheads—even if you had iron heads instead of the stone ones you will be making." He smiled somewhat ruefully. "Why do you think the armored knights of those armies that still have them are anxious to kill crossbowmen on sight? It's because a man with a crossbow is more dangerous to an armored man than one armed with a longbow. He can be more dangerous to the knight than another knight. Certainly, a man with a crossbow can kill an armored knight before the knight can close to fighting range.

"We use crossbows because we can't shoot until the ships are close to each other. Then we need accuracy. And sometimes we need to shoot an officer behind a shield. The crossbow can sometimes send a bolt through a shield when a longbow can't."

Fletcher nodded and returned to smoothing his shafts. "That's all the explanation anyone could want," he said as he sighted along a shaft. "But we are not at sea, and I believe the Jokapcul are not all that heavily armored. My longbow will do well against them, and take them down long before they get close enough to grapple."

There was another thing that occupied them when they made camp for the night: Fletcher had heard about *Lord Gunny Says*, but had never seen a copy and was fascinated by the book. Since he couldn't read Frangerian himself, Spinner and Haft took turns reading it to him during the brief periods between the time they stopped and nightfall.

The men cast lots to determine which watch each would stand. Spinner objected when the Golden Girl insisted on being included in the watch rotation. He lost that argument.

Early in the morning when the others awoke, Fletcher, who had last watch, showed them a freshly killed hawk. "It was too confident while eating its first kill of the day," he told them. "I stunned it with a stone and wrung its neck before it could recover. Now I can fletch my shafts." He quickly plucked the hawk's tail feathers. He tossed the rest of it aside; none of his companions would want to eat it. Maybe if their food ran out and they were hungry enough, they would be willing to eat a hunter. But not just then.

Spinner looked around with mild apprehension; he felt ill at ease but did not know why. "Let's eat as we ride," he said. Nobody raised their voice to disagree. The Golden Girl reached the stallion before he did.

They didn't see the wolf that slinked into the campsite as soon as they were gone and gobbled up the remains of the hawk.

They rode south through the forest for a week. Even though they had enough horses, Zweepee, the smallest of them, usually rode double with her husband. Sometimes, when they trotted for a while, one of the men dismounted and ran—Haft volunteered to run more often than the other men. Sometimes they all got off and walked.

While they walked, Fletcher kept an eye on the ground for anything from which he could make an arrowhead. By the end of the first day he found three pieces of flint and one of obsidian that were suitable. During that afternoon, Haft brought down two rabbits for their evening meal. That night they found a tiny rivulet to camp next to. It provided them with the first fresh water for drinking and cooking they'd come across since leaving the inn. Zweepee found some tubers and onions, and she and Doli made a stew. After they ate and made tea, Fletcher boiled more water to make glue from the rabbit skins. While the skins were boiling down, he used a large granite pebble to flake away at the flint and obsidian. One piece of flint was too flawed, but the other two yielded three usable arrowheads, and the obsidian yielded two more. Rabbit sinew served as cord to bind the arrowheads to the shafts. Five arrows weren't many, but at least he could use his bow. But by then it was too dark to test it.

The bow Spinner had taken from The Burnt Man wasn't a particularly good one, but it was serviceable. Fletcher proved its usefulness the next day when he brought down a small deer for their dinner. Between the men's hunting and Zweepee's broad knowledge of wild plants—knowledge that came as a surprise to everyone except Fletcher—they wound up eating well. And, as they went, Fletcher found more stones for arrowheads and cut more shafts. He soon had a deerskin quiver full of arrows.

Despite the time spent in hunting and gathering, Spinner estimated they were traveling almost twice as fast as he and Haft had when walking through Bostia to Skragland. The horses might not have been twice as fast as moving on foot, but the small party never had to stop to hide from patrols or take detours around villages or enemy campsites; nobody seemed to live in the vast forest. So long as they could ignore the reason for their flight through the forest and not think of the rumored Jokapcul invasion of Zobra, life felt good. They lacked only a stream large enough for them to bathe in and to wash their clothing.

There was enough left of the deer Fletcher brought down two days earlier to last them another day or two, but because they hadn't taken the time to smoke it, the meat was turning. It was ripe enough that none of them had eaten more than lightly of it that night, but thanks to a brace of quail Spinner bagged, no one had to go without meat. What remained of the deer was hung on a tripod over the damped fire in hope that the smoke might render it fit to feed them again.

Spinner had first watch. He was feeling edgy, as he had ever since the first morning on their journey south. He'd had the feeling they were being watched. As soon as the others were sleeping, he walked into the trees as though seeking to relieve himself. Once out of the dim circle of light cast by the banked fire, he softly padded in an enlarging spiral around the campsite. After three ever-wider revolutions without finding a watcher or any sign of one, he decided nobody was there and turned back toward the campsite. Just before he reached it, a scream pierced the night. Spinner burst into the circle of light in time to see a large wolf rip the deer carcass from its tripod and dash into the night. Doli sat upright, her wide eyes staring over the hands she held clapped to her face.

Before Spinner could chase the wolf to reclaim their food, Doli leaped to her feet and threw herself on him, wrapping her arms around his neck.

Instantly, the others were on their feet, weapons in hand, gathering around Spinner and Doli, looking madly about for the attackers.

"Put your weapons down," Spinner said, his voice muffled by the cloud of Doli's hair enveloping his face. "There's nobody here." He pried Doli's arms from his neck. "Doli was frightened by a hungry wolf that came after our venison."

Haft knelt at the remains of the tripod, then picked up the thong that had held the carcass and looked at the others in amazement. "It's not bitten through," he said. "It's not broken either."

Fletcher bent close to look and said, "It looks like someone untied it."

"It—it—" Doli stammered. She swallowed to gain control of her voice, then continued, "The wolf was licking at the thong when I saw it."

Spinner took the thong from Fletcher and examined it. How could a wolf untie a knot in a leather thong? Clearly the thong hadn't been bitten through or broken. He looked at the others with wonder.

They discussed the astonishing wolf for some time before anyone was ready to try to sleep. The wolf did not reappear that night.

They were subdued in the morning, and Haft was the only one to mention their visitor. He cursed under his breath, staring at his meatless breakfast. "That wolf ever shows himself to me, I'll kill him," he muttered.

That day the men killed a fawn, so they had meat that evening and the next morning. During his watch that night, Spinner hid a small portion of the meat to leave behind for the wolf. He no longer had the uncomfortable feeling of being secretly watched; he was certain that what he had sensed was the wolf following them.

Much of the time on their travels south they heard, off to their left and muted by distance, the din of the refugees fleeing north and south, from one invasion into another. But they weren't always close enough to the road to hear its noises; if an easier route opened that took them away from it, they followed that route for a time. And they often followed game trails that took them away from the highway, though they never followed game trails far; game had become too plentiful in the vicinity. Now and then they caught sight of the wolf flitting through the trees. They never saw him long enough for Haft to get off a shot, not even when Haft carried his crossbow armed. Spinner didn't let him chase after the animal. And every night, Spinner left a chunk of meat for the wolf.

During those days on the march, Fletcher made more arrow shafts and found enough appropriate stones to mount heads on all of them; he was satisfied when he had forty arrows. Spinner found an oak tree that was right for a new quarterstaff.

They rarely saw anyone, and when they did, it was always a hungry refugee foraging for food. But on mid-afternoon on the sixth day, they finally saw something other than the unremitting forest and the occasional refugee.

FOURTH INTERLUDE
THE BARGAIN

A Speculation on the Earliest Days in the Alliance Between Lord Lackland, Self-styled "Dark Prince," and the "High Shoton" of Jokapcul

by Scholar Munch Mu'sk
Professor of Far Western Studies
University of the Great Rift
(excerpted from *The Proceedings of the Association of Anthropological Scholars of Obscure Cultures*, Vol. 57, No. 9, Supp. A)

As has been noted in an earlier paper, Lord Lackland, accompanied by a Jokapcul knight whose name has not become known to the international community, stealthily made his way by small ship from the Kingdom of Matilda to Kokudo in the Jokapcul Islands. How the small ship reached Kokudo is not known with any certainty. Some accounts have it that under cover of night the ship slunk timidly to the Kokudo coast several miles from the main harbor of the island, let the two men off in a dinghy, then sailed away before its two passengers even reached the shore. Other accounts claim the ship sailed boldly into the harbor in bright daylight. The most likely scenario, however, is the one that has the small ship intercepted at sea by Jokapcul fisher-craft and escorted into the harbor under armed guard.

By whatever means Lord Lackland arrived in Kokudo, he was under the protection of the nameless knight he had freed and was thus not subject to instantaneous death or enslavement upon arrival. The two men were taken directly to the High Shoton, where Lord Lackland quickly attempted to convince the shoton that he knew a great deal about sea craft and seacraft, information that, as we have seen, he believed would be of great benefit to the High Shoton.

The High Shoton is said to have been impressed by Lord Lackland's knowledge of ships and sailing, but the shoton and his kamazai saw no need to retain the services of the half bastard fourth son of Good King Honritu, and were prepared to have him put to the sword immediately. As has been noted in an earlier paper, the islands of Jokapcul had long since been deforested, thus the Jokapcul had little use for Lord Lackland's knowledge of sea craft, which is to say they lacked the necessary wherewithal to build new, larger, and properly seaworthy ships. So as impressed as the High Shoton may have been with Lord Lackland's knowledge of sea craft, that knowledge was essentially worthless to him. Furthermore, the High Shoton believed, with some justification, that the Jokapcul fishermen had sufficient knowledge of seamanship, rendering Lord Lackland's knowledge of the field of little import or value to the High Shoton's conquistadorial ambitions.

It is possible that Lord Lackland was much chagrined by this turn of events, which deprived him of the use of an arcane body of knowledge he had acquired only through great effort. However, he still had what is called in the common parlance "a trump in the hole." From reports of Jokapcul raids on Matilda that came into his hands, Lord Lackland already knew that these coastal raids were made without benefit of magicians. His surreptitious meetings with the nameless Jokapcul knight imprisoned in the dungeons of Good King Honritu had confirmed that, in fact, the Jokapcul army had no magicians. It is speculated that no shoton was willing to have anyone around him who could control demons; such persons would be too great a threat. Lord Lackland's trump was his knowledge of magic. The High Shoton, despite history going against him, quickly grasped the value of magicians to his army—not to omit mention of magic's equal or greater value to the continuation of his own power—provided he could control the practitioners of magic.

When Lord Lackland presented his trump to the High Shoton, the Jokapcul chieftain stayed the planned execution of his illustrious prisoner so as to consider this new matter. To that end, the High Shoton reassembled the kamazai of his court for an extended consultation on the matter of the military value of magic. Some of the kamazai quickly grasped the merit of using magic; others, more traditional in their approach to military matters, saw no merit in its use at all. Historically, it was said, Jokapcul forces had performed in exemplary fashion without the use of magic, and it was said that such arcana were distinctly un-Jokapculian. The recently converted proponents of the use of magic counterargued that, historically, Jokapcul armies had only engaged other Jokapcul armies, conflicts in which neither of the opposing forces had the service of practitioners of the arcane arts. Moreover, said the proponents, one reason for the lack of success of the Jokapcul raids on the mainland was the use of magic by the mainlanders, which use gave them an advantage over the raiders. However, that particular allegation is disputable, since the army of the Kingdom of Matilda was not known to use magic.

The issue was not resolved until the High Shoton brought Lord Lackland into the deliberations and had him propound the multitude of advantages practitioners of the arcane arts provided to an army, the commanders of which were perspicacious enough to utilize them to greatest advantage. The use of imbaluris as messengers appealed little to many of the kamazai, and gained few converts, as the kamazai were strongly independent and seldom desired to call upon other kamazai for aid or to coordinate their activities. Neither were they greatly impressed by the healing magics; the overwhelming number of their casualties were common soldiers, whose lives they held in what can most charitably be called low esteem. Whilst they were inclined to disbelieve Lord Lackland's tales of phoenix eggs and demon spitters, the doubting kamazai could not fail to see the immense advantages possession of such powers would bestow upon those who had command of them. Should they, indeed, exist.

Consequently, the overwhelming majority of the kamazai recommended to the High Shoton that he grant to Lord Lackland a reasonable, but short, measure of time to demonstrate his command of magic and its value to the armies of Jokapcul. It is likely that, having heard of phoenix eggs, demon spitters, werecats, and other magical implements, the High Shoton would himself have indefinitely stayed the execution of his distinguished prisoner, but it suited him to have his kamazai firmly behind him on the matter. It is said that those kamazai who remained unconvinced by Lord Lackland's presentation did not remain kamazai—or alive—for more than another day.

Lord Lackland was accorded everything he needed to bring demons under his control and to bend them to the uses of the Jokapcul army. The tomes he is reputed to have conjured, once interpreted, are said to have given the Jokapcul army strength far in excess of the power held by any other army of any time or place.

Lord Lackland possessed another area of knowledge that was of value to the Jokapcul—geography. Jokapcul knowledge of the geography and peoples of other lands was, as Lord Lackland quickly learned, abysmal. The High Shoton, upon being appraised of the geographical knowledge possessed by Lord Lackland, commanded his geographers to meet with him for the purpose of determining whether his knowledge was of value to Jokapcul raiders. The geographers, following lengthy consultation with Lord Lackland, concluded that they had a great deal to learn from him of the lands into which the raiders went.

A story has circulated that the High Shoton one day asked Lord Lackland why he would aid the Jokapcul by making them better soldiers and providing them with hitherto unknown

magic and geographical knowledge, thus making them more
threatening to the mainlanders, of whom he was one. Lord
Lackland replied that he desired to overthrow the unjust rule
of King Honritu and claim his own rightful position as King
of Matilda, a position denied him by the basest accident of
birth. The High Shoton is said to have feigned amusement at
the explanation.

As for the High Shoton himself, he foresaw a campaign of
world conquest that would distract the clan chiefs and other
disaffected personages of Jokapcul from their grievances
with him. Moreover, he is thought to have concluded that if it
became known to the nation-states being invaded that Lord
Lackland was behind or connected with the invasions, that
knowledge would deflect some of their anger from Jokapcul
and might cause rifts among the nation-states of Nunimar,
thereby weakening their ability to join forces together against
the conquering armies of Jokapcul, whose armies would consequently attain greater and more rapid success in their cam-
paigns. It is probable that the High Shoton saw great gain for
himself in a public and widely known alliance between himself and Lord Lackland; he cancelled the planned, albeit un-
scheduled, execution of Lord Lackland and agreed to ally
with him.

But the alliance between the High Shoton and Lord Lackland was not bandied abroad for several years, during which
time the tomes were interpreted and their knowledge and
magic incorporated into Jokapcul tactics.

When the High Shoton was assured by his kamazai, his geographers, and by Lord Lackland, that all was in readiness, he
ordered the first invasion of Nunimar that was more than a
coastal raid. That invasion wasn't made against the Kingdom
of Matilda, which would have accomplished the stated objec-
tive of enthroning Lord Lackland as king of his natal kingdom. Instead it was conducted against the Duchy of Rumpole,
directly to the south of Matilda. That accomplished several
things for the High Shoton: it served as a method of proving

the new tactics and the magic of his army, one that would not prove too costly should it go awry; the Duchy of Rumpole was much weaker than was Matilda; and a successful invasion there would drive a physical wedge between Matilda and the coastal city-states along the fringes of the Impenetrable Jungle on the southwestern coast of Nunimar. Success would also mean that the sea lanes of communication between Matilda in the north and Bostia and the Kondive Islands to the south would be disrupted. In addition, victory in Rumpole would allow a wedge to be driven between Matilda and the Land of the Dwarves and Elfwood-Between-the-Rivers, inland from it. It is unlikely, however, that the High Shoton entertained any notion of driving a wedge between Matilda and the High Steppes, where Matilda and the nomads were in a near constant state of war. Lord Lackland was positioned prominently as leader of the invasion. To make the invasion look as if it were inspired by the Kingdom of Matilda, the ka-mazai commanding the expedition left his proper rank at home and took the title of general, and had it broadcast about that he was a mercenary in the employ of Honritu. According to travelers' tales and other reports—not all of which are to be accorded equal credence—during the years of preparation for the invasion of Rumpole, Lord Lackland's ambition grew from becoming king of Matilda to becoming emperor of all of western Nunimar.

For a time the subterfuge worked; the earliest reports of the large-scale invasions on the western coast of Nunimar and on the southwestern coast and the seaways laid them at the feet of Good King Honritu. The subterfuge proved so successful that to this day the Kingdom of Matilda is roundly condemned for its part in the invasions and largely isolated diplomatically. Thus, one of the strongest and most capable nation-states in the civilized world is unable to bring its might in concert with other nation-states to fight off the Jokapcul invasion.

* * *

NOTE: As were the earlier papers by this author on the subject of the Jokapcul attempt at the conquest of Nunimar, this paper has been based on official dispatches, traveler's tales, and the author's three decades of study of matters Jokapculian. In addition to which sources are added confessions extracted from Jokapcul soldiers taken prisoner during military operations in western and southwestern Nunimar.

The author also wishes to note at this time that there was a distressing amount of negative comment about the nonscholarly tone of his earlier paper (*Proceedings* . . . Vol. 57, No. 6), despite the fact that it was clearly labeled a "speculation." A speculation is exactly that. It was the author's intent to inform his readers as to what might have transpired; it was not an attempt at a fully accurate and scholarly biography, which is impossible under the circumstances. It is the author's hope that the more pedantic tone of this paper will quell such negative response to this paper, which in any event is based more on confirmable sources than was the previous paper. (MM)

V
NO OUTLET

CHAPTER
TWENTY

During the afternoon of the sixth day, the forest changed as the small party paralleled the north-south highway. The trees were the same mix of oaks, elms, hemlocks, and their denseness seemed the same. It was the presence—absence, really—of life that changed. When the sun was at its apex, they saw a tree-grazing deer, then didn't glimpse another the rest of the day. They saw their last hare an hour or two later. Even the wolf disappeared from their ken. The farther they went, the less they heard the melodious twirring and chitting of songbirds, until the only birdcalls were the occasional caws of carrion eaters, which grew nearer as they continued south. Tension rose among them, and their pace slowed almost imperceptibly until they were advancing at little more than a creep.

Haft was the first to dismount. He armed his crossbow as he and Spinner communicated with looks and a few gestures. Spinner nodded, and Haft led the way on foot, his eyes probing every nearby shadow, his gaze peering as far into the distance as the trees allowed, crossbow aimed wherever his eyes looked. Spinner, riding the first in line behind Haft, also armed his crossbow as he too stared into the distance and probed the shadows, scanning the crossbow over the range of his vision. He made sure his quarterstaff was loose in its ties. Doli made to ride knee-to-knee with Spinner, and appeared offended when, without looking at her, he brusquely pushed her away and gestured one-handed for her to follow. She gnawed her lip in wide-eyed nervousness, then fell back with the other women. Zweepee hunched over her saddle to make herself even smaller and more inconspicuous than she was and rode tight with the other women. The Golden Girl rode erect, looking about alertly; the hand at the hilt of her knife flexed as though it wanted a sword. Fletcher, as alert as the two Marines, brought up the rear with an arrow nocked in his longbow; he looked backward as often as he looked to the sides, and seldom bothered to look to his front.

In late afternoon Haft froze at the edge of a large clearing then dropped to one knee behind a bush. Spinner instantly raised his hand for the others to stop. He dismounted and gave his reins to the nearest hands, which, as they most often were, happened to be Doli's.

"Wait here," he said quietly. He unlimbered his quarter-staff, held his crossbow ready, and cat-footed to where Haft knelt.

Neither man spoke. What made Haft stop was evident to Spinner even before he reached him. They remained quiet for a time, watching and listening carefully. The clearing was littered with corpses. Vultures hopped about, tearing chunks of flesh from the bodies with great hooked beaks then lifting their heads to the sky as they swallowed. Save for leaves ruffled by vagrant breezes, nothing else moved. The only other sound was the heavy buzz of flies. Spinner and Haft breathed through their mouths to reduce the smell of putrefaction. The faint breeze came from behind them, which explained why they hadn't smelled the carnage earlier.

After a few moments of watching and listening, Spinner stood. "I'll tell the others and send them around," he said.

"Then we'll go in?" Haft asked.

Spinner nodded reluctantly.

Suddenly, there was a flash of gray and both men went into a crouch, threw their crossbows to their shoulders and sighted into the clearing. Spinner recognized the wolf and didn't fire; Haft's quarrel just missed the wolf as it bowled through a knot of buzzards squabbling over the viscera of a corpse. Spinner watched in amazement as the growling wolf raced about the clearing, scattering the vultures and chasing them into ponderous flight. Haft rearmed his crossbow and took aim again at the wolf, but Spinner hit the side of the crossbow just as Haft's finger closed on the trigger.

"Why'd you do that?" Haft shouted angrily, and began drawing the string back again.

Spinner clamped a hand on Haft's wrist and said, "*Look* at what the wolf is doing."

Growling, lunging, and snapping, the wolf pursued the vultures, chasing them away from the corpses. Two of the slower carrion eaters lay motionless on the ground, and another flopped in tight circles around a broken wing.

"So? He just wants the bodies for himself," Haft snarled. "He'll eat his fill, then leave the rest of the bodies for the vultures."

"I don't think so," Spinner said. "Wait."

A few seconds more and another vulture was down, its chest crushed by the wolf's jaws. By then the rest had heaved their way into the treetops around the clearing, where they screamed down at the wolf. The wolf trotted one brisk lap around the bodies in the clearing, looking up at the vultures, then stopped briefly at the far side of the clearing, seemed to look directly to where Spinner and Haft were concealed behind the bush and nod at them. With a parting growl directed at the buzzards, it melted into the trees.

"He was chasing the vultures away for us," Spinner said softly.

Haft gripped his crossbow fiercely, still angry because Spinner had prevented him from killing the predator. "Next you're going to say he was showing respect for our dead."

Spinner didn't reply, but that was exactly what he was thinking. He rose to his feet. "I'll tell the others and send them around."

"What is it?" Doli asked.

"There was a fight in a clearing ahead of us," Spinner said.

Fletcher was slowly looking around, scanning the surrounding forest. He spared Spinner a quick glance but otherwise remained vigilant. Zweepee looked numb.

"A lot of bodies ahead," Spinner said. "The clearing's less than fifty paces wide. Haft and I will search it and see what we can learn. Fletcher, lead the women around the clearing. Wait for us two hundred paces beyond."

"I'll go with you," Alyline said before he could turn back toward the clearing. She dismounted and handed her reins to Zweepee. "There may be something I can use for fresh garments." She made a face. "I've been wearing my costume for more than a week without opportunity to clean it."

"Don't," Spinner said. "There was butchery. And vultures got to the bodies. I don't think there's any clothing left that anyone can wear. If there is, I'll bring it to you. Get back on your horse and go with the others."

"I'll decide for myself if there's anything I can use." She brushed past him, striding to the clearing.

Spinner sighed and shook his head, but didn't try again to dissuade her; that would just ensure that she'd do it.

Fletcher looked at her back and muttered, "Someday that woman will get herself into trouble."

Doli sniffed and looked darts at Alyline's back. "I suspect that's how she became a slave in the first place."

Zweepee, more practical and without the personal interest in Alyline's actions that Doli seemed to have, said simply, "Let's go." She turned her horse to go around the clearing. Fletcher trotted ahead to lead the way.

Doli looked at Spinner. "Take care of yourself," she said softly.

Without a sideways glance, Spinner said, "I will," and followed Alyline. He held his crossbow ready when he entered the clearing. The vultures greeted their appearance with loud caws but didn't dare drop down to resume their meal; in addition to the men, the wolf was looking up at them from the shadow of a tree.

It looked to have been a small battle, as battles went, but to the men who fought it and remained in the clearing, it was the biggest, most meaningful battle they'd ever been in. If the corpses left to rot were indication, it had been a one-sided fight; judging by the uniforms, the bodies were all from the same army. Their mottled green tunics bore a rose emblem over the heart. Spinner and Haft had both ported in Zobra City more than once; they knew the emblem of the Principality of Zobra. The mottled green was the uniform of the prince's warders, the soldiers who guarded the land's borders.

"Nothing," Haft muttered, kicking at a divot lifted during the battle. He examined one of the corpses. One arm was half chopped off, there were massive cuts in the chest, a wide hole all the way through its belly, a leg missing, and the face mutilated. The corpse he looked at was typical. "They did most of this after the fight was over," he muttered. "They won, and then they did this to the men they had beaten." He squatted to look more closely at another body and probed an arrow wound with a finger. "This one was already dead when they shot him again." He spat in disgust. "Barbarians!"

Spinner walked quickly through the battlefield, scanning the ground for anything usable, trying to avoid looking at the bodies. He couldn't remember ever seeing the aftermath of a battle where all the corpses were so abused and the armor so battered. The few peaked helmets scattered about were badly dented or chopped open. The chain mail still borne by some of the bodies was chopped and rent until it was useless. No weapons had been left about, not even arrows. "That tells you what kind of enemy we have," he said, half in answer to Haft, half in explanation to himself. He uncocked his crossbow; there was no threat there, no one but the dead.

The Golden Girl grew more and more angry as she flitted about the clearing from one corpse to another, trying to find a usable garment. Sunlight sparkling on the gold coins of her costume, she looked like a houri come to take fallen warriors to paradise. She picked up a piece of cloth that lay on a corpse. "Look at this," she snorted. "If I took enough scraps like these, I could sew them together and *make* clothing, but I'd never be able to wash out the blood. *Pfagh.*" She threw down the rag and stomped off.

The winners of the battle had taken everything that could be used. If they suffered any casualties, they had removed them as well.

"Who did this?" Alyline shouted angrily. Haft ignored her; only warriors belonged in a place like that—to mourn the dead, to foresee their own fate.

Spinner glanced at her. He didn't answer, though he thought he knew. Then he saw something that proved it. "Look at this," he said as he bent to pick up a rectangular piece of metal still attached to a scrap of red leather.

Haft joined him, took the piece of metal and turned it over in his hands, examining it from all sides, seeing the stain of dried blood on it. "Jokapcul," he said. He looked around at the bodies, then back at the metal-and-leather scrap. "At least the poor buggers did some damage of their own."

Spinner looked toward the trees to their south. "I wonder where they went after this fight?" he said, almost to himself. Then he shook himself and said briskly, "Let's look around," and strode to the trees. He turned to the right inside the trees and started walking around the clearing, examining the ground. Haft followed quickly for a few paces to catch up, then walked a few paces to Spinner's left, also looking down.

"Here," Haft said, and pointed to the ground when they'd made a quarter circuit. He went slowly deeper into the woods.

Spinner joined him and looked at what he saw; the ground was trampled by the hooves of many horses.

"See where they came from," Spinner said. Haft grunted and moved farther from the clearing. Spinner went toward the clearing and circled it for a short distance before stopping to wait for Haft.

"They came from almost due west," Haft said when he joined Spinner, who nodded and pointed at the ground. Not much grew there, under the trees; it was mostly bare earth. But here and there they saw a crushed flower, a broken twig, an indentation in the ground. It was where soldiers had lain in ambush.

"Two score," Spinner said.

"That agrees with the horse tracks I saw," Haft said.

They continued their circuit. Halfway around they found the trail the horsemen took when they left the clearing; they had headed east, toward the highway. They walked a little farther around and found the tracks of the soldiers who were killed. Spinner and Haft followed them a hundred paces into the forest before turning back and following them all the way into the open. The tracks told the beginning of the story. The rose-emblem Zobran warders, about twenty of them, marched more or less parallel to the highway, in a column of twos. They were all in the clearing before the ambushers made their move. That was the story the tracks told. The bodies told the rest of the tale. Arrows rained onto the exposed men, and many of them probably fell before they even knew they were being attacked. More fell from arrows while they were trying to deploy from a marching formation to a fighting one. Not many were still standing when the attackers forayed from the trees and overran them.

Alyline waited for them at the south edge of the clearing. She stood in shadows; no sunlight danced on her garments. With her shoulders slumped, she looked shrunken. Instead of a heavenly body come to escort fallen warriors to the next world, she seemed lost, an abandoned plaything. When they got close they saw her eyes were red and puffy from crying.

"What manner of man does this to the dead?" she demanded. "Why would anyone treat the dead like this?"

"The Jokapcul are a warrior race," Spinner said. "They believe the rest of us are beneath contempt. That's how they treat their enemies." He put an arm around her and she sank into his embrace. He stroked her hair and made comforting noises at her for a moment, then said, "Let's leave here. We'll feel better once we're away."

"But what are we going to do about the bodies?"

"Nothing," Haft snapped, anger in his voice. "We can't do anything about them. There are too many bodies." He stalked into the forest.

Spinner held onto the Golden Girl a moment longer, then she moved out of his arms and followed Haft. Spinner brought up the rear.

Fletcher and the other women were just where they should have been. Doli was visibly relieved to see them—or at least relieved to see Spinner. Zweepee was withdrawn and Fletcher somber. He pointed at the ground a few paces away—at the tracks of many horses coming from the northwest.

Haft walked over to examine them. "Jokapcul," he said. "It's the same shoeing pattern. But that was three days ago." He dipped his head in the direction of the small clearing. "These are from yesterday, early enough in the day that we can find their campsite if we follow them back a short way." The tracks continued to the southeast. "They must have heard the refugees on the highway and decided to follow it."

"Do you think they want to go somewhere east of the highway?" Spinner asked.

"Maybe. Or maybe they want to go to the end of the highway." He didn't have to add that the port of Zobra City was at the end of the highway.

Spinner looked southeast, where the Jokapcul trail went. "That's not the direction we're going," he said after thinking for a moment. "We're going straight south; we won't come upon them." He mounted the stallion and led off to the south. The others knew as well as Spinner did that if two parties of Jokapcul had gone through there in three days, it was likely more bands were also around. Spinner didn't lash his staff under his thigh for riding, he carried it across the pommel of

his saddle, and his crossbow was in his hands. Haft and
Fletcher held their weapons ready as well.

At midday they began to hear sounds far ahead of them. At
first the sounds were muffled, so they weren't sure if their
source was directly ahead or off at some tangent; they couldn't
tell whether the occasional dimly heard clash of steel against
steel, the occasional voice raised in shout, was in their path,
where it might have an effect on them.

"No horses have been by here," Spinner said when the tension had grown enough that he felt he had to say something to
ease it.

"No footmen either," Haft added. Of course they understood that just because they hadn't crossed the path of soldiers didn't mean nobody was ahead of them; they could be
headed straight into an ambush or toward someone else's
battle.

Fletcher started riding with an arrow nocked. Alyline rode
with her reins held in one hand. Zweepee rode behind her
husband and held tightly to him. Doli rode almost touching
Spinner. After a time they heard no more phantom noises in
the distance, but no one's vigilance relaxed. Near the end of
the afternoon, an unnatural silence took up residence, one
that was almost tangible. Haft guided his mare alongside
Spinner. "There was a battle near here," he said quietly, so the
others couldn't hear.

Spinner nodded. "It's too quiet." But there were no bodies
about, no vultures. So where had the battle been? Perhaps
they were passing close by. But if they were, why couldn't
they smell it? Or hear the moans of the wounded? Perhaps it
was a bigger battle and they simply hadn't reached it yet. Neither man wanted to think of a larger battle.

They rode on for a short while longer, then Spinner heard
the bubbling of a brook ahead of them and reined in. "Better
to reach the battlefield in the morning," he said so only Haft
could hear. Haft nodded. In a voice only loud enough to carry

to his small group, Spinner said to the others, "There's running water ahead of us. We'll camp next to it."

When they had the horses unsaddled, he said, "There may be soldiers not far off. We must be quiet. The fire goes out as soon as dinner is cooked. There will be no fire through the night; we don't want to show ourselves to anyone."

There was no discussion, no one gasped in surprise, no one argued; it was what they all suspected. They set about quietly preparing the evening meal.

They still had a haunch of deer. Spinner and Fletcher sliced it into thin pieces that would cook quickly. The women went to the brook to wash the tubers Zweepee found and to get water for tea. Haft made the cook fire. Fire making was a chore the women normally did, while the men prepared whatever game they had for the evening's meal. But fires give smoke, and they didn't want to give away their presence. But Haft could make fire in the Ewsarcan way, so it burned very hot and gave off little smoke. The strips of venison were ready to be spitted by the time the fire was going. The tubers went directly into the fire and weren't completely cooked by the time the party began to eat, but nobody complained.

The brook was the first water they'd found that was more than a rivulet. "I have to bathe myself and my clothes," Alyline announced as soon as they finished with their dinner.

"We all do," Spinner said.

"Shall we take turns, or bathe all at once?" Haft asked in as innocent a voice as he could. He risked a quick, lowered-eyelid glance at the women as he did.

"The men stand guard while the women bathe," Spinner said without a smile. "Then one man bathes while the other two stand watch."

Fletcher nodded.

Spinner stationed Fletcher in the forest behind their campsite to guard against anyone coming from their rear. He and Haft crossed the brook to guard from the front.

Spinner led Haft thirty paces upstream and thirty more into the trees. "This is a good place," he said.

Haft looked back; he couldn't see the brook from there. "We're too deep, we should be closer to the brook."

"Why?"

"Because—Because someone might come along the brook and we won't be able to see them from here."

Spinner chuckled. "And you can't watch the women bathe from here either."

Haft flushed.

"If you can't see, then you have to listen harder. You'll be able to hear if any horsemen come along the brook. And if you don't hear them in time, the women's screams will let you know of their coming." He put a hand on his friend's shoulder and squeezed. "I haven't seen a naked woman for as long as you. We can wait until better circumstances."

"What about that night at the inn?" Haft accused.

Now Spinner flushed. "Well . . . that was different," he said weakly. And it didn't change the fact that they had to allow the women their privacy. He went back to the stream and down it the same distance below the campsite before heading into the trees.

The Golden Girl removed the girdle before entering the water, where she completely submerged herself. When she emerged, she quickly stripped off her soaked clothing and put it on a flat rock by the side of the brook. She scrubbed her skin with sand from the bed of the brook, then pounded her clothes on the rock. Zweepee did the same, and the two women shared the flat rock. They scrubbed each other's backs. They didn't shout or speak much above a whisper but otherwise they splashed and played like children, enjoying themselves as they cleaned.

Doli went primly apart from the other two before stepping into the water. She didn't stand up to remove her wet clothes, but stayed down, submerged to her shoulders, and tried to remain covered by the water when she tossed her clothes onto a rock half in and half out of the brook on its far side. She moved gently hither and yon, letting the rushing water carry off the trail dirt from her skin. Then she rubbed herself all over with the palms of her hands without using sand. When she finally stood and stepped out of the brook, she was a couple of paces from the rock where her clothes lay—very near where Spinner had left the brook's side to enter the forest. She glanced quickly upstream, and when she saw neither Alyline nor Zweepee looking her way, took a few tentative steps under the trees, water dripping off her bare skin. She peered intently into the shadows but saw no sign of Spinner, not even his footprints. She gnawed on her lower lip. The still air made her shiver.

"Spinner," she called out softly. "Spinner," she called again when the forest gave her no answer. She crouched and wrapped her arms around her chest, with her hands on her shoulders. She felt horribly exposed even though she was certain no one could see her. A tree dweller's sudden chittering startled her. She imagined Jokapcul soldiers or slavers to be hidden where she couldn't see them, spying on her, ready to lunge forward and take her. She wondered if they had silently come upon Spinner and slain him.

"Spinner?" she said tentatively. When still no answer came, she stepped back a pace, then another pace and another, and only stopped retreating when her feet were in the water. She looked upstream; the other women still didn't seem to be looking in her direction. She thought they must be paying her little enough attention that they didn't know what she had just done. She nibbled on her lip for a moment, then stood erect. The sun still shined and its rays brought a warmth that removed the gloom and cold she had felt under the trees.

Feeling better, she turned to clean her clothes. At all times, whether she knelt next to or hunched over the rock, she posed herself artfully. She knew she had a good body, a body men liked to look at. Perhaps Spinner was where he could see her at her laundry. If he was, she wanted him to see her as comely, not as a washerwoman. Hoping that he was looking, she worked at cleaning her blouse and skirt until Zweepee's voice came to her over the water:

"Doli, can't you finish that and get dressed so the men can bathe?"

Reluctantly, Doli stood. Facing half into the forest, she wrung out her clothes then crossed the brook, swinging her hips slightly as she went. After all, there was still a chance that Spinner was looking. She might yet distract him from that Golden Girl.

Dressed, she joined the other women and flushed when Zweepee said with a sparkle in her eyes, "One might think you were an entertainer with an audience the way you did your laundry."

Alyline simply looked away.

The men bathed downstream. One stayed at the campsite to guard the women, and a second went farther down the brook, while the third cleaned himself and his clothes. Thanks to Doli, the women had taken so long bathing that it was dark by the time the men were dressed again.

CHAPTER
TWENTY-ONE

"No," Alyline snapped. "That's wrong, it's not fair."

The sun was long down, and little starlight filtered through the treetops. A faint glow from the embers left alive in the makeshift hearth to keep water warm for tea picked out highlights on the six people who sat in a circle around the fire's remnants.

Spinner looked at her, confused. "What's not fair? Fletcher, Haft, and I will each take two hours. I'm only asking two of you to take one hour each. One hour can't be too much to ask of you. You'll get more sleep than we will."

The Golden Girl spat into the embers of the small fire, just missing the teapot. "You are a fool, Spinner! You look at us and you think because our skin is soft to the touch that we are weak and unable. The six of us have been traveling for more than a week. Our pace has been hard at times. We have not stopped for longer than overnight. We have been going as hard as you, and not once did one of us say she needed extra rest, not once has one of us slowed you down. This place is the first we've seen where we could even bathe, and not one word of complaint from any of us. What's more, when we stop at the end of the day to make camp for the night, it is we three who make the fire and cook our meal, while the three of you gather firewood and then take your ease in standing guard." She spat again. "You don't seem to understand that this shows we are as strong as you. We are capable. We can stand watch as well as you. And if we all take turns, then sometimes one of you will get a complete night's sleep instead of losing sleep in guard duty every night."

"She's right, it's not fair to you," Zweepee said quietly. As always, she sat next to her husband.

Spinner started to object, but he didn't know what to say. Alyline was right that he thought the women were too delicate to share in night watch. And the women were standing up to the rigors of travel as well as the men. He looked to Doli, but no help was coming from her.

Silent at first, Doli stared back at him. She didn't want to agree with Alyline on anything, but the Golden Girl was right. "It is wrong for you to always take the watch and have no help from us," she finally said.

Spinner looked at the other men for support. Haft was carefully studying the darkness under the trees as though already on watch, and avoided eye contact with him. Fletcher looked like he wanted to say something else, but nodded in agreement with Alyline. "They can hear as well as we can," he said. "If one hears someone coming, she can wake us."

Defeated, Spinner sagged. But he was not yet willing to admit it. Like all young men, he had an almost overwhelming urge to protect young women in his circle, especially the better looking ones, even when they didn't particularly need protection. It had never created a problem for him in the past, as nearly all young women he met were more than willing to accept the help and protection of young men when there was something heavy to lift or the faintest hint of danger. That was the way of nature, he assumed, and it was a young man's opportunity to prove to a young woman that he could take care of her and their children before there were children to worry about, as it was her chance to see to it that she was pairing off with a man who could care for her and her children when they needed him.

Alyline stood. "I'll take first watch," she announced. "My hearing is sharp." She smiled grimly at Haft. "I'll stay near Haft, and if anything approaches, I'll wake him to deal with it."

Haft returned her smile with a sickly one of his own; he didn't like the idea of the Golden Girl hovering over him while he slept.

"Who wants second watch?"

"I'll take it," Haft said before anyone else could volunteer. If Alyline had to wake him to relieve her, he thought it was unlikely that she would do anything to injure him during his sleep.

Fletcher and Zweepee took the second half of the night.

Doli looked both disappointed and relieved that the four quarters of the night were divided up and no watch was left for her. Her expression changed when she looked at Spinner; she gave every appearance of thinking that she would now have the entire night to entice him.

"Wake me well before dawn," Spinner said gruffly. "I will stand the last watch."

Alyline gave him a smile. "See? With more people sharing watch, we will all get enough sleep tonight."

Spinner stifled a groan as he turned away from her and curled up next to the fire, where he could sleep alone. "Go away," he said in a low, annoyed voice.

Doli started. She hadn't thought she was close enough for him to hear her approach. She turned away with an expression of chagrin and found a space to lay down alone.

During his time with the Frangerian Marines, Spinner had always hated being assigned last watch; the man who pulled last watch was woken too early to have had a full night's sleep and wouldn't have a chance to return to sleep after the watch. And the quiet darkness before the sun rose was a difficult time to stay awake. But last watch was also the most dangerous time of the night, the time when raiders were most likely to strike. Fate had put him in charge, made him responsible for the safety of the people in their small group. It was a responsibility he hadn't sought, one he didn't want. But everyone seemed willing to take his lead—at least no one had stepped forward to challenge his leadership. Since he seemed to be in charge, Spinner felt he should be the one to guard his sleeping companions when they were at their most vulnerable. But that night he also thought last watch would be the best time for him to think about what might lay ahead of them and to plan.

Spinner was glad that Doli hadn't drawn one of the watches; she would have wanted to stay awake talking with him, perhaps even attempting to do things other than talk. Either way, her attentions made him uncomfortable. He wished Alyline had the watch before his, then he could . . . No, that was the same thought he'd had about Doli. It was just as well it was Zweepee who woke him; had it been Alyline, he knew he would have wanted to pay attention to her. He couldn't afford that distraction any more than he could Doli's attention.

So Zweepee woke him, stayed close long enough for him to stand up and assure her he was fully awake, then went back to the bedding she shared with her husband.

Spinner stretched a bit to loosen muscles that had stiffened in sleep, then walked softly around the small campsite. As soon as he knew precisely where everybody lay sleeping, he slowly walked in a circle around the group, stopping frequently to listen to the night. Few sounds disturbed the quiet. A hunting owl hooted in a tree, a bat squeed, a prey animal screamed briefly when a hunter caught it. The distant noises of restless people to the east told him where the highway was. Otherwise all was quiet.

So he thought. Where were they going? To Zobra. Why? To catch a ship home—at least one going to Frangeria, which might be the same thing as going home. What was happening between where they were and the port of Zobra City? That was the big question. The Jokapcul obviously had not ended their invasion of southwestern Nunimar with the occupation of New Bally and the conquest of the Duchy of Bostia; they had invaded Skragland and Zobra as well. But where in Zobra were they? Except for the dead Zobran warders they'd run across two days earlier, the travelers hadn't seen any sign of fighting. There were the faint sounds they'd heard yesterday, and there was the unnatural silence in this area when they arrived the previous evening, but nothing else to tell him where fighting might be.

What kind of planning could he do? He had no idea what to do, except to continue south. What would they do if Zobra City was in the hands of the Jokapcul? That possibility was something he didn't want to think about. If Zobra City was taken, he suspected the way to the Princedons, on the large peninsula southeast of Zobra, would be blocked. He didn't think they could turn and go back the way they'd come; of the many rumors they had heard when they first reached the highway, the one he most believed was that the Jokapcul had invaded Skragland from Bostia. If Zobra City was in Jokapcul hands, the way to the Princedons blocked, and Skragland invaded, perhaps fully occupied, then the Low Desert would be their only route to freedom. Maps he had seen told him the Low Desert led only to the High Desert. He knew nothing of how to survive in the desert, high or low, and he didn't think any of the people with him did either. So he had no idea what to do if Zobra City was taken.

But before thinking of what to do in that case, they had to get to the port. That meant continuing south. Toward where they had heard the distant sounds of fighting. How to avoid Jokapcul patrols—that was what he needed to think about and plan for.

He was still thinking and coming to no conclusions when the rising sun woke the forest birds, whose greeting cries woke the other people.

Spinner feared what the morning would lead them to.

They made little conversation when they ate the cooked venison and half-cooked tubers left over from the previous day. The men kept looking warily to the south, and the women looked in that direction nervously. They all wondered what the day would bring: the men, how many enemies they might have to fight; the women, whether any of them would live to see another sunrise. Except for the Golden Girl; to Spinner, Alyline seemed confident. Perhaps she was looking forward to the chance for revenge against slavers or Jokapcul.

The morning mist wasn't completely burned off by the time they saddled their horses and tied their small amount of gear on them. Without a word, Haft led the way on foot. Spinner followed, also afoot, not far behind him. Fletcher brought up the rear on horseback. Alyline, mounted on the stallion, took the gelding by its reins and led him. The early morning forest was alive with bird song, the chitterings of tree dwellers, the buzz of insects, the triumphant cry of a hunting cat over its kill. The normal forest sounds did nothing to ease anyone's tension. Spinner looked carefully, but no flash of gray told him the wolf was still traveling with them. He wondered if the wolf had merely been escorting them through its range. Perhaps they were beyond its territory.

As they proceeded south, the normal forest sounds diminished. At midmorning the caws of buzzards sounded ahead of them.

The caws suddenly became angry screams, and a great flapping of wings resounded through the forest. Spinner and Haft dropped to their knees behind bushes and readied their crossbows. They looked forward intently. Thirty or so paces ahead the light filtering through the treetops seemed brighter; there was probably a clearing just beyond view. Spinner turned and signaled the others to hold and be ready for whatever came next. Then, in a low crouch, Haft ran softly ahead fifteen paces, lowered himself to the ground, and rapidly crawled to where he could see into the clearing. Spinner covered him, then dashed forward when Haft stopped behind a tree at the edge of the clearing.

There had been a battle. Bodies were strewn about the clearing. From the uniforms on the corpses, it was obvious it hadn't been as one-sided a fight as the earlier one. Nearly half of these dead were Jokapcul. There were two barely seen bodies just inside the trees at the far side of the clearing; perhaps the fight had turned into a running battle.

The wolf that had been pacing the small party was already in the clearing, chasing away the last of the vultures. Then it sat in the middle of the clearing, looked straight at where Spinner and Haft lay hiding behind bushes and said, *"Ulgh!"*

"It's coincidence," Haft said softly. "Tell me it's coincidence. Tell me it's not the same wolf that's been following us. Tell me it's not the same wolf that chased the vultures away before." He aimed his crossbow at the wolf.

Spinner put out a hand and shook his head. "That's the same wolf. I think he's trying to tell us he's on our side." He stood, took his fingers off the trigger of his crossbow and walked into the clearing. It seemed to him that the wolf behaved more like a very well-trained hunting dog than any wild animal he'd ever seen. It must be sorcery, he thought. But good sorcery or bad?

He stopped two paces from the wolf. "You're not an ordinary wolf, are you?" He made a show of pointing his crossbow down and to the side. The wolf sat on its haunches. Spinner watched it closely; if he wasn't prepared, the wolf could easily be at his throat before he had time to react. Instead of leaping, the animal flopped onto its side then rolled onto its back with its legs splayed: it was indisputably male. Its tongue lolled out of its mouth, and its remarkably intelligent eyes looked directly into Spinner's.

Spinner stared back. Finally he said, "No wild wolf would look a man in the eye the way you do. No wild wolf would feel secure with a man looking him in the eye. To a wild wolf, when you look in the eye it means you're about to attack. Right?"

The wolf said, *"Ulgh!"* and swished its tail from side to side on the ground.

Moving slowly, Spinner halved his distance to the wolf,

lowered himself to one knee and stretched out a hand to rub the wolf's belly. "And no wild wolf would expose its belly to a man either."

The wolf arched his back to press its belly into Spinner's hand and growled softly, almost a purr.

Spinner thumped the animal once on the chest and stood up. "All right, fellow, you can travel with us."

"Ulgh!" the wolf said, and spun to his feet. His tongue lapped Spinner's hand.

"But if you're going to travel with us, we have to know your name."

"Ulgh!" the wolf said, and bobbed his head up and down.

Spinner blinked at the so-human nod. "What's your name?"

"Ulgh!"

"Wolf? Is that your name?"

The wolf dipped his head to the side and seemed to shrug his shoulders.

Spinner briefly considered the wolf's response, wondering if he was supposed to play a guessing game, then asked, "It's not your name but it's close enough?"

The wolf seemed to shrug again and let out a low whine.

"We will call you Wolf until we know your real name. Will you answer to Wolf?"

The wolf lowered his head and whined again, then bobbed his head in what could only be a nod.

Spinner looked oddly at the wolf for a brief moment; he was certain it understood everything he said. "All right," he said, "Wolf you are. What can you tell me of who you are, of how you came to be here?"

The wolf's head twisted from side to side, his shoulders writhed, he lifted a paw. A series of growls, barks, and moans came from his mouth. Clearly, the wolf was trying to answer his questions. Of course, Spinner didn't understand a word.

"We will talk more later, Wolf, when we figure out how. But now I have to tell the others that you are with us." He looked at the vultures, which were still in the trees, looking longingly at the bodies they had been driven from. "Stay here, Wolf," Spinner said, just as he would command a dog at home. "Guard the bodies."

"Ulgh!" The wolf remained sitting while Spinner returned to the trees. As soon as Spinner was out of the clearing, the wolf looked at the treetops and barked at the vultures to make them keep their distance. A few of the birds cawed defiantly back at him and stretched their wings menacingly, but none dropped back into the clearing.

Haft was on his feet staring into the clearing when Spinner reached him. "He didn't attack you," he squeaked. "He rolled over and let you rub his belly!" His voice rose to a yet higher pitch. "He acted just like a farm dog does when you go out to slop the hogs!"

"Well, the first farm dogs were descended from hunters' dogs, and the first hunters' dogs were tamed wolves." He put a hand on Haft's shoulder. "He wants to be friends, and we need all the friends we can get. Besides, he can scout for us in ways we can't scout for ourselves." Spinner walked into the forest, back to where the others waited. "His name is Wolf," he called back over his shoulder.

Haft turned to watch the clearing, and to keep a wary eye on the wolf. "His name is Wolf?" he said aloud. "I think Spinner's been ashore too long."

"Fletcher, take the women around," Spinner said after reporting what he'd seen and what had happened at the clearing.

Fletcher nodded and headed his horse around the clearing. Alyline handed the reins of the gelding to Doli, then dismounted and gave the stallion's reins to Zweepee. Spinner ignored her as he returned to the clearing; trying to tell the Golden Girl not to come was a waste of breath.

By the time Spinner got back to the clearing, Haft had already scouted around it.

"These were Palace Guards," he told Spinner. "This time they saw the Jokapcul first. It seems they got the better of it for a while, then something happened. I don't know for sure, but it looks like another troop of Jokapcul came on the scene, and the Guards tried to run away. The Jokapcul pursued them and the battle turned." He pointed at the two bodies half hidden in the shadows at the far side of the clearing. "That's the way they went—the same way we're going." While he spoke, he was glancing warily at the wolf. The wolf ignored Haft and kept watch on the vultures, so they wouldn't return to eating the bodies. It seemed to Spinner the wolf was deliberately ignoring Haft so as not to seem threatening.

The men ignored Alyline as she roamed the battlefield. She gave the wolf one glance when she entered the clearing, then ignored him. Haft quickly busied himself gathering arrows for Fletcher, while Spinner studied the scene to learn more of what had happened.

The tunics on many of the dead bore the red rose over the heart that identified them as Zobran. But where the warders had worn tunics of mottled green, the tunics on these soldiers was the white of the Guards, probably the best-trained soldiers in the Zobran army. Spinner wondered what the Palace Guard was doing so far from Zobra City. So far as Spinner knew, the Guard never left the capital except to provide security for the prince or his family in their travels. He looked, but found no evidence that a royal personage had traveled with the dead Guards. One thing he knew for certain: the Guards had acquitted themselves well against the Jokapcul. As Haft had said, nearly half of the bodies in the clearing wore the metal-plated leathers of the Jokapcul cavalry. And the fight had continued; no one had the chance to mutilate the Zobran dead or to police the weapons and possessions of the dead.

Alyline frequently stooped to pluck something from the ground, squatted to take something from a corpse. When she came near the wolf, she absently reached out to scratch him behind the ear. Then she kept going, peering at everything on the ground. As she did, the wolf sniffed her intimately from

behind. Alyline jumped, spun around and glared threateningly at the wolf, her hand raised to slap him. Clearly she
wasn't thinking of him as a dangerous animal, a killer; to her
he was just another presumptuous male taking unwarranted
liberty with her person.

Wolf ducked his head and looked away. Keeping his head
turned to the side, he rolled his eyes to look innocently up at her.

Alyline's hand stopped in mid-swing. She stared hard at
Wolf. She recognized in the wolf's eyes a level of intelligence
she'd only seen in humans before. "You know exactly what
you did, don't you?" she said quietly. "I allow no male to
touch me without my say. Not even Spinner, who thinks I owe
him that. It goes also for your nose." She looked into Wolf's
eyes and wondered about the intelligence she saw in them.
"Are you ensorcelled, Wolf? Did you somehow cross a sorcerer? Were you changed for that offense?"

Wolf looked down, shook his head. He emitted a series of
whines and low growls.

Alyline gazed into his eyes and wondered if his look meant
what it did if a man looked that way—something had happened, but not a sorcerer's curse. Her look softened. "Take no
liberties with me, Wolf," she said with less threat, "and we
can be friends."

Wolf raised his head and, still sitting, scuttled around until
he was facing her. He raised a paw and, tongue lolling,
cocked his head as though to say, "Friends."

The Golden Girl looked at him a moment longer, then she
took his paw in her hand and shook it. "For now, Wolf. For so
long as you behave."

"Ulgh!" He took his paw from her hand and sat erect and
alert. *"Ulgh!"* he said again, and licked her hand as though
sealing the bargain.

Alyline nodded at him, then returned to her search.

Wolf watched her walk away, then lowered his head. His
chest shook with rapid puffs of breath and his mouth stretched
wide. He seemed to be laughing silently. Had a man acted

thus, anyone could be forgiven for thinking that he thought he'd put one over the woman.

Alyline joined Spinner and Haft a few minutes later. Her arms were filled. She said, "Let's leave this place. Leave these dead to whatever peace they can find."

Haft didn't look at her. His eyes swept the scene, took in the near two score bodies, skipped over Wolf, who was still keeping the vultures away, and then he stalked off, circling around the corpses in their path.

Spinner grunted and followed Haft. He understood the value, even the need, of searching the dead for usable items, but he felt uncomfortable about it. And he didn't want his image of the Golden Girl to be sullied by seeing her carrying off booty from someone else's battle. He absently snapped his fingers, signaling the wolf to follow. Wolf waited until the humans had disappeared into the trees before he stood and left the bodies to the carrion eaters.

CHAPTER
TWENTY-TWO

The others waited for them a hundred paces beyond the clearing.

"We can see where they went just by following the dead," Fletcher said. He spat to the side. "It looks like they kept fighting for a long time."

Spinner and Haft looked through the forest. It seemed there was a body every forty paces or so leading from the clearing. The bodies weren't spread out as though the soldiers were killed in a wide-ranging battle; instead they lay in a line so straight a surveyor could have sighted a line along the bodies. Spinner and Haft somberly looked at the line for a moment, imagining how the fight must have gone. Their reverie was interrupted by the Golden Girl.

"Look at what I got," she said, and dropped the bundle she was carrying. From it she took a scabbarded sword. The belt was too big for her, so she slung it around her right shoulder and across her body so its hilt hung on her left side, just below her breast. She picked up another sword belt, one that also held a scabbarded dagger, and offered them to Doli. Doli turned her head away and didn't take the weapons.

"At least take a knife," the Golden Girl snapped. She picked up a belt that held only a dagger in a sheath, and hung it from the pommel of Doli's saddle. Then she offered the sword belt to Zweepee, who took it. From the way Zweepee touched the dagger, it seemed she thought she could use it.

Alyline then offered swords to Spinner and Haft. Haft spat and took a step away from her. Spinner shook his head and said, "I have my quarterstaff. I'm better with it than with a sword."

"Have it your way," she said. "But sometimes a blade is better than a stick."

Knowing she was right, Spinner hesitated for a moment. Then he took the sword and lashed it onto his saddle. He wasn't concerned about Haft not taking a sword; there were few occasions that a sword could be used where an axe couldn't.

Alyline squatted next to her pile to root through it. She withdrew several pouches, opened one and emptied the contents into her palm. Her hand filled with silver and copper coins. She looked up at them and said half defiantly, "Someday we will need money. The men I took these from will never need money again."

Fletcher nodded slowly. "You're right," he said. He held out a hand, and she gave him several of the pouches, which he suspended from his belt. She distributed the remaining pouches equally among them. No one was reluctant to take them.

One by one, but quickly, Alyline picked up the garments and pieces of cloth she had gathered and looked closely at each, front and back. Some she cast aside, the rest she made into a neat roll, with the money pouches she'd kept for herself in the middle. She tied the roll together with a length of twine.

While she did that, Spinner gave the arrows he'd collected to Fletcher. He examined them carefully, felt the edges of their steel heads, sighted along their shafts, looked closely at how their heads and fletching were attached. "These are good," he said when his inspection was finished. As many of the arrows as would fit, he put into his quiver with the stone-headed arrows he had made earlier. The rest he tied into a bundle with a leather thong and hung it from his saddle's pommel.

Spinner looked around to make sure everyone was ready. He looked into the forest and saw Wolf loping in a circle around them, looking outward as though watching for anyone who might be approaching. "Let's go," he said when he saw all were ready.

"Best idea I've heard all day," Haft muttered.

Alyline glared at Spinner when he reached the stallion before she did and mounted it, but she didn't say anything. She tied her roll of clothing and cloth behind the cantle of the gelding's saddle and mounted it.

They set out single file, with Spinner leading the way and Fletcher bringing up the rear. Except for Wolf. He began by scouting ahead, then sometimes ranged from side to side to make sure no one came at them undetected from the flank. Often he was out of sight, but from time to time he stood in their path, looking toward them, as though to make sure they knew he was still covering their front. Spinner hoped he was right in thinking the animal wanted to help them. He thought it unlikely the wolf was leading them into an ambush, especially as he himself pointed the way each time Wolf waited for them, and the wolf always went in the direction he pointed. Not even Haft objected to the animal's presence ahead of them.

Spinner nodded toward Wolf during one of his brief appearances. "It looks like we have the flankers you wanted," he said to Haft.

Haft snorted and glared threateningly at Wolf, but didn't say anything. As little as he liked the idea of a wolf accompanying the small party, it did seem that the beast was aiding them.

At no time did Spinner make a conscious decision to follow the trail of bodies, and neither had Wolf made that decision for him. But in fact they were following the line of bodies. When Spinner reflected on it, he decided it must be because he wanted to link up with surviving Guards he hoped were somewhere up ahead. There could be safety in numbers,

he told himself, and maybe they could get accurate information from the Guards on what lay ahead. But if he had thought
more carefully about that, he would have known that soldiers
in the field are always the last to know anything about the dis-
position of the enemy.

After a time the line of bodies thinned out, but it remained
surveyor-straight. For a time it disappeared altogether. Then
there were only footprints and spots of blood to follow.

Little more than an hour later they drew near the few surviving Zobra Guards, who were encamped at the side of a
stream. They came into sight just as the Guards were attacked
by more Jokapcul. Wolf was waiting for them, hunkered
down, out of sight of the battle that was beginning.

The company of Zobran Guards had started its patrol three
days before, one hundred men and one magician strong. Along
the way they had encountered and nearly beaten a Jokapcul
company, but were driven off with heavy casualties when another Jokapcul company stumbled upon the fight. The two
Jokapcul companies, one at less than half strength, the other
not as seriously injured, harried the Guards during their
flight, inflicting more casualties. The Zobrans inflicted casualties of their own and finally managed to break off from that
pursuit, only to run into a half squadron of Jokapcul cavalry.
In that skirmish as well, they gave as well as they got, and
those Guards who were still standing were able to get away
without pursuit when the surviving Jokapcul cavalry retreated.
When the Guardsmen reached the stream, they stopped to
rest and bind their injuries. A small Jokapcul patrol stumbled
across them while half of the Zobrans were engaged in minis-
tering to the other half. The Jokapcul patrol was small enough
that the Zobrans were able to defeat them, but only seven Zobran Guards and the magician were left by the time they
did. Three of those Zobrans bore wounds that were painful
but not incapacitating; two more were too badly wounded to

continue their retreat; and those able to travel were too few to carry the badly wounded very far. So they moved a hundred paces downstream, and hoped the relief force their magician had called for would arrive before more Jokapcul found them.

The magician hadn't been of much use in the company's fights; some palace bureaucrat had decided the patrols were strong enough that the magician only needed to communicate, so he carried only a few imbaluris and a handheld demon spitter. The last Jokapcul patrol had a magician with it, one foolish enough to expose himself to a bowman. The Zobran magician was examining the Jokapcul magician's magic kit, a chest the size and rough dimensions of a coffin, when they were attacked by a full hundred-man company. Good soldiers all, the two whole men stood ready, as did the three walking wounded. One of the badly wounded men struggled to his feet and held his sword and shield at the ready. The magician grabbed the first item he recognized. "Phoenix egg!" he shouted as he threw.

There was a clap of thunder as the phoenix egg burst open in the midst of the Jokapcul formation and the freed bird snapped its wings wide, the fire of its feathers spreading and eating through the leather armor, weapons, and flesh alike. A dozen died in seconds. The injured who didn't fall to the ground crying out in their death agonies dropped their weapons and ran away screaming from the intense pain of the hellfire from the phoenix. But more than eighty of the enemy survived to charge the Guards. The magician fired his demon spitter into their mass until the demon popped out of it and demanded to be fed. The magician ignored the demon's demands and frantically searched in the kit for something else to use.

Haft didn't hesitate when he saw the Jokapcul. He threw his crossbow to his shoulder and fired his first bolt before even dismounting—Doli screamed as the crossbow string shrieked next to her ear and the quarrel blurred past her eyes.

By the time his first quarrel hit its target, Spinner's first was in the air. They had taken fighting positions behind tree trunks by the time Spinner's quarrel tumbled a second charging Jokapcul. Within seconds two more Jokapcul fell forward. Fletcher joined them and added shafts from his longbow in raining death into the Jokapcul. Soon there were three broad arrows in flight for every two quarrels. Holes were opening in the ranks of attacking Jokapcul, but the attacking soldiers were so intent on the small knot of men they were charging that they didn't notice.

By the time the Jokapcul closed with the Zobra Guards, another squad was down from quarrels and arrows. The six Zobra defenders who could stand fought fiercely, but their swords were too short to penetrate past the pikes borne by many of the Jokapcul. Most of them fell with fresh injuries by the time the Jokapcul officer saw the man immediately in front of him fall, gurgling, pierced through the throat by an arrow that had barely missed the commander's own neck. Not knowing how strong the force to his rear was, the commander barked out an order, and his subordinate officers screamed it at their men; then the sergeants bellowed out echoes of the officers' orders. The Jokapcul broke off their attack and fled from the crossbowmen and the archer who were whittling them down. Missiles felled four more before the Jokapcul reached safety in the trees.

"Mount!" Spinner shouted when the Jokapcul presented no more targets, and he leaped onto the back of the stallion. "To the rose!" He heeled the horse into a gallop and raced to the aid of the Zobran soldiers.

The others scrambled onto their horses and flew after Spinner. The horses charged toward the stream, dodging and at times leaping over the thirty or more dead and dying Jokapcul who littered the ground in front of the Zobran Guards. Wolf paused twice to rip out the throats of wounded Jokapcul who looked ready to return to the fray.

Spinner leaped off his horse and began shouting orders even as he took in the number and condition of the Zobrans. All of them now bore wounds, three too badly injured to continue the fight, and two were dead. Spinner tried not to show his dismay when he realized how few there were. It was not the force he had hoped to join up with.

"Tend the wounded," he said to the women. Doli and Zweepee immediately turned to the injured men, tearing garments from the dead to use as bandages. Spinner ignored Alyline as she drew her sword and prepared to fight instead of helping with the wounded. He tethered the horses as he continued giving orders to his small force. "Fletcher, ready your bow and watch for the Jokapcul to come again." Fletcher nocked an arrow and ran forty paces toward where the Jokapcul had disappeared into the trees. Without thinking about whether he would be understood, Spinner said, "Wolf, scout them and give warning when they start to move." Wolf barked and padded rapidly along the stream before moving away from it in the direction the Jokapcul had gone. "Haft, hold the left flank," Spinner said, referring to the side closer to the Jokapcul. Haft moved twenty paces to the left and cocked a fresh quarrel into his crossbow. Using hand gestures, Spinner positioned the two Zobran soldiers still able to fight. He turned to the magician.

"The Frangerians are come?" the magician asked in broken Frangerian.

Spinner shook his head. "Only us." Then, "Do you speak Apianghian? Ewsarcan? Bostian?" and a couple more.

The young magician shook his head at the name of each language, then named the three languages he spoke better than he did Frangerian. Spinner had only a smattering of Zobran and none of the other two—and he didn't even recognize the name of one of those languages.

"What do you have that can help us?" Spinner asked in slow Frangerian. In answer, the magician held up both hands; one hand held another phoenix egg, the other an L-shaped object Spinner didn't recognize.

"I fight near." He raised the strange object in one hand and the phoenix egg with the other. He grinned. "We kill many Jokapcul." As he talked he fed the demon in his handheld spitter.

Spinner nodded. As inexperienced as the magician's robe indicated he was, the young fellow couldn't possibly be as powerful as he seemed to be implying. But if he knew how to use the things he held, he might make the difference between life and death for all of them when the fighting started again. "Stay by me," Spinner ordered. The magician stretched himself to his greatest height, which was no greater than Spinner's, and looked down his nose at this stranger who dared give him orders. Before Spinner could demonstrate to the magician who was really in command, the call of a wolf sounded from upstream. Spinner looked toward it and saw Wolf racing toward them. A squad of Jokapcul infantry, blood lust up, ran close behind.

Almost as soon as Spinner saw the squad, one of them staggered and fell forward; the force of his fall jammed the quarrel that Haft shot him with all the way through his body so that its head stuck up several inches from his back. Spinner threw his crossbow to his shoulder and took aim at the closest Jokapcul, but a thunderclap next to him made him jerk violently and his quarrel flew wide of its mark. A Jokapcul soldier jerked to a stop, staggered a step forward, and fell on his side. No arrow or quarrel protruded from his bloody chest.

Spinner looked at the magician, who was holding the L-shaped object out at arm's length. He held it with both hands on its short leg and pointed its long leg at the enemy. The magician muttered something under his breath, and the object bucked violently upward as it discharged another thunderclap. Another Jokapcul staggered and dropped as though poleaxed. Now Spinner knew that it was a small demon spitter; he hadn't known they came in that small size. An arrow in his side, a fourth Jokapcul toppled—Fletcher had turned and fired a shaft.

Nearly at Haft's position, Wolf spun around in mid-bound so he faced the charge when he landed. He took a step backward to kill his momentum, then sprung at the nearest Jokapcul. He eluded the man's outthrust pike and clamped his jaws on his throat. The man collapsed, his feet briefly drumming the ground as his hands clutched at his throat. Wolf released him and dashed to another enemy, who held up his sword to block a leap at his throat. Wolf darted under the blade and his muzzle slashed under the apron of the man's metal-studded jerkin. The man screamed and doubled over, clutching at the ragged wound where his manhood had been ripped away.

Haft rearmed his crossbow and took down another of the attackers.

Spinner was finally able to get off an aimed shot, and saw his target pitch forward.

The action was so fast, had taken so little time, that by the time the officer leading this squad saw the weight of his casualties and barked the command to retreat, eight of his ten men were down. He turned to flee, but a second shaft from Fletcher's longbow killed him. A bolt from the demon spitter brought down another before the lone survivor reached safety out of sight of the defenders.

But the flanking attack was only a diversion.

"Here they come!" Fletcher bellowed as the body of the Jokapcul company, sixty or more men, rushed at them from the trees. Swinging swords above their plumed helmets, the junior officers led the charge as the company's commander ran behind his men, urging them onward, exhorting the sergeants to keep the men running forward.

Fletcher loosed two arrows into the main force of Jokapcul who were charging toward him, killing one officer and a pike-wielding soldier before leaping to his feet and dashing back to the stream bank.

The magician's demon spitter thundered four more times before the demon popped out and demanded, *"Veedmee!"*

The magician rooted inside his robe for food, then continued the fight.

Fletcher had time to shoot three arrows into the oncoming mass of Jokapcul, Spinner one quarrel. Haft left Wolf to guard against another assault on their flank and got off two shots. Each arrow and quarrel found its mark, as did all of the magician's shots; deliberately, more of the marks were officers than men. The magician threw the second phoenix egg, and another officer and more than a squad went down or fled when the bird erupted in fire among them.

Even so, nearly two score Jokapcul closed with five fighting men, one sword-swinging woman, two more women, a magician who wasn't a fighter, and a wolf.

Spinner's twirling and lashing quarterstaff kept the Jokapcul beyond sword's reach and slammed several of them to the ground with cracked skulls, shattered arms, or broken ribs. Still, two or three pikes managed to reach inside his stroke to cut him.

Haft's axe whirred as he lashed out with it, chopping through flesh and splintering thrusting pikes. Bodies piled around him, yet his flesh was gouged as well by seeking blades.

Fletcher fought like a berserker, flailing about with his sword, while Zwccpcc pressed her back against his, protecting him from attack from behind with an awkwardly wielded sword, but she wasn't able to save him from being brought to his knees by a pike-thrust from the side.

The two Zobran Guards stood over their wounded companions and brought down five of their attackers, but the wounds they'd received earlier were severe enough to weaken them and limit their fighting ability. They went down under the press of too many blades slashing and jabbing at them.

The Golden Girl fought with a skill no man would have assumed of any woman, much less one so beautiful, and her beauty caused the Jokapcul to hold back momentarily. That misjudgment cost them three lives. In desperation, an officer ordered all but two to back away and go after the men. He left two men to keep her engaged and prevent her from attacking his other men from behind.

Wolf darted and dashed about, flying over thrusting blades, flashing under defensive ones, crushing throats through helmet flaps, tearing open what groins and lower bellies he could reach under armored aprons.

Even the magician picked up a sword and swung it about. He was untrained in its use, but his very clumsiness saved him for a time—no one facing him could anticipate what he would do next, and his blade bit several Jokapcul who tried to fight him as though he understood combat. Finally, the side of a blade slammed into his head and knocked him insensate to the ground.

Doli ducked and weaved among and under the frightened horses, striking out with her knife at any soldier who came too near. The Jokapcul laughed at her, and turned their attention to those fighting with more serious weapons; they assumed they could easily disarm and capture her when the battle was over.

And soon the battle was nearly over. A blow to the kidney brought Spinner down, and three swords were poised to chop him to bits. Pikemen formed a ring around Haft. Zweepee lay across Fletcher, protecting her downed husband with her own body. Six Jokapcul faced the Golden Girl, her back against a tree, while a seventh crept around the trunk to wrest her sword from her grasp. And two chuckling Jokapcul closed on Doli. Wolf lay on his side, bleeding, his open eyes unfocused and unaware.

Then a mighty war cry shook the trees, and the thud of hooves caused the earth to tremble as a behemoth of unbelievable size, mounted on a steed the size of an elephant and swinging a sword larger than a man, charged into the melee and crashed through Jokapcul, sending them spinning and tumbling like tenpins. In hardly more time than it takes to tell, the remnants of the Jokapcul company were in full rout. But the giant on the mammoth horse gave chase and rode them down. Those Jokapcul would fight no more.

CHAPTER
TWENTY-THREE

"Kind of had a feeling I'd see you again," Silent said when they were settled in a new spot along the stream.

The onslaught of the giant steppe nomad had destroyed the last remnant of the Jokapcul company of a hundred men that had assaulted the Guards. Only one man of them lived, and he was a prisoner.

Silent took charge immediately when the battle was over. He set the women to bandaging the wounded. The men were all bloodied in the fight, but not one of the three women was injured. As soon as each man was bandaged, Silent stationed him in a guard post to watch against the approach of another enemy force while the others were tended to. Even the Golden Girl snapped to when Silent gave orders, and she helped tend the wounded. Spinner wondered whether the fight had broken her spirit, or if she found Silent's size intimidating. He noted with surprise that she ungrudgingly surrendered some of the garments and cloth she had collected to use as bandages. And she saw to Wolf's wounds.

As soon as all the men were patched up, Silent mounted them on horses, including the prisoner, whose arms as well as wounds were bound. He scooped up a couple of massive handfuls of Jokapcul weapons and equipment, including the magician's kit, and tied them onto his huge steed. The women could walk the short distance they were going, he told them, and then led them on foot several hundred paces upstream in the rocky channel. He carried Wolf curled babelike in the crook of his arm.

"We need the water," Silent explained about his chosen campsite. "And we need to be upstream of the bodies so they don't contaminate it for us. And if we don't get careless, it'll be harder to track us."

The place Silent found, at a sharp bend in the stream, was easily defensible. The bend's inner side had a hundred or more paces of open ground, so they had clear fields of fire to rain arrows and quarrels onto anyone attacking from that direction. A high, overhanging bank on the outer side of the bend effectively concealed them from anyone passing in that direction. At the foot of the high bank was a shelf of flat ground wide enough to camp on. At the end of the shelf a strong eddy had cut a deep pool they could use for bathing.

"When we parted, I said we'd meet again," Haft said.

"You did," Silent agreed. He looked at the group, his eyes lingering briefly on the women. "There's more of you than the last time we met. You've even found yourselves a wolf. I imagine you've had an adventure or two."

"We have, and we'll tell you about it," Spinner said. "But first, how did you come to be where you could rescue us? What happened at the border station? Where did you get that horse?" His voice was filled with awe when he asked the last question.

"Slower," Silent said, raising a hand against more questions. "That's many questions, not one. Ask only one at a time. First I'll tell you what happened after you left." He cleared his throat and settled back to tell his tale.

"As soon as the evening meal was finished, just after you left us, Sergeant Pilco had his men finish building what defensive redoubts they could, then stationed his men in them in case the Jokaps decided to attack immediately after they arrived. Except for me. Me, he placed in the trees behind the cottages, where I was out of sight. Well, shortly before dusk, two companies of Jokapcul, one cavalry and one infantry,

showed up, just as we'd been warned. That first night they ignored us. But their officers had them hopping to, making
camp and burying the men we'd killed." He chuckled. "They
kept their distance from that dead gray tabur, though. As
badly chewed as it was by the imps, they still seemed afraid
of it.

"Come dawn, Sergeant Pilco had his squad lined up at the
gate." He shook his head. "I never saw those Skraggers
looking so military as that morning. Anyway, I kept out of
sight. The Jokap officer in command marched up to the gate
big as you please, with an honor guard carrying those flags of
theirs that flop down from a cross piece at the top of the
flagstaff, and demanded to speak to the Skragish commanding officer. He had a lot of barks and growls in his speech,
which made him a little hard to understand, but by and large
he spoke passable Skragish. Not as good as mine, of course,
but good enough to understand. Sergeant Pilco said he was in
command. The Jokap officer looked down his nose like the
sergeant was a bug in his soup, which is a neat trick considering that Sergeant Pilco stood head and shoulders taller than
that Jokap. The Jokap told Pilco that he would only talk to an
officer, not a sergeant, and Pilco told him there was no officer,
he was the commander of that post. The Jokap ignored him
after that, acted just like he wasn't there.

"That plumed dandy looked all around the Skragish side of
the border like he was looking at an overused midden, then
said since there was no officer in command there, it looked
like he was in charge of the border. Then he turned to his own
men and started barking and growling, and a platoon of cavalry formed on the gate while a couple of infantrymen opened
it. Sergeant Pilco objected and ordered one of his men to
close the gate. The man tried, but before the man got to it, the
cavalry platoon came charging through and ran him right down.
Killed him.

"A battle started. I'll tell you, those Skraggers put up one
hellacious fight. I've never seen anyone—except my own

tribesmen, of course—fight so fierce. But they were outnumbered too bad. I came charging out as soon as it started, but
there just wasn't enough of me to save Sergeant Pilco and his
men. I did my best to avenge them, but those Jokaps, they
must've been scared of me, because every time I got close to
any of them, they flat broke and ran away. We wound up with
what you might call a stalemate. I stood at the gate keeping
most of them on the Bostian side. The ones who'd already
crossed over kept their distance from me, but that didn't stop
them finding everybody else who was there and killing
them." He spat in disgust.

He shook himself and continued. "The Jokaps had a magician with them. He had a demon spitter like as I never saw before. Looked like that one there." He indicated the one the
Zobran magician had used. "That thing punched a hole right
through my shield and burned a line on my shoulder." He held
up the shield, on which a patch was evident. He bared his
shoulder to show the scar. "That's when I decided the Skraggers were beyond needing me to avenge them. So I left."

"How did you happen to come this way?" Spinner asked.

"And where'd you find that monster horse?" Haft put in.

Silent laughed. "You mean that pony? I had him out to pas-
ture when you were there, that's why you never saw him. For
coming here, well, there's a big world to see out there, and
I've never been to Zobra." His eyes twinkled as he added, "I
knew that's where you were headed, and thought I might find
you before you found yourselves a ship.

"Right off that last morning, before the sun came up, another imbaluris came with a message for Sergeant Pilco. It
said Jokaps were attacking Oskul. I didn't see much point in
heading there. I decided to go cross-country, thought it would
be safer than the roads if Jokaps were around. And one man
traveling alone cross-country can go at least as fast as two
men following a road." He nodded toward the others. "And
much faster than a group. Yesterday I came across the tracks

of that Jokap bunch that jumped you and decided to follow them, see where they were going and what they were up to.

"I caught up with them just in time.

"That's about all there is for my story. There's a big world to see, and I'm going to see as much of it as I can. I'd like to see it in the company of some folks as might know where we're going, if you don't mind—folks whose company I enjoy." His eyes flicked briefly at the Golden Girl and an eyebrow popped up for an instant.

"You want to travel with us?" Haft blurted. "We could show you a lot of the world, we've been around it several times. Right, Spinner?" He thought of how much help the giant would be if they had to fight again. If? He was sure they would have to do more fighting before they found their way on board an eastbound ship.

Spinner scowled at him. "Right," he said grumpily. He had opened his mouth to formally welcome Silent into their small band and was miffed that Haft spoke first.

"Good! Now that that's settled, tell me about your adventures."

Spinner and Haft took turns telling Silent about The Burnt Man, the slavers, the Jokapcul slavemaster, and what they did about it.

"I'd purely love to see that woman dance," Silent said, looking at the Golden Girl when Haft described her performance and Spinner's reaction to it. "Small as she is, she must truly be a wonder to watch." He didn't look away when Alyline glared at him, but he added with a smile, "When she feels like dancing, that is.

"Glad you were that bright," Silent said when Spinner told about letting Wolf join them. "Some wolves—not many, mind you—can be real good companions for men on the move. He looks like a good one."

Wolf made a noise high in his throat and crawled close to the giant. Silent raised an eyebrow; the wolf seemed to understand what he said. Silent put a giant hand on the wolf's side and rubbed briskly. Wolf rumbled low in his throat, something like a cat purring.

When their tales reached the point where Silent charged to the rescue, the three men sat quietly for a few moments.

"Time to question the prisoner," Spinner finally said.

They went to where the prisoner lay on his side, his arms and legs bound and his mouth gagged. They removed the gag and sat the prisoner against the bank. Spinner squatted in front of the prisoner, with Haft on one side and Silent on the other. The three women arrayed themselves behind the men; Fletcher stood aside as sentry, watching for anyone approaching the stream bend. The magician hovered behind the women.

"Where was your company going?" Spinner asked in Frangerian.

The prisoner scowled at him and didn't speak.

"What was your mission?"

Still no answer.

"Are other Jokapcul units in this area?"

Continued silence.

Spinner stared hard at the man for a moment, then tried again in Bostian. No reply. The prisoner continued his silence when Spinner spoke to him in Apianghian.

"Where were you going?" Haft demanded in Ewsarcan. He tried a couple of other languages, all to no avail.

Silent questioned him in Skragish and in his own nomad language. The magician spoke to him in Zobran. One by one each of the eight people attempted to question the prisoner in each of the languages he or she spoke. The magician rooted through the captured magic kit again, and was disappointed at not finding any demons in it that he could use to make the prisoner talk, or that could translate between Jokapcul and another language.

By the time they were finished trying to question him, they had spoken in more than twenty languages. Not once did the Jokapcul soldier give any hint that he understood a word.

"Now what?" Spinner asked the others; he reverted to

Frangerian, the one language most of them had in common. Doli translated for Zweepee, Haft did the same for Silent. "We have a prisoner we can't take care of. We can't talk to him because we don't have a language in common, so he can't give us any information, or give us his parole."

Haft leaned close to the prisoner and said harshly into his ear, "Then we have to kill him."

The prisoner didn't even flinch.

"We stake him out and see if thirst or the vultures kill him first," Haft said, again harshly into the man's ear. He might as well have commented mildly on the weather.

Silent settled back in momentary thought, then said in Ewsarcan, which Haft translated for the others, "The Jokaps slaughtered the Skragers at the border. I saw that with my own eyes. Stories I've heard tell me they massacre people wherever they go."

Spinner nodded. "We saw them hanging prisoners in New Bally. They simply killed men who were unarmed, unresisting, and under their control."

"The slavemaster at The Burnt Man was a Jokapcul," Zweepee said.

Haft looked around at the others. "Then we are agreed, he must die?"

They were.

Spinner remained squatting, staring at his hands. The idea of killing an unarmed man, a prisoner, was repellent to him. He didn't want to do it, but it was something he couldn't ask someone else to do for him. If he was in command of the group—and he knew they were all looking at him for leadership—killing the prisoner was his responsibility. He had to do it. With a sigh, he stood and looked about for a sword he could use to execute the prisoner.

"I think we should give him to the women," Silent suddenly said in Skragish.

"What?"

"Give him to the women," Silent repeated. "In the olden

days, my people handed their prisoners over to the women."
He grinned. "No warrior wanted to be captured by the Tangonine people because of that; what the women did was worse
than anything a man would do."

The prisoner's eyes opened a fraction and flitted about,
then closed back to the same still slits they had been.

"He understood that," Alyline said. "He speaks Skragish. Give him to me. I'll get him to talk. Tie him down,
spread-eagle."

Spinner looked at her, shocked at the viciousness in her
voice. Haft and Fletcher exchanged a look. Doli looked away.
Zweepee stared at her. The magician studied his fingernails.
The prisoner's eyes briefly flicked about again. Silent moved
to do what she said. In a moment the Jokapcul soldier was
supine, his arms stretched to the sides. Leather cords bound
his wrists to stakes pounded into the ground, and his ankles
were similarly bound to other stakes. The prisoner sneered at
his captors.

"What are you going to do?" Spinner croaked.

Alyline was expressionless. "Get information." She looked
each man in the eye. "Do not interfere. I know what I'm
doing."

They looked at her; no one spoke.

"Zweepee, Doli, join me." She stood straddling the prisoner.
Zweepee immediately came and stood next to the prisoner's
chest. Doli hesitated a moment, then joined the other women
and stood facing Zweepee across the prisoner's body.

Without looking at them, Alyline said to the men, "I think
you should go away."

The men glanced at each other but did as she said.

As soon as the men left, Alyline smiled sweetly down at the
prisoner. "You will talk," she said to him. "You will tell me
everything I want to know." Slowly, sensuously, she lowered
herself until she was squatting on his groin. She leaned forward, placed her hands on the ground next to his head and
lowered herself until her breasts pressed into his chest and her

face nearly touched his. She whispered words the other women couldn't hear. The prisoner growled and bit at her nose, but his teeth snapped closed on air—she moved out of his reach faster than anyone could see.

Still smiling, she lowered her face again and whispered more words. Again his teeth snapped closed where she had been. This time a trickle of blood appeared in the corner of his mouth; he had bitten his tongue. The Golden Girl sat up and, still smiling, slapped him hard. Red sprayed from his mouth and nose as his head jerked with the strength of the blow.

Zweepee dropped to her knees and whispered into his ear. After a hesitation, Doli also knelt and spoke into the prisoner's other ear. Sweat beaded on his face. The Golden Girl drew her golden dagger and held it so the sun sparkled off its blade and flashed into his eyes. Zweepee did the same with her dagger. Doli hesitated less than before and also drew her blade, reflecting sunlight into the prisoner's face.

The three women, their faces mere inches apart, looked into each others' eyes. They giggled. Then they went to work on the prisoner.

He screamed.

From where they were around the bend, the men heard the prisoner's cries and looked guiltily at each other. The man's screams were intermittent, but to the listening men they seemed to go on forever before there was a gurgle and they ended. The men remained where they were, looking at each other but trying to avoid eye contact.

"Well," Alyline's voice snapped after a moment, "we're done. Do you want to know what we learned?"

Spinner's mouth was dry. He didn't try to speak, he simply jerked his head at the other men and led them at a slow pace back to the prisoner.

They tried hard not to look at the body but couldn't help themselves—and, as horrible a sight as it was, looking at the body was somehow easier than looking at the blood-spattered women.

The Golden Girl looked at the men, grimly amused. The other women avoided their eyes.

"He didn't talk in a coherent manner," the Golden Girl said. "Now he said one thing, now another. But I'll put it together for you. Zweepee, Doli, feel free to join in if I overlook anything. His story went something like this: 'You are lost. You may as well kill yourselves now. My company was on its way to Zobra City when we came across you. We were to join in the siege of the city, or more likely in its occupation, as it has probably fallen by now. Mine was only one of many companies and battalions crossing overland from Bostia and Skragland into Zobra. Many others have gone into Zobra City and southern Zobra by sea. Now the High Shoton and his liege, Lord Lackland, control all of Nunimar from Matilda to east of Zobra. We have all of Skragland, or so much as makes no difference. Soon we will have all of southern Nunimar and will be ready to cross to Arpalonia. You have no chance. The High Shoton rules. The entire world will soon be ours, to do with as we please.' "

When the women were through relating what the prisoner had told them, Alyline said in a flat voice, "I must cleanse myself. Get rid of that." She flipped a hand at the body. She didn't look at the men as she strode to the pool. The other women followed her. "Don't anybody look," she snapped without turning her head to the men. The three women were naked by the time they reached the water, bloody clothes in one hand and bloody knives in the other.

The men busied themselves burying the body away from their campsite and cleaning away or covering up the gore that stained the ground.

Sometime later the women emerged from the water. None of the men glanced in their direction while they wrung the water out of their clothing and dressed.

Zweepee and Doli busied themselves with small things that didn't need to be done just then, while Alyline sat cross-legged in front of the collection of garments and cloths she'd gleaned from the battlefield. She selected several, then found her sewing kit and started to work on a new garment for herself.

"Do you think he was telling the truth?" Spinner later asked Silent. Spinner saw himself in command but he was sure the steppe giant knew more about the Jokapcul—and about the situation in that part of Nunimar—than he did, and didn't want to do anything without hearing the other man's opinion.

Silent shrugged. "I think I know them no better than you do," he said. "I know they are arrogant and boastful. But you tell me you have seen sign of many Jokap troops moving south and east. He was probably telling the truth, or something close to it—at least about many companies and battalions entering Zobra." He shrugged again. "About the Jokaps having all of southern Nunimar from Matilda to east of Zobra? That I don't know."

"I don't think it matters if he was truthful or lying," Haft said. "We got out of New Bally when it was occupied. We can get into Zobra City unseen and find a ship even if the Jokapcul are there."

"There were only two of us then," Spinner said, "and we had help from the old man. Now we are nine, and two of us are very obvious. We should not expect help from anyone in Zobra City if it's occupied."

Haft scowled. Nine included the wolf, and he'd rather not include Wolf.

Spinner thought for a moment, then decided. "There's only one way to find out for sure," he said. "We have to continue south."

*   *   *

They stayed at the bend in the stream the rest of that day and all of the next to allow the men's wounds to start healing. They also questioned the magician, whose name was Xundoe.

Xundoe didn't apologize for not having any healing demons or herbs with him, but when he cursed the ignorance of the palace bureaucrats who had sent him out with nothing more than a few imbaluris, it seemed that's what he was trying to do. He also snarled something in Zobran that sounded as if he was cursing the arrogance of the Jokapcul who held their troops in such low esteem that they routinely sent magicians on combat patrols without healing demons.

No, he told them, they were not guarding a traveling member of the royal family. The prince's advisers hadn't believed the reports flooding in about the number of Jokapcul forces invading the country. So the prince sent out several companies of Palace Guards on reconnaissance missions.

What Xundoe saw implied that the reports, if anything, understated the situation in the countryside.

Another time, in answer to a question from Spinner, he said proudly, "I am a mage."

"But mage is the lowest ranking magician, barely above apprentice," Spinner blurted.

The magician blushed; he'd hoped the outlanders would know nothing of the rank structure of magicians. "It's true that I'm only an M-3, but that's only because Zobra has been at peace for a long time and promotions are slow." He hastily added, "If I were elsewhere, I could go before a sorcerers' board and be certified as a full magician, likely a senior magician, soon to be advanced to sorcerer, M-7." He held his head high when he said that. "I've kept up my studies and have learned far more than my grade level, a rank far beneath me, would imply. As you should know; you saw me use all the fighting demons the Jokapcul magician carried in his kit."

Spinner considered the magician's boast and decided he might be telling the truth; his robe was more heavily decorated

with cabalistic symbols than was usual for junior mages he'd
met while on duty with the fleet.

While the men talked quietly, Alyline made new clothing
for herself from pieces of uniforms and other material she'd
scavenged. The new garments were of the same cut and style
as her golden dancing costume: a vest, open between the
breasts but laced together so she wasn't too exposed, and pantaloons with a girdle low on her hips. Unlike her dancing costume, however, the new garments were nowhere diaphanous,
and looked sturdy enough to stand up to wear. Since she no
longer had to wear the golden garments, she packed her golden
adornments away with her money pouches. In place of the
diadem, she wore a broad-brimmed hat fashioned from the
leather of a Jokapcul helmet. She had made slippers from
the leather of a Jokapcul jerkin.

When the men were far enough along the way to healing,
they packed their few belongings and left the stream behind.

CHAPTER
TWENTY-FOUR

They didn't press their movement southward, so the wounds the men had suffered in the fight weren't aggravated by the travel, but continued to heal. Alyline took advantage of their slow pace to collect barks and earths, fruits and roots, with which to dye her new clothes. Fortunately, though they occasionally crossed the tracks of companies of men moving in a generally southerly or southeasterly direction, they encountered no Jokapcul along the way.

On the fourth day of their southward march, in the middle of the afternoon, they came across a narrow road. It was old and well traveled, but the weeds beginning to sprout in it said it hadn't been used in a week or more. They decided it was safe to follow the road for a while. Wolf scouted ahead.

For an hour, travel along the road was good. The roadway was easier on the horses, and the riders didn't have to duck under branches. Songbirds twirred merrily in the trees, and even the buzz of insects sounded friendly. Everything felt and sounded safe; there was nothing to indicate the presence of any danger. If they hadn't known of the invasion, nothing they saw along the road would have reminded them of trouble. They looked forward to finding a village or a farm before nightfall. But after traveling for that hour, Wolf appeared ahead of them, sitting in the middle of the road, facing them, blocking the way. His tongue lolled out of the side of his mouth and his eyes looked sad.

"Ulgh," he whined when they were still twenty or more paces shy of him.

The mare, ridden by Haft in the van of the short column, shied from the wolf, and Haft struggled to bring her back under control.

Spinner dismounted and handed Haft his reins as he brushed past him and moved toward Wolf.

"Hey," Haft objected as he dismounted awkwardly because of the extra reins in his hand and Spinner's horse standing so close.

Spinner dropped to a knee in front of Wolf and briskly rubbed his ruff. "What's the matter, boy?" he asked, looking beyond the wolf. "Is there an ambush ahead? Did you see Jokapcul?"

Wolf whined and shook his head sharply.

Spinner lowered his face to look at Wolf. "Was there another battle, are there more dead soldiers ahead of us?"

Wolf twisted his shoulders and whined again.

"No soldiers," Spinner interpreted. "But there is danger?"

Wolf whined and shook his head once more. Then he lay down and, covering his face with a paw, tightly closed his eyes.

"There's no danger now, but there was. We aren't going to want to see whatever is up ahead. Is that right?"

Wolf yipped, but didn't open his eyes or uncover his face.

Spinner stood. "All right. We'll be careful. You and I will go on, and you show me what's there."

Wolf sprung to his feet and turned south, looking back over his shoulder at Spinner.

"Wolf found something," Spinner told the others. "I'm going with him to see what it is. Wait for me." Without waiting for a reply, he started down the road. He didn't bother to string his crossbow—he was sure he wouldn't need it.

A hundred paces farther along there was a modest clearing in the forest. At one time the clearing had held a farmhouse, a barn, other outbuildings, a stone-walled corral, and a kitchen garden. Now the stone wall of the corral was tumbled down, and wisps of smoke rose from the charred ruins of the farmhouse and other buildings. What looked like several bundles of discarded clothing dotted the garden, which was blackened from a recent fire.

"Yesterday." A voice at Spinner's side made him jump. It was Silent. "Late. Not long before dusk."

"I told you—" Spinner started to say, but stopped when he saw Fletcher beyond the giant, and realized the entire group had come along, though he'd told them to wait.

"We don't need you to protect us from all the evil in the world," Haft said. "And you couldn't even if we wanted you to." He walked into the clearing; puffs of black smoke rose with each step he took. Halfway to the farmhouse he stopped and squatted next to the first of the bundles. He swore, but his voice was too low for the words to carry to those who stood at the edge of the clearing. Muttering, Haft stood and slowly walked through the burned garden to the next pile, which he only glanced at before turning back to the trees. Spinner was walking into the clearing. They didn't speak as they passed. Haft merely shook his head; Spinner grimaced.

Spinner glanced at the first discarded bundle to confirm his fears. It was a middle-aged man, probably the farmer. From the horror frozen on his face and the blood that had flowed from only one wound in his chest, Spinner guessed he was the first to die and was surprised by an unexpected blow. The second was an old man, more severely butchered, probably the farmer's father, or the farmer's wife's father, cut down as he tried to run to the farmhouse. A third, just outside the ruins of the house, was a youth. He'd tried to fight, using the hayfork that lay near his outflung arm. Inside what remained of the walls of the farmhouse were three badly charred clumps that had probably been playful children at the same hour the previous day. It was obvious that the Jokapcul had fired the house while the children were in it.

"Where are the women?" Alyline demanded.

Spinner started; he hadn't heard her come up behind him. "What?"

"The women." Alyline's voice was bitter, as though it was Spinner's fault there were no women. "There are no women's bodies here, only those of men and children."

Spinner turned from her without answering and went to the ruins of what must have been the barn. He found tools in the vicinity, a shovel, a hoe, and a pick. He gathered them and carried them to a patch of bare ground in front of the house to start digging. In moments Haft and Fletcher joined him. Together, they dug a grave. Silent gathered the bodies.

The women stood silently to the side during the burial of the six bodies in the one grave. The magician chanted prayers in Zobran. Wolf stood erect, looking alert, during the brief service, then scouted around the clearing while the humans stood quietly, reflectively, at the graveside for a long moment. Wolf paused briefly near a line of trees, then trotted into it without attracting the people's attention.

"Let's find another place to spend the night," Spinner said when their brief burial service was done. They quickly returned to the horses. Wolf stayed between them and the line of trees.

The next morning they found another farm. That afternoon, a third. Both farms appeared the same as the first—burned out, the bodies of dead men and children scattered about, no bodies of women. They stopped at each place to bury the dead. The following morning yielded two more ravaged farms. They didn't bury the dead men and children at the second farm, since they realized there'd be too many dead ahead to bury them all. They skirted the first farm of the afternoon. At the second, Alyline again demanded, "Where are the women?" Again her question seemed an accusation, directed at the men.

Haft shook his head and chewed his lip but said nothing. Silent and Fletcher looked grim and didn't speak. The magician appeared not to have understood her question.

Spinner shook his head and said, "I don't know."

"Find them," Alyline demanded. She directed the stallion toward a ravine a hundred paces from the burned farmhouse.

Wolf ran to block her way—his nose had told him what was in the ravine. He growled at the stallion, which bucked and kicked out at the wolf, then continued on its way. Wolf whined at Alyline, then turned his head and barked sharply at Spinner before running to reach the ravine before she did.

Spinner swore, urging the gelding into a canter. Reaching the lip of the ravine before Alyline, he stopped next to Wolf and turned his face from the sight that greeted his eyes.

Alyline reached the ravine and sat for a long moment looking into it. The rest of the group followed more slowly. When they all reached it, she said harshly, "Bury them," and turned away. Doli and Zweepee followed her.

The men sat quietly for a moment, looking anywhere but at each other or what awaited them in the bottom of the ravine. Five bodies lay there, their limbs aclutter and torsos twisted. All were female. All were naked. Bruises showed that they had been used hard before they were mutilated and murdered. Scavengers had been at them.

"Let's see if there are shovels," Spinner said at length. He turned the gelding away and headed for the ruins of the farmhouse. Haft went with him. They found a pick head and the blades of two shovels; the handles had burned away. Back at the ravine, they quickly cut and trimmed new handles and fit them to the digging blades. The handles weren't very good, but they only had to last long enough to dig the one hole. The men had no stomach for the job. They quickly dug a pit to dump the bodies into.

"Reverently," Alyline snapped when Spinner and Fletcher picked up the first body.

They avoided farms after that.

At first and last light each day, Xundoe dispatched a messenger to find out what was happening elsewhere, but none of

the flying demons returned, nor did messengers from elsewhere come to him.

Xundoe worried over the failure of his imbaluris to communicate, and his manner became more dejected every time a
messenger did not return. He was sure the failure was neither
the fault of the imbaluris nor of the instructions he gave them,
but he feared the outlanders might think it was.

He did not discuss with them the possibility that no Zobran
magicians remained free to control messenger demons; that
the Jokapcul had captured them all.

On what turned out to be the second to last day of their
journey south, the smoke they saw filling the sky caused them
to advance more cautiously; the enemy had to be somewhere
close to their front. It seemed the prisoner had been right
about Zobra City being besieged.

The next day they crouched under the trees atop a high
bluff overlooking Zobra City. The smoke had diminished; the
fire that caused it was nearly burned out—it came from the
harbor, where the ships that were in port and unable to escape
through the blockade of Jokapcul coast-huggers were burned
to the waterline. They were too far away to see any details of
the people they saw moving about the city, but the banners
rising above it, and above the military encampments around
the city, told them what they needed to know—Zobra City
was in the hands of the enemy.

"We must go overland to the east coast," Alyline said. She
was no longer golden. That day her clothing was a dull, dark
green. A sturdy leather girdle hugged her hips. Her hair was
dirty.

The men looked to the east. Somewhere in that direction,
they hoped, lay safety. But it looked like the Jokapcul were
conquering new lands at a faster pace than they were fleeing.

"What will we do if we run into more of them along the
way?" Doli asked from her usual position near Spinner.

"We fight," Spinner said.

Haft gripped the haft of his axe and hammered its head on the ground.

Fletcher and Silent nodded agreement.

Xundoe again considered the array of demons he had found in the Jokapcul magician's kit and wondered how long they would last if they had to fight along their way.

"We have no choice," Zweepee said, moving close to her husband and hugging him.

Wolf raised his head and sniffed loudly, seeking the safest way to go.

"We've wasted enough time here," Spinner said. He stood and followed Wolf. The others trailed behind.

"We need more horses," Fletcher said. No one responded. The only way they would get more horses was by taking them from Jokapcul cavalry, and none of them was certain they would win the fight.

A week later they were a hundred miles east and to the north of Zobra City. They had the extra horses they needed. Xundoe had a new magic kit with more demons and demon food, including demons he didn't know what to make of. And their party of nine had grown to two score. They had to make another decision—should they attempt to enter the Princedons in hope of finding a ship home? Or should they brave the Low Desert and head directly for the east coast of Nunimar?

Author's Note

The named types of "demons" in this novel come from a variety of mythologies and folklores. While I tried to keep the core of their traditional characters, I changed them unmercifully to meet the needs of the story. The unnamed demon types, I simply made up.